**25 years of celebrity interviews
from vaudeville to movies to TV**

reel to real

David Fantle and Tom Johnson

*Badger Books Inc.
Oregon, Wisconsin*

Published by Badger Books Inc.
Cover design by John Skewes
Edited by Pat Reardon
Photos by the authors or used with permission of the interview subjects.
Printed in the U.S.A.

ISBN 1-932542-04-3

Badger Books Inc./Waubesa Press
P.O. Box 192
Oregon, WI 53575

Toll-free phone: (800) 928-2372
Fax: (608) 835-3638
Email: books@badgerbooks.com
Web site: www.badgerbooks.com

Library of Congress Cataloging-in-Publication Data

Fantle, David.
   25 years of celebrity interviews from vaudeville to movies to TV, reel to real / David Fantle and Tom Johnson.
      p. cm.
   Includes index.
   ISBN 1-932542-04-3 1.
   Entertainers—United States—Interviews. I. Title: Twenty five years of celebrity interviews from vaudeville to movies to TV, reel to real. II. Johnson, Tom, 1947- III. Title.
PN2285.F36 2004
791'.092'273—dc22

                                                      2003027328

To my loving wife Cathy and beautiful children Grace, Max and Maddie, and to my parents, who supported our youthful endeavors in a constant state of disbelief!

— David Fantle

To Mom, Dad, Mark, Anne and Mare, for encouraging a presumptuous teenager from the Midwest to pursue the big fish ... and get it all down on tape.

— Tom Johnson

Contents

I. Vaudeville is Not a Place

II. Hoofers, Warblers and All That Jazz

III. Silver Screen, Pure Gold

IV. Ladies Take the Lead

V. Funny Side Up

VI. Plugged In

VII. Shoot to Thrill

VIII. Your Hit Parade

Foreword

by Cyd Charisse

They didn't call it the "Golden Age of Hollywood" for nothing. And how wonderful it was for me to be part of that artistic ensemble that made up the exclusive fraternity of MGM stars. While that special era of entertainment has been chronicled before, it's so nice to get this fresh look back by two people who share a passion for our glorified show business heritage. What makes this book even more remarkable is that David and Tom, while still teenagers living in the Midwest, traveled to Hollywood and interviewed – two on one - so many immortal stars.

My husband, Tony Martin, and I, worked with and had warm personal friendships with many of the people profiled in these pages, including two gentlemen whose contribution to film dance will never be equaled — Fred Astaire and Gene Kelly. Whether dancing sweetly in the dark with Fred in *The Bandwagon* or sinuously with Gene to a Broadway Rhythm in *Singin' in the Rain,* I loved every minute of it ... including the countless hours of rehearsal, if you can believe it.

But several of the profiles in the book from vaudeville and television stars to directors and songwriters are new to me as well.

It was a pleasure to welcome David and Tom in my living room and share with them some of my recollections of that very special time when there were "more stars than there are in the heavens." The memories are still vivid, and how fortunate that those special moments are captured forever on celluloid as well as in this book for you to enjoy.

— Cyd Charisse
Beverly Hills, Calif.
October 2003
www.cydcharisse.net

Foreword

by Shirley Jones

If you've already bought this book, congratulations — it'll serve you well. If you haven't, go immediately to the register and buy it — and I'm about to tell you why.

For better or for worse, I'm probably the "Queen Mother" of all press interviews — no, not because I'm in such demand, but because, unlike most celebrities, I turn very few of them down. (It's an accepted part of the job, something I learned when I began my Hollywood career in the last days of the studio system.) But the countless interviews have given me the savvy to know "good" interviews from the other kind. And the truth is I wasn't 100 percent sure when Fantle and Johnson, two young guys from the Midwest, showed up at my house with their reporter's notebooks and their tape machine.

It became immediately clear, however, that David and Tom were learned students of Hollywood history. Perhaps because they have the luxury of no green bottom-line interest in one talent or one talent vehicle over another, they've been able to do their Hollywood homework with such sweeping equity — but it shows in the perception and substance of their celebrity conversations. Furthermore, I know most of the stars in their spotlight, and all of them have been meticulously steered out of the familiar hype and hustle trap and into the rarefied "no spin" zone. They are, for you here, as they are at home and on the telephone, plain and simple ... *real* people. (Would that such presence and candor prevail in the penthouse meeting rooms of the general Hollywood hierarchy today.)

So, call me a *Reel to Real* groupie, a believer. Fantle and Johnson's compelling labor of love from John Bubbles to Janet Leigh translates into a gift of love for all of us.

— Shirley Jones
Encino, Calif.
October 2003

Introduction

The year was 1974 and *That's Entertainment,* the compilation film of Metro-Goldwyn-Mayer Studio's most wondrous musical moments had just opened wide in theaters across the country. A new generation of movie fans that hadn't been born during MGM's heyday could watch Gene Kelly joyously dancin' and singin' in the rain, Judy Garland belting out "Get Happy," or Fred Astaire and Eleanor Powell whirling around each other like syncopated pinwheels to Cole Porter's sublime "Begin the Beguine."

For millions of theatergoers, *That's Entertainment* was a revelation; to us — a couple of St. Paul, Minn., teenagers — it was galvanizing. Like many kids growing up in the Twin Cities of Minneapolis and St. Paul, we dutifully watched *Mel Jass' Matinee Movie* on local television in the early afternoons and for years had been treated to campy double bills like *I was a Teenage Werewolf* and *The Brain That Wouldn't Die.* Entertaining as such B-grade fare could be, it could not remotely be classified as art. Artless was more like it.

So, when *That's Entertainment* opened, our interest was piqued far beyond seeing a few choice snippets from those Freed Unit features. We wanted to see the musicals — in their entirety — which gave birth to the clips. We wanted the main course; not just the appetizer. However, in an era before DVDs or videocassettes, viewing what you wanted when you wanted was, to say the least, a problem.

Undaunted, we formed a film society that shuttled musicals (of our own choosing, of course) to nursing homes in the Minneapolis-St. Paul area. By renting 16-millimeter prints of the movies and then splitting the expense among the venues, we kept costs affordable for the nursing homes that signed on. We dubbed the organization "Films On Wheels," which seemed appropriate since most of our elderly audience were on wheels, too.

Later on, at the University of Minnesota, we expanded our hucksterish notion into a new film group — "The Song and Dance Cinema Society" with all proceeds donated to the Ronald McDonald House for children with cancer.

Although eventually sated by seeing practically every musical ever made, our interest took a new turn; we wanted to meet some of the actors and actresses of the films we admired so much. By sheer luck, during the last years of the '70s, many stars from Hollywood's Golden Age were still in the picture ... if not exactly making pictures. What's more, an interview query with a stamped, self-addressed envelope for their reply was often all it took to get an affirmative response in those simpler days.

Just liberated from high school, in the summer of 1978, we snagged the first two interviews that paved the way for the contents crammed between these jackets. Fred Astaire and Gene Kelly (after talking it over between themselves, we always suspected) agreed to sit down and talk with us.

As vendors at Metropolitan Stadium in Bloomington, Minnesota, selling Schweigert hot dogs and Frosty Malts to hungry Minnesota Twins and Vikings fans, we figured we had put away enough money for a quick trip to Los Angeles to meet Astaire and Kelly and then get back in time to work the next Twins homestand. What we hadn't factored in was the cost of taxicabs and buses (we weren't old enough to rent a car!). Fortunately, back then, even the rarefied purlieus of Beverly Hills contained a couple of budget motels with weekly rates and lifesaving kitchenettes.

The visits with Astaire and Kelly, though brief, were transcendent. Kelly and Astaire's protean musical exploits had already attained an almost mythical status for us. In our starstruck minds, the dancers weren't tethered to terra firma (we weren't in a position to see them engaged in such prosaic pursuits as walking the dog or trimming the hydrangeas, something they both did).

So, in a way, it was an eye-opener to interrupt Astaire in his accountant's office while he was busily engaged not in some terpsichorean matter of the greatest creative urgency, but in the laborious chore of balancing his personal checkbook.

Did we experience even a momentary letdown at having our illusions shattered so completely? Hardly. Our appreciation for the hundreds of artists we've interviewed has only deepened knowing that they are indeed flesh and blood — some leavened, perhaps, with a touch of genius.

The next logical step in our fledgling journey toward becoming celebrity chroniclers was writing up notes from our interviews with Astaire and Kelly for the arts section of the *Minnesota Daily*, the University of Minnesota student newspaper (a publication that first published many of the stories in this volume). From there, perseverance became habit and some habits are hard to break as we find that we're still interviewing movie and television stars 25 years later.

"Don't quit your day jobs," Gene Kelly said, laughing, when we once confided to him that we'd like to try and carve out a living interviewing celebrities of the stage and screen. Gene's gentle admonishment proved prescient. Although we've never exited the 9-to-5 grind, we've had tremendous fun interviewing the great, near great, (and merely grating) in our spare time over the past quarter-century. Consider what follows then as our corollary to Kelly's bit of cautionary advice.

— David Fantle
Bayside, Wis.
December 2003

— Tom Johnson
Sherman Oaks, Calif.
December 2003

I.
Vaudeville
Is Not a Place

Sawdust Memories
Will Ahern and Eddie Parks
September 1980

Step, ballchange, flap, step. The hard-driven notes of stride piano played in counterpoint to the steel tones of Capezios in a tap dance, drifted down the steps of Will Ahern's Rainbow Rehearsal Studio in Hollywood. The delightful sounds, however, didn't mesh well with the stifling aroma of garlic and deep dish from Palermo's pizza parlor next door.

"Entertainers come to my studio to train in hopes of making it big in show business," Ahern winked. "They might as well start with the quality of their air intake; they'll face audiences just as bad!"

Will Ahern is a small, silver-haired man with an elfin twinkle in his eye and a smile as infectious as one of Santa Claus' helpers. He had a rhythm in his speech and urgency in his manner. It was his habit to entertain at the "drop of a hat" and to dazzle with his treasured lore of playing the Orpheum Vaudeville Circuit. We were pushovers.

The wonderful world of entertainment started for Ahern in 1909 in Waterbury, Connecticut, where Buffalo Bill's Wild West Show was performing for four days. He was a waterboy, slept in hay on the flatcar, and got kicked in the pants by a mule with rubber horseshoes — all for one dollar a day. "I remember Annie Oakley used to skeet shoot targets with a shotgun," Ahern said. "She would always spray the crowd with spent buckshot."

"When I got older I did a sort of Will Rogers act in vaudeville. I would tie knots in my lariat, and with each knot I would repeat, 'I am a cowboy, I'm not a cowboy, I am a cowboy' … I've been roping for 71 years."

It's a long career that includes more than a few milestones. "I performed for President Woodrow Wilson at the Versailles

Peace Conference. I made films with Mary Pickford in 1913. And I played the Palace Theater in New York," Ahern said.

But admittedly, Ahern's greatest achievement came when he "lassoed" his wife Gladys into tying the matrimonial knot. They've been married for over 50 years.

"On the Orpheum Circuit we were billed as *Will & Gladys Ahern in a Spinning Romance*. My wife did a toe dance inside my rope while I whirled it, then we both danced in it. That was back in 1921."

In their fast-paced 12-minute act, the Aherns pulled out all the stops in song, dance and comedy to entertain.

"I sang 'Rancho Grande' with a sombrero hat on my head," Ahern said. "Gladys would come onstage, take my hat off and exclaim, 'I, Chicita, will do the bolero, yes I'm going to do that, and dance with my beau's sombrero, I will have the need of a hat.' I would grab it back, she would grab it from me and so on. I would then say, 'Who are you?' My wife would reply, 'I am Doña Jose Maria Lopez Diaz Estado. That is my given name.' I would tell her, 'You should give it back!'"

To many people, the term vaudeville might be confused with a two-horse town in North Dakota or with a loud-mouthed performer who has more nerve than talent. In reality, vaudeville as a force died 50 years ago, replaced by the easier access of movies and radio. It remains vivid only in the memories of a handful of men like Ahern. Like a Palomino pony, the vaudevillian is truly a vanishing breed.

Vaudeville was perhaps the best leisure time deal of this century. For 15 cents, the cost of a balcony seat, one could while away three hours with seven acts of some of the greatest traveling entertainment in the country. From the Kita Banzaii Jap Acrobatic Family to Ethel Barrymore in a one-act dramatic playlet, vaudeville had something for everyone.

In the course of his own coast-to-coast travels on the Orpheum Circuit, Ahern acquired invaluable theatrical seasoning that performers can't get today. From Wahpeton, N.D. to New York City, he played to every kind of audience and pandered to most mentalities.

"After a few years on the boards I began to pick up inside information that makes or breaks a really great vaudeville act," Ahern said. "When performing in the southern states, audiences had a different lingo — a sort of drawl. Vaudevillians, to be understood, had to be slower and more definite in intonation. In West Virginia, Ohio and Pennsylvania, you would hit the steel mill and coal mine towns. The crowds were 80 percent foreign, so I eliminated most of the dialogue and did my act in pantomime. New York, Chicago and Philadelphia were cosmopolitan. You couldn't fool audiences there, so you had to snap up the pace of your act."

Orpheum performers played one week in each theater and then moved on. Cities and audiences changed with the frequency of every troupe train out of town and the posting of each new vaudeville bill. But some prejudices remained.

"At the St. Paul Orpheum I shared the bill with four colored boys in a dance act called The Dixie Four," Ahern said. "One of the four came backstage after the show, he was very upset. He said that the restaurant around the corner refused to serve them. I went over and got them sandwiches — to go. The town of Wahpeton, N. D. had a different mania, one against tobacco. Wahpeton is just across the border from Minnesota and they had an absolute rule against smoking of any kind within the city limits. I remember vaudevillians had to buy their cigarettes and cigars in Minnesota and smoke them there."

As a married man, Ahern lived a fairly monastic life. Many vaudevillians were habitual card sharks and pool hustlers when they weren't "knocking 'em in the aisles." In his spare time, Ahern counseled his fellow performers in Ben Franklin's doctrine of thrift, "A penny saved is money not hustled."

"As long as you didn't gamble, you were all right," Ahern said. "During the train junket from St. Paul to Winnipeg I would go back to the men's room and find different acts shooting craps and rolling dice. In a single night a guy would often lose his entire previous week's pay. I used to tell them that they should go to the box-office after the first performance, draw out $150, and send it straight home. That way they would show some profit."

At that moment a gentleman doddered from the other room and smack-dab into our conversation. He announced to us that he would be playing the part of an old vaudevillian who tap dances from Los Angeles to New York City wearing Bermuda shorts in Marty Feldman's upcoming film, *In God We Trust.*

"I'm an old friend of Will's. My name is Eddie Parks of Coogan & Parks Orpheum vaudeville renown," he said. "I first played the Orpheum Circuit around 1909. I was just a 16-year-old kid."

Parks' partner, Jack Coogan, was the father of Jackie Coogan, co-star with Charlie Chaplin in *The Kid* and recently hallowed as Uncle Fester of TV's *The Addams Family.*

"Jack Coogan and I would do comedy, buck, soft-shoe and eccentric dancing," Parks said. "During our soft-shoe number we did dialogue. It was called 'patter between the steps.' It went like this:

Parks: "Do you remember Jones, the playwright?"
Coogan: "I certainly do."
Parks: "Tell me, which one of his productions did you like the best?"
Coogan: "His oldest daughter Lizzie."

Headliner acts like Coogan & Parks usually drew salary figures requisite with the stature of their talent. But often they had to sell themselves with as much élan to the booking offices as they did to vaudeville audiences.

"We drew big salaries because Coogan would go into Orpheum booking offices and say, 'My partner has rich parents so he doesn't need money. He can pick and choose his jobs.' Then I would stroll in and the bookers would fall all over themselves to offer us big money."

Parks was married in 1911, and like Ahern he built a new act with his wife as partner. Although they promised to love, honor, cherish and obey, those vows apparently didn't extend to the performing arena.

"We did a song and conversation. She would sing, 'I will admit I'm fond of animals and such, but when it comes to insects ...' Then she would look askance at me and walk offstage. I would then turn to her and reply, 'Just for that, when you die and are cremated I hope they find klinkers in your ashes.'"

The jousting continued.

"I'd then say that that gorgeous little gal was in a beauty contest in Atlantic City. Last year she was misrepresented and this year she's misunderstood.

"My wife would walk on again as I talked to the audience. She would trip and look at her shoe. Here's the patter:

    Me: "What's the matter?"
    Her: "I've got a loose heel."
    Me: "What?"
    Her: "A loose heel."
    Me: "Now listen Lucille!"

A popular stereotype of old vaudevillians used to be that of a grinning goof whose sunny disposition was totally at variance with the hard realities of life outside the camaraderie of show business. Ahern and Parks have positive personalities they came by honestly.

"I've always liked small towns like St. Paul," Parks said. "When I was a young man I acquired the capacity to enjoy the simple pleasures that every small town offered. Many people in our business become what I call 'show-wise.' They can't go from here to across the street without a bored smirk. They've lost all the wonder and fascination of life."

From looking after the welfare of his vaudeville colleagues

to feeding flocks of nesting birds outside his home, Ahern also remains an unquenchable optimist.

"I take care of about 400 blue-jays, blackbirds and sparrow every day. I spend $30 a week on birdseed," Ahern said. "I have four stray dogs and I don't gamble, smoke, drink or run around — except to and from the studio."

Ahern's Rainbow Rehearsal Hall, in spite of its dust and distinctive odor, is another example of his benevolence. He hasn't raised his rates in 30 years.

"I'm not interested in making money," Ahern said. "I keep low rates to help the singers, dancers, acrobats and comedians who need a place to perfect their routines. You know, when my studio was over a Greyhound Station, the Broadway and vaudeville character actor Jack Barton used to say that if your act wasn't working out in rehearsal, you could catch a bus out of town. Fortunately, Rainbow is a good luck rehearsal hall for Carol Channing and Bob Hope. When I retired from performing, I didn't divorce myself from show business, I just found another outlet. I love it too much."

Vaudeville may be a faint echo to most, but the curtain can never ring down on the exuberance of Ahern and Parks. Their performance of songs, skits and comedy monologues is oral history in action, and it's available to anyone who cares to spare a few moments as audience to a couple of old pros. Best yet, they even waive the 15-cent admission price.

On the Hoof
John Bubbles and Willie Covan
September 1980

American vaudeville ground to a halt over 40 years ago. It is preserved in memory mostly by senior citizens, many of whom treasure that time when, for a 25-cent admission, you could catch seven acts of vaudeville ranging from comic jugglers and Asian acrobats to dramatic monologues and one-act playlets.

Black vaudeville, an afterthought or "poor relation" to the vaudeville that reached most of the American public, is also treasured for its unique legacy. It became the perfect public platform to showcase jazz dance, an indigenous American art form and a continuing heritage, whose pioneers, innovators and stylists range from Bill "Bojangles" Robinson to Sammy Davis Jr. to the MTV gyrations of Michael Jackson.

In Los Angeles recently, we talked with two men who could be considered historical forces in the evolution of black vaudeville jazz dance, specifically the tap dance variety: Willie Covan and John Bubbles. We met Covan in his home in the Watts area of Los Angeles. He talked with an eager, syncopated cadence — much the same way he danced. Covan was a member of "The Four Covans," a bellhop costumed tap dancing family act that toured vaudeville in the early '20s.

Covan said that "The Four Covans" performed five different dances in sequence, one after another, without once leaving the stage. "We danced a jazz number to 'Nagasaki,' a soft-shoe and a waltz in rhythm. After each dance we would back up while the orchestra played the introduction to our next number," he said.

"The reason we never left the stage is because we didn't want to lose touch with the audience. They might walk out to get candy or go to the toilet. I know I was driven to the men's room on several occasions after watching certain acts!"

As physically draining as "The Four Covans" dance act was, Covan said that the hardest gig he ever danced was in Philadelphia. "I was doing two shows a day at the Hippodrome in New York City and then catching the night train to Philadelphia to dance in a 1 a.m. nightclub show. That went on for two endless weeks."

Covan pointed with greatest pride to his introduction of the standard, "Sweet Georgia Brown" at the Palace Theater in New York. "My partner and I were dawdling outside

Remicks Music Publishing House when Maceo Pinkard came out and asked us to introduce this new song of his called 'Sweet Georgia Brown,'" Covan said. "Maceo didn't even have all the lyrics written, and we only had three days to rehearse it, but it brought the house down opening night and I think they're still clapping yet."

Covan then took us into his tap dance studio, a spacious room in his home equipped with a plywood floor — an ideal tapping surface, we learned. His walls were adorned with pictures of dance students he has coached over the years, including Debbie Reynolds, Mickey Rooney and Mary Tyler Moore.

"I don't come in here much anymore," he said. "My wife used to come to the door and I'd show her a step and she would say, 'Oh Will, that's a good one, I love that one.' I used to dance just for her, but she's gone now."

John Bubbles' most recent success has been in the revue, "Black Broadway," which just ended its run in New York. He was George Gershwin's personal choice for the role of "Sportin' Life" in the 1935 black folk opera *Porgy and Bess*. But perhaps Bubbles' most lasting contribution is his rhythm tap dancing, a style he created. In the early 1920s, after months of painstaking and solitary innovation, Bubbles was among the first to elevate tap dancing from the flat-footed stomps, scrapes and shuffles of early exponents like King Rastus Brown to heel and toe steps that really swung.

"I taught Fred Astaire some of my steps for $400 an hour back in 1930 when he was appearing in a Broadway show called *Smiles* with Marilyn Miller." Bubbles said that he would teach the dance steps to Miller, who would then pass them on to Astaire. "For that kind of money I didn't want to give Fred just any kind of steps, but ones I knew he could use."

Bubbles owned a small house in East Los Angeles. When we met him, he was recuperating from a stroke that had paralyzed the left side of his body. Although his quicksilver feet moved at a slow gait, as we sat at Bubbles' kitchen table, his memories of the "good old days" (that might have been even better if show business had been colorblind) flowed, rat-a-tat-tat, like a set of impossibly fast nerve taps.

In the early 1920s, Bubbles teamed up with a pianist named Ford Lee Washington in an act called, "Buck & Bubbles in a Variety of Varieties." As part of the Nat Nazarro Troupe, Buck & Bubbles were a hit on the Orpheum Circuit despite the lukewarm review printed in the *St. Paul Pioneer Press* in November 1921:

"Nat Nazarro presents music, song, dance and comedy in 'A Variety of Varieties' in which Buck & Bubbles, two dusky youngsters assist him. One is a boy-wonder at the piano — the other is clever on his feet. But both are given too much independence. Although they can entertain a long time before they start to get a little tiresome."

"Buck and I were costumed as vagabond tramps in patched clothes and overalls," Bubbles remembered. "We used to do a gag that went something like this:

Bubbles: "C'mon boy, get out of that hole. You're a low man. Look at yer feet, they sure are big: like U-boats."
Buck: "What's the matter with 'em?"
Bubbles: Nothin' … only they're so big, man. How do you get your pants off at night?"
Buck: "I pull 'em off over my head."
Bubbles: "Well, pull this off your head." (Then he'd start playing the piano and I'd start dancing.)

The songs in Buck and Bubbles act back then included such gems of the American popular song canon as: "Mammy 'O Mine," "Rhythm for Sale," "International Rag," "Somebody Loves Me" and "Nobody Knows and Nobody Seems to Care."

The last song, although played straight, effectively

summed up the prejudice that black performers experienced during their circuit tours in vaudeville — segregation that included accommodations in black boarding houses and meals served out the back door of "white-only" restaurants.

That separate but unequal status led Bubbles to compose the following song, "Belittlin' Me," as a way to cope with the prejudice that was rampant, especially down South.

Don't ever try to go too far
don't try to be more that what you are
you'll always get there better by far
than always belittlin' me.

Don't say "ya'll" when you should say "you"
and don't say "George" if you don't know who
the same thing for one is always good for two
when you're always belittlin' me.

It's hard to forget the things that you do
that really grieves me so
Oh my, oh why cain't you be true
I'd like to know
don't make me believe you really care
don't leave me groping in despair
you'll never get nowhere
when you're always belittin' me.

"We just persevered the best we could," Bubbles said matter-of-factly. "One distraction we took with us everywhere in vaudeville was our collection of electric trains. Buck and I were nuts about 'em and had a trunk full of them. We used to lay track all over our dressing room."

Bubbles believes that the black dancers currently performing are good — he cites Honi Coles and Gregory Hines — but couldn't possibly stand up to the kind of competition that existed in the theatrical '20s.

"There used to be a place in Harlem called The Hoofers Club, which was a room where tap dancers could practice any time of the day or night for as long as they wished," Bubbles said. "I never had any time for it. Many of those guys became good dancers, good out-of-work dancers. Meanwhile, I was making big money on the Orpheum Circuit."

John Bubbles said he never "challenge-danced" anyone on a street corner or in a back alley as was the custom among hoofers of a half-century ago. For him, the only challenge came in staying flush at the job he loved so dearly.

Bring Down the Curtain
Harry Delmar
August 1981

"I remember in the early '30s after the advent of sound in pictures, you could drive down Ventura Boulevard the length of the San Fernando Valley and see vaudevillians practicing every imaginable kind of act on their front lawns. There were jugglers, musicians, dancers, contortionists and dog acts all hoping to break into the movies — most never got a job."
— *Eddie Foy Jr. of "Seven Little Foys" vaudeville fame*

About 60 years ago movies supplanted vaudeville as the favorite entertainment genre of the American masses. Yet even in its heyday, just prior to World War I, the force that was to eventually unseat vaudeville was featured at the end of each show. "Animated scenes" and silent motion picture shorts in their embryonic stage of development were screened after each bill as incidental entertainment for patrons filing out the rear exits.

Although the sophisticated technology and popularity of movies sounded the death-knell of vaudeville, some performers like Jack Benny, W.C. Fields and Burns & Allen were able to survive by adapting their talents to the Hollywood film. As an ironic epitaph, these movies then played many of the same theaters in which those vaudevillians had made live appearances a few years before.

Most vaudevillians, however, gravitated to Los Angeles or New York City to be near major entertainment markets and talent agencies — money centers that wouldn't have recognized most vaudevillians' brand of outdated novelty if it had jumped up and bit them in their accounts receivable. Show business has always readily allowed faded glory and good intentions to go justly unrewarded and for the majority of vaudevillians, Eddie Foy's melancholy pronouncement became a fact of life — and unemployment.

In Los Angeles, we interviewed an 89-year-old ex-vaudevillian named Harry Delmar. Even though he shared a chipped and crumbling apartment building with an assortment of panhandlers and petty thieves, Delmar didn't seem to mind. He moved in a waltz tempo of bygone anecdotes that recognized the harsh realities of life as untheatrical, and therefore unimportant.

When we met him, Delmar was busily tapping out an account of his life and career on an old manual typewriter. He was dressed in slippers and a faded checkered bathrobe and he had a shock of silver hair that continually displaced itself and fell across his forehead, blotting out the vision in his left eye. When this occurred, Delmar would bob forward like a chicken on the strut, and mechanically brush his hair back all the while peering intently at us as if to reassure himself that we hadn't, in that instant, left the room.

"I guess I've been living a secluded life out here," Delmar said. "I wanted to move back to New York but there's nobody left there. Here's a photograph of Benny Rubin and me. He was a vaudevillian. I hear he lives right down the block but I don't know where. We listen to different drummers today. What brought us together when we were young no longer exists. You try to find reasons why you fall away. If you want to ask me questions, just be warned that when I start, I go like a jackhammer."

Not an idle threat. Delmar's memories were practically adrenal — as insistent and vital as when the curtain rang down on his last stage performance years before. Anecdotes of SRO audiences, thunderous applause, and his name in lights were clearly at the cutting edge of his experience. Delmar spun them out before us as if they were proof of his singular worth as a human being, but it seemed that for too many years those halcyon days of glory had remained bottled up and uncirculated and that the retelling was tinged blue with loneliness.

"I don't think I'm clever enough to write my own story but I went through it," Delmar said. "I tried to get James Farrell, the author of 'Studs Lonigan,' to ghost for me. He's a fallen away Catholic born in a Kerry patch. His mother took in washing and the whole bit. Farrell refused, saying that my story smacked too much of Studs. Right now I'm writing about when I ran away to Chicago at the age of 15. To make a living, I washed tables and bussed dishes. In my spare time I used to hang around the Majestic Theater, and when people got out of their horse carriages I brushed off the windows for small change. Twelve years later I was headlining at the Majestic and flipping quarters to the bellhops. Are you listenin'?"

Delmar's triumphant metamorphosis from back-kitchen menial to Windy City celebrity was not without cost. As one of the "best hoofers in show business," Delmar has hobbled with a bum leg and danced in extreme pain throughout his career.

"My right leg is about two inches shorter than my left leg," Delmar said struggling to his feet. We noticed that his slippers were really earth shoes with a built-up right sole. "One of my jobs as a kid was in the dining car of the Rock Island railroad line, some euphonious designation like 'third cook.' One day I escaped the kitchen and went out to the platform. There were brass rails on each side and somehow my foot slid off of one and I tumbled off the train. Well, my leg was mangled and they were gonna cut it off. But a doctor named Bohart knew that I wanted to be a dancer, so he wired me together. I've had about five cracks at the final curtain but I'm still celebrating birthdays. Hello, Dolly!"

Delmar might have missed the brass rail but he did grab the brass ring. By 1919, he was making $1,300 a week as half of the vaudeville song and dance team of Delmar and Hackett.

"She would have shot you for mentioning my name first," Delmar said. "Jeanette Hackett was a clever girl who could write lyrics and I was pretty good at staging our routines. We did a 40-minute flash act with a company of 22 chorines and technicians. Everybody in the show could tap dance except Jeanette. She faked the stuff she did with me. Here's the idea of two very successful people who are both strangers to the dance. The only time we really got together was in the opening and during the last 16 bars of music at the finale. Dressed in a cutaway with white spats and striped trousers, I used to run up a large flight of steps and then do splits all the way down. They were called 'Roxy finishes.' Four or five girls would be at the bottom of the steps and I would leap over then into a split and then I would pick one up over my head and swing her over my shoulder."

Although ill equipped to partner Delmar in a syncopated buck-and-wing dance bash, Hackett did have a solo. Delmar said that in order to buy time for the rest of the cast to make costume changes, Hackett danced a Ruth S. Denis type of number complete with exotically tossed veils and hop and skip choreography that passed for high art in the hinterlands in those days.

"The set was a perfumed garden with a misty background," Delmar remembered. "During part of the number, Hackett came out with castanets all over her body. She was the most beautiful girl I had ever met in my life. Jeanette had breasts that were sculpted like they were put there solid as stone — not a droop a second. I was married to her for awhile."

During their eight-year stint as a vaudeville dance team,

Hackett and Delmar performed in Orpheum Circuit Theaters from coast to coast including the St. Paul Orpheum
that once stood at the corner of Fifth and St. Peter Streets
across from the Hotel St. Paul.

"We played St. Paul around 1920, and I always got the
impression that people there weren't as bright as the people
in Minneapolis," Delmar said. "I mean that they weren't as
quick or 'with it' as the saying goes. Our act went over great
in Minneapolis but we laid an egg in St. Paul. I couldn't
understand it and to this day I'm still trying to figure it out.
I run into a brick wall. There aren't any answers, only questions. Are you listenin'?"

Jeanette Hackett died six years ago in a car crash at the
age of 81. After she split with Delmar, Hackett worked for
RKO as a show doctor and costume designer. She ended her
show business career booking entertainment onto ocean lin-
ers. "I saved as much money as I could from our vaudeville
days," Delmar said. "Quite a large chunk of it went to produce my *Revels* which ran for two years on Broadway and
starred people like Bert Lahr and Frankie Fay."

After the *Revels,* Delmar produced a burlesque musical
called *Follow the Boys* filled with bawdy songs, cheesy sight
gags and scantily-clad chorus girls. Another smash hit on the
Great White Way, it elicited a heartfelt testimonial from impresario Mike Todd. "Harry, God damn it. I saw your show
the other day and that's the best piece of shit I've ever seen
produced in my life," he told Delmar.

Looking around Delmar's apartment we noticed many
photographs detailing the highlights of his career. In the midst
of all of those tokens of theatrical remembrance was a colored pictured of Jesus — the kind Christian guilds sell for
nominal prices and that you can't give away at garage sales.

"Heaven must be the ultimate venue," Tom mused looking at the picture (and deciding not to buy).

"That'll be my first command performance," Delmar replied. "There was a time when I couldn't decide if I wanted

to be a priest or an actor."

"I didn't know they were mutually exclusive," Dave piped in.

"You know the path I took," Delmar winked "I like to remember the words of St. Augustine. He said, 'Lord, I'm enjoying myself now, but I promise I'll get around to you later.'" They were words that Delmar lived — and loved — by, for no sooner had he finished St. Augustine than he launched into a soliloquy of distant sexual peccadilloes that would have turned Don Juan beet red.

"When I first rolled into Chicago I checked into a $3 room on Wabash Avenue. The landlady was the first real lay where I saw a lot of hair. I didn't pay rent for four months, and she did all of the leading — for those rates, why not! I was a very hip young guy but I pretended I wasn't. She said, 'Would you like to sleep with me tonight?' I meekly replied, 'I don't know, I've never slept with a woman.' That went on for a long time."

At this point in the interview, Delmar got up, unhitched his bathrobe and wordlessly pointed to a concave depression of scarry tissue near his spine. It was a dramatic gesture as faultlessly timed as one of his dance splits.

"Know where I got that?" Delmar smirked. He could see we were hooked and just waiting to be reeled in. "A gangster's moll shot me in the back during a jealous — what's the word — tryst." Delmar said that a few decades earlier when he was a spry young guy, he was always ready to "tell somebody where to go."

"I had a peculiar quirk," he said. "I disliked mobsters so much that I would bed their girlfriends. I considered it a feather in my cap. One evening while partying at a nightclub, I started to dance with this cheap hood's girl. She kept nuzzling up against me so I took her up to my Riverside Drive hideaway and we got down to it. We began keeping regular company. She was a good lay, that's all I knew, and I thought that was all she cared about.

"About one month into the affair, she woke me up saying she couldn't sleep. She was on the edge of the bed nervously smoking a cigarette. I asked her what was wrong, and she blurted out that she had agreed with her boyfriend to pretend that she cared for me and that after a certain amount of time had elapsed, her boyfriend would 'conveniently find out' and shake me down for some cash. I hauled off and hit her in the mouth. Between spurts of blood, I managed to calm her down. All the time she kept repeating that she had grown to love me. I told her I was going out. I had a date on the sly with a Chinese girl that I didn't want her to know about. She told me not to go because she could be killed for confessing. I slammed the door hearing her scream after me that she would shoot me. I knew that she carried a small pearl-handled pistol.

"I went to a party, and about two hours later I heard an ominous knock (Delmar rapped his knuckles three times on the coffee table to cue the suspense). A detective's knock I call it. I opened the door and there she was — mink coat draped over her nightgown, wearing little pom-pom bedroom slippers. I took off running and made it through one of those brocaded room dividers before I heard the shots and felt the burning in my neck and back. She had the presence of mind to know that all shootings had to be reported to the police, so she took me around to 47th Street and a doctor who was the brother of her boyfriend. Are you listenin'? I couldn't dream up this scenario. I thought I was dying so I tried to get a priest over to administer the last rites and the doctor's bedside manner was, 'Shut up or I'll knock your teeth in.' I'd say I've spent $15,000 on this injury over the years for operations and pain killers. Thanks to Julie Morton. I think that was the girl's name."

A woman scorned and a bullet in the back didn't stop Delmar from continuing to enjoy the carnal pleasures. He said that once he told the lucky woman of the moment that they were going to spend the entire year in bed. It cost him

$60,000 and he never did that again.

"It came easy in those days and you lived, or at least I thought you did," Delmar said. "Now in my old age I spend about three hours a day writing. I wrote this cockamamie thing." Delmar ripped from his typewriter the sheet of paper he had been working on when we first entered the room. "Before you go; read it into your tape recorder," he said. Tom read:

Harry Delmar is the last remaining theatrical producer in the grand tradition of Flo Ziegfeld, Earl Carrol and George White. One time boy wonder of Broadway with "Delmar's Revels" and "Follow the Girls" to his credit, he was also the male half of one of the great dance teams of vaudeville — Delmar and Hackett. Harry Delmar's love affair with the musical theater spans almost half a century. It comprises close associations with some of the greatest stars in show business. Harry Delmar is still active in his beloved field and he can still kick up his heels in a good old soft-shoe routine. A very charming and entertaining gentleman, he can talk with authority about the good old days of the theater and about the stars who made it great.

Harry Delmar is a recluse who funnels his remaining energy into writing a memoir that will never see printer's ink. Are you listening?

MEMORIES OF THE "TWO-A-DAY"
William Demarest
1981

There was a time when live entertainment was inexpensive by today's standards and the shows were consistently first-rate. Early in the century, for the princely sum of 15 cents, you could guffaw with the Marx Brothers, be transported to the last, tragic days of "Camille" via the magnificent stagecraft of Sarah Bernhardt, watch Will Rogers lasso his assistant as the poor lug hopelessly attempted to escape up the theater aisle, or marvel at the juggling prowess of W.C. Fields.

This was the era of the "two-a-day," more commonly known as big-time vaudeville. From the turn of the century to the advent of talking pictures, vaudeville was the presiding form of entertainment for millions of Americans. In Minnesota, St. Paul dominated the cultural scene with its lavish 1,700-seat Orpheum Theatre. Built in 1906, the theater boasted three balconies, nickel candy machines behind each chair, perfect acoustics and a garish French Renaissance interior with winged cherubim floating everywhere. Located at Fifth and St. Peter Streets, what was once the Orpheum is now the Commercial State Bank Building.

During its time as a vaudeville house (1906-23), the theater was one of the most prestigious show palaces on the Orpheum Vaudeville Circuit. The Circuit's job was to book the finest actors, singers, dancers and novelty acts into its own chain of theatres. One of the most unusual acts that frequently graced the St. Paul Orpheum proscenium was "Swain's Cats and Rats." Rats dressed in tiny jockey uniforms would race on the back of felines much to the local audience's delight.

Although the majority of vaudeville performers have faded into oblivion, a few survivors of the era remain and we recently talked to one of them who, since his days trodding "the boards," won a new generation of fans as the irascible Uncle Charlie on the television sitcom, *My Three Sons.*

William Demarest was born in West St. Paul 88 years ago. He is a musician, comedian, singer, dancer and one of America's most beloved character actors. In 1946, he received an Academy Award nomination for his supporting performance in *The Jolson Story,* yet he is best remembered as the loveable but gruff Uncle Charlie.

Demarest now lives in a rambling Palm Springs, Calif. home overlooking the fifth fairway of the Canyon Country

Club. He still golfs daily and is in remarkable health. Sitting in his den bedecked with mementos from his 75-year show business career, Demarest reminisced with us about his vaudeville days and his St. Paul origins.

"When I was a young boy trying to get on stage on amateur night at the Windsor Novelty Theater in the St. Paul Hotel, I looked longingly at the Orpheum Theater across the street," Demarest said. "One day I got a pass, and sitting in the balcony I saw my first big-time vaudeville show, a thrill I will never forget. Six years later, after playing small-time houses around the country, I came back, booked into the Orpheum as a full-fledged vaudevillian.

"The first time I appeared at the St. Paul Orpheum Theatre was in 1914. I worked with a partner named Dennis Chabot, who was a concert pianist and a violinist from Belgium. We did an act where we played music and then for a finish I would do a Russian dance with a roll-over step while playing the violin. Within a few years, I had Chabot standing on his head playing the piano."

After two years with Chabot, Demarest moved to New York and changed his routine. He discarded the all-music format, took on a girl partner and added more comedy to the act. The new team was called Demarest and Colette, and for more than 10 years they were Orpheum Circuit headliners.

"I played the St. Paul Orpheum every year until 1917," Demarest said. "In that year I stood on the roof of the Orpheum cheering the soldiers who were leaving for the war in France, and when I went down to the theater mailbox, there was my draft card! It said that Uncle Sam wanted me to report for duty in Ridgewood, N.J., on Monday. I wanted to finish the week at the Orpheum so I wired them back saying I can't make it by Monday. They wired back and said I'd better show up Monday or be classified as a deserter. So I wired back: 'Class me!' Nobody ever did mention my lateness when I arrived at camp.

"I, too, went away to war," Demarest continued. "When the fighting was over, to my surprise, my first booking was at the Orpheum St. Paul with my wife Estelle Colette. St. Paul audiences were always great … hell, they started laughing when they bought their tickets!"

Demarest's wife and partner's real last name was Cohen, but they angelicized it to Colette in order to ward off trouble during certain bookings.

"Estelle was a Jewish girl and back in those days, around 1909-10, some people were anti-Semitic," Demarest said. "I remember seeing signs down South that read: 'Jew, don't let the sun set on your head.' It said the same thing for black people."

Stars on the "Orpheum Time" were among the most highly paid professionals in the country. "When I first played the St. Paul Orpheum, Chabot and I performed fourth on the bill and were making $250 a week. The last time I performed in my hometown was 1923, and Colette and I were then taking in $750 a week. We were always next to closing on the bill … a good spot."

When Demarest performed with Colette, he had replaced the violin with a full-size cello and started to throw in physical comedy bits, often on the spur of the moment. Demarest pointed to his cello reclining in a corner of his den. "I bought that in a whorehouse around 1914 for $19," he said chuckling.

"We were playing a theater in Pennsylvania and you wouldn't think there was a soul in the audience," Demarest said. "No response whatsoever. And I thought to myself, 'What the hell is this?' So, during a number, I placed my cello on the stage and layed down next to it and tried to do a kip back up to a standing position (kind of like a handspring from a prone position). I fell back down to the stage and it got a big laugh, so for years when I'd tell a joke and it didn't go over, I'd lay down and try to do a kip."

Demarest's penchant (or fearlessness) for crazed pratfalls

came in handy when the actor co-starred in a series of knockabout films written and directed by Preston Sturges.

Recalling his early days growing up in St. Paul, Demarest said in that familiar coarse voice, "I was very athletic when I was young and always wanted to box. My training as a fighter came when I was between five and seven years old. During that time, I had real long hair. When I'd go out in the street, a gang would knock me to the ground and pull my pants down to see if I was a boy or a girl. I got licked many times, but I finally got to be a pretty good fighter."

Ironically, Demarest was once warned that his athleticism could be his downfall. "This doctor saw me perform twice in one day (the so-called 'two-a-day') and warned me that if I continued to rely on physical comedy, I wouldn't live to be 50. And here I am, still active at 88. I sure proved him wrong!"

"Three-Sheeting"
Eddie and Mary Foy
September 1980

In 1955, Bob Hope starred in the popular musical film *The Seven Little Foys*. The movie was about vaudeville entertainer Eddie Foy and his seven gifted children.

Older metropolitan residents may even remember the Foys who appeared at the Orpheum Theater here (in St. Paul, Minn.) before World War I. Their act consisted mainly of Eddie Sr. leading his kids through musical comedy sketches — when he wasn't haranguing them with his deprecating wit.

Although Eddie Sr. died in 1928, five of his seven children are still alive. We visited with two of them, Eddie Jr. and Mary, in the San Fernando Valley home they share. Now in their late 70s, both were eager to discuss their show business careers, which began in 1912.

Going onto the stage was not a matter of choice for the

Foy children, Eddie recalled.

"We got up one morning and we were on the stage," he said. "The old man used to work for theatrical producer J.J. Shubert. Well, one day, Pop hit him and broke his foot. Shubert vowed that he would never work on Broadway again. Finally, my mother said, 'We've got to do something.'

"We started singing and learning a few dance steps. So it was my mother who pushed us and told the old man to form an act. The first thing we did was a benefit in our Catholic church. I remember rehearsing for the show in front of the priest, who barely spoke English. My dad would swear at us for our ineptitude, and the priest would nod his head in approval and say, 'Oh, that is very good! Bravo, Bravo.'"

From those early beginnings in New Rochelle, New York, the Foys became the biggest act in vaudeville, headlining in such cities as Boston, New York, Chicago, Los Angeles and the Twin Cities. Their mother traveled with the act until her death in 1918. After that, the Foys were chaperoned by their aunt.

Mary remembered how her father used to elicit laughs from the audience at the expense of his children.

"Pop used to say that it took him a *long* time to put this act together. He also said that he made New Rochelle a city. These lines got big laughs."

One of the most popular and innovative sketches in vaudeville was "The Old Woman and the Shoe," which they brought to St. Paul in 1917.

"We had a big shoe on the stage and we all lived in it," Mary said. "My dad played the old woman in the shoe and we did our songs and dances and dialogue bits out of the shoe."

Eddie put in, "My oldest brother Bryan — who was 6 feet tall at the time — used to come out on stage and say, 'I'm Little Boy Blue, come blow your horn.' In St. Paul some guy in one of the upper boxes yelled out and told him to join the Army. Well, he jumped over the footlights and joined ...

the Navy. We did gags like, 'Hey, Pop, the chicken laid a goose egg this morning.' To which Dad replied: 'Don't let the rooster know about it!'"

Life on the road was not the best environment for raising seven children.

"I think we probably learned the ways of the world a little quicker," Mary said. But she was quick to add, "However, with a father like we had, you didn't get too wise because he was very strict. If anyone said anything racy in front of us, he would tell them off good."

Eddie intoned: "In the early years we were pretty much set dressing for Pop. He did most of the work. We did harmony singing and dancing. As we got older, we did more and he did less. We didn't go to dancing school, and it showed. We just went out on stage and did it. We tapped rottenly. But I'll tell you, as we boys got older and discovered girls we'd do some 'three-sheeting.' That's what actors called picking up girls in front of the theater. We'd stand just outside and point to our face on the playbill (which was usually three sheets in size) to impress them. Sometimes it even worked!"

Although quick to disparage their own contributions to the act, Eddie and Mary fondly recalled fellow performers that they shared bills with all over the United States. For the sheer bizarre quotient, they recalled three in particular.

… Bert Fitzgibbons "The Original Daffydill." "He would do gags like bring a kid on stage and the kid would be holding a huge chunk of ice. Fitzgibbons would then proceed to tell jokes while the ice melted, damn near freezing the kid's arms off. The act practically gave me frostbite just watching it," Eddie said.

… The Two Bryants. "They were two Germans who played two bums," Mary remembered. "One would take another out of a barrel, but have the toughest time straightening him up. He was like a wet noodle without any bone structure."

… Detso Ritter, "The Man Who Wrestles with Himself." "Detso used to contract his body into all sorts of positions,"

Eddie said. "One day he was late for the train and was literally running to catch it. On one of the cars were a bunch of
nuts being carted off to the asylum. Detso just managed to
jump aboard the last car. The orderly in a white suit was
making a head count "1, 2, 3 ... and so on." When he got to
Detso he said, "Who are you?" Detso replied, "I'm Detso
Ritter, the man who wrestles with himself." The orderly continued counting and included him. True story!"

By the mid-'20s the Foy family disbanded the act and
Eddie Jr. and Mary went their separate ways. Mary's show
business career was somewhat less distinguished than Eddie's,
but she kept performing. "I appeared in my older brother
Charley's Los Angeles nightclub for 20 years. The club was
very successful. Since the place closed down I've been basi-
cally retired," she said.

Eddie, though, has worked steadily through the years gaining a reputation as one of America's most durable character
actors. (He even portrayed his father, Eddie Sr., and traded
ascerbic put-downs with James Cagney as George M. Cohan
in *Yankee Doodle Dandy.*)

"I think Pop would have liked seeing that," Eddie said.

"To the Greats
without a Microphone"
George Jessel
August 1980

We'd heard of Georg(ie) Jessel but never quite knew exactly why he had been famous. To us, he was the self-pro-
claimed "Toastmaster General"; an old geezer who wore a
purple heart medal on his tuxedo, hosted social affairs at the
Friars Club for other stars that hailed from his own era (vaudeville of the early-teens and early 1920s) and delivered eulo-
gies at their funerals.

Definitely old school.

Our earliest recollection of Jessel also included a hilarious late-night TV sketch that Rob Reiner did before he attained fame as a movie director. Reiner lampooned the comedian, portraying him as the oblivious host of a telethon called: "Stop Death in Our Lifetime." His characterization was on the mark, right down to Jessel's toupee, be-ribboned tuxedo and thick, Lower East Side dialect — eerily like the voice of the Carvel Ice Cream TV pitchman that was popular for being so abrasive a while back.

All in all, Jessel's existence, or at least the topicality of how he lived now, reminded us of one of Norma Desmond's "waxwork" dinner party guests in *Sunset Boulevard*.

However, with our ongoing interest in the extinct American art form known as vaudeville came a desire to interview Jessel, who was a staple in that form of entertainment from the time he was a mere 10 years old. He performed along with fellow kids Eddie Cantor and Walter Winchell in acts staged by showman and songwriter Gus Edwards.

During our visit with Jessel in his Los Angeles-area home (in Reseda to be exact), we realized he was much more than an eccentric octogenarian. Attired in a black beret that would have made Albert Camus feel at home, bathrobe and slippers and sitting in a recliner, Jessel played us like we were front-row, center at the Palace Theater 50 years ago.

Jessel's housekeeper seemed nonplussed by our presence (although we thought visitors to Jessel's home must have been a rarity). She sat on a kitchen stool and didn't once shift her gaze from the Sunday *Los Angeles Times*. Flies buzzed around her, and the smoke from her cigarette curled lazily upward creating a smudge pot protective zone around her from the bothersome insects.

"I just talked with Burns (George)," Jessel bellowed. "How is he?" we asked. "Making millions," he said nonchalantly, betraying just a trace of envy, we thought.

Besides Jessel's casual attire, what attracted our attention even more was his home. He was a living endorsement for

Swanson TV dinners with half-eaten meals encrusted on aluminum trays that were splayed all over the kitchen counter. We noticed a few of his cats making quick work of the leftovers that were beginning to ripen and waft in the mid-day heat of the Valley. Aside from the mess, the home was a veritable museum of show business artifacts. And Jessel took great delight in directing us to strategic points on the walls where autographed photos of the queen of England, Golda Meir, Eleanor Roosevelt, several U.S. presidents and dozens of show business celebrities reposed in cheap, thrift-store frames.

"Look over there on the left wall," he commanded us. "Do you know who that is?"

"Rula Lenska," we meekly responded.

"No, it's the Happy Hooker herself, Xaviera Hollander," he boasted.

After the photos, came a blow by blow description of his medals, military uniforms and various awards. Among the collection of oddities was an ivory-tipped cane given to him by Harry Truman, an honorary Oscar, and numerous awards he received for his humanitarian work, much of it in support of Israel.

When the tour ended, Jessel recalled for us his recollections of playing at the Orpheum Vaudeville Theater in our hometown of St. Paul, Minnesota. He first appeared at the theater at the age of 13 in 1911. He was part of a musical-comedy act known as Gus Edwards "Kid Kaberet."

"I never danced in the act, but I did imitations of some of the stars who were famous in those days," he said. "Eddie Cantor used to imitate Al Jolson. Do you want to know an interesting fact? Jolson never saw a microphone until he was 68 years old."

We asked him what type of parental care or protection he received when traversing the country at such a young age.

"At first my mother took care of me. She also was wardrobe master for the troupe. But later Cantor watched over me. He was much older than me."

Jessel remembered our hometown audiences as being rather cold to performers. "And it had nothing to do with your climate," he quipped.

From vaudeville, Jessel went on to success on the Broadway stage. His biggest hit came when he played the title role in the theatrical version of *The Jazz Singer.*

"I did 1,000 performances in that play," he said. "When it came time to make the film, Warner Bros. put out an option to buy it, but they didn't have enough scratch to buy a cheese sandwich. Jolson put up the money, made the film and saved the studio."

After eight Broadway shows, Jessel moved to Hollywood where he produced 20 mostly "B" movies for famed producer Darryl Zanuck at 20th Century Fox. His career in his later years mainly consisted of eulogizing show business friends, hosting dinners and fundraisers, writing a syndicated newspaper column and occasional appearances on TV talk shows. He also made a cameo in the Warren Beatty film, *Reds.* But most of Jessel's time was spent hitting the stump and speaking out against liberal causes and what he said was the moral decay growing in this country.

"I've been banned from network television for nearly seven years. I made an attack on *The New York Times* and *The Washington Post.* I called them the *Pravda* of the West.

"Take television for instance," he continued. "The curse of America is right in that box. It has captured America's mind. The worst thing about TV is its impact on politics. Moses stuttered. He would have been murdered on TV! I was a vice president at ABC for over a year. They had meetings every day with advertising companies. At these meetings the public is never mentioned. If he's got the money he can buy the time and put your Aunt Minnie on. I don't think anyone should criticize any actor on television. When you finish a script it goes to the advertising company and if they want to take out all of the jokes, they do. So you say the guy wasn't funny.

"I'm responsible for the creation of a 90-minute news program in Israel. The county of Los Angeles has 10 million people — they have a newspaper and a half. New York City is down from 13 papers to three. There are 10 in Paris. I can go on and on."

It was quite clear that Jessel could go on and on. Since we seemed to have strayed off vaudeville and show business topics, we asked him for his thoughts on government funding for the arts, a hot topic at the time.

"What arts are there to control?" he asked. "The ballet? Don't make me laugh. I hate to be so pessimistic, but you have to face reality. I only hope Reagan can turn things around."

After leaving Jessel's house, we mused about the long arc his career had taken from a vaudeville and Broadway headliner, to producing movies in Hollywood to anonymity in a shambling suburb of Los Angeles. We wondered what kept Jessel going. Was it distant memories of SRO audiences that he daily nursed and thereby kept intact? Was it the talismans and tokens displayed on every wall, endtable and hutch that kept his eye from straying to a more prosaic reality — the kitchen wastebasket overflowing with TV dinner cardboard boxes?

We looked down at our notebook and found the answer to our question. The Toastmaster General had scrawled something on the last page of notes, probably while we were wandering from one piece of memorabilia to another.

"Here's to the greats ... without a microphone," it read. It could have sufficed as Jessel's own eulogy, a summation of where he ranked in the show business firmament.

Definitely old school.

THE Also-Ran
Benny Rubin
March 1979

Waiter ... taxi driver ... man at bar ... roulette croupier ... janitor. Comedian Benny Rubin's career after vaudeville was a litany of bit parts in movies and on television that could be clocked with an egg timer. Although Los Angeles, after the advent of talking pictures, was chock-full of former two-a-day headliners who couldn't scare up a gig, Rubin was a special case — one of Hollywood's first victims of reverse discrimination.

With dark, saucer-shaped eyes and a large proboscis, Rubin had what casting agents considered a Semitic look. Ironically, in a town largely founded and run by Jewish movie moguls sometimes just a generation removed from the shetls of Eastern European, looking or sounding too *haimish* was a drawback. After all, these powerbrokers had a fervent desire to weave themselves into the American tapestry; they were also dream merchants selling their idealization of America to an overwhelmingly gentile audience. And so the prejudice.

However, trouper that he was, Rubin shouldered the bias and soldiered on, appearing in movies during the 1930s, as a semi-regular on Jack Benny's television show in 1950 and in a slurry of other TV shows from *Perry Mason* and *Adam-12* to *Gunsmoke* throughout the 1960s and '70s. But that was much later.

A self-described "Boston original," Rubin got his start in vaudeville before the 1920s really started to roar, and was shocked when playing the Midwestern theaters of the Orpheum Circuit for the first time in 1922, that he didn't see "cowboys and Indians in the streets."

"Audiences in St. Paul (Rubin was making $62.50 a week then) weren't as fast as audiences in the big Eastern cities like

New York," he said. "It's not that the people in Minneapolis, or wherever, weren't as smart ... it's just that ... if you were living in New York, it was a tough hustle to make a buck. It's tough when you get into trouble and tough to stay out of it, so your mind works faster. In places like St. Paul, your stomach would get into waltz tempo. They are nice people there, they know each other. It's a 'Hey, Charlie, how'ya doin?' kind of thing. So if you made a flip remark and the audience didn't get it, some acts would say that they were dumb. But they weren't. They just moved in waltz tempo."

We asked him about performing on a vaudeville bill with George Jessel, but almost before we got the question out, Rubin pre-empted us with: "Cut! Who next? I don't want any bad talk. I hate a lot of people, and if you mention them, I'll say, 'Cut!'"

The rest of the interview was like negotiating (albeit humorously) a booby-trapped killing field; we never knew what names might trigger Rubin's wrath. It actually became a kind of game with us throwing out names and Rubin punching back remembrances like he was rushing the net at Wimbledon.

Reel to Real: What about Jack Benny?

Rubin: The closest friend I ever had. I was with him in 1926 when he changed his name from Kubelsky to Benny.

Reel to Real: Jackie Gleason?

Rubin: I'm a teetotaler and you'd see a guy like Gleason and he couldn't wait to get on a bill with Pat Rooney so they could get drunk together.

Reel to Real: The comedy team of Wheeler and Woolsey?

Rubin: Didn't like Woolsey much because he lived off Wheeler. Woolsey was a bad straight man who, nonetheless, called himself a comic. If it weren't for Bert Wheeler, he'd have been parking Model-T's.

Reel to Real: Milton Berle?

Rubin: He was a dirty bastard ... still is. His mother would go see other acts while Milton performed. Then she'd go backstage and give him all the best jokes. But then when he found out what was going on … he stole them himself!

In the parlance of the day, Rubin performed his act as a single (no need for unfunny straight men slowing things up) in an act that used his gift for mimicry and dialects. In fact, during the 1930s, Rubin was considered among the greatest showbusiness dialecticians around and even worked for a time as a vocal coach.

"Like I said before, being a Jew kid in Boston was tough. The Irish kids — and later the Wops — used to punch us around. That's where I began to perfect different dialects. That's also the time I took boxing lessons. I had a helluva record, 30 fights and I never won one of them!"

Although Rubin saw Bill "Bojangles" Robinson perform his legendary stair dance, Jack Benny play the violin and Burns & Allen trade barbs with each other on stage, he reserves his greatest praise for a staple of vaudeville, its veritable backbone — the animal acts.

"There was a guy with a dog named 'Louie,' and that mutt wouldn't do a damn thing on stage — which I thought was brilliant," Rubin said. "No matter what he said, the dog wouldn't budge. You can use whips or treats to teach animals stage tricks, but to teach a dog to do absolutely nothing … that's great."

When we met Rubin, he lived in a rather shabby apartment building on Hollywood Boulevard. He told us he was semi-retired but that if his agent called, he'd work at "the drop of a hat." During our visit he showed us a miniature silver star embedded in faux marble and framed in a shadow box. He said that since the entertainment community had never honored him with a star on Hollywood Boulevard's "Walk of Fame," family members had come up with their own commemoration.

To us, the makeshift token seemed sad and defiant at the same time, but Rubin was long past holding grudges (excluding Georgie Jessel). Suffused by the love of family and with memories intact of a long career in show business, Rubin seemed to practically glide across the room to replace the plaque in its prominent position on a credenza. It had taken him nearly half a century (with a life's worth of triumphs and tragedies wedged in between), but Rubin had finally learned to move in waltz tempo.

THE SUNSHINE BOY
Joe Smith
September 1979

This one goes way back.

Joe Smith of "Smith & Dale" and "Avon Comedy Four" vaudeville repute was 95 years old and sharp as tack when we met him one crisp September morning at the Actors' Fund Home in Englewood, New Jersey. It was the unpredictable confluence of chronology that brought us together. We were born in the late '50s and had reached an adult age where we could seek out celebrities. And Smith, for his part, had held on long enough to appear in our gunsights as a potential interview — a harmonic convergence (with distinct Borscht Belt overtones) if ever there was one.

By the time we interviewed Smith — whose "Sunshine Boy" character was immortalized by George Burns in the self-titled movie — his kind of ethnic comedy which relied heavily on German-Jewish and Hungarian dialects and which had been a staple of vaudeville in the first years of the 20th century, had become an historical footnote. Smith himself was all but forgotten; remembered only by a handful of show business archivists, the staff at the Actors' Fund Home ... and Hackensack High School. The spry nonagenarian's only defense against the accumulated early morning dew in the Home's back garden was a pullover sweater with a giant letter "H" stitched on the front. Smith told us Hackensack High had given him the garment — making him *de facto*, the oldest high school graduate in the nation.

"I first met Charlie Dale in 1898 at Child's Restaurant in Manhattan," he told us. Other reports say that the two knockabout comedians met, appropriately, when their bikes collided into each other on Delancey Street on Manhattan's Lower East Side. Smith said that he couldn't know at the time that their inauspicious debut slinging hash would be the beginning of a fruitful partnership that would last 73 years, ending with Dale's death in 1971.

"We both worked a shift from 12 noon to 3 a.m. The rest of the time we looked for stage work. At the time, Charlie and I had a singin' and dancin' act in blackface with some comedy thrown in. In 1901, we hooked up with Will Lester and Jack Coleman and became The Imperial Vaudeville and Comedy Company."

In that era, before automobiles, the foursome played a series of one-night stands all over upstate New York and were transported to their gigs in a horse-drawn sleigh. Smith said that on Saturdays the act would work for room and board and pitch in as waiters and bartenders.

We wondered aloud whether the act's unwieldy title could have been a contributing factor why Smith, Dale, Lester and Coleman, were waiting tables on weekends?

"Eventually we put together a school-type act and opened in a café in New York up on 116th street," Smith said. "As I was leaving the place after arranging the first booking, I looked in the window and noticed it was named Avon. That's how the Avon Comedy Four was born."

Turn-of-the-century bookings at theaters down on the Bowery (New York's theater district long before Broadway supplanted it) led to a gig at the Atlantic Garden, a family beer hall that featured an all-girl orchestra. That's where the Avon Comedy Four met an agent who launched them into the big time — the Orpheum Vaudeville Circuit.

By that time, the act had developed into a full-blown farce

called, "The New School Teacher" — complete with school desks as props. The Avon Comedy Four performed the act, to rave notices, for more than a decade all over the country. Although the comedy creaks plenty after more than seven decades, Smith assured us the lines flew fast and furious. He gave us a sampling.

"The teacher would come on stage and ask us to name two of the principal oceans in the world. A sissified boy would stand up and recite: 'The Atlantic and the Pacific." And the teacher would reply: 'No, that's a tea company.' The teacher would then say: 'I will now call out the roll.' I would hand him a biscuit and say: 'Tomorrow I'll bring you a pineapple.' Flustered, he'd then say: 'Those who are here say, *Here*! And those who are not here, say *Not Here*!'"

Around 1906, Smith & Dale also began developing their own comic specialty — "Dr. Kronkheit and his Patient" — that became a favorite routine amidst the Avon Comedy Four's general zaniness. A typical Dr. Kronkheit exchange would be: "Please, my time is liniment — don't rub it in!"

The act played Orpheum Circuit Theaters for a solid ten years with little more changing than the accompanying musical selections. But in 1918, The Avon Comedy Four, in a furious case of spring cleaning, wrote a whole new act entitled, "A Hungarian Rhapsody."

"We called it that because it took place in a Hungarian restaurant," Smith said. We had singers and dancers ... about six different singing duos. And we had a cubbyhole setup where the waiters would shout orders to the kitchen staff."

Smith remembered that the set was bisected into the restaurant and kitchen with comedy schtick happening in each location. "It was practically two acts," he said. "The waiters would fire orders at me so fast (I worked in the kitchen part), that I would get dizzy. They'd then say, 'Go see Dr. Kronkheit,' and that would lead Charlie and I into our bit.

"Later, Charlie would shout to me: 'Customers are complaining when they order goulash. They want the orchestra to play a Hungarian rhapsody.' I would reply: 'I suppose if they wanted a baked apple, they'd want them to play the William T'hell Overture ... so, t'hell with 'em!' The boss would interject: 'Chef, we gotta hire waiters that can sing, otherwise we'll lose trade.' Then you would hear a waiter singing 'mi, mi, mi' offstage. I would reply: 'Yes, yes, yes. You there, come here!' I would tell the waiter he had to sing or lose his job, whereupon he'd launch into a gorgeous rendition of 'The Song of India.' Then Charlie and I would stick our heads out of the cubbyhole and say, 'They liked that!'"

After the death-knell of vaudeville, Smith, along with Dale, kept busy, often appearing as a thick accented specialty act in movies and later, with a sprinkling of guest spots in television shows. As Smith himself would tell you, it's a long way from horse-drawn sleighs and sleeping berths in Pullman Cars to being electronically beamed into TV sets across the nation. Even more momentous was the fact that Smith lived to see himself immortalized in Neil Simon's *The Sunshine Boys.* That kind of thing is often posthumous, he said.

Two years after our interview, the laugh track finally ended for Joe Smith when he died in his sleep at the age of 97. But, true to form, the old vaudevillian did manage to get the last laugh. He was interred at a cemetary in Valhalla, New York, with the following — prescient — words inscribed on his tombstone: "Booked Solid."

II.
Hoofers, Warblers and All That Jazz

That Nimble Tread
Fred Astaire
July 1978

In a seldom traveled part of the Beverly Hills business district, on Brighton Way — one of the few boulevards without potted palm trees — stands the nondescript office front of a building that contains the offices of several Certified Public Accountants. This would hardly excite interest except that an office on the third floor belongs to one of show business's most cherished legends — Fred Astaire.

The man who has been repeatedly nominated as one of the world's best dressed was, when we met him, wearing a blue sport coat, wide red Christian Dior necktie, blue cotton pants, a red and blue designer belt and Gucci black leather shoes. (We also noticed that his chic attire had the distinct redwood odor of being recently liberated from a cedar trunk.) He greeted us with a "Hi fellas, sit down" off-hand elegance that is his trademark in films. It was just the kind of introduction that at once put us at ease and deflated any notions we might have harbored on exactly how to interview a "certifiable living monument."

After all, Astaire is considered without exception to be the greatest dancer the movies have ever known. His 31 musical films spanning 1933 to 1968 have established a measuring rod of excellence by which all other musical comedy work is judged. Landmark movies such as the series of 10 films Astaire made with Ginger Rogers are today hailed as cinema classics and have been acknowledged as a major influence in the work of dancer/choreographers such as Gene Kelly, George Balanchine and Bob Fosse.

As Astaire settled into a nearby chair, we noticed that his ankles swelled out of his shoes like a couple of globular ballbearings. The effect seemed odd until we contemplated that after the better part of a century stomping the hell out rehearsal hall floorboards, any such ankles — bulbous or not — would be fortunate if they were still attached to legs let alone be proportionately as slender as the rest of Astaire's lithe frame.

To break the ice, we asked Astaire if he had ever visited Minnesota. "About all that I remember positively is that my sister Adele and I performed in St. Paul and Minneapolis as children around 1909 (Astaire was nine years old then) on the Orpheum Theatre Vaudeville Circuit," Astaire said almost apologetically. We certainly couldn't fault him for not remembering 71-year-old specifics about two towns he probably only glimpsed from a stage door.

But after a moment's contemplation he volunteered. "I do remember that the winter weather in the Twin Cities was bitterly cold. "We agreed that was the only specific thing about Minnesota that would endure over 71 years.

We mentioned that we had recently shown his 1948 film musical *Easter Parade,* co-starring Judy Garland, to a St. Paul nursing home audience, and that immediately after the screening an elderly resident innocently asked us if it was one of our home movies.

The statement flabbergasted Astaire. "You mean she thought that *you* guys filmed it yourselves?" he asked incredulously. He cracked a thin, impish smile and gamely fought to retain a measure of self-restraint. But his composure finally shattered into laughter. Eventually he collected himself and said that after a 50-year career of fielding detailed questions on every aspect of his films, this was the first time anyone ever mistook his work for someone else's home movie.

With disco dancing the national rage, we asked if he ever tripped the light fantastic in local Los Angeles nightclubs. Astaire replied that disco was just free-style fun and could not possibly be compared with the exhaustively rehearsed choreography of musical films. As if to make that point emphatic, he improvised a couple of dance steps (still seated in his chair). Astaire did a kind of scissors step crossing his feet back and forth while he thrust one arm out in front. At the same time, he twisted his other arm in back of his neck; his long, tapering fingers sprouting up behind his head like the eagle feathers on a Sioux warbonnet.

The agility of those legendary feet and his marvelously expressive hands demonstrated that Astaire had lost little of the precision that characterized numbers like his adagio with the wooden hatrack in *Royal Wedding* or his synchronized "golf dance" from *Carefree.*

"After seeing *Saturday Night Fever,* I voted for John Travolta as Best Actor at the 1978 Academy Award ceremony," Astaire said. Travolta's tense, sexually charged dancing, was, according to Astaire, an interesting extension of the delinquent character he portrayed.

A direct result of the nostalgia craze of a few years back was a rebirth of interest in the famous MGM musicals and, concomitantly, the effortless flair of Fred Astaire. However, with that rebirth came the inevitable crass commercialism that usually undercuts anything with real substance. In Astaire's case, this took the form of a rash of movie books and unauthorized biographies.

"My 1959 autobiography 'Steps In Time' is, and can only be, the definitive source on my career," Astaire explained. Because of this renewed exposure, he is continually hounded by interviewers and authors intent on asking questions for which he says he has long since forgotten the answers. Astaire said that one writer in particular, British author Michael Freedland, was quite insistent.

"He kept telephoning for days wanting a posed photograph of the two of us for the dust-jacket of a movie book he was writing about me. When I finally agreed to a short photo session, he arrived at my house with his wife and kids, but luckily without overnight luggage."

Astaire's tireless perfectionism has been praised with a trove of theatrical awards, including an honorary 1949 Oscar, the British Academy Award, four Emmys, three Golden Globes, and most recently his induction into "The Entertainment Hall of Fame" by the Kennedy Center for the Performing Arts. While Astaire gratefully acknowledged these honors, his greatest pleasure is in recounting the victories of several racehorses he has owned.

"My filly Triplicate won the 1946 Hollywood Gold Cup," he said proudly and then added with a conspiratorial whisper. "She beat Louis B. Mayer's mare in a hotly contested heat — this when I was under contract to Mayer at MGM."

Our visit at an end, Astaire ushered us out of the office as unassumingly as he greeted us. It reminded us of a certain air of nonchalance that we had first seen in a 1933 film called *Flying Down to Rio,* when Astaire coaxed a lissome gal named Ginger onto a dance floor for the first time, and in the process singlefootedly revolutionized the Hollywood musical.

Elastic Man
Ray Bolger
March 1979

At age 76, song-and-dance man Ray Bolger still has the bounce of a rubber ball. "That's because I practice my hoofing every day," he told us in a recent interview on the set during filming of the television pilot *For Heaven's Sake,* in California's Anaheim Convention Center.

Bolger was wearing a blue cardigan, gray slacks and Pro-Ked sneakers. His thick gray hair was styled and blow-combed and his face (to say nothing of the rest of his body) still had the supple elasticity that has been his trademark for over 50 years.

"Let me tell you a few things about *The Wizard of Oz,* Bolger said as if anticipating our first question — or perhaps anyone's, for that matter.

"Buddy Ebsen (TV's Barnaby Jones) was originally cast as the Tin Woodsman, but he became allergic to the silver metallic paint they were covering his body with. He was hospitalized, nearly died and had to be replaced by Jack Haley," he said. For his own part, in one fell swoop, Bolger was iconized singing and dancing down the yellow brick road as the quick-thinking — and therefore oxymoronic — Scarecrow without a brain in the 1939 MGM classic.

Bolger still has his costume: hat, tunic, pants, leggings and bits of telltale straw (it resides in an upstairs closet alongside the rest of his cardigans) and enjoys watching the film when it is annually rebroadcast on television. Of course, his fondest memories of the film were working with Judy Garland.

"Judy made the whole experience a memorable one. She was a good friend of mine and a remarkable performer," said Bolger.

What does the scarecrow think of the stage musical and recent film, *The Wiz?* "I'm sorry to say, not much. *The Wiz* is overblown and will never have the universal appeal *The Wizard of Oz* has obtained."

All of a sudden Bolger excused himself and ran onto the set to help the director prompt the extras. *For Heaven's Sake,* it was explained to us, was an attempt by the network to cash in on the recent success of the hit motion picture, *Heaven Can Wait.*

The crew was filming a basketball sequence, but only shooting the crowd reaction to the game. Bolger decided to act the role of the entire team and began running up and down court. The camera recorded the faces of the fans swaying their heads back and forth while they watched Bolger jogging and dribbling with an imaginary basketball in his uninhibited crazy-legged style. Surveying the scene was a little like watching a septuagenarian scarecrow that had just been loosed from atop his pole in an Ozian cornfield.

From our vantage, it looked as though Bolger hardly

worked up a sweat after his intense aerobic workout — not unlike if the Wicked Witch of the West's gray-pallored dragoons had just chased him around the castle. When the director yelled: "cut," Bolger literally bounced back into his chair. "What were we talking about?" he asked.

We asked what it was like working with famed choreographer George Balanchine in the "Slaughter on Tenth Avenue" ballet from the 1936 Rodgers and Hart Broadway show, *On Your Toes?*

"Taking dance direction from Balanchine was one of the highlights of my career. It was hard work, but the results were rewarding. The ballet was considered a breakthrough in stage dancing," he said.

Bolger said he didn't think much of Gene Kelly's reinterpretation of the ballet in the 1948 film *Words and Music.* "It was initially a comedic dance. Kelly took it out of context and made it into a serious ballet."

Bolger made some fine musicals during his tenure at MGM, including *The Great Ziegfeld, Rosalie* with Eleanor Powell and *The Harvey Girls* again with Garland.

"I had a great time making *The Harvey Girls.* It gave me a chance to work with Judy again and do some fine solo hoofing." Filming his solo tap dance during a frontier party scene to an instrumental reprise of the Oscar-winning song "Atcheson, Topeka and the Santa Fe," was an arduous experience, according to Bolger.

"I would have to film the number first without using tap shoes. Then I would go into a music stage and re-create the tap rhythms perfectly so they could be dubbed onto the film later."

This was a terribly painstaking job. Bolger's dance style has always been loose-limbed and improvisational. It was "murderous" to dub in the taps so they would match the routine that was shot on film, he said.

Bolger knows only one man who had no trouble performing this task. His name is Fred Astaire.

"What a perfectionist. Fred would work on a single routine until he had every nuance exactly how he wanted it." He called Astaire the greatest dancer in film history.

Bolger has not hung up his tap shoes as so many of his contemporaries have. He still tours the country, performing his eccentric style of dancing and has also has gone dramatic, appearing in the 1979 Stanley Kramer film, *The Runner Stumbles.*

But Bolger's proudest show business accomplishment is no surprise to anyone; it's that the character of the Scarecrow of Oz will be around long after he's gone "over the rainbow."

"Beautiful Dynamite"
Cyd Charisse
April 1996

"She came at me in sections,
More curves than a scenic railway.
She was bad. She was dangerous.
But she was my kind of woman."
    —*Fred Astaire upon first encountering Cyd Charisse,
    "Girl Hunt Ballet" from the film,* The Band Wagon

Cyd Charisse, with legs that stretched into infinity and a smoldering sensuality that no other dancer in Hollywood could match, has become a reigning icon of the Golden Age of MGM musicals that peaked in the early-1950s. Nicknamed "Beautiful Dynamite" by Astaire, Charisse proved to be a perfect duet partner for Fred in *The Bandwagon* and later in her favorite role as Ninotchka in *Silk Stockings.*

It's true. MGM had no shortage of talented dancing ladies in those days. Ann Miller's tap dancing could approximate a pneumatic drill gone berserk; Leslie Caron was ballet-trained with a gamin quality; and Vera-Ellen could tap or toe dance with equal aplomb. But Charisse's routines had an added dimension guaranteed to appeal to red-blooded American males in theaters across the country. In the "Broadway Ballet" from *Singin' in the Rain* for instance, when Charisse sinuously wrapped her legs around Gene Kelly's torso and then rubbed his steamed-up eyeglasses on her inner thigh, enough heat was generated to melt stone. More than 40 years later, the effect on movie audiences is still the same.

These days, Charisse, along with her husband, singer Tony Martin, lives a mostly retired life in a luxury highrise off Wilshire Boulevard in Los Angeles. Slim and chicly dressed, Charisse, in the short walk from the front door to the sitting room, displays an effortless grace that seems as natural as a deep breath. But in reality, such equipoise did not come easily. From the age of six, the practical consideration of overcoming a handicap was the motivating factor in Charisse's decision to dance.

"Growing up in Amarillo, Texas, I had a slight case of polio which resulted in an atrophied shoulder and me being very skinny," she says. "People were afraid to touch me. So in order to exercise my muscles and become part of the community again, I took dance lessons." It helped that Charisse's father was a self-professed "balletomane" who loved to see his daughter dance and encouraged her every step of the way. Before long, Charisse's precocious talent required an outlet beyond what her West Texas hometown could provide. She began studying dance in earnest in Los Angeles with a former partner of the great *danseuse* of Diaghilev's Ballets Russes, Anna Pavlova. It was during the strict regimen of daily classes that the ballet master of the Ballet Russe de Monte Carlo saw Charisse. The world-renowned troupe was performing at the Los Angeles Philharmonic Hall. In short order, she was offered a spot in the company.

After trekking home to Texas to receive her father's blessing, the teenage Charisse joined the company in Cincinnati. However tragedy struck, and Charisse's father fell gravely ill.

She left the troupe to be with him when he died. Then, at the age of 16, Charisse got a second chance to join the company during another stopover in Los Angeles. Proceeding to Europe, the Ballet Russe de Monte Carlo was about to embark on a tour of the great capitols starting with Berlin. "We were scheduled to perform there on September 1, 1939," Charisse says. "Unfortunately, Hitler chose that day to invade Poland and begin World War II. At the behest of the State Department, I found myself on a steamship back to the United States."

Back for a third time in Los Angeles, Charisse auditioned for the MGM film *Ziegfeld Follies* which starred just about all the high-octane musical talent the studio could command. "Arthur Freed, the producer of the picture, became my mentor," Charisse says. "He needed someone who could dance *en point* in a sequence that — portentously — featured Fred Astaire." The number, entitled "Bring on the Beautiful Girls," also showcased Lucille Ball who brandished a bullwhip to keep a bevy of "feline" chorus girls in line.

"Fred was in a top hat and tails and I did this tentative little toe dance around him, but not with him," Charisse remembers. "The problem was these huge mountains of soap suds that were part of the number. Showgirls were gathered on a big staircase that I was supposed to pirouette down. But the bubble machine went crazy and started to cover the girls with suds. They started to scream and ambulances were called. In the final print all you see is one small scene of me pirouetting through the mess."

Her movie debut opposite Mr. Bubble notwithstanding, Arthur Freed liked what he saw and signed Charisse to a standard seven-year contract at $350 a week. With one fell swoop of a pen Charisse became a cog in the greatest dream factory in history.

"It was fabulous," she says. "I took singing lessons, acting lessons and had a vocal coach who worked with me to get rid of my Texas twang. MGM in those days had the greatest writers, directors, costumer designers — you name it. Everything was at your fingertips, and everything was done in-house."

According to Charisse, MGM "built stars to last." "Today," she says, "an actor is lucky if they're in a film big enough to sustain them to stardom. In my day, you had an army of gifted people, all experts in their fields, tailoring parts for your particular talent."

Charisse's breakout role was as the object of Gene Kelly's affection in the "Broadway Ballet" from *Singin' in the Rain.*

"Gene was going to use his dance assistant, Carol Haney, in the role," Charisse says. "Carol was a wonderful dancer, but Freed didn't think she photographed well. All the moves were already blocked out by the time I was brought in. The 'vamp' part of the ballet was hard to do because of all the nuances. It was really like a mini-drama within a number. We rehearsed the Salvador Daliesque 'Crazy Veil' sequence until my shoulders were chapped — they had to blow so much wind on me in order to make the veil go up into the air."

When queried about her favorite dance number, Charisse responds without a moment's hesitation. "'Dancing in the Dark' with Fred Astaire from *The Bandwagon* was so simple, yet so lovely," she says. "I loved Astaire's style. He had a quality when he walked in a room that was his and nobody else's in the world; a charm, elegance. He was also extraordinarily gentle. He would never confront you with a criticism directly for fear that he would embarrass you. But he wasn't a pushover. With Fred, you would invariably come in early and work late. You had to have stamina."

It's logical to assume that Charisse, 76, might want to relax a little and accept the plaudits her talents have earned over decades spent in front of the camera. It's logical, but it would be wrong. A couple of years ago, to help her mother combat a severe case of arthritis, Charisse, in tandem with a chemist friend, developed a product they dubbed Arctic Spray.

The curative is now being marketed at drugstores throughout the country.

Charisse may be driven by a work ethic underscored by arduous hours spent rehearsing in drafty sound stages, or maybe her newfound career owes it's provenance to memories of a little girl in Amarillo, Texas, who triumphed over some tough odds of her own. In any case, Charisse says with just the faintest hint of incredulity, "I now find myself a business executive. It's a whole new dance."

With a Song in Her Heart
Kathryn Grayson
April 1995

We wore suits for this interview — that's the prime difference between hip, young tinseltown circa 1995, where dressing down in mixed company is as acceptable as dressing up, and the rules of decorum that governed Hollywood a half century ago.

Kathryn Grayson, 76, Metro-Goldwyn-Mayer's reigning diva in musicals and operettas of the 1940s and '50s commands that token of respect. And if we had any doubts that our pinstripes (we looked like a couple of accountants come for a tax audit) paid appropriate fealty, they were dispelled the instant we met her.

After being led by Grayson's longtime housekeeper from the foyer of her rather baronial mansion in Santa Monica through a darkly paneled corridor, we surfaced in a small library anteroom. There, Grayson reclined in a highbacked chair, gussied up for the occasion in a chiffon dress that pulsated its bright red hue like a feathered ladies chapeau in a Renior painting. To add to the dramatic effect, Grayson was suffused in what could only be described as a weird theatrical glow. It was a couple of seconds before we realized she was benefiting from an uplight hidden from view on the floor behind the chair.

It might have been ages since her last movie, but Grayson still knew how to entertain "the gentlemen of the press," as she quaintly called us. We felt glad we dressed up; moreover, Grayson ranks as one of the very few stars we ever interviewed that could make an entrance just by sitting down.

Under what she said was Louis B. Mayer's watchful yet benevolent eye, Grayson told us she literally grew up at MGM, enfolded and protected by the all-powerful studio system. She came to believe she was special because everyone in MGM's "extended family" was special.

The solid grounding Grayson managed to get at MGM is evident even today. In a transient town where the only regularity seems to be the fleeting nature of fame, she's lived serenely in the same 20-room home for 50 years.

"I moved here with my husband (singer/actor John Shelton) from Bel-Air just after the war," she said. "He had been shot down over the Solomons and was rescued by a submarine off a Japanese-held island. After getting back stateside, our old house made him feel claustrophobic. Now my neighbors include Mel Brooks and Anne Bancroft, Julie Andrews and Michael Crichton."

Grayson came by her singing ability early — perhaps even genetically. Surrounded by brothers and sisters with four octave ranges, Grayson would sing coloratura soprano to RCA Red Seal recordings of Enrico Caruso (she would later record for that label); and with her siblings, perform impromptu quartets from *Rigoletto* and *Lucia Di Lammermoor.*

"A friend and I used to climb over the fence of the St. Louis Municipal Opera Amphitheater in Forest Park," Grayson said. "We would sing arias for the janitor who worked there. He always applauded and said we were as good as the singers who played there on tour. Well, we thought we were pretty hot stuff until we learned that the janitor was stone deaf!"

Grayson was in California studying to be an opera singer

when MGM expressed interest in signing her to a contract. On Saturday afternoon (so as not to conflict with high school), Grayson and her singing teacher visited the studio for an audition. "I sang Deanna Durbin's songs, Judy Garland's songs, Jeanette MacDonald's songs and even Grace Moore's songs," Grayson said. "I must have sung for two or three hours." She made the cut and was signed to a standard contract with an option for renewal and a salary increase at year-end.

"I didn't think I was pretty enough for pictures," Grayson said. "Edward Johnson who was head of the Metropolitan Opera in those days, approached me and asked if I wanted to sing 'Lucia' on stage. I loved the opera and wanted to do it desperately, but Mr. Mayer said no. He told me that if I made my operatic debut before releasing my first picture, I would be known forever after as an opera singer. However, if I was a hit in movies, then I'd be internationally famous for the rest of my life."

However, according to Grayson, who was the "spoiled brat of the lot" at MGM (against the advice of studio executives, she used to make the commute from home to studio on her Harley-Davidson motorcycle in nine minutes flat), Mayer's advice went unheeded. "I was still furious," she said. "We had this tremendous tete-a-tete, until finally he said, 'Kathryn, you're such a little rebel! I want you to go to a mountaintop and yell, 'Go to hell!' and then listen to the echo coming back to you. I then want you to yell, 'God bless you!' and listen to that echo.'"

According to Grayson, that's when Mayer's philosophy sank in. "He saw the big picture. He wanted all of us to have happy lives," she said.

Grayson made her film debut in 1941 in *Andy Hardy's Private Secretary* with Mickey Rooney. "Those 'Andy Hardy' films were a training ground for MGM starlets," Grayson said. "Judy Garland, Lana Turner, Donna Reed and Esther Williams all got their start in those pictures. I didn't realize until quite recently that my 'Andy Hardy' movie was one of the top ten moneymakers in 1941."

Grayson's initial success was followed up with starring roles in a series of lighthearted musicals, including *Anchors Aweigh*, co-starring Gene Kelly and Frank Sinatra.

"Frank was one of the sweetest people with whom I've ever worked," she said. "During *Anchors* we would do our close-up shots at the end of the day. Frank and I would feed lines to Gene during his close-ups, but Gene would be mysteriously AWOL when it came time to feed lines to us for our close-ups. Gene was very ambitious about all aspects of filmmaking and would be off somewhere learning about cameras or some such thing. Frank, on the other hand, didn't have to be ambitious. He was Frank Sinatra — already a star."

Grayson remembers recording the whole score of that film in one or two days. "Sometimes the music would come into our hands wet, still smelling of ink," she said.

Living under a strict dietary regimen of steak and tomatoes for lunch (high-energy protein) and soup and salad for dinner, Grayson starred in and recorded the soundtracks for *Kiss Me Kate, Showboat* and two movies starring another operatic sensation; former Philadelphia truck driver, Mario Lanza.

"I went to the Hollywood Bowl in 1948 with Mr. Mayer, his secretary, Ida Koverman and my husband to hear Mario sing with the Bel Canto Trio," Grayson remembered. "He had such a beautiful voice. He came to the studio the next day and we sang together for the benefit of the sound technicians. Their verdict was that we sounded great together. The only problem was Mario's weight. He was heavyset."

Trimming a few pounds wasn't much of a hurdle for a studio that boasted of creating "more stars than there are in the heavens."

"I lent Mario my masseuse to help him trim down, and in a few months we were ready to start filming our first picture, *A Midnight Kiss,* which was followed soon after by *The Toast of New Orleans.*"

The only memorabilia from those halcyon days that Grayson kept is a dress she wore in *A Midnight Kiss.* "Everything is gone now," she said. "The MGM backlot is leveled. The whole studio system fell apart when Mr. Mayer left MGM. He loved quality. I hear the Sony people who now own the former MGM studio have beautiful gardens there ... I wish they'd make beautiful pictures instead."

A lyrical lament from one of MGM's storied songbirds.

SETTING THE RECORD STRAIGHT
Gene Kelly
June 1978
March 1994

Hollywood isn't cherished for its long memory. In fact, it's often derided as incestuous and infested with a particular brand of shark that jealously devours those whose movies don't excel at the box office. However, even a town as insecure and unapologetically larcenous as Hollywood can sometimes reach a meaningful consensus about real art.

That happens to be the case concerning the legacy of song-and-dance man Gene Kelly. He is venerated everywhere in the film capital as a true original — no small achievement in a place with more than its fair share of poseurs and mere technicians. Since Fred Astaire's death in 1987, Kelly has stood alone as the reigning high priest of a joyous and uniquely American art form — the movie musical.

It was the summer of 1978 when we first met Kelly. As newly minted high school graduates, we had put in three hard months selling beer at Minnesota Twins baseball games to come up with the airfare to get us to Los Angeles. After nearly two years of persistent correspondence, Kelly had finally green-lighted a "brief visit" to his home in Beverly Hills.

To say we were fans of the Golden Age of Hollywood musicals, and in particular Kelly's huge contribution, would be understating the case. Our consuming passion for that era had inspired us to found a film society that brought the musicals of Kelly, Astaire, Garland and others to shut-ins at Twin City area nursing homes. True confession: Under cover of that humanitarian guise, we were able to indulge our obsession by viewing obscure, forgotten musicals that didn't even make it on TV's late, late show.

For almost half a century Kelly has lived in the same French colonial house with red window shutters on Rodeo Drive in the Beverly Hills flatlands just south of Sunset Boulevard. On the appointed day, he strolled over to us from his favorite room, the library, with an almost syncopated bounce in his step. We had seen it dozens of times before in his movies; whether gliding alone down a backlot *rue* at MGM as *An American in Paris,* or with two buddies in New York City out for a day *On the Town.* It was a jaunty, confident and athletic stride.

Kelly said that he and his two children, Tim and Bridget, had been over at neighbor Harry Warren's house using the tennis court, as they often did, for a few quick sets. In 1950, Warren, a three-time Academy Award-winning songwriter, had written the score for *Summer Stock* starring Gene and Judy Garland.

"Wonderful, wonderful Judy, she was the greatest," he said. "She wasn't a trained dancer but she was such a hard worker. We did a number in that film in a barn called 'The Portland Fancy.' She was terrific, picked up the steps so quickly. And it wasn't an easy dance to do."

We asked him about *Singin' in the Rain,* perhaps his most enduring film and a benchmark by which all other musicals are measured. The movie is a timeless treasure trove of great numbers, but the "Moses Supposes" dance with Kelly and Donald O'Connor tapping out a rhythmic Morse Code like a couple of pneumatic drills, never fails to electrify audiences.

"Donald and I rehearsed that dance for days, but most critics dismiss it as a zany Marx Brothers romp," Kelly said. "They remember the clowning around with the vocal coach that precedes the number, but not the dance itself."

Kelly told us that he didn't own any prints of his movies. "MGM had a strict policy; they never gave out any films, even to the movies' stars," he said. Now videocassettes make buying most movies a $19.95 proposition.

As he walked us to the door, Kelly gave us the thumbs-up signal, which he said he had also given to Barbra Streisand when he directed her in *Hello, Dolly.* It was his message to her at the end of each camera take that she was on cue.

Every Christmas thereafter, without fail, we would receive a greeting card, some picturing the Kelly clan posed in their backyard along with whatever family pet was within grabbing distance when the shot was taken. For our part, we kept Gene supplied with copies of our various entertainment articles when they were published.

After 16 years of sending these missives to each other, we had the great pleasure to return to Kelly's home on Oscar night, 1994, where we chatted some more about old movies and future aspirations.

Dressed in chinos, a white, Ralph Lauren polo shirt and leather loafers, Kelly, now 83 years old, slowly made his way over to greet us. His steps were halting and measured due to "nursing a bum leg." Shortly after the interview he was hospitalized in San Francisco with cellulitas (a potentially dangerous infection) in his leg. In July 1994 and in early 1995 he was hospitalized again — this time as a result of mild strokes. He's now back home and on the mend.

For an instant it was hard to reconcile Kelly's enduring movie image of explosive athleticism with the reality before us — that of a slightly enfeebled octogenarian. But if the march of time has slowed Kelly's machine gun footwork to a slow shuffle, age had also sharpened his wit and deepened his memory.

"Historically speaking," Kelly said, "I'm one of the last ones left who can correct inaccuracies about MGM musicals in show biz books these days." As an example, he cited Hugh Fordin's "World of Entertainment," a book about producer Arthur Freed and his creative unit at MGM. "I, along with Vincente Minnelli, Judy Garland and dozens of others, was part of that unit in the 1940s and '50s," Kelly said. "You'd think that when the author was compiling facts, he'd have wanted to consult me. He didn't, and there are several mistakes as a result."

Kelly says history continues to be rewritten to this day. The misinformation ranges from an erroneous birthdate in a popular biography of his life, to a German journalist who recently reported that MGM studio chief Louis B. Mayer "foisted" Debbie Reynolds on Kelly as his co-star in *Singin' in the Rain.*

"That is patently untrue," Kelly said. "Mayer wasn't even at the studio in 1952 when we shot the picture."

Some undisputed Kelly history was evident last year with the selected market release of *That's Entertainment! III,* another time capsule of classic MGM musical moments that began with the release in 1974 of the hugely successful *That's Entertainment!* Kelly, along with stars June Allyson, Cyd Charisse, Lena Horne and Mickey Rooney host segments of the anthology. The film is now available on video.

"One clip features Cyd and I dancing the 'Heather on the Hill' number from *Brigadoon,*" Kelly said. "Another segment is an outtake from *Annie Get Your Gun* with Judy Garland cast as Annie Oakley. Betty Hutton eventually replaced her and starred in the movie."

Truth to tell, Kelly says that the best musical material from those days has already been used in the two prior *That's Entertainment* films. "But there are some historical oddities — like footage of vocal dubbing — that MGM would never have released to the public during its heyday," he says.

On the Town, which Kelly co-directed with Stanley Donen,

remains his all-time favorite musical, mainly because it was his directorial debut at MGM and the opening number, "New York, New York," and some establishing shots were filmed on location in New York City. "That was no small achievement back in 1949, especially when you consider the studio had a standing New York set that looked more authentic than parts of the real city," Kelly said.

In an issue of *The New Yorker* magazine (March 24, 1994) author John Updike, in a tribute to Kelly, cited *On the Town* as his favorite movie, too. However, he lamented the fact that Kelly rarely seemed to pair up with a female partner to good advantage, the way Fred Astaire did throughout his career.

"I thought Updike did a good job of summing me up," Kelly said, "but he should know that the roles I was given were way different from Fred's. The mode of dance in the 1940s and '50s was no longer ballroom like it was with the Fred and Ginger pictures in the 1930s."

In spite of such comments, ample evidence exists to dispel the notion that Kelly's best dances were solo numbers. "My few quick turns with Rita Hayworth in *Cover Girl* to those beautiful strains of 'Long Ago and Far Away' were akin to the kind of dancing Astaire did," Kelly said.

Kelly admits that, overall, movie musicals are largely icons of the past. Their decline might be due to savvy audiences that just can't bring themselves to suspend disbelief when an off-camera orchestra begins to swell moments before a song number. However, others see MTV, with its quick-cut camera work geared to short attention spans, as the modern-day spawn of old-time musical numbers. Kelly agrees.

"Film editors have become the choreographers today," he said. "Everything is 'bam!' a tight shot of a shoulder, a leg, half a pirouette, an ass. In my day, editors were simply called 'cutters'; now a whole musical can succeed or fail based on the editing."

Up until suffering the strokes, Kelly traveled the college

lecture circuit discussing his old movies to sellout crowds. "If they can meet my price, I'll give 'em a spiel," he said. Last year Kelly lectured in Atlantic City and was surprised when his old friend and other *Brigadoon* dancing partner, Van Johnson, showed up in the audience.

Future plans include finishing an autobiography for publication in 1995 and quashing the curious notion that he had died.

"The mix-up started with those GAP print ads, 'Gene Kelly Wore Khakis,'" he said. "Besides myself, the first group of ads included Arthur Miller, Marilyn Monroe, Humphrey Bogart and a few others. Along with the phrase being in the past tense, all the other personalities were famously dead, except Arthur and me. People leapt to the natural conclusion. You wouldn't believe the number of phone calls I got from friends trying to figure out whether I was still here or not," Kelly said.

Now that's setting the record straight!

Shirley's Many Guises
Shirley Jones
April 1995

The name Shirley Jones conjures up different images for different people. To a generation now in their "golden years," she was the fresh-faced young songstress in such musical films as *Oklahoma!, Carousel* and *The Music Man.* To baby boomers, she was Shirley Partridge, the ever-smiling matriarch of TV's singing Partridge Family in the early '70s. And to film buffs, she was a dramatic movie star who won a Best Supporting Actress Academy Award in 1960 for her role as the hustling prostitute in *Elmer Gantry.*

Making it big in show business has been likened to winning the lottery, and Jones is the first to admit that her meteoric rise to superstardom was more of an accident than a carefully charted career plan. Now, 43 years after she burst onto the scene as Laurey in *Oklahoma!*, Jones, 64, in a recent interview in her Beverly Hills home, which she shares with husband Marty Ingels, told us she attributes her success largely to happenstance.

"I never really set out to make anything happen," she said. "I was always able to sing — that was a God-given gift, but the pieces of my career just sort of fell into place."

A native of Smithton, Pennsylvania (population 800), Jones appeared in amateur theatrics, but really aspired to become a veterinarian. On a family trip to New York City, she met a pianist who insisted she sing for an agent friend of his. Within a matter of days after that chance meeting she was auditioning for Richard Rodgers and Oscar Hammerstein and was immediately cast in a chorus role in *South Pacific*. A part in another Rodgers and Hammerstein show, *Me and Juliet,* led to her being cast in the 1955 film *Oklahoma!.*

During location filming in Arizona, the 21-year-old film novice was surrounded by screen veterans, including Gordon MacRae, Rod Steiger, Eddie Albert, Gloria Grahame and director Fred Zinnemann (who also directed such classics as *High Noon* and *From Here to Eternity).*

"I was very lucky," she said. "Fred was very patient, to the point where he was really Svengali. He asked me if I had ever performed before a camera. I said 'Never,' to which he replied: 'You're an absolute natural.' I was really like a sponge and quite malleable. I had not done enough work on the stage to form any bad habits. I was very open to being directed, and Fred loved that. I was also so naive, the camera didn't scare me."

Neither did Rod Steiger. Ingels, dressed in a ratty bathrobe that fit his image as a former comedian who'd do anything for a laugh, had been kibbutzing the interview from a nearby chair. He leapt up, left the room and returned momentarily with a large black-and-white picture (one that had been blown up into huge dimensions from a still photograph) of the *Oklahoma!* cast. In it, Steiger, with a grin a Cheshire cat would envy, is posed clinching Jones's shapely waist in a kind of backwards bear hug.

"Funny story about that," Ingels chimed, "Rod had the hots for Shirley during filming and could barely contain himself."

"That's true," Jones said. "I was young and kind of naïve about the ways of the world. But Rod's ardor kind of cooled quickly. Later I found out that Fred Zinnemann had extracted a promise from him that he would keep his paws off me for the sake of the picture. In fact, he blackmailed Rod into becoming my protector on the set! 'Judd Fry' … my hero … how do you like them apples?"

Just as quickly as her star had risen, the imminent death of the musical film by the late '50s almost counted Jones among its many casualties.

"My movie career was over when musicals weren't being made anymore because I was typecast for those roles," she said. "I was forced to take television parts at a time when it was considered beneath a 'movie star' to do television."

It was Jones' Emmy-nominated performance opposite Red Skelton in a Playhouse 90 production of *The Big Slide* that caught the attention of Burt Lancaster, who was about to star in the film *Elmer Gantry,* based on Sinclair Lewis' satirical novel about a phony evangelist. After convincing director Richard Brooks that she was right for the part (he preferred Piper Laurie), she was cast in the role of the prostitute who blackmails the hustling preacher played by Lancaster.

Jones' first day on the set was particularly difficult, as Brooks — still brooding from not casting Laurie — offered her no direction. "I went home that night in tears thinking he really hates me," she recalled. "The next day, Brooks took me aside and said, 'Shirley, I want to apologize to you. I left you alone because I wanted to see if you'd fall on your face. You didn't, and, as a matter of fact, I think you're going to win an Academy Award.'"

Although Brooks' prophesy came true, Jones herself didn't hold much hope for winning. "I really had no clue that I would win," she said. "Janet Leigh was taking home all the awards for *Psycho.* When they announced my name I was in shock."

"I would not have had a career if it wasn't for *Gantry,*" she added. "That film and winning the Oscar gave me a chance to star in movies throughout the '60s."

With feature parts now assured, Jones starred in a string of mostly romantic comedies opposite such stars as Marlon Brando, Glenn Ford, David Niven and Tony Curtis. By the end of the decade, she felt she needed a change. When an offer came along to star in a weekly television series about a single mother and her brood of aspiring pop singers, called *The Partridge Family,* Jones eagerly accepted it. Whereas *Elmer Gantry* saved her movie career, *The Partridge Family* effectively ended it.

"The show killed my movie career," she said. "Do I regret doing it? Absolutely not! I had traveled the world making movies and I needed a change. I had three young children to raise and my marriage was teetering. I needed to stay near home with as close to a nine-to-five job as possible. *The Partridge Family* gave me normalcy. It also paid me a lot of money."

During the five-year run of the show, Jones' co-star and real-life stepson, David Cassidy, became a teen idol. "The experience was really tough on David," she said. "He nearly had a nervous breakdown. After the show he left the business for a year, went to Hawaii, sat in a field and played guitar. That kind of overwhelming adulation is tough on a young kid."

In light of the success a few years ago of *The Brady Bunch Movie* — a pastiche of another California "family" of the period, there has been talk of transferring the Partridge brood to the big screen.

"We've been approached about a sequel or some type of

remake," she said. "But we never could get it together because David didn't want to get involved again. With the success of *The Brady Bunch Movie,* I wouldn't be surprised if somebody remade our show with a new cast. The adults of today grew up with our show and they're the ones going to movies today."

In 1980, Jones found another outlet for her considerable talents when she performed for the first time with the Milwaukee Symphony Orchestra. She now regularly appears with orchestras throughout the country.

Concerts and summer stock consume most of her performing these days. She's also a regular host on cable's American Movie Classics channel.

"I'm very choosy when it comes to the projects I select," she said. "I don't want to do something for the sake of being back on television or in a movie. I don't need the money and the roles are just not there for women in my age bracket."

Entering the Lion's Den
Ann Miller
April 1998

Tap dancer Ann Miller was, perhaps, the quintessential female MGM musical star of the early 1950s. Whirling like a dervish around prehistoric bones in a natural history museum *(On the Town),* the disembodied arms and instruments of a hot swing band *(Small Town Girl),* or kicking out a staccato rhythm on a coffee table *(Kiss Me Kate),* Miller was tops in taps for a studio famed for its musicals.

Miller's MGM movies were pure confection; cookie-cutter, cotton-candy escapism spun from a studio system geared to making audiences forget their troubles. As Frank Sinatra, another alumnus of MGM's Golden Era, has said: "Musicals were fantasy trips; boy meets girl, boy loses girl, boy sings a song and gets girl. The plots were that simple."

More important was the certainty that at least three times during a 100-minute musical, Miller could be counted on to beat out a tattoo with her feet that rivaled any pneumatic jackhammer on a Manhattan street corner.

At 79, she claims she can still click out 500 taps a minute. "I still know how to lay down the iron!" she exclaims proudly.

Today, Miller is late for a hair appointment that, unfortunately, will cut our interview short, too. "I get my hair done once a week if it needs it or not," she tells us in a hurried Texas drawl that has the strange, sentient effect of drawing us in and making us instant confidants. From our angle, as she descends the curved staircase from the second floor of her Beverly Hills home, Miller doesn't need it. She's as well coiffed as the two large airdales that flank her every move. In fact, the troika reminds us of her haughty Nadine character and the two Russian wolfhounds she took strolling down Fifth Avenue in *Easter Parade* — a 1948 hit that co-starred Fred Astaire and Judy Garland.

"It was the culmination of a dream dancing with Fred Astaire," she tells us. "But I was really too tall for him. I had to wear ballet slippers and when the dress flares out during our number, 'It Only Happens When I Dance With You,' you can see them. Now I've shrunk an inch and a half and would be the perfect height for either Fred or Gene Kelly. Cyd Charisse was the same height I was and so was Rita Hayworth. Cyd sort of crouched down in more of a ballet bent-knee thing so you didn't notice the disparity as much."

Miller's home is decorated in what could best be described as a kind of French Roccoco style, as if a bit of gilt and guilding from the Palace at Versailles had errantly plopped down on the west side of Los Angeles. A couple of cement lions stand guard at her front door and bring to mind not the royal crest of French despots, but the roaring trademark of MGM — the king of dream factories that boasted having "more stars than there are in the heavens."

Although the day of studios with dozens of stars on exclusive retainer is a historical footnote, Miller takes pains to maintain vibrant connections with her MGM contemporaries. As she points out, although the U.S. Senate is considered the most exclusive club in America, the fraternal order of MGM leading ladies has an even more rarified pedigree. "Politicians abound, and Congress is always in session, but they're not making any more of us," she laughs.

Point well taken.

"I hosted a luncheon not long ago with Debbie Reynolds; just a little get-together at a Chinese restaurant off of Wilshire Boulevard for some of us who used to work together at the studio," she says. "MGM was like our alma mater because many of us never went to college — we were working. Esther Williams came and so did Ann Rutherford, Janet Leigh, Cyd and Margaret O'Brien. June Allyson even flew in. We had a ball. It started at 12:30 and we didn't get out of there until 5:00 p.m. All the dishing that went on — thank God we didn't invite the press!"

Miller's favorite film is a toss-up between *Easter Parade* and *Kiss Me Kate,* but *Parade* does contain her favorite number, "Shakin' the Blues Away."

"Maybe it's because I'm out there on the stage all alone. And the tune, by Irving Berlin, is so good," she says. That's the great thing about tap dancing; it's very electric. No matter what you're doing — reading a paper, washing the dishes — when a big tap number starts, it commands your attention instantly."

At that moment Miller gets a phone call. She picks up the receiver from a sidetable near her chair and chats amiably for a couple of minutes. After she hangs up, she tells us that her caller — Robyn Astaire (Fred Astaire's widow) — has just invited her out to dinner later that week.

"Robyn's a sweet girl," Miller says. "You know the whole flap about her partnering with the Dust Devil vacuum cleaner people and using Fred's image superimposed dancing with the vacuum is really nothing. She needed the money to help finance an air cargo business she runs. She's a pilot, you know."

We remembered that particular television commerical. It involved a clip of Astaire taken from when he danced with a coat rack in the 1951 film *Royal Wedding*. The commercial, the subject of more than a few newspaper editorials, caused a negative stir, especially among film purists who thought the idea of substituting a vacuum cleaner for the wooden hat-stand bordered on sacrilegious and was an affront to the memory of Astaire.

During the late 1940s Miller was heir apparent to the reigning tap dance queen on the MGM lot, Eleanor Powell. Although, at age 12, Miller studied ballet alongside Tula Finklea (who was 14 at the time) at the studio of Nico Charisse, the man Tula would eventually marry (changing her name to Cyd Charisse in the process), Miller herself never took a tap lesson.

"There was a Capezio shoe shop across the street from the dance studio on Sunset Boulevard where we practiced," she says. "I would go over there and the owner, a man named Morgan, would let me practice on the tap mat at the back of the shop. He made me a pair of tap shoes that had little jingles in the toe taps. That's where I developed my high-speed tapping. It all came from the man upstairs. I don't mean Mr. Morgan, I mean the other Guy!"

Movie musicals flourished with the advent of sound and began to wane as staple entertainment in the late-'50s. Miller laments that audiences these days are hard-pressed to sus-pend disbelief long enough to let film musicals thrive, espe-cially in light of the fact that they, along with jazz, are America's only indigenous art form — our gift to the world.

"You have to have a good story now," she says. "The great thing about the old musicals were that they were so innocent and sweet. You left the theater with a lift and there is nothing wrong with that. But today's audiences — even the children — have become so sophisticated. Musicals can't compete against the special effects movies now. They'd be going up against aliens and rubber toys that talk ... there's a thought! Maybe a pornographic musical or one with an animatronic dinosaur doing a big tap number would work!"

Sidestepping the nauseous thought of a chorus line of gyrating Barneys, we remind Miller that tap dancing has achieved new currency with the popularity of the Riverdance troupe of Celtic high-steppers.

"Michael Flatley, the lead dancer stole two of my steps," she says. "And they're the two best steps that he does — always get big applause. I even bought the video to revisit the steps again."

The legendary Bill Robinson once said that if you could copyright a step, nobody could lift a foot. "Bojangles" knew that the true art of terpsichore lay not in individual steps, but in how thrilling tap combinations were strung together to create a memorable cohesion — the signature Morse code of American musical theater.

Miller smiles the all-knowing smile of someone who's traversed that territory many times ankle-strapped into her own flying tap shoes.

THE GREAT AMERICAN FLYERS
The Nicholas Brothers
December 1999

Nobody ever got "air" like the dancing Nicholas Brothers, not even Michael Jordan in mid-leap during a monster jam. Fayard and his younger brother Harold were, by almost unanimous consent, the greatest airborne flash act in show business history. Their specialty was somersaults into mind-boggling leg splits from which they rose almost in slow motion, and rapid-fire tap dancing that sounded like short bursts from an angry Gatling Gun. For the record, the Nicholas Brothers were running up walls and doing backflips (into splits) long before Donald O'Connor's justifiably famous "wallies" in his "Make 'Em Laugh" routine in *Singin' in the Rain.*

The Nicholas Brothers were a legendary act at Harlem's Cotton Club during the 1930s where they gyrated and flipped to the swingin' bands of Cab Calloway, Chick Webb and Duke Ellington. Later on, their specialty numbers in such movies as *Stormy Weather, Orchestra Wives, Down Argentine Way* and *Sun Valley Serenade* stopped those shows cold in their tracks.

Harold and Fayard started their show business careers as a child act in their hometown of Philadelphia in 1930 where their mother played piano and father played drums in an orchestra called the Nicholas Collegiates. It was Fayard who caught the dancing bug first, lingering after his parents' stage performances to watch other acts on the bill.

"I liked what I saw," he said. "They were singing, dancing and telling jokes ... having fun up there. So, just by watching, I taught myself how to perform."

When we met, Fayard was garrulous about the Nicholas Brothers and their legacy. He was dressed in a blue leisure suit and sported a Planet Hollywood baseball cap. Harold, more taciturn, wore thready sweatpants and a gray sweater and had his gray hair tied back into a nubby ponytail. His inscrutability seemed even more so accented as it was with a wispy Fu Manchu goatee.

The Nicholas Brothers started out as pint-sized performers and remained lithe, super-charged and hobbit-sized throughout their careers. There must be a physics postulate somewhere about minimal body mass and lightning-fast propulsion leading to spectacular aerial dynamics. Just don't make the mistake of calling Fayard and Harold a flash act.

Harold: We weren't a flash act. We did tap and acrobatics.

Fayard: Yes, "flash" is a bad word. When you say, "flash," you think flashy. But we did classical tap. In our routines you'd see a little bit of ballet, eccentric dancing and you see acrobatics and classical tapping. We can do a routine without any splits, just tap dancing.

Reel to Real: Outside another great flas— sorry, acrobatic act — The Berry Brothers — you guys were unique. You tapped and they didn't.

Fayard: They did flips and spins. They did a sort of jazz split with the back leg doubled up underneath. We never hurt ourselves the way we did our splits. We tried to do them the correct way with both legs fully extended. When the Berry Brothers did their splits, they hit the floor so hard. I remember Ananais Berry had corns on his knees and buttocks so he would take a razor blade and just cut them.

Reel to Real: Watching various dance acts that followed your parents' act on stage whetted your appetite for performing.

Fayard: I would go back to our apartment and try to do what I had just seen. I could do all the tough steps, but never get that damn time step down. That was the hardest thing for me to get. After I learned it, I never used it. They say that the time step is the basic building block step for tap dancing. I went and saw a show and they would start off with a time step, do another step, go back to the time step ... and I said, "That's monotonous. Don't they know other steps?" Right then I said I wouldn't do the time step anymore ... and never did.

Our father saw me rehearsing one day — in the living room — and said, "Son, what you are doing you are doing well, but don't do what other dancers are doing. He told me not to look at my feet. "You're entertaining an audience, not yourself," he said. He told me he liked the way I gestured with my hands.

Reel to Real: We read in Marshall Stearns' wonderful book, "Jazz Dance: The Story of American Vernacular Dance," that the film choreographer Nick Castle said your hands were as beautiful as Astaire's.

Fayard: Actually, he said that my hands were the best in show business. I love Fred Astaire. He was a perfectionist and he did all those wonderful things. He used his hands like I do. I just did more of it. I went to a rehearsal hall in Philly and rented a room with mirrors so I could see myself. I figured I was going to do more with my hands, and work with my whole body — to give this Nicholas Brother style! That's what I taught Harold.

Reel to Real: Do you have a favorite routine from all your movies?

Harold: I thought the thing we did in *Stormy Weather* was great — the one where we slide down the gutters in a split for our big finish. We did that number in one take. You know Astaire said that was the best number he had ever seen in a movie.

Fayard: I liked all of our routines because I could see progress in all of them.

Reel to Real: You worked with Gene Kelly in *The Pirate* in 1948.

Harold: It was the first time we did straight dancing … no tricks, or tumbling or anything. But it was interesting because the three of us synchronized our moves. Gene had seen us in New York and told us that some of the stuff we were doing was what he'd like to do.

Fayard: Producer Arthur Freed at MGM called Gene into his office one day and said: "Gene, I've got the story that you can do with the Nicholas Brothers." It was the script for *The Pirate,* but Freed warned Gene that any number he might do with us could be cut out when the picture played theaters in the South. Gene said: "I don't give a damn! It'll play the same all over the world, so why do we have to just think about the South?" The movie played in the South and they never cut us.

Reel to Real: Was it ever tough when you toured the South in live shows?

Fayard: We did a Southern tour in, I think, about 1946.

I told our manager I didn't want to go down there, but the bookers said it would be OK because we would have our own road manager and a private bus ... and these dollar signs were flashing before my eyes. So, we went. After our first show, in Tennessee, all of these white people were coming up to us. Then this blue-eyed, blonde-haired girl came and was hugging and kissing me and I was thinking: "Is this really the South?" People would come backstage and tell us they had seen all of our movies.

Harold: Times back then weren't as peaceful as they are nowadays, so to speak. But we had a good time. In those days, black people enjoyed life. That's how we were all the time ... just happy. Things change — a whole lot has changed since we were growing up. Europe was a different scene altogether. I just felt that they idolized us. My brother left and I did a single, and they loved me.

Reel to Real: Who was the greatest dancer you ever saw?

Harold: "Baby" Lawrence was fantastic. Guys today are dancing like Baby danced back in the 1940s and '50s. Savion Glover ... he's thinking Baby Lawrence even though he may have never met him. I know that's the kind of rhythm he's doing.

Fayard: We danced with about every dancer there was. Outside of my brother, I would name Eleanor Powell. She could do ballet, tap, ballroom, splits, acrobatics ... everything. And she could do it all well. Some say she was the world's greatest female dancer, but I say she's the world's greatest dancer. She's better than everybody.

Reel to Real: She had a relatively short film career, though.

Fayard: Yeah, but when she was on screen, you paid attention. I remember one of her friends threw a birthday party for her and they transformed her garage into a theater. We watched all her movies and then they played the Nicholas Brothers movies over and over. And she sat next to me and held my hand and would say: "Did you see that?" And she kept squeezing my hand, never taking her eyes off the screen and saying: "Watch this," like I had never seen the routine before. Then, after she blew out the candles on her birthday cake, I said: "Eleanor, I don't count when I dance." And she said she didn't either, and I said: "Well, we do have something in common." I then said: "Eleanor, I pick up a lot of steps that I don't have names for." And she said: "Me, too!" Then I said: "Wow, we really have something in common."

I guess you're wondering why the Nicholas Brothers lasted so long — we performed for 68 years.

Reel to Real: What's your secret?

Fayard: It's because we did so many things ... we were versatile. We'd sing, dance, play drums, tell jokes, stories. And we could do a show made up only of the Nicholas Brothers — nobody else. We could be on stage for an hour or even two. That's why.

Fred Astaire's Silent Partner
Hermes Pan
August 1988

Cole Porter, in his song "You're the Top," described "the nimble tread of the feet of Fred Astaire," thereby positioning the dancer alongside such all-time, world-class greats as the Louvre, the Eiffel Tower, Whistler's Mother and camembert cheese. The only other thespians Porter bothered to refer to in the same breath with Astaire in that song were Garbo (her salary), Durante (his famed schnozz) and Mae West (her shoulder).

Of all the stars manufactured in the '30s in the great Hollywood dream factories, only one, with the possible exception of Charlie Chaplin, has given more sheer joy to more people than Fred Astaire. The movies he made with Ginger Rogers remain as testaments to a golden era of filmmaking, a time in our collective history when movies could be innocent, witty, elegant, exuberant and fun — and still attract a mass audience.

Even today, the nine landmark musicals that Astaire and Rogers made at RKO retain a freshness and vivacity that are astonishing. During the Great Depression, they helped people escape the harsh realities of unemployment and bread lines. Today, they still have the power to transport us out of our own time. The Astaire-Rogers movies didn't just break old, shopworn molds of how to portray dance on film; they became a measuring rod of excellence by which all other dance films were — and still are — compared.

What most moviegoers may not realize is that the Astaire-Rogers duo owes a large measure of its success to Astaire's silent partner, a Greek-American rarely seen on the screen (and never seen in an Astaire-Rogers movie). His name, however, is invariably there, rolling by on the final credits. He is Hermes Pan, choreographer of all the Astaire-Rogers pictures from *Flying Down to Rio* in 1933 to *The Story of Vernon and Irene Castle* in 1939.

Pan was born in Memphis, Tennessee, in 1910, and a couple of years later moved with his family to Nashville, where his father was employed as Greek counsel to the southern states. On the side, he also operated a restaurant that Pan remembers as one of the best in the state. In Nashville, Pan was exposed for the first time to jazz dance, rhythms and riffs.

"Sam Clark was a black kid who was our houseboy and drove for us," Pan says. "He was a little older than I was and he used to teach me all kinds of shuffles, the Black Bottom and the Charleston. From those beginnings, I got my show business start, dancing in speakeasies in the 1920s at the age of 16."

Young Hermes also squired his sister in a dance act that landed the team specialty spots in a few Broadway shows.

"My sister's name is Vaso. It was taken from Vassiliki in the Peloponnesos," Pans tells us. When he wasn't gigging with his sister, he danced in the chorus of *Animal Crackers,* starring the Marx Brothers.

"Groucho was too sarcastic, I never did like him," Pan recalls. "Chico was alright, but he was always skirt chasing. Harpo was the nicest." Zeppo Marx, the brother whose presence amounted to a bit part in most of their shows and movies, became Pan's agent in Hollywood.

"He never did a damn thing for me," Pan recalls. "Everything I ever did I got on my own." That included mustering the gumption to motor West for a shot at the movies.

"I drove out to Los Angeles in 1930 with my mother and sister," Pan remembers. "Busby Berkeley was doing things along with such dance directors as LeRoy Prinz and Seymour Felix. I had worked for Felix back on Broadway in *Top Speed* and I thought it would be a cinch to land a job."

Unfortunately for Pan, in the early '30s the camera covered more ground than most chorus lines did. "I never got picked once," Pan says. "I remember Berkeley would line all the boys up and say, 'You, you, you and you ... the rest of you can go home.' Half the time the selectees didn't even have to audition. In those days, choreographers weren't dancers. Busby Berkeley couldn't dance a step — he was an idea man. They let the camera move for them. They'd have 500 pianos floating around or girls with violins in geometric configurations. It wasn't dancing at all."

In 1933, Pan got his big break as dance assistant to Dave Gould in *Flying Down to Rio,* a picture featuring a fresh young dance sensation from back East — Fred Astaire. Pan himself had just "happened" back into town after an abortive road trip with a traveling dance troupe.

"We had played one-night stands up and down the California coast," he says. "We were stranded every other week. In fact, one time we were stranded in Modesto and we had a booking in Antioch for three days. We told the hotel management that we would come back and pay the bill, but they wouldn't budge. I had to leave my mother for security. Years later, when I won my Academy Award for *A Damsel in Dis-*

tress, one of the kids came up to me and said, 'Don't forget, I remember when you had to hock your mother!'"

Fortunately for Pan, he was able to pay the bill, retrieve his mother and follow a tip that led to Dave Gould's office at RKO Pictures. "I had gotten together with my sister and worked out about a chorus of steps to "The Carioca," a tune from the movie. I showed the routine to Dave and he liked it. I was in."

On his first day of work, Pan was told to, "Go over to stage eight and see if Fred Astaire needs any assistance." A daunting proposal to anyone, the idea terrified the neophyte Pan. "It scared the life out of me because Fred was already an international star," Pan says. "I introduced myself by saying my name is Pan. Fred called me by my last name from that moment on. He had been working on a solo tap dance, which he hadn't quite finished. He was stuck for a little break step and asked me if I had any ideas. At that moment something clicked in my mind and I remembered a break that Sam Clark had taught me back in Tennessee. I showed it to Fred and he loved it. After that he always called for me, never for Dave Gould, who had two left feet. Fred would yell: "Pan, Pan … where is Pan?"

Astaire once said that dancing for the screen was approximately 80 percent brainwork; that only 20 percent of the strain was on the feet. According to Pan, that 20 percent part of the ratio seemed to yield a disproportionate share of callouses, shin splints and bruises.

"We'd knock ourselves out," he recalls. "We would come in usually at 10 o'clock in the morning and work until one. After an hour's break, we would come back and rehearse until we got too tired — around five or six o'clock. It was almost constant dancing."

The braintrust of Astaire and Pan extended beyond just mentally mapping out the five or six necessary dance routines for each film. When it came time to actually do the dance, Fred always rehearsed the duet numbers with Pan as his partner — long before Ginger Rogers ever appeared on the sound stage. "A lot of times Ginger would be working on another picture," Pan says. "Also, we liked to work without her because in the initial stages we weren't always sure what we were going to do. I would do Ginger's part and then Ginger would come in and I'd teach her the steps."

Pan also dubbed in the taps for Ginger's routines, drudgery she was glad to avoid. "We would shoot the numbers to pre-recorded music and then post-record the taps, days or even weeks later.

That kind of perseverance paid off when Fred cited Pan as his "best dance partner" — a subject not open to critical debate since the Astaire-Rogers films were always shot on closed sets. Pan, on the other hand, feels that in Astaire's career of over 35 musical films, Ginger Rogers holds the coveted position as his best partner.

"Ginger wasn't the greatest dancer, but to my mind she was Fred's best partner. There was a quality when Fred danced with Ginger that didn't occur with any of his other partners. I worked with Cyd Charisse and Vera-Ellen when they teamed with Fred. They were better dancers than Ginger, but the same magic wasn't there."

Astaire wrote in his 1959 autobiography, "Steps In Time," that Pan had an uncanny knack for coming up with great trick dance ideas. The golf dance in *Carefree* and the title number from *Top Hat* solidified Astaire's renown as a solo performer and Pan's reputation as a surefire "idea man" in his own right. But it is the "Bojangles of Harlem" dance from *Swing Time* that contains a perfect balance of screen gimmickry and fancy footwork. The number, an acknowledged classic, has Astaire dancing (in blackface) in and out of syncopation with three huge shadows of himself projected on a wall behind him.

"The idea for that dance came one morning when I was sitting with Hal Borne, our rehearsal pianist, waiting for Fred to arrive," Pan says. "Hal started playing and I was dancing around the stage when someone flipped on some overhead lights in the rafters. They shone down on the dark stage and I could see three shadows of myself. I commented to Hal on what a great effect it made and said I was going to tell Fred about it when he came in. Well, Fred arrived and I said, 'I think I've got a great idea.' He replied, 'It better be good!' Anyhow, I told him and then we went to the special effects department and they said it would be no problem."

Pan was also capable of choreographing more intimate solo numbers for Astaire that eschewed special effects. One of his best came in an unheralded 1950 Paramount film called *Let's Dance*. It was during those years, when Astaire was Gingerless, that he would often rely on knockout solo numbers to maintain the forward momentum not only of the film, but also his career. The solo, called "The Piano Dance," is considered a tour-de-force of versatility and ingenuity by no less a terpsichorean authority than Rudolf Nureyev.

"Fred didn't originally want to do that number," Pan remembers. "I had laid it out so that at one point he would be hanging over the top of the baby grand with one leg dangling in the air. Fred was adamant that he just couldn't do that. I showed him, he tried it, and then said, 'My God, that was easy!' At the end of the number he has to exit the club while dancing over some chairs. He was also skeptical about that. He said he might break a leg. I told him, 'Look, hold my hand, step on the seat of the chair and put your foot on the top, balance, push with your right foot and push back with your left and you can go over as slow as you want to.'"

During the 40-year span of his movie career, Pan choreographed pictures that starred Rita Hayworth, Marge and Gower Champion and Shirley MacLaine. He even worked in *Sun Valley Serenade* with the greatest flash dance act the movies have ever known — the Nicholas Brothers. "Those guys had so many backflips, splits, riffs and steps, and they did them all at the speed of light," Pan says. "I gave their numbers for that film some cohesion, but I can't do a backflip into a split, so I mostly just let them go."

In 1968, 35 years after Pan made his visit to stage eight to "assist" Astaire, both men were reunited to work on *Finian's Rainbow.* The film proved to be their musical swan song. Astaire died last year and Pan lives a life of retirement in Beverly Hills, sauntering forth occasionally to accept an award for his body of work as a choreographer. The tributes that come his way are well-deserved, but as Pan might concur, they are just the afterbeat to a film legacy that remains as imperishable as the Louvre, the Eiffel Tower and Whistler's Mother.

Taking a Bet on Las Vegas
Debbie Reynolds
1994

Long before there was Madonna, Princess Di and other tabloid favorites, there was Debbie. In fact, the life of entertainer Debbie Reynolds has served as some of the juiciest media fodder over the past 45 years.

America has watched Mary Frances Reynolds grow up on screen. The perennial ingenue appeared in dozens of featherweight comedies and musicals in the 1950s, as well as the 1952 classic *Singin' in the Rain.*

Her on-screen persona was in stark contrast to the real-life soap opera she played out under the unsparing klieg lights of the world press. Her stormy four-year marriage to crooner Eddie Fisher ended in 1959 when he jilted her for Elizabeth Taylor, reputedly Reynolds' close friend at the time. The heartache Reynolds experienced in her personal life added an edge and maturity to future film roles, including *How the West Was Won* (1961) and her Oscar-nominated performance in *The Unsinkable Molly Brown* (1963).

Reynolds proved herself really unsinkable when her second husband, shoe tycoon Harry Karl, spent the '60s squandering his personal fortune of $15 million and Reynolds' show business earnings of $10 million.

Bankrupt, divorced and distraught, Reynolds rose again and scored personal triumphs in the Broadway musical revival of *Irene* (1973) and *Woman of the Year* (1983).

Reynolds is a little bit like the Eveready battery bunny that "keeps going and going." She's now gambling her name, reputation and assets on what she describes as the biggest challenge of her life — that of Las Vegas hotel owner.

In the game of high stakes hotel and casino management, Reynolds is admittedly a small-time player.

"I'm not in competition with the big players on the Strip," she said. "They're huge conglomerates. I run a real 'ma and pa' hotel. I'm here all the time. I don't think you'll see Mr. Wynn (Steve, chairman of several Las Vegas mega-properties) signing autographs or singing songs. In fact, Mr. Kerkorian (Kirk, the MGM Grand mogul) comes here to relax. My place is small. You can bring your girlfriend and sit in a quiet corner."

Reynolds might just as well have added a codicil to that statement. Seated at a ringside table with our wives, we were the youngest fans at Reynolds' show by half, adrift in a sea of blue hair and Chanel No. 5. As she went through her paces, singing, dancing and introducing film clips of her performances in a raft of vintage musicals, Reynolds eyed us warily, as if we were a guerrilla troupe planted there for effect by a provocateur like Howard Stern.

Before long, Reynolds started integrating us into her show, saying to her audience: "Look at these youngsters, they don't know me from a hole in the head, but I bet they're familiar with my daughter Princess Leia ... (then a stage whisper aimed directly at us) ... that's Carrie to you." Drawing first blood, Reynolds became the provocateur. She needn't have bothered.

Grainy film clips and grainier comedy schtick aside, after the show, we witnessed a ploy as remarkable as it was simple and effective. Reynolds came out from the wings, walked down the center aisle and positioned herself at the back of the theater where she patiently signed showbills, old albums and glossy photographs for any fan that came forward (and there were dozens). The septuagenarians were uniformly thrilled, and we learned a surefire marketing technique.

"I don't forget my fans," Reynolds remarked as she wielded a Sharpie marker over a black-and-white still of her as Kathy Selden from *Singin' in the Rain*. "Once you commit that treason, it's over."

The Debbie Reynolds Hotel, Casino, and Hollywood Movie Museum is located just off the Las Vegas Strip on Convention Center Drive. Reynolds bought the former 200-room Paddlewheel Hotel & Casino at an auction in 1992. After an extensive renovation, including decorating the hotel in a Hollywood motif and building a new 500-seat showroom, Reynolds reopened the hotel under her name in July 1993.

Her energy boundless, Reynolds took time after her main stage performance to visit in the hotel's Hollywood Palm Cafe, a 24-hour full-service restaurant that plays host on weekends to a "Jazz & Jokes" marathon (from 10 p.m. until 2 a.m.) featuring Reynolds, the comic slapstick of Rip Taylor, a trio of local musicians and a steady stream of drop-in guests. At 63, Reynolds, dressed in a purple and black pants ensemble, still evokes the girl-next-door image that she parlayed to stardom in MGM movies of the '50s and '60s.

The only entertainer who owns a hotel and casino, Reynolds said she bought the property primarily to showcase her estimated $30 million worth of movie artifacts. The museum opened earlier this year.

"Initially, I just wanted a museum to house my collection of movie memorabilia," she said. "This place happened to be a hotel I could fix. The museum is the only one of its kind in America.

"I think my hotel really is different," she added. "I call it a unique boutique. In Europe you have small hotels and big hotels and everyone gets along real well. I think you can have that in Vegas, too. I don't have an amusement park and I don't want one. I don't want noise and I don't want to be knocked over by crowds. This hotel is very quiet when compared to the major players on the Strip."

Born in El Paso, Texas, Reynolds along with her brother and parents moved to Burbank, California, when she was eight years old. Even living in the shadow of Warner Bros. Studios, she said she harbored no ambitions of ever seeing her name on a theater marquee.

"I went to the movies as a fan, but I had no dreams of a show business career," she said. "I wanted to be a gym teacher. Making pictures was really accidental."

The "accident" occurred when at age 16 Reynolds entered a local beauty contest. Her lip-synching impersonation of Betty Hutton won her the title of "Miss Burbank." As fate would have it, two of the pageant judges were talent scouts at Warner and MGM. With a toss of a coin, the Warner scout got dibs on Reynolds, filmed a screen test and signed her to a contract. At the insistence of studio head Jack Warner, Mary Frances became Debbie, a more appropriate name he felt for his perky new starlet.

After her screen debut in *The Daughter of Rosie O'Grady,* Reynolds was signed to a long-term contract at MGM. By 1950, the studio system was beginning to fall victim to a new competitor — television. MGM, which once boasted of "more stars than there are in the heavens," was pillaging its roster of high-priced talent. Reynolds was one of the few exceptions, and she proved herself a bankable asset to the studio.

While many stars fought the indentured servitude inherent in a studio contract, Reynolds said she never felt a creative noose around her neck.

"It didn't bother me because I never had lofty ambitions," she said. "I wasn't a Gene Kelly who was a great director, a

brilliant dancer, a person driven to succeed. I was happy with
a steady salary and free acting, singing and dancing lessons
all day."

Will her foray into hotel ownership ever replace her zeal
to perform?

"I hope I'm always foremost an entertainer," she said. "I
have a president and general manager who run the hotel. To
get people to come to a small hotel it has to have something
that's different. That's what the museum provides.

"This hotel has been the biggest challenge of my life,"
she added. "I run it like a home and worry about everything.
I'm vacuuming. I'm cleaning. If you're not involved it doesn't
come out your way. Who knows your dreams? Who can read
your mind? It's impossible. I'm trying to make everything
excellent. That's what I'm trying to do."

That Debbie, always a crowd pleaser!

A VERY SHORT INTERVIEW
Mickey Rooney
December 1998

An interview with Mickey Rooney is as close as we've
ever come to spending time with a live-action cartoon. He
didn't just enter the lobby of the Hyatt Hotel in Westlake
Village, California, near where he lives; he trundled in like a
miniature tank and waved us down with such theatrical ex-
aggeration, we thought he was in the finish step of a Busby
Berkeley dance fantasia at MGM.

"My car ran out of gas down the street and I had to get a
refill can from the filling station," he implored, wheezy and
red-faced. "I'm almost never late and I hate when other people
are."

At age 77, Rooney exudes inexhaustible energy. We're
winded just witnessing him scuttle from one topic to the
next with the same manic energy he employed in jumping

over fence posts with Judy Garland in those lovable, ridiculous *Andy Hardy* show-in-the-barn epics.

Fifty years and about three career incarnations later, Rooney is a world-class gnome with barrelhouse arms and legs that seem to spring akimbo out of the solid mass of his torso. His face, with oval eyes, is round as a pie plate and the full figure effect is as if someone had precariously balanced a dove's egg atop the larger hen's egg of his body. Oddly, Rooney brings to mind those old Victorian children's book drawings of a perfectly symmetrical Humpty-Dumpty.

For sure, Rooney has certainly had as many ups and downs — and even some egg on his face — in his long, honored and erratic career.

"I'll tell you anything you want to hear, including how bald I am," he laughed.

He also had some free advice for a middle-aged autograph-seeker that had been circling our couch like a raptor honing in on a field mouse. We could tell she was biding her time while trying to positively fix in her own mind Rooney's identity. When she did, she swooped.

"Mickey ... I think you're just great ... I just want to —"

But Rooney cut her off in mid-sentence with: "Dear, I'm doing an interview right now and it's rude of you to interrupt like that." He waved her off like a potentate dismissing a vassel at court. It was really quite funny, although we did feel some sympathy for the lady who reacted with a confused grimace as if she had just stubbed her big toe.

At least Rooney cured her of any future career as a celebrity stalker.

In solidarity with the LAPD (and to cover his barren pate), Rooney wore one of the department's baseball caps along with a stripped Izod sport shirt. With pride he showed us a giant silver ring bearing his real name, Joe Yule, that his wife had made for his last birthday.

"I've done more pictures than anyone in the business — 300," he blurted. "Twenty-seven of them alone were *Andy*

Hardy movies." His latest, the sequel to *Babe,* called *Babe: Pig in the City,* was released in late November. Rooney speaks mostly in short declarative sentences and keeping him on topic is fruitless, unless, of course, it's a topic he can make a short declarative sentence about.

The interview soon takes a bizarre turn where, as journalists, we become comically impotent and seem to have out-of-body experiences in which we can spy ourselves on the couch sitting limply by while Rooney holds forth grandly.

Literally and figuratively we've been slipped a Mickey!

"At MGM all the contract players had a home," he mused. "And nobody was coddled, despite what a lot of the leading ladies at MGM have said. We were considered part of the family. We had a place to hang our hat, a place to sleep. We had a job when a lot of people around the country were on the bread lines."

For three consecutive years during the 1930s — including the pivotal blockbuster year of 1939 — movie exhibitors voted Rooney the number one box office star in the country. In today's terms it's like Leonardo DiCaprio having a solid three-year run of superstardom complete with the unearthly adulation he received after the release of *Titanic.* The weird thing is that Rooney's dismissive about his own achievement.

"It was nothing, really," he said sounding like he means it. "There was no difference in my life. The great kick about it was that I was opposite the best of the best at the time; men like Cagney, Gable, Tracy and Bogart. Being a nice person was more important to me because with being number one, someday inevitably you'll be number 15. And now I'm not even on the chart.

"I've had a 76-year career in the movies," Rooney continued. "I was in pictures when I was one-year-old. I'm a writer, director, painter and pilot. I play golf and tennis. That's the secret of remaining forever young and getting through the tough times in life. And believe me, I've had a few. You need to be enthusiastic."

The contagion of Mickey's irrepressibility has led him and some of his limited partners to investigate such schemes as Mickey Rooney's Feel Great Insurance Company ($50,000 life/health policies for $25 a month); Movie Moguls (a Hollywood board game that resembles Monopoly); and Complete: for the man who wants to be (a spray-on hair tonic for baldness).

"It does away with toupees," Rooney said. "You shake it up and it frizzes out like cotton candy and then you just rub it in."

And so the interview ends much like Rooney began in Hollywood when he portrayed a series of fresh-faced hustlers wrapped in a kind of innocent Americana that might have struck a false note, but that was MGM's stock-in-trade.

"I hate the word seniors," Rooney said, off topic for the last time. "I like to think of us as experienced people, that way it isn't such a brand. Just remember; our lives are in front of us, not behind us. We all have new vistas to conquer."

Go Mickey!

In the Swim
Esther Williams
May 1996

Talk about carving out a niche. While MGM was loaded to the gills with actors, singers and dancers, there was one — and only one — aquatic star on the Culver City lot, Esther Williams. And the 20-foot-deep swimming pool built on Stage 30 on the lot, complete with hydraulic lifts, hidden air hoses and special camera cranes for overhead shots, was built especially for Williams.

Long before "strong women" were in vogue in Hollywood, Williams packed a combination of youth, beauty and athleticism, often schlepping her leading men, including Van Johnson, Red Skelton, Ricardo Montalban, and future husband Fernando Lamas through the water. And unlike her pretty boy co-stars, Williams usually wasn't afraid to get her hair wet.

Like ice skater Sonja Henie before her, Williams was one of only a few athletes to make a splash in movies. She went from championship swimmer to model to Hollywood star with a persona she knew couldn't easily be replaced by the studio brass.

"I worked through three pregnancies in bathing suits," she said. "Thank God my kids kept their knees in! But even pregnant, it got to a point where the studio couldn't replace me. It was a whole world that was mine. It was my terrain. The only one I worked with that could really swim was Fernando. He was a swimming champion in Argentina."

Still luminous at age 74, Williams looks shipshape and appears ready to challenge Olympic swimming star Dara Torres in a 50mm freestyle heat. It was fitting then that Williams shared career remembrances with us poolside at her Beverly Hills home. On an adjacent table rested two signature books: "Pools" by Kelly Klein and a copy of the "The MGM Story." Williams was dressed in a white smock with gold lettering that read: "Swim with Esther" stitched on a front breast pocket.

A championship swimmer at 16, the Los Angeles native lost out in her opportunity to swim for the 1940 Olympic team because the games were canceled due to the war. Williams' form, however, did catch the eye of show business impresario Billy Rose, who cast her opposite former Olympian and screen Tarzan, Johnny Weismuller in *Aquacade,* a live musical extravaganza performed in and under water.

Williams barely had time to dry off, when she caught the eye of MGM executives who offered her a screen test. As Williams recounted, this was not just *any* screen test. She was to make her test opposite arguably the biggest movie star of them all — the *king* himself — Clark Gable. It was a circumstance she called a "crazy fluke."

"Louis B. Mayer was mad at Lana Turner because she

married Artie Shaw without asking him," she said. "He wanted you to tell him everything. He said to me, 'I want to be a father to you.' I said, 'Mr. Mayer, I have a father.' That line of his worked on a lot of girls."

As "punishment" for Turner's insubordination, Mayer threatened to replace her in an upcoming Gable film with an unknown. Williams unexpectedly was that unknown, and Gable willingly played along.

Williams fully expected her screen test to lead nowhere, and in fact, she was swimming laps in the Beverly Hills Hotel pool when she was summoned to Mayer's office in Culver City. Dressed in old clothes and wearing no make-up, Williams dutifully reported to the studio. When the time came to enter Mayer's office, much to her shock, there sat Gable.

"It's the knees that go," she said. "I loved him so much in *Gone With the Wind* when I was in high school. I thought this was the man of my dreams, if I could only find someone like him when I got married. And there he is! He put out those big paws. I'm touching him. He shakes my hand and I said, 'Oh Mr. Gable, I've heard so much about you.' He very sweetly smiled and said, 'I've heard a lot about you, too.'"

Director George Sidney was assigned to make the test, and no one, including Williams, actually thought Gable would report to the set to shoot it. Williams rehearsed the scene with actor Dan Dailey, who fully expected to film the scene with her, when Gable walked in, tapped Dailey on the shoulder and said, "OK, kid, I'll take over now." Dailey stormed off the set leaving the neophyte Williams even more flustered. To make matters worse, Gable's wife, Carole Lombard accompanied her husband.

"Lombard is situated right under the camera and she's so blonde and she's wearing a black velvet suit with a beret with black fox everywhere and diamonds in her ears," recalled Williams. "I thought she's going to sit there and watch this barely out of the chlorine swimmer do a scene with her husband. So I said to myself, 'OK, swimmer take your mark.

I've been under pressure before and I've gotten to the end of the pool. So now I just got to get out of the pool first.' "

No sooner did Sidney yell "action," than Gable planted a big juicy kiss on his young, unsuspecting leading lady.

"There's no kiss in the scene," she said. "Not a single kiss. This screen test is to determine whether I'm going to get this role. Recovering from the kiss I say my line, 'Do you really have to go?' And he says, 'No, I'm not going' and gives me another kiss. That's not the line, and he's not supposed to kiss me again. After the fifth kiss, I look at Georgie (Sidney), and he said, 'cut.' Gable said, 'This is great. Good luck. Hope you get the part.' He gets up and leaves with Lombard on his arm and the two of them are laughing and having a wonderful time. As they walked off the stage, Gable says to his wife, 'I told you I was going to kiss me a mermaid today.' I'm sitting there not realizing that they often played jokes on each other. That was legend. I was the joke of the day. This is something you could cry over, but I didn't. I just didn't get to the end of the pool first."

At the time, Williams thought the test an "exercise in futility" and said, "I'd have something to tell my grandchildren."

Much to her surprise, the test resulted in a long-term contract, and although she never made the picture with Gable, Williams made her film debut opposite Mickey Rooney in 1942's *Andy Hardy's Double Life.*

The venerable *Andy Hardy* series served more as an official screen test and helped launch the careers of such stars as Donna Reed, Lana Turner and Judy Garland. Audience response to Williams was positive, and she was cast in *Mr. Coed* starring Red Skelton. Midway through production, studio brass, after viewing the rushes, renamed the movie, *Bathing Beauty* and awarded Williams top billing. It would become Hollywood's first swimming movie and launch a series of successful aquatic musicals starring MGM's very own diva of the deep.

Williams estimates she swam more than 1,000 miles through such movies as *Neptune's Daughter, Pagan Love Song* and *Easy to Love.*

While making those pictures, Williams worked through three pregnancies. Throughout it all she managed to stay in her size 9 bathing suit. However, she said the pregnancies did wreak havoc on the shooting schedule and with producer Joe Pasternak.

"They had to rearrange the entire shooting schedules so I could get into the size 9 swimming suits and be photographable because we didn't finish those pictures until five or six months," she said. "I remember calling Joe and telling him, 'Joey, I'm sorry. I know we've had this conversation before, but I'm pregnant.' And he said, 'God damn it, why do you keep doing this to me?' And I said, 'It's not being done to you Joe, it's being done to me!' And he replied, 'I know, I know, but if you don't tell that husband of yours to knock it off, he'll be barred from the lot.' And I said, 'Joe, it doesn't happen on the lot!'"

All told, Williams was married three times (last to Fernando Lamas) and has three children, Benjamin, Kimball and Susan, from her second marriage to radio singer Ben Gage.

In addition to being America's swimming sweetheart, Williams was one of the first stars to parlay her name recognition into successful business ventures. Williams stuck to what she knows best; her name has long been attached to a line of swim suits as well as above-ground pools. However, her first venture into swimwear was more of an educational experience than a profitable venture.

"I guess life imitated art," she said. "I played a swimsuit designer in *Neptune's Daughter.* Fred Cole from Cole's California called me and said I should have a tie-in with him. What he did was get me for peanuts. I was doing fashion shows from movies and, after seven years, I finally smartened up."

Williams got out of the swimwear business, but dove headfirst back into it after the death of Lamas in 1982.

"He really didn't want me to do anything, but wait for him to come home," she said. "It's just the way he was. My sister Maureen asked me one day, 'What do people in show business call it when you take time off and then go back?' And I said, 'A hiatus. A 20-year hiatus.' And she said, 'From the time they said swimmer take your mark and you became a swimming champion, you had a spotlight on you and maybe you needed a rest.'"

Williams has been making up for lost time. She's a popular fixture at film festivals, and newer audiences are seeing her thanks to cable channels such as Turner Classic Movies. Movie star, businesswoman and mother, Esther Williams has plunged back into life!

III.
Silver Screen,
Pure Gold

Roasting a few Chestnuts
Ernest Borgnine
(1998)

That guttural belly laugh with its accompanying gap-toothed smile, and a portly frame that infers the phrase "second helping" might just be the most sublime in the English language. It's all part of the Ernest Borgnine brand that has worked so well in hundreds of movies and episodic television shows now for half a century. Whether he's killing Frank Sinatra in *From Here to Eternity,* playing the nebbishy title character *Marty* in an Oscar-winning performance, or bilking Joe Flynn's Captain Binghamton character in the TV sitcom *McHale's Navy,* Borgie, 81, is a crowd-pleaser that has always been warmly received by audiences. Spend a little time with Borgnine, and you feel like family. All that's missing is a plate of fettuccine and a glass of chianti.

Call it old school, but unlike many of today's younger stars, Borgnine *gets* publicity and makes himself readily available to the media. This was no different on a hot summer day when he hosted us in his trailer while making an independent feature, in, of all places, a farm field near Kenosha, Wisconsin. He nodded agreeably when we mentioned we were situated only a few miles from the birthplace of two other show business heavyweights — Orson Welles and Don Ameche.

Borgnine has long been a believer in alternative modes of transportation. Like a latter-day Ralph Cramden, he can be seen tooling around the country behind the wheel of his retro-fitted "Borgie bus." "I have a ball with it," he said. "I drive it and take it all over the country. Don Rickles can't get over it. Milton Berle said, 'God I wish I had his courage.'"

Born Erness Effron Borgnine on Jan. 24, 1917 to Italian parents, Charles and Anna Borgnine in Hamden, Connecticut, he grew up in New Haven. An only child, Borgnine took to sports but showed no interest in acting. After high school he joined the Navy, where he stayed for 10 years (reaching the rank of Chief Gunner's mate) at the end of World War II. After he toiled in various factory jobs, his mother suggested that young Ernie, with his forceful personality, could channel that energy into acting. He enrolled in the Randall School of Dramatic Arts and later joined the Barter Theater in Virginia, where he plied his newfound profession for four years. His big break came in 1949, when he landed a role in the Broadway production of *Harvey*. In 1951, Borgnine moved to Hollywood and made his film debut in *China Corsair* (1951).

Borgnine's reputation as a screen heavy was laid when he played Sgt. Fatso Judson in *From Here to Eternity* in 1953. Two years later he broke out of the mold, portraying the sensitive New York butcher Marty Piletti in *Marty*. Talk about good company, Borgnine won the best actor Oscar, besting Spencer Tracy, Frank Sinatra, James Dean and James Cagney.

Other screen credits include: *The Catered Affair, The Dirty Dozen, The Wild Bunch, The Poseidon Adventure* and *Escape from New York*. On the small screen, Borgnine starred as Lt. Cmdr. Quinton McHale on the popular sitcom, *McHale's Navy*.

Off-screen, Borgnine has been married four times, including a hugely publicized marriage to entertainer Ethel Merman, which lasted all of 32 days. He's been married to his current wife, Tova, a successful cosmetics company owner, since 1972.

Reel to Real: We have to ask you about *The Wild Bunch*, which was recently selected by the American Film Institute as one of the 100 best films of the century. There's a scene where William Holden and the men are getting laid in a brothel, and you're the lone gang member sitting outside whittling on a piece of wood. Some say that scene — purposely placed there by director Sam Peckinpah — signaled to audiences that your character was a closeted homosexual.

Any truth to that?

Borgnine: Oh my God almighty! Ain't that something? I always tell people this. I'd already finished up in the brothel! How stupid could people be? No, it was just like this. The man was done and he was out there waiting for the rest of the guys to come out. Period. That's it, you know.

Reel to Real: Do you think that *The Wild Bunch* was too violent?

Borgnine: No, it's nothing compared to what we have today. And yet at the time it was considered very violent.

Reel to Real: Playing a heavy as you did, you also had a lot of interesting death scenes. Are those fun to do?

Borgnine: Well, it's always paid me well. It all started with *From Here to Eternity*. Then I got into being a bad guy, killing Lee Marvin with a pitchfork. One thing led to another. Finally when I did *Marty*, somebody asked, '*Marty?* To be played by Ernest Borgnine? He's a killer!'"

Reel to Real: Rod Steiger played the role of *Marty* first on live television. Did you see his performance?

Borgnine: No, not until much later. They asked me if I wanted to see it and I said, "What for?" I wanted to give my own performance. I won't comment on his, but he did win an Emmy for it, which, hey, people thought was good. I won an Oscar for mine.

Reel to Real: Winning an Oscar makes you a fraternity member of a very small, select club. How important was winning for you?

Borgnine: I'm very proud of my Oscar for the simple reason that I think I got it on my own, through my own merit, through my own work and I'm very proud of it. I only received $5,000 for the film, with a promise of $5,000 more if I signed a seven-year contract. I never got it.

Reel to Real: Winning the Oscar has got to be worth more than $5,000.

Borgnine: Oh my lord. I'd have done it for nothing.

Reel to Real: You didn't even pursue acting until after

you got discharged from the Navy, correct?

Borgnine: My mother asked me one day after I came back from the service, "Ernie, have you ever thought of becoming an actor? You always like to make a darn fool of yourself in front of people. Why don't you give it a try." And I said, "Mom, that's what I'm going to be." It opened up a whole new life for me and 10 years later, I'm very happy to say, I had an Academy Award.

Reel to Real: You took a supporting role in the NBC sitcom, *The Single Guy*. Why didn't that show last longer?

Borgnine: Well the thing that makes me mad and angry right now is the fact that they don't want people over 50 years of age on television anymore. That's unfortunate because there are so many of us out in Hollywood that would love to be working. They canceled the show because of some political reasons at NBC. The ratings were still good. It was fun and it was a challenge but I originally didn't want to get into it.

Reel to Real: So if you weren't working, what would you do?

Borgnine: I could be out in my bus. But then again, how many thousands of miles can you do? Right now, I'm in the midst of writing my book. Do you want to hear how I came up with the name for the book?

Reel to Real: Sure.

Borgnine: I think some of the oldsters will get a kick out of this. I was walking along 10th Avenue in New York City contemplating my fate about becoming an actor. And I'm saying to myself, "Why did I become an actor? I could be doing anything else that would at least be keeping my home and family together. And here I am running from pillar to post trying to find a job and I can' t find a job." In those days you could only work once a month on television because they were afraid if you were seen too much you'd be out of business. The only ones who were working steady were people like Charlton Heston and Jack Lemmon. And I said, "Wait a minute. I can act as well as Charlton Heston, if not better, right?" So I'm walking along and suddenly I smell the hot chestnuts. The vendor at the corner is selling hot chestnuts. I walked up and it reminded me of my mother when she used to cut the chestnuts and cook them. And the whole house would be permeated by the beautiful smell of the roasted chestnuts. So I walked closer to the vendor. Not to buy any because I couldn't afford them — just to catch a smell. And I saw a sign on the vendor's cart that became my philosophy of life and the title of my book. It said: "I don't want to set the world on fire, I just want to keep my nuts warm."

Reel to Real: As a movie star, wasn't it a big career risk for you to take a role on a television sitcom, *McHale's Navy?*

Borgnine: Yes, it was. As a matter of fact, when my agent called and asked me if I wanted to do this, I said, "No, no, I'm through with television now." As far as I'm concerned, I'm an actor now, you know a motion picture actor and I'll stay with movies. He said, "Well, if you change your mind, call me." OK, fine. So the next morning, as the good Lord would have it, there came a knock at my door. A young man is selling chocolate bars for some private school out in the San Fernando Valley. He said, "would you like ... and I said, sure, sure, how much are they?" I started digging for the money. And he looked at me and said, "Mister, I've seen your face before, are you in show business?" I said, "Yes, I am." He asked me my name. And I kiddingly said, James Arness. He said, "No, he's on *Gunsmoke.*" And I said I was just pulling his leg. "My name is really Richard Boone," I said. He said, "No, he's in *Have Gun Will Travel.*" All this kid had to do was look around the door corner and see my Oscar. I thought I'd get him now, so I said, "My name is really Ernest Borgnine." Absolutely no recognition of any kind! He said, "But I know I've seen you." I said, "Thanks a million son, here's your money." I picked up the telephone, called my agent and said, "Is the part still open?" he said, "Yes." I said, "I'll do it." He asked me what changed my mind and I responded, "None of your damn business." A year later I'm on the road up in Oregon looking for a place to park for the night. And I stuck my head into this cabin and this fellow looked at me and said, "McHale, what are you doing here?" I thought, "Boy, that kid was right!"

Reel to Real: Tom Arnold starred in a remake of *McHale's Navy* in which you had a small role.

Borgnine: I was in it. They paid me well for it, and I can't say another word about it. In the TV series, I had a chemistry with these guys that spewed forth a sense of comedy. I'm sorry to say in the film they made, there was just nothing there.

Reel to Real: You spent 10 years in the Navy. Did you ever see anything there resembling the *McHale's Navy* hijinks?

Borgnine: Oh you'd better believe it. I was stationed on board a yacht during the war. And on this yacht, believe it or not, I had my own stateroom and I was the gunner's mate onboard. We had the run of the Atlantic Ocean you might say. It was the greatest thing since cut bread. We'd go out and get boxes of food for ourselves, steaks and everything else during the war mind you. And we'd trade in another box full of stuff just to get whisky and beer and everything else. And then we'd go out and have a ball on the beach.

Reel to Real: After *McHale's Navy* you had no trouble going back into feature films?

Borgnine: Oh yeah. That's what made it so easy, and people just couldn't get over it. They asked, "How come you can go back and forth from motion pictures to television and everything else? You are one of the few who can do it." I said, "There's nothing different between television and motion pictures." It's the easiest thing in the world, you know. A lot of people are great on that small tube. You get them up there on the great big tube, and they can't do it.

Reel to Real: Have you always been comfortable with your character actor status?

Borgnine: Absolutely. I don't want to be a star all the time. You know how many headaches these people have? Let's see, I've got to carry this picture on my shoulders. That's why they have best supporting actors. I'm one of the very few actors that ever won an Oscar for not being a leading man, really, but rather for portraying a character.

Reel to Real: You don't seem to wear your political leanings on your sleeve like many others in your profession. Is that an accurate statement?

Borgnine: It's a pretty private thing for me, but I did shoot six commercials for a group of people who are pushing for a national sales tax, instead of the IRS. What the heck ... I'm 81 years old and I like to speak my mind. As a legacy, on the day I die, I'd like to have a newspaper publish all the things that I find wrong in the United States today. And my first would be to get rid of the politicians. We put politicians into Congress and the Senate for what? For representation. But who do they represent? They represent not only their party, but the people who give them the money, the lobbyists.

Reel to Real: On a lighter note, what really keeps you going at this breakneck pace?

Borgnine: My mother told me when I was a young man, "You know, Ernie, if you can make one person laugh in the span of 24 hours, you have accomplished a great deal." And that's what I try to do, make somebody laugh in the span of 24 hours. That's it. If you can do that, it keeps you young, keeps you happy, and hey, what more can you ask out of life?

MEASURINQ UP
James Cagney
March 1979

James Cagney was no tough guy.

The man who died Easter Sunday at age 86 was the antithesis of tough. He was a doting husband and father with a penchant for poetry and a soft spot for song-and-dance men. He was a gentleman of the old school.

It was 1979, on St. Patrick's Day, that we went to Coldwater Canyon, in Beverly Hills, to visit the legendary screen star. Until then, Cagney had granted few interviews since his retirement picture, *One, Two, Three,* in 1961. Shortly after our visit, however, he was deluged by reporters in conjunction with his comeback appearance in the movie *Ragtime.*

We entered Cagney's very private life as college journalists. At the time we were freelance writers who hustled our stories to any newspaper or magazine that would print — and pay for — them. In additon, we wrote a regular celebrity interview column in the University of Minnesota's student newspaper, the *Minnesota Daily.* Our specialty was old Hollywood. The previous summer we had cadged a couple of sit-downs with Fred Astaire and Gene Kelly.

"If Freddie will see you, so will I," Cagney wrote us in late 1978. He informed us that he would be spending the winter months in his Southern California home and that's where we could reach him. He preferred to stay year-round at his upstate New York farm, but his wife, Billie, of more than 60 years, liked the warmer weather, he explained to us. So we planned our spring break trip to Los Angeles.

Immediately upon our arrival at our Beverly Hills hotel, we phoned Cagney's unlisted number that he had included in his note to us. A woman answered.

"Hello, we were told to call Mr. Cagney to arrange a short visit," Dave told her.

"Who told you that and how did you get this number?" She asked, bristling.

"Mr. Cagney," Dave said.

"Well, he can't see you." With that, she hung up.

We had not journeyed two thousand miles to get the heave-ho from some anonymous voice on the end of a telephone line. We called again. This time, Dave was more assertive.

"Listen," Dave said, "We're students from the University of Minnesota and we flew from Minneapolis to see Mr. Cagney at his invitation."

"Hold on a moment," the woman said. The few seconds she was away from the phone seemed like an hour and a half.

"OK, be here in a half-hour. No cameras and no tape recorders," she commanded. It was like we were caught in some old '50s noirish melodrama directed by Sam Fuller and stocked with his hardboiled dialogue.

"We'll be there," Dave said trying to channel Richard Widmark in *Pickup on South Street*, and hung up the phone. We quickly hailed a taxi for Coldwater Canyon — a boulevard that bisects the Santa Monica Mountains and links West Los Angeles with the sprawling San Fernando Valley to the north.

When we arrived at Cagney's house perched on a sloping shoulder of the canyon, a woman who appeared to be in her mid-50s answered the door. She introduced herself as Marge Zimmerman, Mr. Cagney's assistant. We could tell by the brusque voice that she was also the telephone mystery woman. We didn't know it at the time, but Zimmerman was soon to be embroiled in controversy chronicled in a feature story in *Life* magazine. According to many of Cagney's old show business friends, Zimmerman had taken complete control of all aspects of his life — professional and personal. Some of Cagney's friends claimed she was motivated by profit.

But Zimmerman was not without her defenders. Many said she helped keep the ailing Cagney stay vital by pushing him back into film and television roles. To this day, her motives and the exact role she played in his life are unclear.

In all fairness, she was extremely friendly and cooperative toward us once we made eye contact. She ushered us into the den where Cagney was waiting. "Cag, I'd like you to meet two young men from Minnesota," she said.

"Minnesota," he said with astonishment. "What brings you here?"

"We came to meet you," Tom said. Seated on a rocking chair, dressed in a terrycloth bathrobe and with a severe case of early morning bed-head (his unruly white hair stood almost straight up as if he had just seen a ghost), Cagney replied, "Hell, you must be a six-footer!" What immediately struck us was that classic, instantly recognizable Cagney voice. Age had not diminished that unique high-pitched, Irish-by-way-of-Yorkville, New York, pitch and machine-gun cadence.

While Tom tried to live up to Cagney's assessment of him, Dave scanned the room. Like the rest of the house, it was decorated in what might be described as Western Americana with about a sequoia's worth of wood paneling and Western artifacts, including a large Frederic Remington sculpture. The room also contained a large oil portrait of Cagney as Admiral Bull Halsey in the 1960 film, *The Gallant Hours,* painted, we later learned by Cagney's good friend and instructor, Sergei Bongart.

Cagney looked every bit his 80 years. He suffered from diabetes, strokes and a heart condition. Shortly after our visit, he entered a hospital for treatment of sciatica, a painful lower back disorder. But like the characters he portrayed on the screen, he still seemed larger than life.

"What can I do for you boys?" he asked.

"We'd like to talk to you a little about your musical film career." His face lit up with a broad grin.

He told us that as a self-taught dancer, when he was young,

he would "acquire" steps from stage performers as he sat in the audience watching vaudeville acts, and then immediately swap them with other aspiring hoofers on the streets of New York.

There was nothing deviant in this and it was considered an accepted practice, Cagney told us, provided one used the proper discretion and didn't cop an entire routine outright.

Tom said that he had read an anecdote about how the great black tap dancer Bill "Bojangles" Robinson once gave a recital for a group of dance experts and how they all stared intently at his feet during the performance. "They should have been lookin' at my face, 'cause that's where I was sellin,'" Bojangles said.

"Right, right," Cagney laughed. "He knew."

Cagney said that in the early days, choreographers charged a large amount of money to tailor a routine for a dancer, and it was just common sense for those less wealthy to pay 15 cents admission to the local vaudeville house and get it second-hand at a much lower price.

It was during those early years — in the 1920s — that Cagney formulated his distinctive stiff — but rhythmic — style of dancing and his raspy enunciation of song lyrics. This combination meshed to a pinnacle in his Academy Award-winning portrayal of George M. Cohan in *Yankee Doodle Dandy*, admittedly his favorite screen role.

Cagney cited veteran hoofers Johnny Boyle and Harland Dixon as brilliant all-around dancers who had great influence on his own personal style, but he acknowledged Fred Astaire to be the master of cinematic song and dance.

Cagney said that he and "Freddie" had talked of making a musical together in the early 1950s, but due to previous commitments (Astaire was contracted to MGM at the time) their schedules never coincided long enough to make it a reality.

In 1961 Cagney retired as a movie actor and has since felt no great urge to perform again in front of the cameras. He did intimate to us that the only film offer he felt a tinge of regret in not accepting was the role of Alfred Doolittle, Eliza's father, in *My Fair Lady*, a character whose tremendous *joie de vivre* had impressed Cagney when he saw the Broadway version of the musical.

Besides movie musicals, Cagney's other interest is raising Morgan horses on his New York farm. He told us that Morgans are utilitarian and are good for work or riding. Tom mentioned to him that his grandparents, of Irish descent, raised horses on their farm in Iowa.

"Well I'll be darned, my wife is from Iowa," he said. Cagney's marital status is unique among show business couples. He and his wife "Bill" (as he calls her) have been married for 58 years.

As for that perennially asked question of all great movie stars, "Do you watch your films when they're shown on TV?" Cagney says, "Not the hoodlum ones, but if it's one of my musicals I might stick around for the dance numbers."

Because we had traveled by taxi, we planned to make the two-mile walk down the canyon to Sunset Boulevard, but Zimmerman wouldn't hear of it. Instead, she insisted on driving us back to our hotel in Cagney's 1961 Bentley. As we rode, she invited us to the Gingerman Restaurant the next night to hear the Beverly Hills Unlisted Jazz Band, featuring actors George Segal (*The Owl and the Pussycat* with Barbra Streisand) and Conrad Janis (*Mork and Mindy*). It was a weekly tradition for the Cagneys to attend when in town.

When we arrived at the Gingerman, we found a line that extended around the block. After name-dropping to the hostess why we were there, we were promptly seated. A few minutes later, Zimmerman arrived.

"Order anything you want," she said, sounding this time like the Army sergeant from Fuller's *The Big Red One*. "Enjoy the tunes."

After dinner, Zimmerman returned. It was time to meet the Cagney party. Sitting next to Cagney and his wife was the owner of the Gingerman, Archie Bunker himself — Carroll O'Connor, who sized us up silently with a penetrating glance that would have stiffened even Meathead. Cagney, wearing a Russian sailor's cap and blue blazer was having a grand time as he tapped his foot in time to the Dixieland stylings of the band. (What *wasn't* grand was the procession of tipsy wellwishers who crowded the table, including a soused character dressed in yachting regalia who was a dead-ringer for Thurston Howell III of *Gilligan's Island*.)

Via Zimmerman's urging, public excursions had become commonplace for Cagney during the last couple of years. After we exchanged pleasantries, Cagney, wordlessly, reached over and gave us a couple of signed postcards taken from one of his own paintings — a still life of a vase of flowers, doubtless painted under the close tutelage of his instructor, Bongart. It was a touching gesture from a man famed — at least in the movies — for being a hardcase; a tough guy.

We returned to our table to listen to jazz; feeling, you guessed it, six-feet tall.

Living Life in the Affirmative
Tony Curtis
June 1998

Tony Curtis readily admits that he broke into movies much the way a thief enters the second story window of a mansion — surreptitiously, almost undetected. "People didn't know who I was — I just snuck in," he says, laughing the same incredulous laugh he did in 1948 when Universal first put him, a largely unknown acting quantity, under the standard studio contract. "I was like a weed that grew out of a crack in the cement, only that crack happened to be located on a studio lot."

Thanks to an irresistible combination of darkly Semitic matinee-idol looks and an engaging grin that illuminated the screen, Curtis escalated his stealthy break into the business to a four-alarm fire. Separately, and with his equally photogenic wife, Janet Leigh, Curtis became a sex symbol long before hype and marketing spin made such phenomena easy to construct.

"Janet and I ended up being a movie couple, but without intending to be," he says. "We fell in love and the next thing we knew, all the magazines went *ga-ga* over it. Eddie Fisher and Debbie Reynolds could have been our maids in comparison ... Elizabeth Taylor and Richard Burton could have been the couple who lived in our gatehouse and looked after the garden. That's how big the buzz around us was in those days."

Half a century later, the march of time — not the ravages of it — have tempered Curtis' good looks into a formidable, but not vestigial presence. The rippling chest of yore, barrel-shaped now, still emanates powerful strength. And he still can highbeam that Pepsodent smile at will, which he does unstintingly.

Curtis, 73, lives in a gated community in the hills of Bel-Air about a Henry Moore stone head's throw across the 405 freeway from the new Getty Center art museum. It's a propitious location for Curtis, since acting in movies has largely, though not completely, given way to his second career as a painter. He tells us that at last count he has perhaps 1,500 canvases and 2,000 drawings stacked in a studio he keeps in Woodland Hills. Much of the overflow seemed to recline against all available upright surfaces in the living room of his hacienda-style house. Matisse-like still-lifes were propped next to framed animation cells of Tony as Stony Curtis from *The Flintstones* cartoon show, and blow-up photos of him and Jack Lemmon dressed in drag and reclining on a divan on the set of *Some Like It Hot.*

But apart from the multicolored neck ribbon of Curtis' *Legion de Honneur* medal (bestowed by the French government for meritorious cultural achievement) which peeks at us from its half-opened box, very little chronicling Curtis' show business career is visible.

"You wouldn't know to look around here that this is the home of a movie actor. You'd think a painter lives here, and that's the way I like it," he says in that familiar low-clipped tone that conjures images of a boyhood spent on New York City streets.

Back to that medal. An impression many people have of Curtis the last few years, largely through his appearances in the media, is of a loose cannon. Flouncing into gallery and nightclub openings with the Legion of Honor hung prominently around his neck like the "flair" of badges and pins on a Denny's waitress smock, Curtis brings to mind a younger version of Georgie Jessel in all his ersatz military regalia. It would be easy to dismiss Curtis' eccentricity, like it was Jessel's, as a joke, a publicity ploy. But that would be wrong. Curtis, you see, makes it abundantly clear that he doesn't give a shit! To wit; he's seen and done almost everything, and, good or bad, he's come out alive on this end wiser for the wear. To Curtis' way of thinking, that clarity also provides the liberating freedom of not having to buckle to peer pressure — or pretty much any pressure. Curtis has, in effect, achieved a zen-like state of placidity these last few years.

"My dear friends, every minute of the day it can't get better than it is right now," he recites, in the clunky, wilful cadence unique to 12-step program literature (Curtis tells us he is indeed a program graduate after liberally abusing cocaine and heroin in the 1970s). "And that minute will give way to the next 'best' minute. I'm not jerking myself off here. I've never been busier. I've never looked better in my life. Everywhere I go people love me. I get tables anywhere in the world. And I love it all!"

An ego successfully rehabilitated? Almost. Curtis does confess to a kind of wistful *ennui* about receiving recognition from his peers in Hollywood for what he considers to be about 20-25 great films out of 110 movies in which he's starred. "That's part of the uniqueness of my situation," he says. "I've done some excellent films, like my favorite, *The Boston Strangler.* But I guess I'll have to leave any affirmation in the hands of the gods."

But wait! Affirmation of sorts comes almost daily for Curtis. There's a mural of him in a white T-shirt, painted by an itinerant artist that looks across the Hollywood Freeway. More famously, Curtis is depicted on the cover of The Beatles' *Sgt. Pepper's* album and, of course, there's Stony Curtis. Not bad for the former Bernie Schwartz from 'Da Bronx.'

"Those tiny little pop-culture affirmations prove that I made my mark during a period of time," he says. "They make me feel good."

What didn't make Curtis feel good, at least at the time, was working with Marilyn Monroe during *Some Like It Hot,* one of the very best comedies ever filmed. "She made it tough for everybody," Curtis says. "If you're in a chain gang and you're tied to someone else, who's also tied to someone else, and so on ... and the fifth guy down the line is screwing around and not paying attention, it will delay everyone else. That was the case with Marilyn. You're being paid good dough to work and you're doing 10- to 12-hour days. You don't want to have to baby someone unless the script calls for babying.

"She would play Jack Lemmon off against me or me against him, and Billy Wilder against both of us," Curtis continues. "Marilyn was getting even with every guy who ever fucked her! That's my read on her. But I never said kissing her was like kissing Hitler! I don't know where that came from."

A full frontal barrage with Curtis telling it like it was — with no particular axe to grind or anything to purge. He tells us he exorcised all his demons years ago. "There's nothing for me to be upset about," he says. "There isn't anyone alive who wouldn't want to be a major player in Hollywood. Walk down the street and point to anybody. You get everything you ever wanted."

Through the years, various actor friends and artists have shared with Curtis pearls of wisdom that he has filed away and learned from. One was from his acting idol, Cary Grant. "Cary once told me the way to judge a fine bottle of white wine was that after chilling, it should taste like a cool glass of water," Curtis remembers. "It's so artful that it's artless, Cary said." Curtis instantly related Grant's sommelier advice to his own profession and considered it one of the best acting tips he ever received; that less is more. Indeed, underplaying scenes may have helped ensure the long run Curtis enjoyed in movies.

"One thousand years from now the films I made will probably still be around in some form," he says. "If you look at it that way, they have their own kind of perpetuity."

Who could ask for better affirmation than that!

On Hiqh with Moses
Charlton Heston
May 20, 1996

It's strangely appropriate that the actor who portrayed Moses and other historical heavyweights during an illustrious 48-year movie career should himself live atop a mountain. That happens to be the case with screen legend Charlton Heston. For more than 30 years, his piece of the rock has been a secluded parcel of real estate perched on top of Coldwater Canyon in Beverly Hills. Heston's land adjoins undeveloped acreage managed by the Los Angeles Water Department, thus furthering the illusion of a pastoral retreat, albeit a hideaway set against one of the largest urban areas in the U.S. — greater L.A. that recedes endlessly in either direction from Heston's aerie.

Ascending to Heston's hilltop retreat does not come close to approximating his biblical journey up Mt. Sinai under the watchful eye of Cecil B. DeMille, but it does require all the torque our sub-compact can muster. Still imposing at 73, Heston sports an Adidas polo shirt and shorts as he greets us at the door. His broad shoulders and barrel chest taper down to a thin waist and muscular (although slightly knock-kneed) legs — the product, no doubt, of hoisting cast-iron swords and the dead weight of flintlock rifles to the ready position in scores of films over the last four decades.

Since screen images are so indelibly linked in the public's collective consciousness, for just an instant, we half expect Heston to perform a miracle and part his swimming pool for us as we move to a workout room located just a short forehand stroke away from his tennis court.

Heston, alas, proves to be a mere mortal, humbly admitting that lucky casting has afforded him the opportunity to play larger than life characters on the screen — Moses, Andrew Jackson, Judah Ben-Hur, John the Baptist and Michelangelo, to name just a few.

"I've been a public face for more than 40 years," he says. "It has advantages and disadvantages. But don't get me wrong, the positives far outweigh the negatives."

The interview takes place in a glass-enclosed hallway that affords a ringside view of the action on Heston's court. The hallway is stocked with buckets of tennis balls, a wealth of rackets, even a Universal Gym for weight training. In what seems an unconscious attempt to dispel any thought that he might be guilty of conspicuous consumption, Heston says he is fully aware his hard-earned good fortune as an actor has allowed him to indulge in pleasures of the good life.

"The time I spent as president of the Screen Actors Guild gave me a wide and embittering understanding of the mortality rate in the acting profession in Hollywood," he says. "More than three-fourths of the members of the guild made less than $2,500 last year. The brutal fact is that the overwhelming majority of actors don't act at all. To be in a tiny band of perhaps a dozen men and five women who can choose what film projects they want to do is a shining stroke of good fortune."

Heston believes that the rampant unemployment among actors is a problem that can be credited to a historical lack of autonomy in the entertainment profession.

"The actor alone among artists can work only if someone gives him a job," he says. "A painter can pump gas all week for a living and then paint masterpieces in his furnished room or backyard. The novelist needs only to earn enough money outside his living to be able to buy pen and paper. But the actor cannot act at all unless someone volunteers, 'Here's a part, there's a stage, go do it!' It's a unique frustration."

The concern Heston feels toward his fellow thespians isn't blind sympathy. He served a stint as co-chairman of President Reagan's task force on the arts and humanities and in accordance with the tighten-the-belt doctrine of Reaganomics, Heston believes arts funding shouldn't be exempt from cutbacks.

"If you're cutting school lunches then you'd better cut support for the San Francisco Ballet," he says. "I think the public marketplace has to be an appropriate factor in judging the validity of art. While some creative undertakings are less well-equipped to thrive in the marketplace than others, they all have to accept the responsibility to test themselves there. I understand that ballet productions are expensive to mount and that grand opera with a full house can't break even. If you can't break even, then what's happening? Theaters, orchestras, or any artistic endeavor that seeks to insulate itself entirely from mass public consumption can't make a very good case for itself for government funding."

Throughout his career, Heston has shown a penchant for starring in epic box-office winners. He has practically cornered the market in adaptations of stories from the Old and New Testaments. *Ben Hur* and *The Ten Commandments* are two biblical opuses that Heston admits profoundly influenced his career. Working with Cecil B. DeMille (on *The Ten Com-*

mandments and the Oscar-winning circus epic *The Greatest Show on Earth*) made an equally strong impression.

From the religious prophets of the ancient world to Elizabethan England and the tragedies of William Shakespeare, Heston has always had an unerring eye for quality scriptwriters.

"I've had the supreme satisfaction an actor can have, and that's the chance to try the great parts over and over again. I first performed *Macbeth* in school and I've done it five times since then. I figure I have one more left in me. Those combats at the end are the toughest fights in Shakespeare. They absolutely drain you. I fight with a broadsword and shield and sometimes with heavy war clubs — none of that light foil stuff like in *Hamlet*. Any actor properly trained can do combat, but the problem with the great roles is that you are already pouring on the energy knocking the bottom out of the barrel and then to come to the fifth act of *Macbeth* and say, 'OK, now the fights.'"

The great roles notwithstanding, Heston believes that art also means compromise and frustration.

"I have never made a film or done a play where I felt the potential was realized," he says. "The whole creative process is one of failure, that's why you can spend a lifetime in quest of perfection. It is like Michelangelo (whom Heston played in *The Agony and the Ecstasy*) standing back from the Moses statue after working on it for two years, then throwing his hammer at it and saying, 'Why don't you speak?' If Michelangelo could be dissatisfied with his work, then the rest of us bloody well better be."

While younger audiences may not know him as Moses, despite the regular Easter-time TV airing of *The Ten Commandments*, Heston's continued appearances in films, such as the 1994 hit *True Lies*, in which he played Arnold Schwarzenegger's menacing, eyepatch-wearing boss, have introduced him to a new generation of filmgoers. Add to that his portrayal of a nefarious poacher in the 1996 film *Alaska* directed by his son Fraser, and a co-starring role in Kenneth Branagh's *Hamlet*, it's no wonder when pressed to name his favorite film, Heston replies, "I don't know, I'm not through yet!"

Reel to Real: In *Alaska* your son, Fraser, directed you. How would you assess your son as a director, especially vis-a-vis some of the all-time greats with whom you've worked?

Heston: Fraser is a good director. He also has the enormous advantage in directing me because he knows me very well and he knows that I like to be pressed. Nowadays I almost always work for directors who are younger than me, and dare I say, greener in reputation. This situation usually results in an extraordinary deference, which is not useful to me as an actor. They'll say, "Oh Chuck, that take was marvelous. Could we perhaps do just one more take to be sure." I'll reply, "Hell, let's do five takes until I give you exactly what you want!" Fraser understands that those niceties are trivial and he gives me a frank assessment."

Reel to Real: You've even taken a turn at the helm, directing such actors as John Gielgud.

Heston: My major flaw is that I am too kind to actors. Being an actor myself, I know it is hard when you are striving to get something that by definition is probably unattainable. I tend to praise actors too much — and some need a lot of coddling. Gielgud, for one, was not interested in praise. He presumed he would be good, and he was. Many directors and actors like to talk endlessly about their scenes. It's like jacking-off; it's fun, but it really doesn't accomplish anything. If you have questions, explore them, but the time to talk about a scene is on your own time with the director, over a beer. Shooting time is too important.

Reel to Real: You worked with directors William Wyler and Cecil B. DeMille on two biblical blockbusters, *Ben-Hur* and *The Ten Commandments*. What were their particular styles like?

Heston: Wyler's instinct for performance was the best I've ever seen. He would shoot several takes, but he wouldn't tell you what he wanted done differently because he really didn't know himself. He was just probing and searching for the best performance he could extract. DeMille was always very courteous to me and especially to actors at a time when it wasn't very fashionable to be polite to actors. He would always address them as ladies and gentlemen, not, "Hey you!" If he shot in the fall of the year, he would take great pains to shoot long and elaborate sequences that required a lot of extras. That way, he felt, these people would be employed at a time when they could use a little extra money for the holidays. He gave me my first big break as the circus manager in *The Greatest Show on Earth*. If you can't make it fly with two DeMille pictures, it ain't gonna get off the ground.

Reel to Real: Your recollections of DeMille don't jibe with some reports that he was a real fire-eater.

Heston: I think he earned that reputation in his younger days. The two pictures I made with him were the last films he ever directed. He was in his 70s then. Don't get me wrong, he was quite authoritative. You've got to remember that for more than 40 years he had been one of the best known directors in the business and that shaped his personality. He was formal and really quite magisterial, I guess you could say.

Reel to Real: Have you ever *not* taken on a Shakespearean role? You always seem to jump at the chance to play the great parts, the latest being your role in Branagh's *Hamlet*.

Heston: Every time you get a chance to waltz with the old gentlemen, you have to do it, especially as an American actor, you don't get that many chances. Obviously, I was never right for the title role in *Hamlet*: bass voice, 6 foot 3, broken nose — that's not right. It would be a one-act play. The great parts are all unachievable, really. I've done *Macbeth* five times and still have not gotten it right. I'm striving in roles that other actors have been trying to whip for four fucking centuries! As far as Shakespeare is concerned, I was attracted to parts that I was physically right for — Henry the Fifth, Macbeth and Marc Anthony. I first played *Macbeth* — badly, no doubt — in high school. I got the part because even at 14, I had a bass voice.

Reel to Real: In *The Big Country*, another Wyler film from 1958, you had to be persuaded to take a supporting role as the hot-headed ranch foreman. Cut to 1994 and your small part in *True Lies*; are you comfortable at this stage of your career to cede the leads and assume character parts?

Heston: Of course. Jim Cameron (the director of *Titanic* and *The Terminator*) offered me the part and I asked him, as I ask every director, "Why do you want me to take this role?" He said that he needed me for the role because he required someone who could intimidate Arnold Schwarzenegger in his agent role. I told Cameron I could do that because I've been playing those kinds of parts all my life. To make the guy more menacing I came up with the idea of wearing the eye patch. I figured the guy had probably been an OSS guy during World War II, parachuting into Yugoslavia to cut German throats. Along the way, it's conceivable that he lost an eye.

Reel to Real: You are perhaps Hollywood's best-known political conservative. What do you see as your role in political campaigns?

Heston: I think the role of surrogate, which I play in political campaigns, is widely misunderstood. Happily, it's most often misunderstood by Hollywood liberals who think they're contributing to a campaign by hitching a ride on Air Force One, or going to a White House dinner. That has nothing to do with a campaign. A president or presidential candidate really feels perfectly capable of electing himself — and he'd better believe that. They sometimes want you to show up at the big rallies. I think I can make more of an impact on behalf of congressional and senatorial candidates. I do two things for a campaign — I get people to show up at fundraisers, and I can usually turn out the media to cover an event.

Reel to Real: Liberal causes have always been *de rigeur* in Hollywood. Do you think your outspoken stance on such issues as less government and the right to bear arms has had an adverse effect on your ability to land certain film roles?

Heston: The obvious presumption is that I lose roles because I'm a conservative. I refuse to accept that. I would be deeply distressed if that were true. It's different for younger filmmakers who happen to be conservative. They tell me, "Chuck, nobody's *not* going to hire you because everybody knows you are a political conservative, you've always been a conservative, like John Wayne. But it's different for us." If they think that is true for them, OK. But I have never had that feeling about myself.

Reel to Real: Many people don't realize that you were active in the early Civil Rights Movement.

Heston: That fact insulates me from some criticism. There are certain things that political opponents dare not say about me — for instance, that I am a racist. The Democratic Party shifted to the left in the 1960s after Jack Kennedy was killed. I don't think that's why the shift occurred, but nonetheless it happened. My politics are exactly the same as they were at the beginning.

Reel to Real: You met your wife Lydia while attending Northwestern University outside Chicago and have been married for more than 50 years now. Can such a long and exclusive run be chocked up to Midwestern family values?

Heston: It really depends on picking the right girl in the first place. I suppose you could say, though, that I believe in the strength of Midwestern values. I am a Midwesterner. It's the center of the country — it really is.

Nice and Easy Does it Every Time
Karl Malden
1998

That famous schnozz — like a small mass of unshaped modeling putty — reaches your eyes first. It dominates the face of Karl Malden, and, taken together with his other features, seems to telegraph in an instant several verities about the man; his unfailing good cheer, his naturalness, his candor. In fact, talking with Malden about his recently published book, winning an Oscar, or working with Marlon Brando, is like chatting up your neighbor over the back fence during a break raking the Fall leaves. It's easy and informative.

Although consigned by his looks to supportive roles as best friend, father confessor, or the occasional heavy, Malden, over the span of 50 years, has shown the world just how indelibly he could etch those characters. *A Streetcar Named Desire*, for which he won a Best Supporting Actor Oscar in 1951, *On the Waterfront, Baby Doll* and *Patton*, as G.I. General Omar Bradley, are just a few movies that wouldn't be quite as good without Malden.

"Nonsense!" Malden says with genuine self-effacement, over coffee and Danish at a small hotel on Sunset Blvd., just down the slope from the new Getty Center that hulks over the landscape for miles like a white elephant. "Honest, upright and honorable is the way I've been described. Just watch me screw that up right now."

Perhaps it's the face allied to the distinctive baritone; maybe it's the long track record of memorable movies, or Malden's 21 years of "don't-leave-home-without-it" American Express commercials, but a flicker of recognition comes slowly into the eyes of our busboy. He's a young Hispanic kid to which English does not come readily. But he's all smiles as he approaches us for a refill. To us, it serves as a neat reminder of the true measure of fame that American pop culture provides — the kind that pervades everyday life and every ethnicity. Innately, Malden knows this as he furtively smiles back at the busboy one of those unspoken, I-know-you-know-I'm-famous smiles. Everything is understood without a word being spoken.

It's disconcerting then, to hear that Malden received only three calls for movie work last year. One of them, *The Long Kiss Goodnight*, starring Geena Davis, Malden termed "terrible."

"I don't belong in the movies they're making today," Malden says who is dressed this day in a blue windbreaker and Tommy Hilfiger shirt with it's wreathy coat-of-arms. "They've kind of passed me by, but I don't care. I used to do two or three films a year and then the five years on *Streets of San Francisco*. But, as Ecclesiastes says, 'To everything there is a season.' That's it, my friends. Either enjoy it or die miserable. I'm not going to die miserable.' "

Far from it. Along with his daughter, Carla, Malden took advantage of his enforced hiatus and wrote an autobiography, *When Do I Start?* which Simon and Schuster published this year. "When I found that suddenly I had nothing to do, it was untenable. My dad used to ask me at the dinner table, 'What did you do today, son?' Sometimes I would say nothing and he'd say, 'Well, that's one day shot to hell, isn't it?'"

Working daily for three or fours hours over the last two years, Malden and his daughter shaped the richly anecdotal book.

"To write a book with a family member is amazing," he says. "They laugh and cry right along with you — and they learn."

What Carla learned, if she didn't already know, was all about the underpinnings that made Malden such a staunch everyman in many of his films. In his best work, Malden seemed to be shot through with the same kind of steel he helped pour in the mills around Gary, Indiana, where he grew up. "I learned a lot about life there," he says. "Richard Widmark says we're all ditchdiggers. All actors go out there and dig a ditch. Sometimes it's deep and sometimes it's shallow, but we keep digging that ditch.

"I think the best that can be said about me is that I never shirked my duty whether it was in a steel mill or in a movie. I came ready to work. That's it."

Although Malden cut his teeth theatrically with The Group Theater in New York (*Golden Boy* was his Broadway debut), audiences rarely saw the Method behind his acting. It seemed as effortless and natural as breathing. "During that time I began to hear phrases like, 'What's the beat of the scene? Where's the spine?' I didn't know what the hell anybody was talking about, but gradually I came to understand."

Malden came to understand so well that one day director Elia Kazan approached and asked him to read for a part in a gothic Southern drama just completed by Tennessee Williams called *A Streetcar Named Desire*.

"When Kazan gave me the play to read, my wife and I were living in New York in a one-room apartment. I read the play while she ironed some clothes. I then asked her to read it. We both felt it was the greatest play either of us had ever read — and I've read a lot of plays. It was pure poetry."

Malden worked with both Jessica Tandy who originated the role of Blanche DuBois on Broadway, and Vivian Leigh who portrayed her in the film version. "Vivian, sadly, had many of the tragic qualities of Blanche," Malden says softly. "Jessica was a sensational actress; one of the most beautiful human beings I've ever met in the theater. Marlon and I have talked about this. Everyone says Vivian was the greatest Blanche, but Kazan could control the film by cutting it and putting the emphasis where he wanted it — on Blanche — if he wanted. It's an unfair comparison.

"Besides," he continues, "No one noticed anything else when Marlon came on stage, I don't care who was in the scene. He changed the style of acting in America with his role as Stanley."

According to Malden, Brando's untapped abilities as a director were every bit as prodigious as his actor gifts. In his single directorial effort, Brando directed the Western, *One-Eyed Jacks*, co-starring Malden as a corrupt sheriff.

"The industry lost a great director when they didn't give him another movie to do," he laments. "Marlon had something that I didn't have as a director. He couldn't be pushed. Producers would say, 'Hurry up, you're two days behind schedule, pick up the pace! Faster, faster!' On the other end, as a director, he had to motivate the actors. Marlon was a sergeant caught in the middle trying to do a good job. He did it on his own time. He couldn't be pushed and I respect that and wish I had that quality."

Life as a film actor-cum-diarist seems to suit Malden. He says it gives him more time to spend with his wife of 58 years, two children who live close by, and assorted grandchildren. For a man who approached acting throughout his career by the book, now he's interested only in what's in the book — his own.

"After you buy it, don't leave home without it," he quips, waiting for the laugh he knows is imminent.

The Karl Malden Method ... foolproof.

Of Mockingbirds and Maniacs
Gregory Peck
August 1981

Gregory Peck was out stumping for "unpopular" liberal causes long before Screen Actors Guild president Ed Asner became vocal about rebels in El Salvador. Unlike his contemporaries Ronald Reagan and Senator George Murphy, Peck has never used his elected positions in the entertainment business as an entrance to the national political arena

— a curiously popular enticement for movie and television stars these days.

"I've been called the Hollywood equivalent of John F. Kennedy because of my devotion to liberal politics," Peck told us during an interview at his Bel-Air home. "Naturally, I am flattered, but I'm afraid the comparison ends more or less where it began."

Dressed in khaki shorts and an old dress shirt rolled up at the sleeves, Peck asked if we'd like something to drink. Momentarily, a houseboy appeared with a tray of flavored teas and coffees from which to choose. The late afternoon sun was beginning to slant so we moved out to an upstairs terrace and watched as Peck's son, Tony, tossed a football back and forth to a friend. From our plush vantage point (tantamount to the owner's box at, Anaheim Stadium, probably), Tony looked to have the bionic arm of Joe Namath; bulleting 50-yard passes with ease.

"He's putting together a rock band right now," Peck said with the bemused detachment of a parent used to his children's fevered — and ever-changing — enthusiasms. "We'll see," he added dolefully.

For eight years, from 1966-68 and 1970-76, Peck served on the embryonic National Endowment for the Arts Commission (NEA) with such luminaries as John Steinbeck, Agnes DeMille, Isaac Stern and Leonard Bernstein. Following the passage of the Arts and Humanities Act of 1965, the NEA was afforded a whopping $4 million annually in scholarship and grant subsidies. The money was intended to blanket the cultural needs of the entire United States.

"We would meet six times a year and quarrel for hours over which writer, regional theater, or ballet company best deserved a $2,000 grant," Peck said. "I think we got pretty good results, but I do remember a certain politician from Iowa who used to eternally wail to his colleagues on the floor of Congress, 'Tax money for toe-dancers over my dead body!'"

The confounded reality that in 1966 a city the size of

Hamburg, Germany, gave $7 million to their local opera company alone while the entire U.S. muddled through with a mere $4 million in cultural subsidies made Peck's social consciousness crawl.

"The total amount has grown now to $160 million in the United States, which is still not much," he said. "Most of the performing arts don't pay their way back at the box office with the cost of production and other expenses."

Wouldn't it be hard for the Reagan administration to justify increased spending on cultural programs at the expense of cutbacks in social welfare?

"I know it's hard for many people to accept. They feel that cultural groups should pay their own way," Peck said. "But if we want our young people to expand their horizons and personalities and to reach their highest aspirations, then the arts must be nationally subsidized. The private corporate sector has already taken up most of the slack."

On The Beach, Gentleman's Agreement, and *To Kill a Mockingbird,* for which Peck won an Oscar, were entertaining films that crusaded for timely social issues. They were Peck's dream movies, killing two birds with one stone.

"*Gentleman's Agreement* was a cause celebre around Hollywood because it was the first movie to deal directly with anti-Semitism," Peck said. "When Darryl Zanuck decided to do it, people advised him not to rock the boat. 'Business is great,' they said. 'Why deal with such a controversial subject?' Zanuck replied that it was a very good dramatic story that also made observations about racial prejudice. We all felt we were pioneering in a small way. Nowadays it would be nothing, but in 1948, it mattered."

The era of movie producers like Zanuck, who were passionately interested in every line in the scripts of their movies, has given way to a generation of movie mogul conglomerates who look only as far as their profit margins.

"I don't know any studio heads today and I don't want to know them, because they probably won't be here next year,"

Peck said. "They all seem to be a page in Gulf and Western's portfolio. That fellow in the tall building in Columbus Circle in New York, Charles Bluhdorn, he turns the pages, and if a company like Paramount didn't do well last year, he'll throw the rascals out and get some new rascals in. They are essentially crapshooters. Zanuck was a walking computer. You could call him from the set if you had trouble with a line and he'd rewrite the line with you right there on the telephone. If you call one of those fellows today, chances are they won't know what the hell you're talking about."

In 1962, Peck portrayed Atticus Finch, the morally courageous lawyer who defended a black man accused of rape in *To Kill a Mockingbird*. The character is strongly reminiscent of the quiet determination of Frank Capra's everyman idealist of the 1930s and '40s. It is Peck's favorite role, and was one of the most challenging of his career.

"I think one of the hardest things to do as an actor is to make a good man interesting, because they can be awfully dull. If a man is predictably nice, he can put audiences to sleep," Peck said. "Atticus was a good man if anybody anywhere was ever good. We managed to make him compelling. Today when I'm with my wife and we walk down Fifth Avenue in New York, people will come up to me and say how much *To Kill a Mockingbird* meant to them. One young man even said that his decision to become a lawyer was formulated at the age of 14 after he saw the film."

The Boys from Brazil, in which Peck played the part of Dr. Mengele, the diabolical Nazi death-camp experimenter, was a world away from his restrained performance as Atticus Finch, but didn't require flexing too many acting muscles.

"To play Mengele, a raving lunatic, was not difficult," Peck said. "I got down the German accent, blackened my hair, shaved the hair-line back a couple of inches, and affected a kind of laboratory pallor. It has been said that the greatest role an actor could play would be a dipsomaniac dope fiend being dragged to the electric chair. You can climb the walls and claim it's great acting."

Peck can be considered dogmatic in more than just a political sense. He was chewed to pieces by salivating canines in the finales of two of his more recent films, *The Omen* and *The Boys From Brazil.* But apparently he holds no grudges. "I don't want to make a career as dog food," he said. "The only thing my German Shepherd, Roger, has a fondness for teething on is old Hawaiian Tropic Suntan Oil bottles." (The dog was busily engaged perforating one during the course of our interview.)

One of the *old guard* Hollywood directors Peck remembers fondly is William Wyler, a master of light comedy best known for *Ben Hur, The Best Years of Our Lives* and *Funny Girl.* His economical direction would give any Stanislavskian pause to rethink his method.

"Wyler's direction was considered to be death on wheels to method actors," Peck said. "When I was working on *Roman Holiday* with Audrey Hepburn, he'd say, 'Audrey, get mad; you have to cry in this scene.' She had to produce tears without analysis. On the contrary, method actors might say, 'Grandma hurt my feelings when I was five, and if I can recall that, I can cry for you.' It's kind of like dry fly fishing. You drop the fly in the water and when the trout grabs it, you set the hook. There are directors who wouldn't recognize a valuable nuance if you hit them in the face with it. But Wyler was omniscient. He'd wait until a scene was right if it took three days."

Peck will make a rare foray into network television later this year, starring as Abraham Lincoln in *The Blue and The Gray*, an eight-hour CBS mini-series based on the Civil War writing of Pulitzer Prize-winning historian Bruce Catton.

"Television is more meticulous now because networks have more money to spend," Peck said. "They aren't scrambling to shoot 20 pages a day whether it's good, bad, or indifferent. Historical drama can be very good on TV and still be a pleasant change from sophomoric comedy and escapism, which someone once said was just a euphemism for junk."

If he's lucky, Peck's Lincoln might even harken back to the quality of his old movies — four-score and seven years ago. ...

The Battle for Respect

Rod Steiger

March 1995

Rod Steiger is a fighter who has been waging the same titanic battle ever since he left the mean streets of Newark, N.J., at the age of 16 to join the Pacific Fleet during World War II. In those days, with the vicious murmurings of his classmates cutting into him like a razor, Steiger would be called out of school on a regular basis to pick up his inebriated mother from the neighborhood saloon.

Steiger's struggle then, as now, is for respect. It has never changed.

"I am convinced that my success and intensity in the movies comes from the fact that I have sworn somewhere to myself — deeply, psychologically — that I will succeed so spectacularly that the Steiger name will never be laughed at again."

During a long and rambling interview on the deck of his Spanish-style villa in the hills above Malibu, he said the anger and rage that didn't find an appropriate outlet a half century ago makes money for him on the screen. "If I didn't fall into acting," he said, "I probably would've been a mean drunk who ended up with a knife in his ribs after a barroom brawl."

Dressed in a long, flowing black bathrobe, wearing sandals and a large silver medallion around his neck, Steiger, with his bald pate gleaming in the mid-morning sun, conjured images of a groovy West Coast shaman about to impart to us the healing mysteries of the universe instead of regaling us with acting anecdotes. Steiger did however confide to us that for years he suffered bouts of debilitating depression that waxed and waned without warning. He said that medication and the writings of Antoine de Saint-Exupery were helpful in combatting what fellow sufferer Winston Churchill called "the black dog on my back."

"I would recommend reading Saint-Exupery's *The Little Prince* for anyone who has the blues. It's just magical," Steiger said. After all, it was Saint-Exupery who said: 'It is only with the heart that one can see rightly; what is essential is invisible to the eye.'"

Steiger, who won a 1968 Best Actor Academy Award for his performance as a bigoted Southern sheriff in *In the Heat of the Night*, and was nominated for an Oscar in *On the Waterfront*, opposite Marlon Brando, has carved a career playing social misfits or outsiders on the fringe. They are roles (given Steiger's rough and tumble background) with which he has a certain empathy.

Indeed, his favorite starring role is the misanthropic Jewish pawnshop owner tortured by memories of the Holocaust in *The Pawnbroker*. Although raised a Lutheran, Steiger, now a self-professed agnostic, grew up in a Jewish neighborhood and drew on his memories for the critically acclaimed and Oscar-nominated performance.

"As a boy, my best friend was Jewish and he invited me to his house one day for a steak dinner," Steiger remembered. "When I saw his mother put the meat into a frying pan with a 1/4 inch of water, I nearly died. They were kosher, but what she did to the steak should never happen!"

These days, to get parts in films, Steiger has had to do something he never had to do before — sell himself. "Nowadays, I walk in to see studio heads who are about 34 years old and experts in marketing," Steiger said. "Unfortunately, they know little about creating. One of them asked me if I could do a Southern accent. My first animal instinct was to hit him with a chair, then I told him I won an Oscar playing a sheriff of a small Southern town."

Moments like that convinced Steiger of the possibility

that he might be a cipher to a whole generation of moviegoers. "My part as the Cuban mob boss in the Stallone film *The Specialist* was a $40 million commercial to that generation that I exist," he said.

The commercial seems to have paid off. Steiger has been working continuously and will be seen in no less than three films in 1998 — *Incognito*, with Jason Patric; *Animals*, with Tim Roth; and *Revenant*, a vampire movie.

An alumnus of the Actor's Studio in New York, Steiger hit Hollywood right on the cusp, when the old guard comprised of actors like Humphrey Bogart started to cede power to the avant-garde led by the protean talent of men like James Dean and Marlon Brando. Steiger worked with them all. Here are some of his reflections:

On Brando … In *On the Waterfront*, we didn't get to know each other at all. He always flew solo and I haven't seen him since the film. I do resent him saying he's just a hooker, and that actors are whores.

On Dean … Jimmy was a friend of mine and extremely talented. But he hadn't quite got his technique together. At the time of his death, he was working too much on instinct. He'd be brilliant in one scene and then blow the next.

On Bogart … In *The Harder They Fall*, Bogey and I got along very well. Unlike some other stars, when they had closeups, you might have been relegated to a two-shot, or cut out altogether. Bogart didn't play those games. He was a professional and had tremendous authority. He'd come in exactly at 9 a.m. and leave at precisely 6 p.m.

I remember once walking to lunch in between takes and seeing Bogey on the lot. I shouldn't have because his work was finished for the day. I asked him why he was still on the lot, and he said, "They want to shoot some retakes of my closeups because my eyes are too watery." A little while later, after the film, somebody came up to me with word of Bogey's death. Then it struck me. His eyes were watery because he was in pain with the cancer. I thought: "How dumb can you be Rodney!"

On Gary Cooper . . . I had great respect for him as a survivor. Acting had moved on a little bit from where Cooper was, and in the interim his career had gotten a little shaky. To publicize our movie, *The Court Martial of Billy Mitchell*, we did a live scene on *The Ed Sullivan Show*. He was as white as a piece of chalk; perspiration was dripping out of the cuff of his uniform. A couple of times during the scene he got lost a little bit, but he had the guts of a lion. Of course the other side of Cooper was every time we had a scene to shoot during the movie, I had to pound on Elizabeth Montgomery's dressing room door to get him out of there!"

Steiger, 72, is father to a five-year-old son. Although he wants to continue to work in estimable projects in order to leave a legacy to his child, he faces a potentially debilitating handicap.

"I'm a lazy lion," he said. "I sit around all day and read magazines, gaze at the ocean, have lunch and then dinner with my wife and child. But get me interested in a project, and I'm alive again." At that moment, Steiger drew a corollary to his mother. He told us that during the last 11 years of her life, she was sober and a regular attendee of Alcoholics Anonymous meetings. "I was so proud of her," he said. "She turned herself around. She came alive again."

In his own lifelong campaign to win the respect of his peers, Steiger, like his mother, fought the good fight and prevailed. For proof, just rent a video — *On the Waterfront . . . In the Heat of the Night . . . The Pawnbroker . . . Dr. Zhivago . . .*

IV.
Ladies Take
the Lead

Tippi's Pride and Joy

Tippi Hedren
May 1996

The godforsaken edge of the Mojave Desert, north and west of Los Angeles, is hardly the habitat of choice for most movie stars. But, then again, Tippi Hedren is not your garden-variety leading lady.

Hedren, 62, the stunning blonde with the icy reserve of Alfred Hitchcock's *The Birds* and *Marnie*, doesn't give a whit about the Hollywood fast lane. And she "doesn't do lunch" unless the end result benefits her one consuming passion — Shambala Preserve, a wildlife sanctuary of more than 70 exotic animals that roam over 60 acres of Soledad Canyon that she and her then-husband Noel Marshall set aside for that purpose in 1972.

"I think we were put on this earth to do more than just watch television and stuff our faces," she offers in a tone that suggests she does little of either. Hedren, for one, lives by that platitude telling us that if she can't zip up her bluejeans in the morning, she doesn't eat that day. Dressed in a leopard-print shirt and wearing a lion head ring and Shambala chain around her neck, Hedren seems every bit as sleekly feline as the cheetahs and leopards that stalk her menagerie.

The days start early for the 11 people on Shambala's staff (the word is sanskrit for "a meeting place of peace and harmony for all beings, animal and human"). Hedren, who lives in a house on the grounds, tells us she's been up since 4 a.m., attending to business.

"Back in '72 there was nothing here," she says, giving the preserve a rather desultory scan. "We planted eight hundred trees, redirected the creek and dredged the pond over there." Hedren motions to a marshy slough where Muscovy ducks and Mallards are busily paddling around. In stark contrast, across the creek, Shambala's two resident elephants are giving themselves the dustiest mud bath this side of a Tarzan movie.

"All of Hollywood thinks this is what I do," she protests, "but I need to work in movies because Shambala doesn't provide me with an income. It's strictly a nonprofit enterprise that gives sanctuary to animals that need a home — mainly the big cats; the predators."

Hedren underscores the point by mentioning her latest role, a small part as a charismatic leader of the pro-choice movement in the very funny political satire, *Citizen Ruth*.

"Shambala hasn't usurped my interest in movies at all," she says, "but the preserve and its attenuating foundation, The Roar Foundation, is run entirely on donations, including my own." Hedren's daughter Melanie Griffith and her husband Antonio Banderas, are on the foundation's advisory board, along with Betty White, Linda Blair, Loretta Swit and many other actors and non-actors.

Since starting the preserve, Hedren has put a couple of her homes and at least one large piece of commercial real estate on the auction block to keep the Chapter 11 creditors at bay. After nearly 25 years, her enthusiasm — maybe her calling — for providing a refuge for animals remains unabated.

"None of the animals at Shambala have ever been in the wild," she says. "All of them depend on human care. Many arrived having suffered from gross mistreatment and neglect. With the expert care we provide, they are brought back to health and live out their lives in dignity."

Hedren refers to her life-long love of animals as a "birth affect" — something she's harbored since she was a little girl growing up in the tiny farm town of Lafayette in southwestern Minnesota. Back then she also dreamed of becoming a champion figure skater with the Ice Capades, and practiced incessantly on area ponds and, later, on frozen lakes after the family moved to Minneapolis.

Hedren, who began her career modeling at Dayton's and

Donaldson's Department Store fashion shows, still has family in the Twin Cities and, until very recently, went back once a year to visit.

"Like most natives, I love Minnesota in the fall and spring, but you can have it the rest of the time," she laughs, referring to the bleak, exhausting winters.

After seeing her in a television commercial for a dietary product that aired during *The Today Show*, Hitchcock called Hedren and asked whether she'd like to appear in an animal movie — of sorts; *The Birds*. Hedren, who felt her modeling career was waning, accepted. After the most expensive screen test in Hollywood history (it was shot over three days), she was offered the role of Melanie Daniels, the chic mantrap who fatefully pays a call on Rod Taylor in Bodega Bay just as the birds are massing to attack.

"Everything culminated with that last scene where I go up to the attic," she says. "They had a cage built around the attic door that I opened, and three prop men were there wearing leather gauntlets with huge cartons filled with ravens and seagulls which they began to hurl at me. The scene took five days to shoot.

"On Wednesday, Cary Grant visited the set and told me I was the bravest woman he ever met; by Friday they had me on the floor of the attic, my dress torn to shreds from the talons of the birds."

According to Hedren, to achieve a more realistic effect, her dress was fitted with elastic bands that were then tied to the legs of some of the birds. "One broke loose and scratched me right under the eye," she says. "I freaked and started to cry from sheer exhaustion." Hedren did suffer a sort of nervous shutdown after that scene and remembers sleeping for a solid week — against the strenuous protest of Hitchcock who wanted to proceed with the filming.

"I have a dichotomous feeling about *The Birds*," Hedren says. "On one hand, it's a one-of-a-kind picture that everyone has seen, and the shocks still hold up after all these years.

I'm proud of that. But Hitchcock really ruined my career. He was obstinate and possessive. After a while I couldn't stand it anymore, but he wouldn't release me from my contract and so for two years I didn't make a movie; I just sat around drawing my $500 a week salary. After that, we never spoke to each other again."

Future plans for Hedren include the possibility of co-starring with her daughter Melanie in a movie. However, much more tangible are the frequent visits from her grandchildren to the Shambala Preserve.

"My advice to anyone contemplating acting as a profession is to be independently wealthy or have another vocation as a backup. Melanie and Antonio are well set, but most actors make a pittance."

Hard-won advice from an actress who has had to stretch every dime following her true vocation ... her call of the wild.

Just a Girl Who Can Say No
Celeste Holm
January 1998

Celeste Holm and Hollywood were never an easy fit.

In the 1940s and '50s, an era of studio-manufactured starlets, girls often just couldn't say no — not if they placed any value on their careers. Holm could, and did, much to the chagrin of studio heads like 20th Century Fox's Darryl F. Zanuck.

"When I went out to Hollywood, I was already established on the stage," Holm says. "That's just what the head office people were afraid of; that they couldn't control me. Zanuck had seen me as Ado Annie in *Oklahoma!* — the original girl who couldn't say no — and he was astonished to find I was an actress, not a girl. He preferred girls who would say, 'Yes Mr. Zanuck, right away!' Women made him nervous.

Women disagree, and I used to do it in French!"

Audiences soon learned that the characters Holm inhab-
ited were as dependable as death and taxes. In *Gentleman's
Agreement* for which she won a Best Supporting Actress Oscar in 1947, *High Society, The Tender Trap* and *All About Eve*,
Holm offered rock-solid support. She was knowing, poised,
and unflappable in a way that seemed alien to many of the
actresses who were insty-products of the studio dream machines and who had not come up through the slow, galvanizing process of the Broadway stage.

"I really was mystified at how some of the studio contract
players could get married and have children because they never
had to make a decision, not even on nail polish," she says.
"During the filming of *Three Little Girls in Blue* (1946), one
day I came in and June Haver wasn't on the set. She had been
there that morning and then she left. They told me she had
decided her roots were too dark, so we had to wait three
hours while she had her hair done. That, to me, is uneco-
nomical."

Economy in words and action, and a certain stoicism, is
something that Holm learned early on, particularly from her
Norwegian father. When at the age of two and a half, after
seeing the great Anna Pavlova dance in New York City, Holm
announced to her family that she was going to be a prima
ballerina, it was her father who offered the only gentle dis-
sent. "Wanting to be a great dancer and getting there might
be two different things," he cautioned.

Pictures of Holm's family grace every possible flat surface
in her pre-war apartment on Central Park West in New York
City. Books, sometimes stacked six-deep, cover every other
available flat plane. Holm says that the floor-to-ceiling windows drink in the light once the sun clears the phalanx of
high-rises that line Fifth Avenue on the opposite side of Central Park. Her grand piano is festooned with awards from the
Mental Health Association for years of charitable work. (She
starred in *The Snake Pit* (1948), a shocking expose on abuses

of the mental health system that broke ground toward meaningful reform). Less prominent is Holm's Oscar for *Gentleman's Agreement*, barely visible on a side table and partially hidden by the lush overhang of a summer flower arrangement.

"The only thing that happened to me after I won my Oscar," she says ruefully, "was that I couldn't get into another musical. I was suddenly an ACTRESS. I was asked to star in the movie *Sitting Pretty*, where I was supposed to stand around plumping pillows while talking to Maureen O'Hara. I agreed to do it if I could knit through the whole movie something that gets more and more shapely — a sort of running gag. Also, I wanted to wear glasses and whenever I took them off, I'd run into walls. They told me no and then let Marilyn Monroe do all my bits in *How to Marry a Millionaire*."

Smartly dressed in a navy blue pants suit, with her hair brushed back, Holm looks every bit as beautiful as several pictures of her in younger days that hang around the apartment. Her appearance now somewhat suggests an affluent clubwoman, but her manner reminds us more of a wisecracking Rosalind Russell straight out of *His Girl Friday*; an irresistible combination, especially to a couple of reporters. What is truly mesmerizing is that Holm's face, with its million inflections, is the perfect outward reflection of each verbal nuance. Zanuck was right, this girl (sorry, woman) is an actress!

"At our family farm at Schooner's Mountain, just north of Hackettstown, N.J., my mother and I used to do a weird kind of acting exercise," she says. "My mother stood on one hill and I stood on another and we would enunciate bits of stage dialogue back to one another. It was great practice in the days before everyone got a stage microphone. Kind of like Demosthenes speaking with pebbles in his mouth against the roar of the Aegean to get rid of his speech impediments."

Life on the farm held Holm in good stead when she auditioned for the role of Ado Annie in Rodgers and Hammerstein landmark musical, *Oklahoma!* During her audition for Richard Rodgers, Holm even had the temerity to let out a long *Suueeee!* hog call for the composer.

"To this day I don't see productions of *Oklahoma!*," Holm says. "Invariably, they get my part wrong. Ado Annie was very simple. She was cute, not cornpone, like everyone seems to play her. Before Gloria Grahame died, she wrote me a letter apologizing for having ruined the part in the film version. How do you like that?"

Holm currently stars in the CBS series *Promised Land*, playing Hattie Greene, the spunky matriarch of a close-knit family traveling across American in a battered RV. In conjunction with the show and in real life (Holm has three grandchildren), she was recently named "Grandparent of the Year" by the National Grandparents Day Committee. She also appeared, last year, in a movie, *Still Breathing*, co-starring Joanna Going and Brendan Fraser, which is making the rounds of the festival circuit.

"I love doing *Promised Land*," Holm says, "because the show always takes the tack of helping other people. We get something more out of it when that happens. It's fun. Also, I appreciate the opportunity to rebut the negativity about aging now prevalent in this country. There's a wealth of wisdom and a capacity of consideration that seniors can share with our younger generations."

THE ART of CROWD CONTROL
Janet Leigh
May 1996

Once upon a time in Hollywood (the early 1950s to be exact), there lived a beautiful princess named Janet Leigh and her crown prince, Tony Curtis. Their union in 1951 had been properly sanctified by an ordained minister and by God. Beyond that, it earned the beneficence of another — perhaps higher power — Metro-Goldwyn-Mayer Studios.

You see, the star-crossed couple generated considerable box office heat in those days. With the hegemony of television making Pepto-Bismol the aperitif of choice for most movie executives, the king of studios responded enthusiastically to balance sheets in the black. And Leigh and Curtis certainly delivered the requisite numbers along with a large and soothing dose of old-style Tinseltown brio.

Generally, life was simpler back then — or perhaps just simply repressed. In any case, even media-generated hype and spin had an innocent hue and took longer to build than the egg-timer industry average of today. However, in the case of Leigh and Curtis, as the rpm of their individual careers increased, their combined "celebrity" became a veritable juggernaut drawing unruly crowds that literally buckled seaside piers during personal appearance tours.

According to Leigh, the big difference between her and, say, today's crop of young media icons is that she was schooled by the studio to court publicity and, if not the adulation that sometimes came with it, at least in how to take it in stride. Howard Strickling, head of publicity at MGM, taught her a valuable lesson in the 1950s, one that held her in good stead; it was the fine art of crowd control.

"The surge comes because the crowd thinks you are going to run away from them," she explains. "So if you remain calm, they settle down because they think you're extending yourself. It really works, but you've got to keep moving — never stop. If you stop, they'll corner you."

Leigh's explanation isn't disdainful — far from it — it's a thoughtful, if somewhat dispassionate, deconstruction of crowd dynamics. For us, it conjures certain advice Midwestern farmers used to dole out when working around livestock. " ... Move slowly, deliberately, no jerky movements; always keep a watchful eye on the bull . . .

Cattle calls, we surmise, must be the same all over, be they of the four-hoof or two-legged variety.

Leigh greets us at her 10-foot-high driveway gate. It effectively screens the house from any Peeping Toms who venture into these oxygen-thin reaches of upper Beverly Hills to gawk at the immortal star of *Psycho*.

"I've been stalked," Leigh says matter-of-factly. "Jamie (her daughter, Jamie Lee Curtis) has had several stalkers, so she's nervous. You just have to take precautions."

The house itself which she shares with her husband, Los Angeles businessman Bob Brandt, seems like a continuation of the steep mountainside incline on which it is built — all angular rooms and vaulted ceilings.

"It's where I draw the line between my public persona and my private life," she says.

Looking svelte from a regimen of regular tennis matches with friends like fellow MGM star, Jane Powell, Leigh, 71, plops on a sofa and tells us that contrary to F. Scott Fitzgerald's famous pronouncement, some American lives do have second acts.

"I've become a writer during these last several years," she announces proudly. To date, Leigh has written an autobiography entitled, *There Really Was a Hollywood*, and a well-received book on the making of *Psycho*, which was published in 1995 to coincide with the 35th anniversary of the film. That same year she published her first novel, *House of Destiny*.

"The first time I saw my name printed on the dust jacket of my first book, it was every bit as thrilling as seeing my face up on a movie screen for the first time in 1947 in *The Romance of Rose Ridge*," she says. "As an actress, you are such a small part of the overall movie, just a cog in the machine. But writing a book is introspective, personal and you go at it 100 percent alone."

According to Leigh, writing and performing are definitely aligned. "You prepare for a role the way you prepare a character for the written page," she says. "For example, when I played Marion Crane in *Psycho*, I constructed her whole life.

I knew what she was like in school; her tastes, frailties, strengths. I knew what kind of sister she was, and what kind of daughter."

Just as Leigh these days faces a blank sheet of paper alone, she also flew solo developing her character in Hitchcock's most disturbing suspense thriller. "Hitch had a hands-off policy unless you really were blocked," Leigh says. "He was the consummate shot-maker and he trusted his actors to come up with their own motivations. I do remember that he didn't feel there was enough passion between John Gavin and I in the opening hotel room scene, even with me just dressed in a slip and brassiere, so he told us to turn up the heat, which we did."

It's no shocker that Leigh remains unimpressed with the quartet of *Psycho* clones that have been made in the intervening years — although she's seen them all. When pressed to choose the least objectionable entry in the series, she picks the 1990 made-for-cable prequel version. "In that one you saw what a loon Norman's mother was, so you figured out why he went bats," she laughs. Leigh adds she has no intention in appearing in the upcoming big screen remake of the film.

The apple doesn't fall very far from the tree in the Leigh household. Jamie Lee Curtis, 40, started in the movie business starring in horror films such as *Halloween, Terror Train, Prom Night,* and *Friday the 13th.* To a generation of spooked teenagers, she earned the endearing appellation, "The Scream Queen." She is currently appearing in the sequel to *Halloween,* and mom is playing — what else? — Jamie Lee's mom!

In another career parallel with her mother, Jamie Leigh wrote a children's book a couple of year's ago for her daughter, entitled, "When I was Little: A Four-Year Old's Memoir of Her Youth."

Separately or in tandem, with Janet Leigh and Jamie Lee, blood — along with a little bloodletting — does tell!

Baked Alaska
Virginia Mayo
May 1997

It was as campy as it was unexpected. At the chic Boccaccio restaurant in the Los Angeles suburb of Westlake Village, screen star Virginia Mayo had just received her flaming Baked Alaska from a proud waiter who, as if auditioning for a part himself, served it up with pomp and circumstance that would have suited a four-star cafe straight out of the *Michelin Guide.* It was a dessert as overpriced and overproduced as any musical production number from Hollywood's gilded age.

That's when Mayo, not to be topped by the third course of any meal, said it — right on cue — and with the appropriate parrot-like vocal inflection. She aped the famous line delivered by her co-star James Cagney in the classic 1949 film *White Heat,* right before he blew himself to smithereens in the oil refinery finale. "Made it ma, top of the world!" she said, as she eyed the blazing confection as if it were a dividend check from Exxon. We cracked up and the waiter, for all his trouble, minced back to the kitchen with a surefire anecdote he'll doubtlessly unload at cocktail parties for years. Mayo just sat back in anticipation, waited silently for the flames to abate, then ate her fill.

With the recent deaths of movie legends James Stewart and Robert Mitchum, only a few stars from Hollywood's Golden Age remain. Mayo, who made her film debut in the 1943 film *Jack London* (starring her future husband, Michael O'Shea), is emblematic of that increasingly small fraternity of studio contract players who appeared bigger-than-life on the silver screen and left a legacy of indelible performances.

A dishy blonde in her heyday, Mayo displayed early the versatility that was required of stars that were routinely signed to long-term studio contracts. In her case, she toiled mostly for Samuel Goldwyn and Warner Bros. In some 50 films, Mayo proved that she could cut it up with Bob Hope in *The Princess and the Pirate*, and Danny Kaye in *Wonder Man*, tap dance with Gene Nelson and James Cagney in *The West Point Story* or play it icy cold in *The Best Years of Our Lives* and *White Heat*.

Born Virginia Clara Jones 77 years ago in St. Louis, Missouri, Mayo says it was not her mother, but an aunt, who nurtured her early ambition to become a performer. At age six, she enrolled in her aunt's School of Dramatic Expression.

"My aunt was very famous in St. Louis," recalls Mayo. "In fact, Thomas Eagleton, who for a brief time ran for vice president with George McGovern, took elocution lessons from her. In addition to diction, we learned movement and how to be comfortable performing before an audience."

Ironically, Mayo says her aunt was a real taskmaster, who never offered her much encouragement.

"She didn't think I had any talent," she says. "I was kind of ugly and awkward. She tried to help me as much as she could, but she had other pupils who she felt could sing, act and dance better than me."

With a steely determination that seemed to compensate for any artistic shortcomings, Mayo landed a prestigious role in the St. Louis Municipal Opera Company, where she performed in the popular musicals of the day. At age 17, she left St. Louis, changed her name to Mayo and toured the United States in the musical comedy act, Pansy the Horse. After four years with the act, she moved to New York City and joined legendary nightclub impresario Billy Rose's new revue at his famed Diamond Horseshoe. It was while appearing at the Horseshoe that Mayo caught the eye of two Hollywood studio moguls, David O. Selznick and Samuel Goldwyn.

After appearing in a screen test, Selznick took a pass proclaiming that Mayo was in need of more "dramatic experience." However, Goldwyn, who also tested Mayo, detected

something in the erstwhile performer that apparently eluded
Selznick, and signed her to a long-term contract.

Goldwyn, more than anyone else, says Mayo, was responsible for making her a star. In fact, he took almost an obsessive interest in his new starlet inviting her into his office almost daily to review the previous day's film footage and cri-
tique her performance. He also invited her to his home, which
was a launching pad for some famous Hollywood parties.

"Mr. Goldwyn was very much a gentleman and only interested in high-class movies," she says. "He never put junk on the
screen and I admire him for that. I remember while shooting
the *Princess and the Pirate* he was always coming on the set and
glaring at me when the cameras were rolling. During one scene,
I was supposed to act frightened because of this imminent pirate attack. Mr. Goldwyn, said to Bob (Hope), 'look at her,
she's so nervous.' And Bob replied, "Leave her alone, Sam, she's
supposed to act nervous. She's great.'"

The crowning achievement for Goldwyn was his 1946
post-war drama, *The Best Years of Our Lives*, directed by William Wyler and starring Fredric March, Myrna Loy, real-life
double-amputee Harold Russell, Dana Andrews and Mayo.
The film swept the Oscars winning nine, including Best Picture. As Marie Derry, Mayo played the slatternly wife of
Andrews in a convincingly unsympathetic manner.

Mayo says she had no inkling of the classic status the
movie would almost immediately attain. "You never know
in advance how a film is going to turn out," she says. "All
you really know is your part and you try to inject as much
believability into the character as you can."

Another memorable role was that of Verna Jarrett, James
Cagney's tough gun moll in, arguably, the last great Warner
Bros. gangster film, *White Heat*. Mayo credits Cagney with
adding "little touches" such as the cluster headaches that made
the film more than just a run-of-the-mill mob movie.

"At that stage of his career, Jimmy wanted to do different
kinds of parts and then they handed him *White Heat*, which

was just another tough-guy role. After talking with Jack Warner, he was convinced that by working with the director (Raoul Walsh) he would be permitted to add touches that would make the part more interesting. Jimmy had great ideas. He was very creative."

When the studio system petered out in favor of one-picture deals in the early '60s so did, for the most part, Mayo's screen career. "I would have liked to go on, but it ended," she says casually. "The younger movie executives have selective memories. I don't know what they think. And the scripts that I saw weren't great anymore."

Mayo continued to appear on stage in musicals and comedies and on television in such shows as *Remington Steele* and *Murder She Wrote*. She shares her Thousand Oaks, Calif., home with her daughter, son-in-law and three grandsons. O'Shea died in 1973. Her off-camera vocation is painting, primarily in oils and watercolors.

Spying a picture of a familiar looking Hollywood star on Mayo's dining room wall later that afternoon, Dave cheerily piped up with the *faux pas* of the day: "Is that Andy Devine?" He was referring to the jowly character actor with a voice that sounded like a braying mule who starred as an affable sidekick to the hero in dozens of Westerns. Truthfully, the oil painting did bear a resemblance to Devine. Taken aback, Mayo curtly replied that the picture in question was her portrait of *her* husband, O'Shea. Ouch! ... for a brief instant, Mayo generated some white heat of her own that would have baked the *state* of Alaska!

About the possibility of penning her show business memories into an autobiography, Mayo says, "If you don't tell the truth about everything, it's not worth reading. I would have trouble telling the world about my romances except, of course, to a priest."

Mayo prefers to let her work in front of the camera speak for itself. By that measuring rod, there's little doubt that Virginia Mayo has "made it ma, top of the world!"

A Delicate Balance
Eva Marie Saint
May 1996

Success can be defined many ways in Hollywood. Comedian Jim Carrey's measuring rod, oft reported in the press,
was the $20 million payday he received for starring in *The
Cable Guy*. Others benchmark success by how many Academy Award nominations/wins they rack up over the course
of a career or the number of "A-pictures" in which they star.

For Eva Marie Saint, a Best Supporting Actress Oscar winner herself for her 1954 film debut *On the Waterfront*, fame,
fortune and choice parts were all well and good but they
never supplanted — even for an instant — her devotion to
family matters.

Indeed, for nearly a half century, Saint has achieved a
delicate balance between her life and her career. Against the
capricious backdrop of a "company town," where real life
relationships are often more ephemeral than the ones portrayed on celluloid, two statistics attest to the success of Saint's
balancing act — a marriage of 46 years to director Jeffrey
Hayden, and a son and daughter miraculously scot-free of
the crippling neuroses that often plague celebrity offspring.

"It really wasn't that hard balancing everything because I
made it my plan to never do more than one film a year," she
says. "When I made *Exodus*, it was in the summer and I took
my kids, husband, mother, father and mother-in-law. Along
the way there were many things I turned down — like a role
in *Quo Vadis*. My agent said, 'Eva Marie, you'll never be a
superstar.' I told him that I just wanted to be a working actress with a home life that worked."

After raising their two children in a house they owned for
22 years in the Mandeville Canyon section of West Los Angeles, "It's always in the news because the canyon is always

on fire," Saint says, she and her husband "simplified" to a luxurious high-rise apartment on Wilshire Boulevard near UCLA.

Saint, 74, greets us at the door with the same perky enthusiasm she must show neighborhood kids knocking for handouts each Halloween. After ushering us into the living area, she excuses herself and is back before we can blink with a couple of glasses of her favorite fruit juice, Tropicana pineapple-orange.

"I have a life and it is not lived on the set," she says. "I felt that way when I was raising my kids and I feel that way now. I don't want make-believe children. When Donna Reed, the perfect American mother to millions of TV viewers in the 1950s, ended her show, her kids were teenagers. She said to me, 'Now I'm going to get to know my kids.' I thought that was so very sad.

"My kids never had the feeling that we were both in show business," she continues. "I remember our son came home from a school field trip and said, rather excitedly, 'Mom, I saw Gregory Peck's chair with his name on it.' I said, 'Honey, I think you met Mr. Peck when you visited me on the set of *Stalking Moon*."

Saint gave birth to her boy, Darrell, just two days after she received the Oscar for *Waterfront*. You don't need a crystal ball to guess which event overshadowed the other. "Once you get an Oscar, it becomes an appendage that you carry around the rest of your life," Saint says. " … Announcing Eva Marie Saint … Oscar winner. But working with Marlon Brando and Elia Kazan was worth it."

According to Saint, *Waterfront* producer Sam Spiegel and director Kazan "scouted" her on Broadway where she was appearing with her lifelong mentor, Lillian Gish, in *The Trip to Bountiful*.

"They asked me to come over to the Actor's Studio to audition for the role of the 'blonde,'" Saint remembers. "I was to improvise a scene with Marlon Brando, who I was in awe of from my time as a student there.

"Just before I went on stage, Kazan set the scene for me. I was a very religious girl who went to Catholic school. Marlon was coming to see my sister who was out of the house, and it was my mission to keep him from worming his way into the house. Now I don't know what instructions 'Gadge' (short for 'Gadget,' Saint's — and others' — nickname for Kazan) gave Marlon, but during the scene he charmed his way in. He then swept me off my feet and asked me to dance. I was sort of crying just a wee bit, but then, as we danced, I became more attracted to him. Gadge could see there was chemistry between us. I guess that's what the improvisation was supposed to show, or not show, in the first place."

During shooting, Saint remembered Brando to be a princely, cordial man who would often lend her his overcoat to wear between scenes on the chilly set. "It was cold in Hoboken on the waterfront where we shot the film," she says. "I would wear red flannel underwear for warmth, and every so often would lift up my skirt — red bloomers aflutter — and do an impromptu can-can dance for the cast and crew just for a laugh. You know the simple act of laughing would warm us up."

After *Waterfront*, Saint, as an independent contractor not tethered to any studio, starred in a series of major motion pictures including *Exodus, Grand Prix, The Sandpiper* and, perhaps most memorably, as another enigmatic blonde in Alfred Hitchcock's *North By Northwest*.

"I was very impressed that Hitchcock had his bacon flown in from Denmark," Saint says. "During the auction scene I was decked out in a very expensive red dress, and during a lull I went and wandered off to get a cup of coffee which I proceeded to drink from a Styrofoam cup. Well, Hitchcock stopped me dead in my tracks. He said, 'Eva Marie, you don't get your coffee, we have someone get it for you. And you drink from a porcelain cup and saucer. You are wearing a $3,000 dress and I don't want the extras to see you quaffing from a Styrofoam cup.'"

Although Saint admits that assessing the relative merits of Hitchcock and Kazan (two of the cinema's great auteurs) is like comparing apples to oranges, she is unstinting in her praise and affection for her mentor, Lillian Gish, who starred in silent movies before Kazan was wearing long pants. Saint appeared with Gish in the original stage production of Horton Foote's *Trip to Bountiful*. Decades later, Geraldine Page won an Oscar reprising Gish's role in the film version of the play.

"Lillian had that odd mixture of strength and vulnerability which I feel I have at times," Saint says. "She was the first one at rehearsal and the last one to leave at night. And she was at all times, unfailingly honest.

"I remember years after our *Bountiful* experience, I was starring in a television adaptation of a George Kelly play, *The Fatal Weakness*. I wore bangs in the part because I thought it was right for the character. Anyway, at a party in Malibu that was being held for Lillian, I arrived and was told by the host that Lillian wanted to see me — alone. 'You should never wear bangs,' she scolded me. 'You have a nice forehead, why do you want to hide it!' The funny thing was that my husband never liked me in bangs, but it took Lillian's remonstration for me to cut them."

Despite the flurry of activity that continues to fill her days, Grandma Saint never misses the opportunity to squire her two grandchildren to the latest Disney animated feature. It's her latest role, and one she thoroughly enjoys — after all, "that is really a labor of love," she says.

Truer words were never spoken — on balance.

V.
Funny Side Up

PLAyiNq Jazz "ToNiqHT"
Steve Allen
August 1980 and 1993

Conjuring up the singular Steve Allen isn't easy. It may be impossible, a contradiction in terms. Characterizing his talent is like encountering the proverbial fork in the road — or more appropriately — a railroad roundhouse with dozens of tracks stretching out infinitely in every direction.

Creator and first host of *The Tonight Show* ... acknowledged master of ad-lib comedy ... author of 43 books ... playwright ... jazz pianist ... composer. They all describe the artist Noel Coward once called, "the most talented man in America." But it his gift for musical composition that Allen himself ranks above all others, with ad-lib comedy a distant second.

"Somebody once compared me to the great old Hollywood songwriter Harry Warren," said Allen. "Harry wrote a lot of good tunes but never made it into the front rank of his peers like Berlin, Gershwin and Porter."

The comparison is apt. Of the 5,200 songs (at last count) Allen has composed during the last half century, 1,000 have been published and a few have achieved bonafide hit status including, "This Could Be the Start of Something," "Picnic," "Impossible," "Gravy Waltz," and the Bing Crosby-Andrews Sisters hit, "South Rampart Street Parade."

However, Allen points out laughing, in order to have a hit, it helps to have the song published, and that means automatically ceding 50 percent of the profits over to the publisher.

Allen, 73, works out of a nondescript office building in Van Nuys, Calif. — his nerve center where we talked music with him recently. Amid a phalanx of file cabinets containing *Tonight Show* stills, radio and television scripts, kinescopes, etc., hangs a framed one-sheet poster of *The Benny Goodman Story*, the 1955 biopic that starred Allen in his feature film debut as the King of Swing.

This day Allen was a bit late getting started and caromed into his office with a large leather valise (jammed with books, scripts and files) slung over his shoulder. Dressed casually, Allen wore his trademark horn-rimmed glasses low on his nose and despite the flurry of his entrance — which created a momentary tizzy among his small staff — his other trademark (a toupee so flat you could practically land a fighter jet on it) remained unruffled.

"The great kick of doing the Goodman movie was getting to hang out with Lionel Hampton, Gene Krupa, Teddy Wilson, Harry James and all the guys," Allen remembered. "I didn't get to know Benny, nobody did, not even the men who played with him. His emphasis was on the music — other people didn't exist for him."

For the role, Allen was coached in correct fingering techniques by veteran clarinetist Saul Yaged. "Saul is still the world's number one Benny Goodman fan — perhaps to his own detriment," Allen said. "He knew all of Goodman's solos, his tone, everything. He was to Goodman what Oscar Levant was to George Gershwin. But at least Oscar composed his own melodies, whereas what Saul did for a living was be Benny."

According to Allen, the decision of who would play the lead in the movie came down to a choice between himself and Tony Curtis. "Leonard Feather once told me that Benny cast the deciding vote himself," Allen said. "Benny thought Tony looked too much like a 'pretty boy' and that I resembled him more. Secondly, Benny said that as a jazz musician, I would have the right attitude. Tony would have to fake it."

Allen's jazz pedigree was an outgrowth of the popular music he grew up listening to on the radio in Chicago in the early 1930s. "I was a big Eddie Duchin fan in those days. He was as influential as Sinatra and Presley to kids my age, 12 or

14," Allen said. "Duchin created a certain style to a medium-tempo ballad. Every American teenager who had access to a piano learned them very fast, including myself."

While attending Hyde Park High School on Chicago's South Side (Mel Tormé was a classmate), Allen discovered jazz.

"Chicago has always been a good music town. I had heard jazz before, but to me, it was just one of 19 different aspects of the popular music that I loved," Allen said. "Many classic jazz performances are built around popular tunes by Berlin, Gershwin, Johnny Mercer, etc. Take Coleman Hawkins' rendition of 'Body and Soul.' He didn't write the song, but thank God he recorded it."

For the record, Allen's show business debut wasn't cutting up in comedy clubs, but playing jazz piano as a teenager in trios and with a small band on the South Side. "My first gig paid 50 cents," he said. "It sounds comical now, but in those days, 50 cents could buy a meal in a restaurant. I remember I played for two hours in a saloon near the corner of 63rd Street and Cottage Grove, just down the street from my high school. Later I gigged a couple of times with Mel Tormé, who was a drummer then."

Allen always played by ear and to this day can't read music. "I wish I had taken the time to learn," he said, "but after a while it seemed like it would have delayed the progress I was making in the clubs." Any regrets are tempered by the knowledge that his idol, Erroll Garner, never learned to read music either.

"To this day, I think Erroll can swing a room or a record better than any other pianist. Great as some of the others are, there is just some little extra mystery ingredient that knocks me out," Allen said. "And then there is the other totally separate Garner brain that plays ballads in the lacy, romantic, emotional style that may or may not be jazz depending on how you define it."

Years later, Allen realized a dream by booking Garner as a

guest on *The Tonight Show*. "It was like being a kid in a candy store," he said gleefully. "I would say, offhandedly, let's get Lester Young and we would get him. One night I was on stage before we went on the air and suddenly I saw Lester walk in. Nobody paid attention to him; they were all doing 40 different things. But I recognized his porkpie hat and tenor case. I had never met him and didn't know how much TV he watched. I said, 'Mr. Young, welcome to our show.' At that point he realized he was talking to the host. He looked real close at me; we were standing practically nose-to-nose, and replied 'Many eyes.' It was a hip reference akin to 'I only have eyes for you' or 'I have eyes to quit this job.' Lester had his own special language and it influenced many jazz musicians."

Allen themed many of those early *Tonight Shows* around jazz. One memorable episode featured Hoagy Carmichael, who had offered kind words of encouragement to Allen as early as 1948. "He was one of the first people to record a number of mine," Allen said. "It was a tune called, 'An Old Piano Plays the Blues.'"

Allen's favorite show had Richard Rodgers in the spotlight performing his songs for 90 minutes. "We had Andy Williams, Steve Lawrence and Eydie Gorme and Pat Kirby all sitting unrehearsed around the piano with Dick," Allen said. "It came off like a sing-along in somebody's home, it was that intimate. In those days I think the only person we didn't get was Charlie Parker. But we got almost everyone else."

A quarter century after the airings of most of those shows, Allen is rediscovering gold in the record vaults of his office. "Just a few days ago I came across three different piano performances by Bill Evans. We'll make a 30-minute video out of that lovely find."

In the show's early days, Allen staffed the *Tonight* orchestra with the best jazz sidemen to be found in New York. In the tradition, subsequent hosts Jack Paar, Johnny Carson and

Jay Leno all recruited excellent jazz musicians including such leaders as Doc Severinsen and, until recently, Branford Marsalis.

By Allen's own estimate, he has written and recorded material for six jazz CDs. His latest, *Steve Allen Plays Jazz Tonight* (1993, Concord Jazz, Inc.), contains a baker's dozen of swinging tracks, including a few Allen compositions.

"I've always been puzzled when I read that some rock group called the Four Garbage Cans are now into the seventh month of production on their new album," Allen said. "I don't put it down, but I don't understand it. I did my *Tonight* CD in one night."

Indeed, inspiration for a song can hit Allen anywhere; driving down the freeway, at home noodling with chords on the piano, or even during a deep sleep. Allen respects his peripatetic muse by keeping a handful of tape recorders within reach at all times.

"My biggest hit, 'This Could be the Start of Something' hit me in a dream," Allen said. "I was writing the score of *The Bachelor* — the first television musical. Just before I awakened in the morning I thought of the melody and the first seven or eight lines of the lyric. Thank God it was a morning dream, because you never remember your early night dreams."

Allen likes "96 percent" of the jazz he hears today, much of it on radio station KLON in Los Angeles. "Just take the piano players he said," "The good players of today stand up very well to the legends of 30 or 40 years ago. The young players tend to have more chops. In the old days there was only Art Tatum who had that facility. One CD I particularly like is *Kenny Barron Live at Maybeck Recital Hall* (Volume 10, Concord Jazz, Inc.).'"

After musing long and hard about his abundant contribution to so many different areas of show business, Allen shrugged. "I haven't directly decided anything much in my life."

Perhaps expecting a pat answer from a man who spent a career refusing to be pigeonholed is just too easy. Whatever the object of Allen's labors in the coming years, it's certain he'll bring the same enthusiasm that held sway the day he started out tickling the ivories 60 years ago.

... On Comedy

The quick wit and nonstop flow of quips and puns were not evident during our interview with Allen. Instead, a sense of smugness pervaded his office when we got around to discussing the how, what and why of being funny. That's not to say that Allen was uncooperative or unfriendly. We learned quickly that talking about comedy is serious business.

"I get laughs in quite a few different ways," Allen said. "Most comedians don't, I suppose. I do some very broad, burlesque, vaudeville, slapstick sort of things in my nightclub act. I do a character called 'Senator Phillip Buster' who wears a silly wig, mustache, baggy pants, and tells big, broad jokes. On the other hand, some of my material is more sophisticated or controlled. My brain works in some of the same ways as Groucho's did in that whatever someone says, I turn it around and make some dumb joke out of it."

We reminded Allen of the time Groucho had a contestant on his show from Pottstown, Pennsylvania. "I remember Pottstown very well," said Groucho. "I played there years ago. I was heavily panned in Pottstown."

Allen laughed in his familiar staccato fashion (kind of like a Buick backfiring short bursts out the exhaust pipe) and said, "Yes, that's an acceptable example of the type of play on words I would do."

In an unusual analogy, Allen compared sports to variation in comedic style. "There really can be no such thing as a decathlon champion of comedy," he explained. "You can make up such a category in your own head and elect your own man. It's like taking the best guy in high jumping and the fastest guy in the 100-meter dash and saying which is the best athlete. You can't. You're talking about two different ballgames. The same specialization is found in the field of comedy. The reasons we laughed at Groucho have nothing whatsoever to do with why we laugh at Steve Martin. They're just funny in two different ways."

We were surprised when Allen admitted he enjoys the work of almost all other comedians. "The real mystery is why five percent of them don't amuse me," he said. "I really don't understand that because some of the ones that don't amuse me are quite successful. I probably am entertained by more comedians than any other comedian. That may strike you as odd. The fact that I'm at the head of the list doesn't mean a damn. The more important fact is that most comedians aren't amused by their peers. I never quite understood why. I don't know whether it's an unconscious jealousy, misunderstanding of different styles, or whatever it might be."

The only brand of comedy Allen doesn't enjoy is dirty humor. "I laugh not only at comedians, but people, dogs, wallpaper, whatever."

On July 27, 1953, Allen originated and hosted what has become a television institution — *The Tonight Show.*

The original *Tonight Show* was a talk show only on certain nights, Allen said. The show would occasionally present a live 30-minute drama, a political debate or it would book the Basie Band to jam for 40 minutes. Allen said the material was 97 percent spontaneous and only 3 percent written.

"It takes no talent to host a talk show. I don't mean that as a cute statement," he said. "Yet on the other hand, of the few hundred talented people in the business, very few can run a talk show. Marlon Brando would fall off the desk in three seconds, as would most movie stars. And yet there are some people with no talent whatsoever who are very successful at talk shows. I run into journalists who are better than any of these guys and they're not on the air. It has something to do with one's projection over the air."

Intelligence is also not a prerequisite for being a talk show host, according to Allen. "It certainly makes it easier for those of us who are intelligent. I won't give you any names of those in the other category," he said with a laugh.

Kicking Back with Lucy
Lucille Ball
September 1980

Her career has spanned 25 years in an industry with a talent turnover as rapid as some South American dictatorships. Her last name has bounced from Ricardo to Carmichael to Carter with regularity. But she has never really needed a last name, because to the world she is simply known as Lucy.

The acclaim she earned when her first series, *I Love Lucy*, premiered in October 1951 was long overdue. Lucille Ball — first as a platinum blonde and later as the redhead we all came to know — arrived in Hollywood in 1934 as a "poster girl" in the Samuel Goldwyn film, *Roman Scandals*, which starred Eddie Cantor.

So began a 17-year apprenticeship in movies, where she could be seen in the background of a few Astaire-Rogers musicals, on the receiving end of cream pies thrown by the Three Stooges and as the object of the collective desire of the Marx Brothers. Occasionally Lucy would land some meatier assignments such as the role of the crippled singer in Damon Runyon's *Big Street*, the title role in *DuBarry Was a Lady* and good parts in a few Bob Hope pictures.

We interviewed Lucy in her home on Roxbury Drive in Beverly Hills, where she lives with her husband, comedian Gary Morton.

It was slightly uncomfortable walking up to her front door while people in cars and buses sneered at our impetuosity, exclaiming in loud tones, "Those two have nerve — knocking at her door." Luckily Lucy's public relations man, Howard

McClay, was expecting us and we disappeared inside without a backward glance.

Lucy was waiting for us in the living room. Looking fit and trim, she wore a brown pants suit, tinted brown glasses and a green kerchief. Her 25-year trademark, red hair, practically pulsated with an orangish tint.

We seated ourselves on the couch next to her white toy poodle that looked to be as well coiffed as any Angeleno just released from a Jon Peters Salon rinse and set. Lucy spoke candidly about her life and career, with some scorching insights on the present state of television that would give any self-respecting network executive pause to pull the trigger.

Only once did she get into a momentary snit and that's when we asked her why, according to facts printed in a volume of *Current Biography*, she ran away from her upstate New York home at an early age ready to embark on a stage career on Broadway.

We surmised the question would be a cute lead-in to recollections about her childhood and budding show business ambitions. Instead, Lucy fixed us with a cold stare (at least that's what we figured; we couldn't see her exact expression behind the tint of her sunglasses). You'd have thought we just strangled her dog.

Lucy slowly rose from the couch ready to kick our abashed asses out her faux French chateau front door and to the curb, when we redirected … quickly.

Reel to Real: Why did the article in *Current Biography* say: "much of the information about Lucy's early life is vague and contradictory?

Lucy: You'll find out if you read some of the scurrilous unauthorized biographies that have been written about me. They take the first two pages and make you out a bum that ran away from home and had an unhappy childhood. You are 80 years old or there must have been some reason why you left. I went to dramatic school when I was 15 and there was nothing vague or contradictory about that, except in the three unauthorized book versions of my career. There is one good book by Bart Andrews. (*Lucy and Ricky and Fred and Ethel*, Popular Library, 1977.)

Reel to Real: Have you ever had any formal musical training?

Lucy: I never studied, musically, and God knows it looks like it. I attempted to take up what is called eccentric dancing but teachers told me I was ill equipped for that. They wrote my mother a letter saying that she was wasting her money, which she was, because I couldn't do anything. I've gotten away with my dancing in many musical films only because I could rehearse for weeks. The little stuff I did on my television show was satirically done. I don't mean that each step was out and out satire, but it was easy enough for me to master. Same with my singing. I never could sing, although I've done a lot of singing. My mother also wasted her perfectly good money on piano lessons, which I can't play.

Reel to Real: Were there any tell-tale signs of inherent comedic ability when you were young?

Lucy: I certainly didn't notice any. All I knew was that I wanted to perform, and I took every chance that I got at school … church … Kiwanis and Elks clubs. Wherever I was needed — sweeping up, selling tickets — I would pitch in.

Reel to Real: Have you always been as physical and vivacious as you appear on the screen?

Lucy: I've always loved physical comedy. I don't do one pratfall after another, inasmuch as people have made such a thing out of that. Our show was void of a lot of things that television is doing in triplicate these days. I counted once, and in all my 25 years on television, there have not been more than five or six shows where I threw pies or did deliberate pratfalls. I've used trampolines, stilts, animals and even jumped out of planes, but these flowed naturally out of the plot predicaments. People don't really hear me when I say this. I'm glad you have your tape recorder on.

Reel to Real: What did you do to survive during those early struggling years in New York City?

Lucy: I literally starved. I was young, very backward and awkward. Vaudeville was the only thing I knew so I tried to break in. Unfortunately for me, vaudeville was already dead and gone. The lack of food and work forced me into modeling. I finally became a showgirl and my first job in Hollywood was as a showgirl. I came out here to Los Angeles only expecting to stay for six weeks. I've never left.

Reel to Real: You worked with the Marx Brothers in the film *Room Service*. Were they as crazy offstage as they were onstage?

Lucy: Yes, all except one, who was an extraordinary, sensitive, intelligent and adorable man. That was Harpo.

Reel to Real: Would you prefer the old studio contract system to the way actors make their way in show business today?

Lucy: In retrospect I'm sure everyone would. I certainly would. I never objected to any of the hype. I have always been very much in favor of the big umbrella, the poppa, the help and the build that a star would get from the public relations department. In addition, they took beautiful publicity photographs. Nowadays the kids are begging for the old departmental specialization. They have to do everything themselves, including writing, producing, directing, raising funds and selling their project.

Reel to Real: Do you watch your television shows, and what do you look at when you view them?

Lucy: I usually watch Vivian (Vivian Vance, who played Ethel on *I Love Lucy*, died in 1979). God bless her! I used to enjoy working with Vivian. We would almost play act and pull a little extra out of each scene. I would rather look at a compilation like the *25 Years of Lucy* special than just watch one particular show. There are, of course, a few exceptions such as the special I made with Dean Martin.

Reel to Real: What was the production schedule like for *I Love Lucy?*

Lucy: The first couple of years it was 'round the clock, seven days a week because we were innovating so many new things. We trained hundreds and hundreds of people. We invented three-headed monsters for shooting close-ups, medium-shots and long-shots at the same time. We also shot in sequence like a play. We didn't make our audience sit and wait for hours. They came in to watch and we got them out as quickly as possible.

Reel to Real: How did you manage to get stars of the magnitude of William Holden and John Wayne to appear on your show?

Lucy: There was a time when people weren't doing television. Desi had the idea of trying to get these stars for guest appearances once television became accepted a little more. When we got Duke Wayne and Bill Holden, we didn't have trouble getting any more stars.

Reel to Real: How important were audience ratings in the early days of television?

Lucy: They certainly were not as stupidly important as they are today. But there is no way of accurately gauging the effect because there was less competition back then. *I Love Lucy* never had any problems with the ratings.

Reel to Real: How much, besides your acting, did you contribute to the show?

Lucy: I just acted. I had great writers. Vivian, Bill, Desi and myself would naturalize the dialogue a bit, especially where Desi was concerned. Soon writers would write the scripts just the way we talked naturally. Throughout all the years, we did very little ad-libbing. That was not our forte.

Reel to Real: Your shows are seen all over the world in rerun syndication. Why do you think the show remains so fresh and popular?

Lucy: I think it covers many generations of understanding. The little kids understand it, the next generation understands it, mom and pop understand it and remember it, as do grandma and grandpa. For sheer escapism, I don't think there has been a better executed show. People can watch our show and get away from all of the sex, violence, blood and guts and all of that. Even before our show was dubbed in other countries, people could identify with our domestic predicaments.

Reel to Real: Do you watch much television?

Lucy: I never watch soap operas but I do enjoy game shows. I never had a chance to watch game shows when I was doing a weekly series. The other shows I get to look at are the news, *60 Minutes, 20/20 ...* 15/15, 8 1/2 — whatever they call them. I'm not saying I don't enjoy shows like *The Incredible Hulk* or *Real People*. It's just that I get more out of a show like *60 Minutes*.

Reel to Real: How would you evaluate the present state of television?

Lucy: Chaotic, downhill, leaving us.

Reel to Real: Do you have any favorite current performers, comedic or otherwise?

Lucy: Alan Alda in *M*A*S*H* and some other people in that show and *Taxi* are two of the finest programs on the air. I really don't watch many other shows.

Reel to Real: Can you understand why *Laverne and Shirley* is often compared to your show?

Lucy: Well, it is about two girls involved in different situations. Many others have done it besides us. But those slapstick premises were all copied from the *I Love Lucy* writers. There are only so many jokes that people can do, only so many situations that a comic can get in or out of. I like *Laverne and Shirley*, but I don't laugh at it.

Reel to Real: Who can make you laugh?

Lucy: In person I laugh at Dean Martin, my husband Gary Morton. Ann Sothern and I used to laugh at Betty Grable. Very few people can give me a real belly laugh.

Reel to Real: In the early '70s you came back to the big screen in a musical version of *Mame*.

Lucy: The film broke all box office records in New York City. If they hadn't stopped the public relations work, the film would have been a bigger hit. Warner Bros. Studios were going through some terrible happenings with that horrible picture *The Exorcist*. They had seven deaths on that film! All the people at that studio were out on extremes working on that movie. They were like a bunch of paramedics running around the world trying to catch up with the violence that was plaguing their crew. The whole studio was spooked with *The Exorcist*. That in itself is a story that should be written. Not everyone knows this.

Reel to Real: You recently made news when you were hired by NBC President Fred Silverman to act as creative consultant for that network.

Lucy: There is a certain expertise in knowing how to do my type of half-hour comedy show. The network still feels the need of having more situation comedies. People are still packaging such shows, but the network is not doing a very good job of selecting any after they have been put together. That's why I took the job.

Life's Never a "Drag"
Milton Berle
March 1995

Milton Berle saunters into the Beverly Hills Friars Club with his longtime gagman Buddy Arnold in tow, and the staff and fellow Friars greet him with a reverence usually reserved for royalty. Berle relishes the kudos and his exalted position and returns the salutations with what everyone expects from a comic legend — a quick one-liner, a gentle insult or an off-color joke (in this case, all three simultaneously).

Once upstairs in the main dining room (aptly named the Milton Berle Room), Berle complains about the temperature. "It's so damn cold in this room," he bellows. "What are they doing, hanging meat in here?" Score one for the old-timer. A few minutes into the interview, Berle has warmed up sufficiently to shed his fedora and trench coat which he wears rain or shine (giving him a 1950's-era businessman look that seems more at home in New York's garment district than in the palm-treed purlieus of Beverly Hills).

These days Berle, 86, holds court in his private corner booth. With trusty cigar in hand that he waves for emphasis like a conductor's baton, he regales us with anecdotes from his rich traveling trunk of show business memories. Berle, who holds the title *abbot emeritus* at the Friars has been a fixture there since the age of 12 when entertainer Eddie Cantor brought his young and impertinent new find into the New York branch to show off to show business cronies Fred Allen, DeWolfe Hopper and Enrico Caruso.

"I'll never forget that day," recalls Berle. "I put on a long pants suit and dark glasses. Cantor introduced me as a young entertainer who was going to be famous some day. Fred Allen smirked, 'That'll be the day!' So there I was, this kid clowning and trading lines with the big guys."

Cantor's prophecy for young Milton quickly came true. Berle, was one of five children born to Moses and Sarah Berlinger in New York City. "Stage Mother" Sarah elected young Milton to become a star and bring financial security to the family. With his trademark Bugs Bunny jowls, Berle played "the kid" in dozens of silent films starring the biggest names of the day — Charlie Chaplin, Douglas Fairbanks, Mary Pickford, Marie Dressler and Mabel Normand.

But when growing pains cut short his cute kid status in films, Berle began a slow but steady climb to vaudeville stardom, eventually headlining at New York's famed Palace Theater. Berle's career was nurtured every step of the way by his mother.

"My mother was with me all the time," he says. "She was my chief helper and my main stooge in the audience. She was with me at every show I did in vaudeville, even the lean days when I was playing five shows a day for a paltry sum. She was also my severest critic. But her instinct was right on the nose most of the time."

The 1930s and '40s brought Berle continued success in vaudeville, radio and the legitimate stage. While other comics such as Bob Hope and Jack Benny ruled the radio waves, Berle admitted he had only limited success on radio.

"I never made it big on radio because I was too visual," he said. "You had to see me. It was because of this realization that I took the early plunge into television although a lot of people thought I was crazy."

In June 1948, Berle entered the newfangled world of television and Tuesday nights would never be the same again. He became, literally, an overnight sensation and his *Texaco Star Theater* soon was responsible for selling more televisions than the collective sales effort of Philco, Admiral and Zenith.

TV proved the perfect medium for Berle's no-holds-barred style of physical comedy and sight gags. He admitted that the Texaco show was, in effect, a televised vaudeville show. Early in the run of the program, Berle was dubbed "Mr. Television." Another nickname, "Uncle Miltie," came about by accident.

"I received a lot of complaints from parents who wrote and told me their kids wouldn't go to sleep until our show was over," Berle says. "So I went on the air and told all the children watching to 'listen to their Uncle Miltie' and go to bed right after the show. Shortly after that spot I was in a parade in Boston and a couple of workmen in hardhats yelled 'Hi, Uncle Miltie.' I had no idea when I first used it that the name would stick."

During his seven-year run on primetime (including two years under the sponsorship of Buick), Berle would go to any lengths for a laugh. A pie in the face, a pratfall — even dressing in drag — was all part of his repertoire. Ironically, milking laughs was the farthest thing on his mind when he first donned women's clothing in the 1930s.

"It had nothing to do with show business. It had everything to do with making it with a girl I met," he says. "I was in my 20s and met this gorgeous girl from Texas who came to New York to become a model. I took her out for a couple of weeks all the while trying to figure out where I can make love to her. You see, she was staying at an all-girl's hotel and I was still living with my mother!" Finally, Berle devised a way to circumvent both his mother and the hotel desk clerk.

"I went to the Brooks Costume Company and picked out a dress, complete with padding for a bust," he says. "I wore these high heels that just about killed me. I put on a wig and makeup. I made it past the desk clerk and into the elevator where this one girl gave me a look like she just met the elephant man. It was well worth it until the next morning when I tried to leave. My feet were swollen from the shoes. So here I am in drag, barefoot and walking back to where I lived, about 10 blocks away."

About 10 years later Berle again dressed in drag, this time for a larger audience.

"Our show aired on Valentine's Day so we thought it would be funny if I'd come on stage in drag, rip off my clothes to reveal my suit underneath and go into my monologue. That's how it started. Later we did a June bride in drag, Cleopatra and a lot of different things."

Berle has been married three times, first to Joyce Matthews in 1941. They divorced and later remarried in 1949. The couple adopted a daughter, Vicki, but the union broke up for good a year later. In 1953, he married Ruth Cosgrove and they adopted a son, William. The marriage lasted until Ruth's death in 1989. Berle remained a widower only a year before he married Lorna Adams, who owns a clothing design business in Los Angeles and is about 30 years his junior.

Berle refuses to live in the past and continues to pick and choose projects that go against the Uncle Miltie persona. As proof of how far he'll stretch as a non-comic actor, he recently played an Alzheimer's victim on an episode of *Beverly Hills 90210.*

He has also forged a niche as a fitness spokesman for older Americans. Berle's new video called, *The Milton Berle Low Impact/High Comedy Workout for Seniors* includes an ample dose of the old shtick. Don't expect to see Berle himself doing deep knee bends. He leaves that to the other oldsters, ranging in age from 70 to 101.

"I believe that laughter is a very important thing," he says. "It takes away all stress. I'm integrated into the video, discussing the importance of laughter and dressing up as Jane Fonda and Richard Simmons." Old habits die hard!

Milton Berle's life story has recently been optioned by director Gilbert Cates for a possible TV mini-series. Who would Uncle Miltie like to see portray him on the small screen he single-handedly popularized?

"I favor Jeff Goldblum (*The Big Chill, The Fly*) because I hear he sings, dances and can do comedy," Berle says.

Although the lanky Goldblum stands well over six feet, filling Mr. Television's shoes is one tall order.

"Say Goodnight, Gracie!"
George Burns
1978 and 1994

Our meeting with George Burns was roundabout, to say the least. We were waiting one night outside the Dorothy Chandler Pavilion in downtown Los Angeles after seeing a show. We'd just put in a call to the Beverly Hills Cab Company for a lift back to our hotel. After a few minutes of utterly mundane, pointless debate over which Los Angeles cab company offered the most courteous service, a paint-chipped cab pulled up. Our cabby introduced himself — immodestly perhaps — as Seymour Barish, "God's gift to West Coast public transportation."

He was a bewhiskered old coot dressed in hightop tennis shoes, a grimy knit stocking cap and blue jeans that were so streaked with motor oil that they looked as if they had seen service as his dipstick wipe rag. We asked to be driven to our hotel in West Hollywood. Barish immediately flipped the meter, raced the engine and we were off.

Barish's cab had to be one of the dirtiest in Southern California. Besides the absence of one door handle, there was a gaping hole the size of a basketball in the passenger floor of his taxi — through which we could view the passing of each white stripe of highway divider as Barish drove (he didn't exactly adhere to the straight and narrow). We worriedly asked Barish if the opening was to be used as a passenger foot brake. "No," he replied, "it's the emergency exit in case of fire, but no one gets out of here without paying first." We could understand the need for an emergency exit; the back seat was littered with trash of every description, including empty Coke bottles, skanky cigarette butts and a generous padding of back issues of the *Los Angeles Times*.

One of the articles, we noticed, contained an article about Barish. It said that he had recovered more than $1 million in stolen government bonds. Barish explained to us that when driving home from work one day, he stopped his cab because he saw an abandoned wooden box that he thought he would convert into a "dandy breakfast table for use in the kitchen." But after discovering the amount of money inside, he took it down to the police station where he was summarily arrested.

"It seemed the police thought I had stolen the money," Barish said. "But what really burned me us was that after the whole mess blew over, I wasn't even offered a reward."

Barish also mentioned that he knew our hotel intimately, having lived there briefly two years before. He said he had driven the "clientele" of some young ladies to it. This was startling news to us, especially since we were paying $29.50 a night for our rooms and thought we deserved better than a brothel. When we expressed our outrage to Barish, he suggested we double up with one of the ladies.

We wondered if Barish had driven any movie stars around town. (This was a question we methodically asked of all our Los Angeles cabbies). He pulled out an autograph book — we had thought it was his dispatch book — that contained such names as Humphrey Bogart, Lauren Bacall, Groucho Marx and George Burns. After 35 years of driving the Beverly Hills beat, he said it might be more appropriate to ask which film stars he hadn't driven.

We were particularly interested in Burns' signature. Barish said the he and Burns were the best of friends, and that if we wanted to meet him, he could drive us to George's house right away. We thought Barish was putting us on — we weren't born yesterday, after all — and dared him to prove he wasn't joking.

As we cruised down Maple Drive in Beverly Hills, we began to squirm, and when we turned up Burns' driveway we realized that Barish had told the truth. We had an acute case of stage fright and decided we couldn't just knock on Burns' front door unaccompanied and unwelcome — Barish would have to come with us.

The three of us then trouped up the sidewalk and rang the bell. Barish, with the unnerving spring of a bullfrog leaping off a dock, disappeared into a flower bush just off the landing. A drowsy houseboy answered and tersely informed us that Mr. Burns usually slept in the evening. We shot a glance at our watches: it was only 9 p.m. Taking pity on a couple of flummoxed rubes, the houseboy gave us the number to Burns' office.

Embarrassed, and with a haste prompted by the long leash of Burns's pissed-off Doberman, we returned to the car. Barish, acting as if everything was status quo and we hadn't noticed his reenactment of the *The Celebrated Jumping Frog of Calaveras County*, asked if we wanted to go anywhere else.

"To the hotel," we huffed.

"The bordello it is," Barish said.

Upon arriving, we noticed the meter had been run up to around $60. We paid Barish and watched as he gleefully drove off in the direction of Sunset Boulevard, rhythmically tooting his horn. We both figured it was probably a feint and that in due course he'd soon double back to pay the houseboy.

Next day ...

After putting in a call to Burns' office located not far from our hotel in a place called Hollywood General Studios, we met with some initial resistance from Burns' longtime assistant and all-around man Friday, Jack Langdon.

"You want to interview George? Well, he's pretty busy these days, and besides, he happens to be out of town right now."

"That's not what his houseboy told us last night. We could practically hear Mr. Burns snoring upstairs." (a little impertinent perhaps, but what the hell).

"Damn, you caught me," Langdon laughed. "If you can get your butts over here pronto, I'll work you in, but you've gotta move fast!"

We made tracks.

The unmistakable smell of cigar smoke hit us like a third stage smog alert. The odor and its attendant thin blue veil greet all visitors to George Burns' Hollywood office.

The office itself was spartan, with surprisingly few mementos from Burns' 80-plus-year show business career. What was conspicuous was the framed photo on the wall of Burns' late wife and performing partner Gracie Allen.

Burns was seated in a director's chair, inscribed with his name, clutching his second favorite partner, a cigar. In between puffs, he sipped tea from a mug, appropriately inscribed with the word "God," a tongue-in-cheek reference to his starring roles in the two *Oh, God!* films.

The deity notwithstanding, at a first glance, Burns, stoop-shouldered with squinty eyes and a sparse gray toupee barely covering a bulbous cranium that tapers narrowly into a V-shaped chin, looked startlingly like Dr. Zaius — the chimpanzee scientist — from the *Planet of the Apes* movies. We *didn't* mention the likeness.

"Here boys, have a cigar," he offered.

It was an 85¢ El Producto Queens ... no expensive Cubans for Burns.

At age 98, the travails of aging may have slowed his gait to an intermittent shuffle, but they have not impaired his mind. The almost centenarian still smokes at least a half dozen stogies a day, "more when I'm working," he said between drags.

Burns ritual almost ended recently when the Hillcrest Country Club banned cigar smoking. To accommodate its most venerated member and quash his potential defection, club management amended the rule to read "cigar smoking prohibited for anyone under 95."

Burns looked alarmingly thin, an observation we shared with him. "I'm not a big eater," he responded. "That's maybe why I'm still here. Look at what happened to John Candy (the obese comedian who died earlier this year from a heart attack). Did you read what he used to eat? He never stopped eating."

And Burns has never stopped performing. The old vaudevillian still travels the circuit with 1994 bookings in Cincinnati, Richmond, Atlanta, San Antonio, Dallas, Houston, San Diego, Tucson, Phoenix, Boston, Orlando, Providence, Tampa, Las Vegas and Atlantic City.

In fact, Burns will celebrate his 100th birthday (Jan. 20, 1996) on the Caesar's stage in Las Vegas (it's already sold-out), followed by a performance soon after at London's Palladium. He can still put over spirited renditions of "Old Bones" and other songs as steeped in antiquity as he is. All in all, it seems to be a prescription for longevity that has worked exceedingly well for the diminutive man born Nathan Birnbaum on New York City's Lower East Side.

Burns has not let the passage of time or the passing of

show business cronies alter his routine. He still plays bridge regularly at the posh Hillcrest Country Club, drinks a double martini before dinner, and escorts comely Hollywood starlets to celebrity functions.

He spoke about his well-publicized propensity for dating younger woman."Oh sure, I date seven or eight girls a day," he said. "I used to date 25 a day, but I'm a little older now." Burns recently escorted *Basic Instinct's* Sharon Stone to a Hollywood gala.

His assessment of the screen siren: "She's too tall for me."

Ask him about the recent Los Angeles earthquakes and Burns shrugs his shoulders in nonchalant indifference.

"I was playing bridge when the quake hit," he said. "I'm used to quakes. I don't feel good unless we have two or three a day. It's my form of aerobics."

Burns' career spans more than seven decades, from vaudeville and radio to motion pictures and television. The anchor for more than 40 of those years was Gracie Allen. She retired from the act in 1958 due to ill health and died in 1964.

Burns has always been the first to credit Allen for the success of the team, but he said playing the role of the straight man was not as easy as it appeared.

"You think it's easy being a straight man," he asked? "I just walked on stage and asked Gracie, 'How's your brother?' She'd go off on a long comic routine and then I would say, 'Is that so?' I had seven or eight of those. To be a straight man you have to have good ears. When the audience laughs you don't talk. The minute they stop laughing you say, 'Is that so?'"

Following up on the vaudeville tack, we flurried a few questions at Burns about the halcyon days when he and Gracie played the St. Paul Orpheum Theater (situated in our hometown) in the 1920s. George was in fine form firing back one-liners with the confident aplomb of a comic master. We, on the other hand, came across like the most wooden straight men who ever tossed a set-up line. (Vaudeville may have been termed "the two-a-day," but we were definitely "two-by-four!")

Reel to Real: When were you first hired by the Orpheum Circuit?

Burns: In 1925, I was 83 then.

Reel to Real: Did you play the St. Paul Orpheum before you teamed with Gracie?

Burns: No. Before I met Gracie, they wouldn't let me into St. Paul.

Reel to Real: What did your act consist of when you teamed with Gracie?

Burns: We did an act called "Burns & Allen in 'Lamb Chops.'" I said, "Gracie, would you like a kiss?" She said, "No." I said, "What would you like?" She said, "Lamb Chops." And that joke made us both stars.

Reel to Real: What are your specific recollections of the St. Paul Orpheum?

Burns: Large, beautiful — and with indoor toilets.

Reel to Real: What were your impressions of playing St. Paul?

Burns: Gracie and I always did love playing St. Paul because there was *a* great restaurant there ... I forgot the name of the hotel I stayed at in St. Paul because I lost the towels I stole.

Reel to Real: What did you and Gracie do between shows in St. Paul — to kill time?

Burns: We went to Minneapolis.

Reel to Real: How was the audience in St. Paul?

Burns: That's why we went to Minneapolis.

Reel to Real: What were some of the most unusual acts that you shared the bill with in St. Paul?

Burns: Power's Elephants, Fink's Mules, Madame Burkhardt and her Cockatoos and Dainty Marie.

Reel to Real: What was your salary on the Orpheum Circuit?

Burns: The team got $400 per week. That was good

money in those days.

Reel to Real: Were there any other unusual incidents or events that happened while playing St. Paul?

Burns: I would say that during our careers Burns & Allen played the Orpheum Theater in St. Paul about 15 times, and we were never cancelled. That was *very* unusual.

In the last two decades Burns has carved out his own niche as a "single" act. Going it alone has produced a Kennedy Center Award, a Best Supporting Actor Oscar for *The Sunshine Boys,* and a doctorate of humanities degree from Brandeis University. Not bad for someone who never finished the fourth grade and was a self-admitted show business flop long before he met Allen.

Sandwiched between his other star turns, Burns became a recording star in the late '70s with the hit "I Wish I Were 18 Again." He also recorded a duet with Willie Nelson. Why the foray into country music?

"They asked me and they paid me," Burns said. "If Nelson wants me to sing with him again and he pays me, I'll do it. For free, he'd have to sing one of my songs like the 'Red Rose Rag.' "

The air in Burns' office may be stale, but his outlook on life is amazingly fresh. In a rare serious moment, Burns explained his formula for staying young and offered a topical message for today's youth who are easily sidetracked by societal temptations such as drugs.

"Get out of bed, keep working and love what you're doing. The most important thing is to fall in love with what you're doing. If kids focused on one thing that they would eventually like to do and just did it, they wouldn't have to be turned on by drugs. Your future will turn you on. I get turned-on by show business. I smoke cigars and drink martinis, but I don't use any stuff. I don't need it."

George Burns has made performance art out of growing old. Retirement has never been a word in his vocabulary.

"Listen boys," he said. "You can't help getting older. But you don't have to get old."

On the Road
Bob Hope
August 1980

In 1980, when we had our first interview with Bob Hope, he was long established as a show business stalwart. Yet, at the mere mention of his legendary status, Hope blanched and squirmed uncomfortably on the couch on which he was sitting.

"Oh Christ!" he told us, "A legend is someone who had a great past, and I just don't like to think about that. I look forward to what I'll be doing tomorrow. I'm an entertainer. I have to worry about my next show. If you start believing this legend stuff, you're in trouble."

There's no doubt that his name conjures up different emotions among the several generations he touched. For the veterans of every American conflict from World War II to the Gulf War, Hope and his band of show business gypsies brought humor and a bit of home to war-weary troops stationed in all corners of the world. To the anti-Vietnam War protesters of the 1960s, Hope represented a right wing hawk who never met a conflict he didn't like; and to the people who grew up in the '80s and '90s, he was an elderly cue-card-reading comic who sleep-walked through some rather unfunny sketches with the likes of Brooke Shields and Connie Stevens.

Throughout his career, Hope publicly paid credit and expressed deep appreciation to his army of writers who — at a moment's notice — provided him with topical gags tailored to meet any occasion. A comedian performing without good material is like being exposed to an audience naked. And throughout his career, Hope was fully clothed. To Hope's enduring credit, he brought something else to the equation that rivals the importance of the material itself — masterful timing. Like two of his contemporaries, George Burns and Jack Benny, Hope had impeccable sense about when to deliver the kicker. His gags often had the speed of a Gatling Gun ("Rapid Robert" was a nickname of his) and the insouciance of a Saturday night drunk.

Because of his continually booked calendar, Hope doesn't figure on anyone's list of most accessible movie stars. Yet during a recent week of performances at the Carlton Celebrity Room in Bloomington, Minnesota, he sat down with us in his hotel suite for a few minutes of supervised chat.

Hope's dinner show at the Carlton presented a patriotic medley of songs, jokes, a couple of tunes sung by his wife Delores, and a cameo appearance by his poodle, Tobey, who scampered onstage and ate off the dinner plates nearest the stage.

With Hope were his wife Delores, a muscle-bound bodyguard (a former "Mr. Minnesota" we later learned), and their ravenous pooch.

Reel to Real: You have such a constant lack of privacy. How do you deal with it?

Hope: Delores and I have so much privacy in our schedule, my goodness. We go down to Palm Springs and stay there 10 days. Nobody bothers us. We live high up on a hill, and we get to the golf course and meet just the people we want to meet. It's only when I travel that I get so many requests to meet people.

Reel to Real: How did you first get involved with the United Service Organization (USO)?

Hope: I started working for it at its inception in 1941. I went to an Air Force base not knowing what I was doing. The audiences were so great that I decided to do more and kept doing it and doing it. When war was declared, it became very dramatic. We went and did our radio shows for five years at military bases. We did only two shows in those five years back in Hollywood. Then we quit for two years and did the Berlin Airlift. We did USO shows for 31 years, and it's the most gratifying experience I've ever had. I get letters every day from people I entertained at those shows. Tonight somebody brought back a USO picture of all of us in Africa for me to autograph.

Reel to Real: How did you land your first motion picture contract?

Hope: I was in the *Ziegfeld Follies* singing "I Can't Get Started With You," which I introduced. I was singing it to a redheaded showgal who later turned out to be Eve Arden. A producer and director saw me, and they said, 'We want you for *The Big Broadcast of 1938.*'"

Reel to Real: How long did it take before you realized that "Thanks for the Memory" was going to be your signature song?

Hope: I got a pretty good idea of it when the song was voted an Oscar and BMI named it the song of the year. I adopted it immediately for my radio show — *The Pepsodent Show* — way before you were born. It turned into something, I'll tell you.

Reel to Real: What are your remembrances of working with W.C. Fields in *The Big Broadcast of 1938?*

Hope: W.C. Fields was something else. He was tremendous and a great ad-libber. They used to let the camera run on him hoping he'd say something brilliant. After a scene, they wouldn't yell cut, they'd just keep rolling. I remember a shipwreck scene when he ad-libbed, "Ah, they're jumpin' overboard. There go the women, the women are jumpin' before the kids, the men are jumpin' before women ..." He kept talking. Finally he looked into the camera and said, "They'll run out of film pretty soon."

Reel to Real: How did you first get teamed with Bing Crosby?

Hope: We worked together for two weeks in 1932 at the

Capitol Theater in New York. I was master of ceremonies
and Bing was singing. We got to fooling around and doing
bits together. When I was contracted to Paramount Studios
in 1937, Bing owned a piece of the Del Mar racetrack, and
he invited me down for the Saturday night gala. We did the
bit that we had done five years earlier at the Capital. There
was a producer there, in fact, the same producer who hired
me for *The Big Broadcast of 1938*. He saw us work together
and exclaimed, "Those guys really hit it off!" That's how *Road
to Singapore* came about, and we were on our way. We made
seven *Road* pictures together and were due to make the eighth
when Bing died. I would like to do the eighth with George
Burns.

Reel to Real: How much, if any, were the *Road* pictures
ad-libbed?

Hope: I would say 20 percent. Those writers were marvelous; they knew construction so well. They knew how to
get us into trouble and how to get us out. I had just started a
radio show with 13 of the best writers who ever lived — now
they're all producers and directors; Mel Frank, Norman
Panama, Jack Rose, Jack Douglas. I would give them the
script, and they would dash off material for me. I would then
go to Bing and say, "What do you think of this, and this ..."
He'd say, "Oh, that's marvelous." So we would use the lines.
Now the first picture, we ad-libbed so much, and they laughed
so much on the set that *Time Magazine* said we had ad-libbed
the entire script. It hurt Don Hartman, one of the original
writers. He was really wounded. He came onto the set one
day during the filming of *The Road to Zanzibar* and was listening to the dialogue. I shouted to him, "If you hear one of
your lines, yell bingo." That made him furious. But when
the picture was selected for the New York Film Critics Award,
he started smiling and saying that our spontaneity was what
made the films so successful. Audiences used to die, they
didn't hear half the jokes, they laughed so much.

Reel to Real: How do you think comedy has changed

Between acts with Will Ahern and Eddie Parks.

An earthbound John Bubbles.

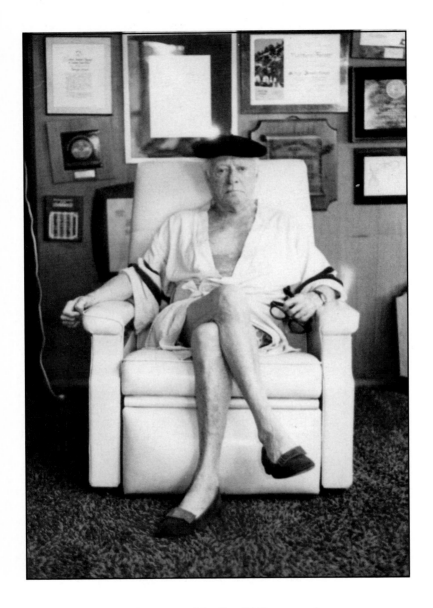

George Jessel in La-Z-Boy mode.

**Festering with
Jackie Coogan.**

**William Demarest and his
"whorehouse" cello.**

Eddie Foy Jr. points to his portrait.

Hackensack High's No. 1 grad: Joe Smith.

Benny Rubin and his wooden clogs.

Hitting a high note with Kathryn Grayson.

Ann Miller dances cheek-to-cheek with Fred Astaire in *Easter Parade* (1948).

Ray Bolger: Scarecrow memories.

Starting at the top with Fred Astaire.

Cyd Charisse: "Beautiful Dynamite."

Harold — half of the high-flying Nicholas Brothers.

Mickey Rooney: Andy Hardy grows up.

The "unsinkable" Debbie Reynolds.

"Neptune's Daughter" — Esther Williams.

A Partridge without her pear tree — Shirley Jones.

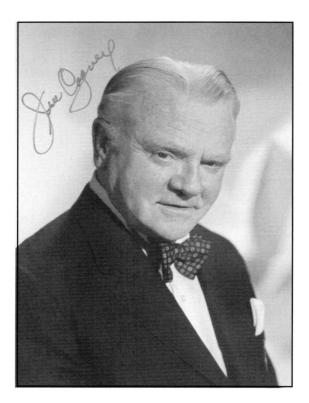

Everyone's favorite tough guy — James Cagney.

Charlton Heston on high.

The importance of being Ernest ... Borgnine.

The artistic Tony Curtis.

Don't leave home without him — Karl Malden.

Gregory Peck

Gene Kelly — on tap.

In the heat of the day with Rod Steiger.

At home with Janet Leigh.

Tippi Hedren and one of her companions.

Virginia Mayo

Eva Marie Saint   **Celeste Holm relaxes in Central Park.**

Steve Allen composed ... or possibly composing.

Cigar aficionado Milton Berle.

George Burns between puffs.

Eddie Albert

Lucille Ball

Bob Newhart

Thanks for the memories — Bob Hope.

Mel Blanc, man of a thousand voices.

William Shatner   **Peter Falk**

Carroll O'Connor

Carl Reiner

Robert Stack

Ed Asner   **Ted Knight**

Director George Sidney in his Beverly Hills office.

TOP: Mel Brooks hams it up with authors Tom Johnson, left, and David Fantle. LEFT: Frank Capra is not dressed for the weather.

Vincente Minnelli makes a point.

Director Robert Wise with posters of his films behind him.

The informal Sammy Cahn.

Happy hour with Hoagy Carmichael.

Song writer Harry Warren has come a long way from 42nd Street.

Burton Lane

Jay Livingston, Ray Evans and their Oscars.

Artie Shaw shares a couple of his favorite CDs.

through the years, if at all?

Hope: Comedy has changed in the last 25 years. They're doing things in person and on the screen that I would never have dreamed they'd get away with. I think it is a sad commentary to see total crudity in comedy. I hate to see it in pictures or anywhere, but especially in pictures because they are endorsements and documents that we send around the world. People must think Americans are a bunch of dirty-mouthed, oversexed people. But thank God you can see pictures like *Raiders of the Lost Ark, Superman II,* and *Star Wars,* which make all the money. It's shaking up a lot of people. I remember when *I am Curious (Yellow)* came out. That dirty stag film cost about $35,000 to make and they grossed $15 million. That was the start of all those dirty pictures. The producers said, "Oh, we can get away with it," then everybody started hopping into bed. There was a film I went to see when I performed here a few years ago called *North Dallas Forty.* I love football. Mac Davis was in it, and he's a good friend of mine. We play golf together so I had to see it. I took a cab out to a neighborhood theater, the Roseville IV. Let me tell you the filth in that picture. At the finish there was one word on the screen that I had never heard before. I walked out disgusted.

Reel to Real: What do you think of President Reagan's budget cuts for the arts?

Hope: I'm baffled by it all. I just don't know how he is going to make it work. He's got the confidence of the people, thank God. And the polls show that they're going to give him a great chance, which is something new. He's got a wonderful group of guys around him, so I think they'll work it out some way. He's got more guts than any president I've seen. To stand up in front of the air traffic controllers union, say what he thinks, and get away with it.

Reel to Real: Do oriental countries that you perform in really appreciate your brand of humor? Can they understand it?

Hope: In China I had a good interpreter at the Peking College. I showed them my picture *Monsieur Beaucaire,* and I went around back to listen to them. They laughed like hell at it, I mean they really dug it. Because it was about a poor barber fighting the system. I was amazed at how fast they caught on to my humor.

Reel to Real: Working on a film doesn't allow you the luxury of immediate audience feedback. Is that why you haven't made more movies lately?

Hope: Not at all. The reason I haven't made so many films is because I haven't seen anything I've wanted to make. A movie is a document that lives forever — I have 60 of them out. I was performing in a little town called Owensboro, Kentucky, recently, so Sunday morning I turned on the television. *My Favorite Brunette* was showing with Peter Lorre and Dorothy Lamour. Delores and I were enjoying it I must say, when on comes a commercial and right after that they started to repeat the previous reel of the movie. I tried to get hold of the station manager, but it was being broadcast out of Indianapolis. The guy in charge probably pushed the button twice and then went back to sleep. At the finish of *Brunette,* I'm about to be executed in the electric chair, but I get a last minute reprieve. Bing did a cameo as the warden. He was heartbroken that I got off scott-free.

Reel to Real: Have you ever been asked to run for public office?

Hope: Yes I have. There was a radio poll held up in Seattle asking if they'd vote for me if I ran for the presidency. I didn't know anything about it, but 81 percent of the people said yes. The news got back to Washington, and a couple of senators came out to see me about it. One was Senator John Tower of Texas.

Reel to Real: Last political question. You supported Reagan for the presidency, yet you came out in favor of gun control. Why?

Hope: I asked him about it, and I think his argument is

very weak — especially since he's been shot. You know, a lot of states have gun control. California has gun control. I wish they would get real tough about it. I don't know why a guy can get doped up, buy a gun and then shoot up a town. If there would have been gun control in Memphis when they first found Hinckley with those three guns, they might have grabbed him and looked into his head — there were a few things mixed up there. I don't know why the hell they ever let him go. Jim Brady looks like he's ruined forever. Reagan is damn lucky.

Reel to Real: I guess it's a reflection of the times. It does seem a sad state of affairs when you now see police on horseback patrolling Hollywood Boulevard at night.

Hope: Hollywood Boulevard is a real zoo. I hate to think what those loonies are doing to my cement star in the Walk-of-Fame. They're probably cleaning their feet on it!

Reel to Real: It's no secret that you've been an outspoken conservative, yet you remain extremely popular on college campuses. How do you account for that?

Hope: That's easy to understand. Students are very fair about everything. They look for ideals. They told me Columbia University was a nest of liberals. I did a show there and they turned out to be one of my best audiences ever. I've found that students have the ability to separate my personal political beliefs from the bipartisan comedy I perform on stage.

Reel to Real: How do you account for your amazing longevity?

Hope: It's a tough, tough business. You have to keep coming up with things all the time. When I started at Paramount in 1938 I had the invaluable grounding of stage and radio behind me. I worked my way up until I was number one. From that time on I had a pretty solid rock to stand on.

Reel to Real: Why is it that after the 1960s you, for all intents and purposes, stopped making films?

Hope: I haven't read anything I've liked. First of all my television and personal appearance schedule has been tremendous. I am doing a film on newspaperman Walter Winchell, which should be released in April or November of 1981. The picture will be along the lines of the *Seven Little Foys*, a film I made about 25 years ago. I'll enjoy doing this because the story will have a lot of everything — drama, comedy, music, show business and journalism.

Reel to Real: What's your secret for staying so active and vital?

Hope: The secret to staying youthful is to have fun. If people could only get a laugh every day, I think it's the most important thing in the world because many people never exercise their laugh lines. They stay grumpy. When an audience laughs at one of my jokes I get a good feeling inside. My wife once said to me, "Boy, this is a lot of work." This isn't work to me. It's fun. When you do one show a night and play golf every day and meet a lot of friends, you're having a ball.

Television's Funniest Shrink
Bob Newhart
August 1981

The Hotel Bel-Air in Los Angeles is a three-star hideaway favored by such dignitaries as Princesses Astrid of Norway and Margaretha of Sweden, H.S.H. Grace de Monaco ... and Bob Newhart. In an undeniably Southern California style, predicated on a movie mania only Southern Californians would take credit for, the Bel-Air management displays signed glossies of everyone of significance who has stayed there — from international royalty to those with merely a Hollywood pedigree.

So much for anonymity.

Last summer in the dark recesses of the hotel's café, we met Newhart for breakfast (he favors corned beef hash straight out of the can). That quiet spot was his choice, and it seemed to be in keeping with the proper manner we had always associated with his character on *The Bob Newhart Show*. Considering the outlandish tenor of today's sitcoms, memories of Newhart's low-keyed approach and unruffled demeanor should be treasured.

"One of the keys to the success of my character was that I let the ensemble on my show grab a healthy share of the laughs," said Newhart. "It worked for Jack Benny on radio and television, and it worked for me."

Newhart's left-handed entry into show business was the result not of any particular burning ambition on his part, but rather of his ineptitude as a Certified Public Accountant.

"I used to balance the petty cash box where I worked with money out of my own pocket," he said. "If it was a dollar under, I'd take it out of my pocket. If it were a dollar over, I'd put it into my pocket. My boss kept telling me to balance it correctly but I said that you're paying me $3 an hour to find 50 cents. It doesn't make sense! I guess that's when I knew I wasn't cut out to be an accountant."

Soon after, nightclub comedy work gelled into riotous monologues on comedy albums such as *The Button-Down Mind of Bob Newhart,* in which his routines "The Driving Instructor" and "The Submarine Commander" gained Newhart national fame.

"I know albums tend to use a comic's material faster than he can replenish it, but for me it worked in reverse. The album was the only reason for my gaining prominence at all," Newhart said. "I think that era ended with *Laugh-In* and its quick blackouts. You couldn't do seven- or eight-minute monologues, you had to do three- and four-minute skits."

It was while performing in Las Vegas that Newhart first developed a friendship with another comedian that has stood the test of time — 16 years of each other's insults.

"Don Rickles was playing a hotel lounge in Vegas. His wife knew my wife, so we all arranged to meet for dinner before Don had to go back and do his third show," Newhart said. "During the meal, he asked my wife questions about how old our kids were and I thought, 'What a lovely man!' As you know, Rickles' act is different from what our conversation was based on that day. Well, we went to see his act and he came out from the wings and promptly called me a stammering idiot and my wife a former hooker from Bayonne, New Jersey. We've been friends ever since."

The Bob Newhart Show came about because Newhart said he had high regard for the quality and professionalism of the Mary Tyler Moore Production Company.

"Lorenzo Music, who wrote for *The Smothers Brothers* program and who was Carleton the Doorman on *Rhoda,* and Dave Davis were a writing team. They came up with the concept that I should play a psychologist. It was a great idea but my only reservation was that it was a potentially dangerous area. I didn't want to portray really sick people like schizophrenics. As it turned out, I did have the distinction of being on television six years and never curing a patient. Mr. Carlin was probably worse off at the end of the show than at the beginning."

The pilot for Newhart's series lacked many of the show's now familiar faces. Marcia Wallace and Bill Daily weren't featured, and the whole show had to be reshot because the network, for unknown reasons, objected to the script's use of the word "condominium."

If they were halcyon days for Newhart, the nights were pure halcion.

"One director we had had absolutely no sense of humor," Newhart recalled, bemused. "We rehearsed with him for five days when I finally told our producer Michael Zinberg that I thought one of the essential ingredients a comedy director should possess is a sense of humor. It's like a team having a ball player with poor eye-hand coordination. After that, we hired Dick Martin to direct. God bless him! He sat in the director's booth for three months watching us block and rehearse, in order to acquaint himself with the show."

The show's six-year run provided high points that still

manage to conjure up what Woody Allen would call "legiti-mate laughs" during re-runs.

"Bill Daily is responsible for many of the biggest laughs in the show," Newhart said. "His part of Howard Borden was so nonsensical that he seldom had anything to do with an episode's particular storyline. In one show he had just returned from the Fiji Islands and he came in and said, 'Bob, do you think I'm getting shorter? … Because I think I'm engaged to a Fijian princess and if I don't marry her, the chief said I will be cursed. To seal the ceremony, they gave us two cows. Do you think the state of Illinois will recognize the marriage?' I said, 'I'm sure they will. You'll be the couple with the two cows.' Stuff like that was totally off the wall. The writers loved it."

Newhart also credits Daily with the biggest laugh line in the show's history.

"I was working with a prison group and Emily and I both had our hands against the wall. Howard came running in and he thought we were holding up the wall. When we walked away he said, 'Hey, aren't you going to help me? I can't hold this up all by myself.' The studio audience died.

"A new television series for myself might be in the off-ing," Newhart hinted. "But it won't be one detrimental to an audience's intelligence. I had the experience a couple of years ago where I couldn't find a program from Tuesday through Saturday that I felt like watching. I guess most television is like sitting in front of a microwave oven — eventually it will rot your brain."

Wide Awake and Ready for Action
Carl Reiner
April 1998

Carl Reiner is in desperate need of a Starbucks jumpstart — or a little more shut-eye. It's unconscionably early (before 8 a.m.) in his office on the Warner-Hollywood Studios lot in Los Angeles, and he is visibly tired at such an early morning start, a fact he soon makes quite audible, too.

"I'm a little sleepy right now," he slurs, squinting out at us intently with sacks under his eyes that bring to mind two puffy bagpipes. "I don't feel funny as I'm saying this right now. It's like the serious actor who announces, 'I'm going to do a comedy this year!' I feel like that guy right now. I can't prove at this moment that I'm funny at all."

Despite the self-deprecating disclaimer, in a way, Reiner, 76, proved his comic chops with that gentle jibe culled from a mammoth joke depository hidden deep in the recesses of his sleep-deprived cerebellum.

Clearly, this is a man who "knows from funny." Since the age of 17, when he made his theatrical "debut" of sorts as second tenor in an ersatz version of *The Merry Widow,* in New York, Reiner has been downloading jokes and bits of business with the alacrity of an IBM mainframe computer.

"My greatest strength is that I appreciate all kinds of comedy and have worked with different kinds of comedians," he says. "As a director, I have a feel for what's funny, I think. For instance, in *The Dick Van Dyke Show* (created, directed and co-starring Reiner), Dick had no trouble doing pratfalls. He loved doing them. So we liberally laced the show with them. He always said he was born 30 years too late and should have been a silent film clown. On the other hand, falling down would be anathema to someone like Mort Sahl or Woody Allen. You just have to know what's right and work with the actor's strengths."

Perhaps nowhere more than on the legendary late-1940s television variety program, *Your Show of Shows,* did Reiner's penchant for working to an actor's strength come more sharply into play. Television was a new animal then; an insatiable monster, really, that voraciously consumed scripted material while always demanding more.

"Luckily I had done some shows at Catskills summer resorts, so I knew how to turn over material quick," Reiner says. "In those days you would need three different acts for vacationers that stayed, on average, three weeks. But in television you needed new sketches every week for 39 straight weeks. It was chaos, but we were young and that was the job. You never thought of not doing it. Just do it … like the Nike commercial."

Reiner did more than just survive the grueling pace of performing and writing for network television; he thrived, winning 12 Emmys in the process. His latest was for a reprisal of his role as the megalomaniacal TV star Alan Brady from *The Dick Van Dyke Show.*

"Paul Reiser, the star of *Mad About You,* came up to me at a party and wanted me to guest on his show as Alan Brady," Reiner says. "I hadn't done a sitcom in 35 years and didn't want to be unfaithful to the *Van Dyke Show*, so I turned him down. But Paul countered with, 'I don't want you, I want Alan Brady!' I thought, 'What a great idea. Alan Brady is alive and well and still an entity unto himself.' Great potential there."

Reiner didn't reacquaint himself with the rapid-fire neurotic tics that made the original Alan Brady so memorable by renting videos of the old show or watching re-runs on *Nick at Night;* he just winged it.

"I'll tell you one thing, though; I was at Sidney Sheldon's house the other day and he said that he and his wife always tune in *Nick at Night* before going to bed and watch *The Dick Van Dyke Show.* They told me they want to go to sleep with a good feeling in their heads."

A nice wrinkle — comedy as sleep-therapy.

"I don't know if it's better than counting sheep, but, hey, whatever works," Reiner says, playing once again to his strengths — this time to an audience of two that yawns, but for the right reasons, at his jokes.

Late last fall, Reiner resurrected another classic from his repertoire, the decades old recording of, *The 2,000 Year Old Man,* with his partner in crime, Mel Brooks. Acknowledging the approaching millennium, Reiner and Brooks recorded a new CD which they dubbed, *The 2,000 Year Old Man — In the Year 2000.* In addition, Harper Collins released a book version of the CD, which includes ancient sage wisdom on marriage, self-help books, rap music and the Spanish Inquisition. Reiner is also looking forward to the opening of movie he directed starring old friend Alan Arkin and Marisa Tomei called *The Slums of Beverly Hills.* And, if continued professional success wasn't enough, he can also look with pride to a marriage that has lasted 53 years to Estelle, a jazz vocalist.

All in all, it's a long way from graduating at the age of 16 from Evander Childs High School in The Bronx, to trading outrageous puns about Ovid with Mel Brooks.

"Brooks' household was funny because Brooks was funny as a kid. My home wasn't funny but my mother and father knew what was humorous. During the Depression there wasn't a lot to laugh about," Reiner says, curiously eyeing a statue in his office of the Maltese Falcon (a prop from *Dead Men Don't Wear Plaid* which he directed starring Steve Martin). Reiner promptly picks up a black Sharpie magic marker and starts detailing some of the scuffed surface of the bird.

"It's the stuff dreams are made of," isn't it?," we say, aping Bogart with an impression that wouldn't get us a job parking cars in the Comedy Store lot.

"It's the doorstop my door was made for," Reiner replies. "C'mon guys, wake up and smell the coffee! Wait! maybe I should follow my own advice."

VI.
Plugged In

IT AIN'T EASY BEIN' GREEN
Eddie Albert
March 1994

He's best remembered as the eternally optimistic "Mr. Douglas" on the campy '60s sitcom *Green Acres,* who abandoned his citified existence and thriving legal career on Park Avenue for a hardscrabble farmer's life somewhere near Hooterville, USA.

In reality, Eddie Albert, 86, lives in the posh West Los Angeles community of Pacific Palisades. However, he truly does have a green thumb, managing to make his lawn yield more of a bumper crop than his television farm ever did.

"My front yard is nothing but vegetables," he told us during a recent visit. "I eat what I grow, and I grow just about everything — you name it!" Indeed, in a spot where most Angelenos plant orange trees and yucca plants, Albert had row upon furrowed row of carrots, beans, lettuce and herbs coming up.

Albert's commitment to the environment reaches far beyond subsistence farming. He has been a vocal activist speaking out for years in support of such causes as preserving family farms in the Midwest and particularly the nation's dwindling topsoil.

"I was a citizen long before I was an actor," he said, responding to the question of whether his status as a performer has hurt his credibility as an expert in environmental matters. "Most people don't realize that the whole world hinges on a little thing called topsoil. When Europeans first settled this continent, we had 18 inches of it, on average. Now we're down to about five or six inches. When it goes, we're finished as a nation."

Down and dirty pronouncements notwithstanding, Albert believes we have "a couple of generations" to reverse this trend.

The conversation moved from Albert's sitting area in front of a large fireplace to a bench in his tree-shaded backyard. Crowned with a healthy shock of snow-white hair, Albert was dressed in a white T-shirt and a blue downfilled vest, continuing (visually at least) the environmental guru theme to which he adheres. Capping off this "clean look," Albert was shod in a pair of boots constructed from some indeterminate synthetic fabric that made him look like he was ready to play a round of lunar golf with an Apollo astronaut.

Edward Albert Heimberger began his show business career as a "song-and-dance-patter-man" on a radio broadcast out of Minneapolis, Minnesota. Announcers kept referring to him as Hamburger instead of Heimberger (food analogies resonate throughout his life and career), so he dropped his last name altogether.

"I was pretty bewildered back then, without a clear-cut profession. It was the Depression and after 1929 only an idiot would study business in school; it wasn't very chic," Albert said. "Show business felt the effects of the Depression later than almost anything else. I guess that's why I gravitated toward it."

After landing some desultory radio work and small theater parts in New York, Albert was cast by the legendary stage director George Abbott in the Broadway play, *Brother Rat,* followed in short order by another Abbott production, *Room Service.*

"Most people are familiar with the Marx Brothers movie version of that show," Albert said. "They brought their own kind of frenetic energy to the thing, which wasn't the way it was originally intended. The brothers were marvelous, but the show never really worked as a movie."

Albert made his film debut in the Warner Bros. production of *Brother Rat.* His co-star in the movie also had an activist bent that he translated into a long run in the White House — Ronald Reagan.

"Ronnie wasn't a very good comedian, but as a straight

man he was fine," Albert remembered. "Even in those days — 1938 — he liked politics. And when he was asked to speak, he was better than anyone else."

With World War II looming, Albert took time out of his contract work at Warner Bros. to trek to Mexico and turn up facts about Nazi activities south of the border. For cover, he joined the Escalante Brothers Circus as part of a "trapeze act." In between shows he gathered information that he promptly turned over to Army intelligence. When the Japanese bombed Pearl Harbor, Albert enlisted in the Navy.

"I was with the first wave of Marines at Tarawa," he said. "I piloted a Higgins Boat, and when I neared the beach there were about 600 dead Marines floating in the water. The tide was too low and all the boats got hung up on a reef hundreds of yards from the beach. We had to unload the guys and they had to make it to shore on their own through a hail of machine-gun fire. It was hell. To this day, I often think of those brave Marines."

The bucolic pastures of Hooterville are literally a world away from the war-torn coral atolls of the Central Pacific, a place Albert said he never wants to revisit even as a tourist. Ironically, *Green Acres,* aired between 1965 and 1971, paralleling another turbulent period in our history. Perhaps the absurdity of the show was an effective metaphor for what was taking place thousands of miles away in Vietnam.

Quite naturally, memories of working with Mr. Kimball, Mr. Haney, Sam Drucker, Eb, and even the prescient pig, Arnold Ziffel, evoke fonder memories. "It was the most fun I ever had," Albert said."It was superior writing, really quite subtle in its own way. And working with Eva Gabor was great."

Albert is also justifiably proud of his film work, which included two Best Supporting Actor Academy Award nominations for *Roman Holiday* and *The Heartbreak Kid* and co-starring roles with the likes of Erroll Flynn and Humphrey Bogart.

A widower since 1985, Albert was married for almost 50

years to singer, actress and dancer Margo. They had two children, Maria, and Edward, who has followed in his father's acting footsteps and etched his own distinguished show-business career.

Ultimately, however, reminiscing about the past is a zero-sum gain. Albert is too busy thinking about his next road trip, a junket to Washington, D.C., where he'll talk to some senators about the topsoil threat. Then it's on to Europe to spread the "manure" there. (His word, not ours. After all, Albert says, "If manure can make crops grow, maybe the verbal version will plant a few ideas with people.")

For Albert, it ain't easy bein' green.

Read All About Him
Ed Asner
September 1980

"Mary, you got spunk ... I hate spunk!"
— *Lou Grant to Mary Richards*
The Mary Tyler Moore Show, *1970.*

Spunk. Whether he likes it or not, that word characterizes Ed Asner, both personally and professionally. The Lou Grant character that Asner created in 1970 on *The Mary Tyler Moore Show* had a gruff exterior tempered by underplayed sensitivity. From the WJM newsroom in Minneapolis to the *Los Angeles Tribune* city desk, the Lou Grant spunk remains, 10 television years later, a commodity an audience can count on.

Asner's personal grit was seen recently during the Screen Actors Guild strike that closed down Hollywood entertainment production for nine weeks. He was the last actor to cross the musicians' picket line after an agreement had been tentatively reached with the Guild. It reflects a political and professional bent that can be traced to his years as a journeyman laborer doing odd jobs throughout the Midwest.

"One of my first jobs was selling encyclopedias," he said during a recent interview in his office-trailer on the CBS TV lot. "I threw up from the training. It was scumbag time, the degrading hard sell. I tried to sell shoes and then went to work on an auto-assembly line in Kansas City. That didn't work out, so after nine or 10 months, I traveled to Chicago and worked as a taxicab driver. I finally wound up in a steel mill in Gary, Indiana. I really appreciate the blue-collar worker."

Asner's first professional acting experience came as a member of Paul Sills' Chicago Playwrights Repertory Theater, a company that fostered Elaine May, Mike Nichols and Barbara Harris among others.

"Before I got out of the Army, I was stationed in France, and I got a letter from Paul Sills who I had known from the University of Chicago Theatre," Asner said. "Sills wrote that he was starting a little professional theater on the near North Side and asked if I wanted a job. He said hopefully he could pay me $50-$60 a week. Suddenly my life fell into place. It was a 180-seat theater, which we slept in. The second floor had been an old chop-suey joint and bookie front."

The Chicago Playwrights Theatre was not an immediate hit among the city's theater critics. The avant-garde stance and presentation of modern playwrights was not always appreciated or understood.

Asner was first cast in *La Ronde*, by Schnitzler, but the play incurred the displeasure of the Catholic Church and closed after only two performances. He was then cast as the lead in *Woyzeck* by Georg Buchner. It was a hit and ran for two years. Asner quit the Chicago Playwrights Theatre when it became improvisational.

"I felt it was too much fun to improve," he said. "I wanted to seek renown as an actor, not an improvisationalist. I wanted to be tested. You can put that down to feelings of Jewish middle-class guilt."

As an out-of-work actor in New York City, Asner cobbled together a workable method for canvassing the city with his resume and headshots.

"I began looking for work by making the rounds, looking up anybody and everybody I could. One of the few times I ever did anything intelligent for myself, I came to New York expecting nothing. I set myself up a grid pattern of the city. I would drop off my picture and resume to any and all agencies knowing full well that most of them were dumped in the wastebasket before I reached the door."

For six years Asner acted in such plays as *The Three-Penny Opera*, *Ivanov* and *Henry V* for Joseph Papp's Shakespeare in the Park. But Asner's decision to move to Hollywood was not a natural outgrowth of his experience on the stage.

"I could have stayed in New York forever, but I was discovered by the Burt Leonard people, who did the television shows *Naked City* and *Route 66.*'"

Asner's success led to his first TV series role as a character on *Slattery's People*. It was short lived. "They couldn't find a way to use me properly. In the first 10 shows they didn't use me in two of them."

Asner said that he, and just about every other actor in Hollywood, tested for the part of Lou Grant on *The Mary Tyler Moore Show*.

"I read for the two producers and then came back a week or two later and read with Mary. I think that Gavin MacLeod tested for my role. The producers didn't think he was right for it, but asked him if he would be interested in the role of Murray Slaughter. Happy ending."

During the eight-year run of *The Mary Tyler Moore Show*, Asner remembered only a couple of occasions in which artistic disagreement among cast members flared into personal vendetta.

"Most of the time we were secure enough with one another that no animosity was aroused. A couple of times, however, Ted Knight and I got into personal conflict, even though we are and continue to be the best of friends. Once during a Friday night performance, I brought my hate with me onstage. I was deadly. I learned that it is a professional necessity to quell any anger before going onstage, or else everyone's performance will suffer."

Asner believes that there is an "everyman" aspect to his role of Lou Grant that has allowed the character to grow, develop and most importantly, remain popular for 10 years.

"No amount of adversity can keep him down for long. As Chuckles the Clown on MTM used to say: 'A little song, a little dance, a little seltzer down your pants.'"

Still, the character has changed. "The first season of *Lou Grant*, we found that the old MTM character wasn't working. Everyone was miserable. The Jamaican episode was the old comedic Lou Grant, but some of the scenes on the beach were somber and they augured in the new Lou Grant."

During the last two years, the *Lou Grant* show had begun to use its newspaper-related episodes to explore such complex social issues as race relations, spousal abuse and abortion. We asked Asner if he thought that a one-hour format was enough time to do justice to such weighty subject matter.

"If you are dealing with a newspaper, and not an all-out comedy, then you have to deal with issues that a newspaper deals with. I'm amazed that we handle these problems as completely and succinctly as we do."

Professional journalists applaud *Lou Grant* for its realistic depiction of the workings of a newsroom.

"In the beginning I felt guilty about that," Asner said. "They applauded us so loudly, it really helped. But I challenged that we were that dramatically effective. In the third year I felt we began to merit their praise."

How does Asner handle criticism of his work?

"I think I always find outlets. I was in a production of *The Tempest* in New York, and Brooks Atkinson reviewed it. It was his next-to-last review before retiring, and he likened my voice to that of a train conductor. I diverted myself from his criticism with the thought that I would not have time to get on stage in something else and make that son-of-a-bitch eat his words concerning my talent."

Asner is not generally known as a movie actor, but his work includes the films *The Slender Thread, Skin Game* and *Fort Apache, the Bronx,* due to be released in 1981.

"I have yet to enjoy feature movies because of the slowness and tender loving care that each moment of film seems to require," Asner said. "I would say that if you promise to keep my busy enough, I would be glad to do features. You know I made *The Wrestler* in Minnesota. It's a beautiful piece of real estate. It was always so comfortable up there — even in winter."

LOONEY TUNES
Mel Blanc
September 1980

Given the "flaked out" reputation Southern California has acquired over the last several years, it was just another weekday afternoon. There we were, talking with Bugs Bunny, Tweedy Bird, Porky Pig, Daffy Duck and Barney Rubble in Beverly Hills. Was the Los Angeles "laid-back" lifestyle starting to affect us after only two weeks, or were we really talking to these characters? Luckily for us, it was the latter. This wasn't a chance meeting on Rodeo Drive, but a prearranged interview with the man who is responsible for creating these immortal animated cartoon voices along with more than 400 others — Mel Blanc.

We chatted in the offices of Blanc Communications overlooking the constant traffic snarl of Wilshire Boulevard. Blanc was not wearing the customary three-piece suit and rep tie that might be more emblematic for the founder of an immensely successful advertising firm. Instead, he wore a green open-collared shirt with his favorite and most famous character stitched onto his pocket — Bugs Bunny. He greeted us with, "Eh, what's up youse two?"

Blanc was born in San Francisco in 1908. Even as a child growing up in Portland, Oregon, he realized that he had the unique ability to create different voices.

"I was quite popular in school," said Blanc, whose non-affected speaking voice is a close approximation of Barney Rubble's. "I used to entertain the kids and teachers at assemblies. The kids would laugh and the teachers would laugh. In fact, the teachers showed their appreciation for my entertainment by consistently giving me lousy marks."

During the '20s and early '30s, Blanc went through what seemed like a mandatory struggling period. His musical talents, not his voices, landed him much of his early work in show business. An accomplished musician on the violin and bass, Blanc got a job on the NBC Radio Orchestra in San Francisco and later worked as the pit orchestra conductor at the Portland Orpheum Vaudeville Theater.

Along with his wife, Estelle, Blanc moved to Los Angeles in the mid-'30s hoping to land a job in motion pictures or network radio as a voice specialist. After months of hounding the offices of Schlesinger Productions, the animation factory that later became Warner Bros.' "Looney Tunes" and "Merry Melodies," he was given a chance to audition for director Frank Tashlin.

"He asked me if I could do a drunken bull. I thought about it for a minute and said, 'Yes.' When he asked me how he would sound, I told him that he would sound like he was a little loaded and looking for the sour mash. Tashlin loved it and gave me my first job in cartoons."

The idea that in his career Blanc has managed to create over 400 distinctly different voices is mind-boggling.

"They would show me a picture of the character that was going to be in the cartoon. And then a storyboard that showed me what the character was going to do throughout the picture. Porky Pig, for example, was a timid little guy. I had to give him a timid voice. When I lecture at colleges, I tell the kids that I wanted to immerse myself in the life of a pig so I could authentically create a pig's voice. I went to a pig farm and I wallowed around with the pig for a couple of weeks. I came back to the studio and they kicked me out and said, 'Go home and take a bath.'"

"Then they showed me a picture of Bugs and told me that he was a real stinker. I knew he was a tough character. I had to get a tough voice. So I thought either Brooklyn or the Bronx. I compromised and put the two of them together. That's how I got the voice for Bugs ... doc."

Almost as famous as Blanc's characters are the catchphrases associated with many of them. Such phrases as "Eh, what's up, Doc?," "I tawt I taw a puddy tat," and "That's all folks" have become part of the American vernacular.

"'Eh, what's up, Doc?' was popular around 1932-33," Blanc said. "They were going to have him say, 'Hey, what's cooking?' and I said, 'Instead of that corny saying, why don't you use a modern expression like 'Eh, what's up, Doc?' They thought it was a good idea, and the expression has become synonymous with Bugs.

"Strange enough, Warners had all the catchphrases and the characters copyrighted and trademarked. I gave them all of those damn things and now I have to ask permission to use them."

The most successful prime-time TV cartoon show of all time and a personal favorite is *The Flintstones*. Blanc supplied the voice of Fred's neighbor and best friend, Barney Rubble, as well as the Flintstone's pet dinosaur, Dino. Blanc said that the producers of the show, Hanna-Barbera, wanted him to pattern Barney after Art Carney on *The Honeymooners*. He refused and demonstrated with a "Hey, Fred" the difference between Barney and Carney.

On January 24, 1961, Blanc was involved in a horrific traffic accident that broke every bone in his body. He was in a coma for three weeks and wore a full-body cast.

"I was in the obituary column in Honolulu," he said.

"But the old adage 'The show must go on' held true. After two months in the hospital, I was brought home and put in a full-body cast. We recorded eight months of *The Flintstones* from my bedroom. My son fixed up a beautiful recording studio right in the house."

The technology of making cartoons has changed radically over the years, but Blanc feels some of the artfulness has been sacrificed to speed and other economies.

"What they're doing now I called limited animation. The old Warner Bros. cartoons were full animation. Every frame was drawn separately, whereas in limited animation they draw the face, you see the eyes blink, the mouth moves a little, the background is on a turntable, and you see the same damn thing over and over again."

According to Blanc, years ago, a six-and-one-half minute cartoon employed 125 people, took nine months to make, and cost about $50,000. Today it takes the same number of people, one-tenth of the time to make a cartoon that costs around $350,000.

At age 72, Blanc has no immediate retirement plans, yet he is grooming his son, Noel, to assume the voiceover chores. He is already president of Blanc Communications, an advertising firm that handles the accounts of such companies as 9-Lives cat food, Pepsi-Cola, Oscar Mayer and Paine-Webber. On a recent installment of the TV show *That's My Line,* Noel demonstrated his uncanny ability to duplicate his father's voices.

"I have found that you can count on your fingers the number of people who can do more than two creative voices," Blanc said. "Most of them are impersonators or copyists. A lot of them will do a voice and say that they created it. I say bullshit! It was created by Schnozz Durante or one of those other guys."

And that's all, folks!

Common and Preferred
Peter Falk
May 1996

"You can't use an umbrella as a prop when the sun is out, but you can use a cigar under almost any circumstances," Peter Falk announces in that gravelly, clutched rasp known to millions worldwide as the voice of Columbo — everyone's favorite rumpled television detective.

Falk, 71, imparts that sage bit of actorly wisdom not while chewing on a cheap stogie (Columbo smokes cigars, but Falk tells us he never does), but in between puffs on a True 100 cigarette, which is seldom out of his hand. "I've been chain-smoking cigarettes for 55 years," he says, hunched in a chair in the office/studio of his Beverly Hills home. "My mother is 91 years old and still lights up. I'm trusting to luck that I'm blessed with her constitution." Throughout our visit, so many ashes accumulate in the folds of Falk's paint-smeared Oxford shirt and chinos that by visit's end he seems to have morphed into a walking, talking smudge pot. The overall effect is, in a way, oddly charming.

Perhaps more than anything else, meeting Falk face to face is like running into a Damon Runyon character fresh off a three-day gambling bender. Following him as he pads around his beautifully appointed studio, we wouldn't be too surprised if he decided to launch into an impromptu version of "Luck Be A Lady Tonight" from *Guys and Dolls*.

As Falk points to a low shelf where four of his Emmys from the series rest, it becomes apparent that the actor and his Columbo character are closely intertwined; that the non-plused absent-minded professor demeanor of his award-winning police lieutenant is really no affectation. However, something seems amiss. We finally realize it is Falk's house; the kind of Beverly Hills brickpile the intrepid detective would fearlessly invade searching for clues armed with just the tiniest pin to deflate the ego of its cocky owner. It's a spread that would dazzle "everyman" Columbo, but Falk seems right at home. (He lives at the house with his actress/wife Shera Danese. Falk has two grown children from a previous marriage.)

"I'm a Virgo Jew, and that means I have an obsessive thoroughness," Falk says making the correlation between himself and Columbo. "It's not enough to get most of the details, it's necessary to get them all. I've been accused of perfectionism. When Lew Wasserman (legendary Hollywood powerbroker, Steven Spielberg's mentor, and until recently, head of Universal Studios) said that Falk is a perfectionist, I don't know whether it was out of affection or because he felt I was a monumental pain in the ass."

However, Falk's mania to excel is tempered in the sweet-natured television detective. "Columbo has a genuine mistiness about him. It seems to hang in the air," Falk says. "He's capable of being distracted. I remember one case where it was 20 minutes into the teleplay before he realized he hadn't taken off his pajamas. Columbo is an ass-backwards Sherlock Holmes. Holmes had a long neck, Columbo has no neck; Holmes smoked a Meerschaum pipe, Columbo chews up six cigars a day at a quarter a piece."

The connection Falk feels — that Columbo is some sort of tattered stateside reincarnation of the famous Baker Street sleuth — is underscored by the fact that in a position of prominence, on a bookshelf right next to a copy of *The Columbo Phile,* is the *Complete Sherlock Holmes* by Arthur Conan Doyle. Volumes that speak volumes about where the poor man's Hercule Poirot ranks in the crime-solver firmament.

"The show is all over the world," Falk says with genuine amazement. "I've been to little villages in Africa with maybe one TV set, and little kids will run up to me shouting, 'Columbo, Columbo!'" When people are not calling out the name of their favorite shamus, strangers invariably yell to him, "serpentine," in reference to a hilarious, bullet-dodging scene in the 1979 film, *The In-Laws*. Director Arthur Hiller and co-star Alan Arkin had to convince a reticent Falk that the scene would work. He says he's thankful now that he capitulated.

Curiously, Falk isn't particularly enamored by his unique voice which is as much a signature as the trench coat he wears that has never seen the inside of a dry cleaners. "I never considered my voice part of my acting arsenal," he says. In fact, he believes his performances play much better when they are dubbed into foreign languages — especially French.

Whatever the combination, the voice allied to Falk's peculiar brand of American unpretentiousness caught the eye of director Frank Capra, who cast him in *A Pocketful of Miracles* (1961). The film, Capra's last feature, was not the critical or commercial success he had hoped it would be, but in his autobiography, *The Name Above the Title*, Capra gushed about Falk's performance.

"The entire production was agony ... except for Peter Falk," Capra wrote. "He was my joy, my anchor to reality. Introducing that remarkable talent to the techniques of comedy made me forget pains, tired blood, and maniacal hankerings to murder Glenn Ford (the film's star). Thank you Peter Falk."

For his part, Falk says that he never worked with a director who showed greater enjoyment of actors and the acting craft. "You could see his shoulders shaking with laughter when we nailed a scene," Falk says. "And there is nothing more important to an actor than to know that the one person who represents the audience to you, the director, is responding well to what you are trying to do.

"One time I remember we kept doing a scene after Frank had yelled, 'Cut and print.' I asked him why, and he laughed and said that he loved the scene so much, he just wanted to see us do it again. How's that for support!"

During another scene Falk says he learned a valuable object lesson from Capra about playing comedy.

"I had a scene where I was mad and had to rather dis-
tractedly put on my overcoat and leave a room. The scene
called for me to have trouble putting on the coat with the
idea of mining a few laughs out of it. We did several takes
but it never seemed to come off right. It looked too much
like I was faking having trouble putting on the coat. Frank
called for a five-minute break and during that time had some
crewmember sew shut one of the sleeves of the coat — unbe-
knownst to me. Well, when we did the scene again, I went
crazy trying to put the damn thing on. Frank's solution was
perfect and truth came to the scene. His films are filled with
moments like that. They are what you remember. After the
scene was over and I realized what Frank had done, I went
over and hugged him."

For Falk, art has always been in the details, and not just
in an astrological sense or as the lever that makes a scene
succeed in a movie. Until he was in his mid-20s he pursued a
career in public administration as an efficiency expert for the
Connecticut Budget Bureau. But he soon grew tired of bottom lines and balance sheets and became involved in amateur theatricals. In 1955, with the encouragement of Eva
LaGallienne, he turned professional and his performance in
the off-Broadway production of *The Iceman Cometh* led to
more work on Broadway, in television and films.

During the filming of *Castle Keep* with Burt Lancaster in
1969, Falk broadened his artistic horizons in an area that
seemed to take him by surprise. "I was holed up in this cell-
like hotel room after the day's shooting and I noticed an
Italian leather valise on the floor half hidden under my bed,"
Falk says. "I picked up a pencil and began to draw it. Instantly I became a compulsive sketcher."

Although Falk admits that a couple of years can go by
before he approaches an easel, his devotion to charcoal sketch-
ing (particularly nude figure studies) has been as constant in

his life as, well, the ratty trenchcoat Columbo wears and which currently hangs in Falk's upstairs bedroom. Falk has sold his work at galleries just twice, nine years ago and again about six months back. Prints of his nudes sell for about $400, he says.

"They command a certain price because Columbo drew them," he laughs. "If *you* drew them they wouldn't be worth shit!"

All things considered, Falk would prefer regular movie and *Columbo* work with ample time in between spent in his airy studio trying to fathom the confounding beauty of the human form. He shows us several sketches on buff-colored paper.

As a parting shot, we try to bait him out of his artistic languor with a question about what it was like to work with Frank Sinatra and the rest of the Rat Pack during their heyday in *Robin and the Seven Hoods*. "The whole swinger scene is very hip in a retro way now," we proclaim.

Falk stiffens us with a glassy stare as if perhaps we had spent too much time confined in our own castle keep somewhere and says, "I don't know or care about all that. I just like to draw."

Straight to the point. For Falk as for Columbo, bullshit comes in various advanced degrees. And on those occasions he's ready with that tiny pin!

THE LAST OF THE
GREAT ANCHORMEN
Ted Knight
August 1981

One of the uproarious quirks of the Ted Baxter character in *The Mary Tyler Moore Show* was his "gentleness with a buck." Ted's pathological stinginess was as reliable as WJM-TV's low ratings. After all, who but Ted Baxter would take his wife on a dinner date to a restaurant with drive-up service? And who but Ted would consult a personal tax attorney not yet out of law school?

It was with mild surprise then, that we declined an offer of financial assistance when we interviewed Ted Knight, who played Ted Baxter so convincingly for eight years on *The Mary Tyler Moore Show*. During our meeting in Los Angeles over lunch we let slip that we were anticipating some lean cuisine in order to make ends meet during our three-week stay.

"Reporters don't become wealthy working for the *Minnesota Daily*, just tired."

"You be sure to come to me if you get strapped for funds," Ted said.

Our steadfast refusal to endorse one of Knight's blank checks has haunted us to this day, because avaricious friends now consider us the worst kind of bubbleheads for not taking him up on his generous offer. One of the most unaffected celebrities we've ever met, Knight's has a carefree demeanor that might be traced, ironically, to the type of television roles he played early in his career.

"I played five lead Nazi parts in *Combat* and I got killed in all five episodes. If you spot me now in those old shows, you'll probably get a good laugh. I also portrayed a KAOS agent on *Get Smart*," Knight said. "I think you'll find historically that many actors who play sinister roles have unusually happy home lives."

Why was Knight typecast early on as a Hollywood heavy?

"When I came out here, the thinking that prevailed was a complete turnaround in terms of what criminals should look like," he said. "Instead of the pockmarked thugs with scowling faces, they wanted clean shaven, all-American types. Since I have Aryan features, I fitted the bill perfectly. I had one speech memorized in German that I recited at every casting call. Translated in English it said that I had a terrific headache and wanted to go to bed. But I acted it with such venom and anger, I got cast in a lot of heavy roles."

In a career that began in the first grade, Knight has worked as a ventriloquist, puppeteer, and narrator of documentaries and commercials and —in a weird foreshadowing — as a broadcast journalist.

"I fell off the couch playing Santa Claus in the first grade because I had forgotten my lines," he said. "I got such a big laugh, so I fell off the couch three more times and got bigger laughs and that's when I realized my future — the disease hit me. I'll probably wind up my career falling off couches as Santa Claus.

"Actually it all started for me in 1947 in Hartford at the Randall School of Fine Arts ... [morphs into the booming *basso profundo* Ted Baxter anchorman voice] ... in a small 500-watt radio station in Hartford, Connecticut. It wasn't easy in those days — you had to work hard and own a good suit with an unspeckled tie."

In case you're not an MTM trivia buff, that speech was Ted Baxter's opening statement at any banquet where he was fortunate enough to be nominated for an award.

"The character of Ted Baxter is entrenched in the lexicon of American entertainment," Knight said. "Baxterisms in word and deed can be readily identified in many characters on television today. I loved doing him."

And Knight is *still* doing him! At that moment, he joined in singing "Happy Birthday" to a crowd gathered at a nearby lunch table in the commissary, ending the song by rhythmically banging his soupspoon on the table. Knight then made an impossibly long lean over his salad bowl and stuck his beaming mug (with Pepsodent teeth so bright you'd think you were looking at a whitewashed house on the island of Crete) point-blank into the face of a pretty young starlet he thought was Deanna Lund.

"Would you like to become a nun," Knight said, leering, "because I'm feeling very priestly today? I want to hear your confession." [And then to us] "My wife knows I'm a flirt but that's as far as it goes. You can't cut me off completely."

The experience of performing on one of the few sitcoms — *The Mary Tyler Moore Show* — that is admired as a sterling example of near flawless writing and execution is not lost on Knight.

"Comedy is one area I've learned an awful lot about," Knight said. "Eight seasons on MTM has helped and hindered me because I now have such high standards where TV comedy is concerned. I cringe more than I should. The MTM writers were very good, but in retrospect you tend to glorify or flatter more than is necessary. A moment I'll never forget is that emotionally charged last show when everyone in the newsroom was fired but me. That caterpillar crawl over to the Kleenex box on Mary's desk. It was our last scene together after eight years of performing.

"The tears, everything, it was all genuine. We were all very close. It was a very rare moment. We knew as actors, characters and human beings that we were stepping out the door for the last time."

Too Close for Comfort, the only new series from any of the three networks last season that became a hit, is Knight's first bow as lead star.

"I have more responsibility as the top banana," he said. "I enjoy it more. There is no sibling rivalry and I don't have the agony of fighting for more lines or being upset when someone else has more lines. All actors experience that whether they admit it or not. Actor's paranoia is more intense when you're a supporting player. Paranoia develops into another area when you're a STAR — if you let it, that is. The aging process kind of mellows you out after a while so that you don't give a rat's ass. I've got money. I've got enough to keep me happy and my family solvent for the rest of my days. The success has kind of worn thin all the attendant glamorous aspects that you envision when you're young. It has a tendency to rust with time. It doesn't have the meaning it once had. It's still work, a job, a workplace, something I enjoy doing, the challenge of making something work that looks impossible.

"And I'll tell you another thing," Knight continued. "My co-star on the show, Nancy Dessault, is a brilliant comedienne who has yet to be discovered as such. She's got everything Lucille Ball ever had and she's a better singer. She's very inventive."

Knight feels the success of *Too Close for Comfort* is because of a retrenchment of traditional values in this country.

"The prevailing mood of the country is a swing to the conservative right," Knight said. "We try to exemplify the family cell structure in an accelerated society on our show. Mom and Pop trying to make it with the kids — not literally I mean! You know what I mean."

According to Knight, a capacity for hard work and a matter-of-fact receptiveness to sudden change are the main criteria for longevity on network television.

"You have to sweat blood to get a good product," he said. "If you go with the cheap shots, miss days, goof off, take dope, or just go with the original lines, then that will show. You have to have the integrity to really care about what you are doing."

Shooting from the Hip
Carroll O'Connor
May 1998

Carroll O'Connor is a contrarian — and that's a good thing.

During his heyday as Archie Bunker on *All in the Family,* O'Connor's roly-poly physique and impish smirk conjured images of a wiseacre; a wingless cherub complete with a halo of wispy white curls to cap it all off. It really was a long, lateral stretch from his role as television's most celebrated frothing bigot. And it's a credit to his acting prowess that all those years O'Connor was playing against type quite convincingly when he baited Jews, blacks, hippies or pretty much anyone who didn't conform to his narrow definition of what constituted the "right sort of person."

In reality, then as now, O'Connor abhors injustice or prejudice in any form. Discuss those topics with him and a pall of dark seriousness descends like a total eclipse of the sun; muscles become rigid, facial features taut, words emphatic. The cherub has winged it on outta there!

"I don't care anymore, I say what I believe," O'Connor says in a low matter-of-fact tone, without a trace of impudence. "We shy away from characterizing people as being bums, or whatever. It's too terrible a generalization in polite society."

After the roller-coaster ride of a long career in front of the cameras and the life-changing event of losing his son Hugh to drugs in 1995, it's as if O'Connor these days has galvanized into a survivor with a teflon coating who isn't shy about speaking his mind. Far from it, he's eager. Like his doppelganger, Archie Bunker, O'Connor still calls a spade a spade, however, this time he's arguing the right — color-blind — side of the equation.

We're visiting this day with O'Connor in the Spanish-style home that he shares with his wife of more than 40 years, Nancy Fields O'Connor. The house is charmingly situated on a picturebook little knoll near the UCLA campus in Bel-Air.

If we thought for an instant that O'Connor would enjoy downtime after the four-year run of his hit TV series, *In the Heat of Night*, we were mistaken. His autobiography, "I Think I'm Outta Here: A Memoir Of All My Families," was recently published by Pocket Books. In addition, he and his writing partner, Patrick Houlihan, have finished a screenplay called *The Long, Long Gallows* about a group of Irish mercenaries who fought on the Mexican side in the Mexican-American War. O'Connor also says he has a novel in the computer and is currently shooting a movie based on his son. So much for taking it easy!

"It's not at all hard to keep energized about my crusade against drugs because it's what I have to do," O'Connor says. "And there has been some forward momentum. I helped get anti-pusher laws enacted in about eight states. You can now sue pushers where you couldn't before."

In California, O'Connor's model bill was signed into law as the "Drug Dealer Liability Act," but in his estimation, it doesn't go quite far enough. "The next law I want to get on the books is a tax law that allows us, on probability cause, to investigate whether a known pusher has filed his tax return. I talked to Senator Orrin Hatch about it, but he was cautious. He thinks it might smack too much of Big Brother."

On the subject of movies, and even television, where he found enduring fame, O'Connor is circumspect. "On an artistic level, movies have been a total failure," he says. "They have the potential for being the most powerful performing art, but are, in fact, the weakest. Television isn't far behind. The only TV series that ever aspired to art was, I believe, *All In The Family*. We satirized American society and all its foibles. We opened a door, but nobody else came in!

"Archie was a totally new character on the scene and very funny and human," O'Connor continues. "For 13 years it was a great part to play. I've seen my (Archie's) chair in the Smithsonian Institution and it's great. But I'm incurably selfish. Now they have stuff from *The Jeffersons* ... Fonzie. It was a great honor when my chair was the only thing in there."

Although O'Connor admits that Archie Bunker is the greatest character he ever played, Sheriff Gillespie from *In the Heat of the Night* was, in his view, the best. "What I brought to Gillespie was a willingness and an unexpressed fervent desire to make up for a lot of bad racial mistakes," O'Connor says. "I tried to make him symbolic of the white South in his regretfulness. I also played him as a tough man, but a calm man who didn't tolerate bad language. He was a very moral guy and a gentleman at all times."

O'Connor's actorly instincts have been vindicated by the thousands of letters he's received, many from Southerners, lauding his characterization.

Thirteen years as Archie and several years as Gillespie have nothing on the long run O'Connor has shared with his wife, Nancy. They met in the late 1940s when he was attending the University of Montana at Missoula and have been together ever since.

"We're not superior people," O'Connor explains, making a stab at defining their chemistry, "we've just had better luck than most couples. We're pretty equally matched."

At that moment, Nancy enters the foyer and in a stage whisper intended for all to hear, tells us, "You want to know the real scoop on Carroll, just see me before you leave!"

Equally matched? To the contrary ...

A Real 'Starship Trooper'
William Shatner
2001

In the box-office hit, *Miss Congeniality* starring Sandra Bullock and Oscar-winner Michael Caine, William Shatner plays Stan Fields, an over-the-top beauty pageant host. (Sort of like Bert Parks on Ritalin.) *TV Guide,* in its assessment, said Shatner nearly stole the picture.

Everyone's favorite starship captain, however, begs to differ.

"There was no 'stealing' the picture or anything like that," Shatner said in a conversation from his Los Angeles home, but he did admit that he was given some freedom to improvise in the part. "It was a small role, but Don Petri, the director, was kind enough to let me wander and rummage around a bit. He gave me some freedom to work. But it was just such a pleasure to work with Sandra and Michael and enjoy their company. They are so wonderful. The pleasure of their company was extraordinary. I feel like I made some new friends with those people."

To baby boomers raised on '60s television, it might come as a surprise that their favorite starship trooper is now 70 years old. Yet, with the exception of a slight paunch, and nursing a damnably persistent cold, Shatner looks and feels fit enough to do battle again with the Gorn (a reptile-like alien nemesis from a *Star Trek* episode).

"I don't feel any age," he said. "I feel as strong and as passionate about everything as I did when I was a young man." As proof, he offered as evidence the warp speed schedule he has been on since the middle of last year. "I looked at my schedule last June and realized that I was making a major motion picture (*Miss Congeniality*), performing in a low-budget film in the desert *(Shoot or Be Shot)* and then launching into the even more daunting prospect of directing a film *(Groom Lake)*. I thought to myself, 'I hope I can physically do all this.' When it was all over, I ended up in better shape. The schedule was intimidating, but I had to prove to myself that I could do it."

In *Groom Lake*, a low-budget independent film scheduled for release later this year, Shatner takes on writing, directing and acting chores. No stranger to working behind the camera, Shatner directed several episodes of his hit television series, *T.J. Hooker* in the early '80s and then went on to direct the big budget box-office hit *Star Trek V: The Final Frontier* in 1989.

Not surprisingly, the story takes on science fiction aspects as a dying young woman seeks affirmation of life after death by going in search of a UFO. The movie was shot in 20 days, a light year's difference from the shooting schedule of a *Star Trek* feature, Shatner said.

"In *Groom Lake* we shot 10 pages of the script a day, or the equivalent of about 10 minutes. With *Star Trek V* we maybe completed two-thirds of a page a day. Any movie is stressful if you're the director, but with that stress comes a good deal of joy. I felt a great deal of exaltation during that 20-day shoot. We were all fueled by passion. I was willing to keep everybody running right to the end of the schedule. You don't have that necessity in a larger budget movie. There's plenty of backup built into the schedule. If you miss a day or two, it's written into the budget."

Shatner's nonstop work schedule came less than a year after his third wife, Nerine, accidentally drowned in the swimming pool of their Studio City, California, home. With a quivering voice, Shatner said, "Nerine was an alcoholic and died as a result of that accident." In tribute to her memory, Shatner worked tirelessly to raise funds and in January, dedicated the Nerine Shatner Friendly House in West Los Angeles. The Friendly House is a non-profit, private facility for women in need of help in overcoming drug or alcohol dependency.

Long before his involvement with the Friendly House, Shatner has used his passion for horses (he owns a horse farm in Kentucky) to raise more than $1 million for a variety of charitable causes dedicated to helping physically challenged children. A successful horse breeder and competitive rider, Shatner founded, more than a decade ago, the Hollywood Charity Horse Show at the Los Angeles Equestrian Center.

A Montreal, Canada, native, Shatner received a bachelor's degree in business from McGill University. Although the business he's in is called "show business," Shatner deprecatingly said as an actor he possesses little financial acumen. "It (the degree) hasn't helped me. What it's done is given me an arrogance that has led to one humiliating fall after another!"

But he might be just being modest. When Shatner signed a deal with online travel discounter Priceline to be its pitchman, he took stock options in lieu of salary and later cashed in his shares for millions when the stock was trading in the $90 per share range. Priceline, like so many other dotcoms, is now trading as a penny stock, its value virtually nil. Shatner's contract expires in October, and he said he has no knowledge of the company's future plans to use him. Priceline did, for the first time, begin airing ads this year not using the actor. About his enormous windfall, he said, "I just got lucky." As for his own investment advice, "People should ask me when I'm going to invest and then just sell!"

No conversation with Shatner would be complete without a few questions about Captain James T. Kirk, the character that put him on the map and sealed his lasting legacy as one of the seminal figures of episodic television. Like a good sport, Shatner handles the questions with aplomb.

"You wouldn't be talking to me if there wasn't a Captain Kirk," he said. "The point that we're even talking today is because I was on *Star Trek*. The wide things that opened up for me came as a result of that performance many years ago led me not to think in terms of 'I wished there never was a Captain Kirk.' I constantly pat myself and say, wasn't I lucky there was that character.' "

And with little prodding he admitted his favorite episode is "City on the Edge of Forever," with guest star Joan Collins — an episode in which he closes the show with a classic line, "Let's get the hell out of here."

We asked Shatner, a prolific science fiction author, if his interest in the genre was piqued after appearing in *Star Trek* and another classic '60s series, *The Twilight Zone*.

"If I recall, I was interested even before that," he said. "Sci-fi is an interesting literature niche. Part of the mystery of life is what happened before — why did the dinosaurs destruct? — and the other part of that is what's going to happen tomorrow. Since they've speculated on what happened to the dinosaurs, you can equally speculate on what's going to happen tomorrow or the day after."

With the success of *Miss Congeniality* and his appearances on the TV sitcom *Third Rock from the Sun*, Shatner, with his penchant for blustery performances, would seem a natural for comic character actor parts. He bristles at the thought, not wishing a return to the Captain Kirk typecasting days he worked so hard to exorcise.

"When I was working on Broadway I only did comedies," he said. "My whole background is comedy. But why push me in a hole? I'm an actor. If somebody has written a funny line, you act a funny line. If it's sad, you perform a sad line for the character. That's just part of my repertoire, my bag of tricks."

FESTERING

Jackie Coogan
August 1980

"Gomez, I'm so hungry I can eat a horse."
"Come, come Fester, you had one for lunch."
— *Jackie Coogan to John Astin from "The Addams Family,"* *1964*

In a show business career that has spanned more than 60 years, Jackie Coogan is best remembered for one role — Uncle Fester. It doesn't seem to matter that Coogan has worked in just about every entertainment medium including vaudeville, motion pictures, radio and the stage. For millions of people who have seen the television show *The Addams Family* in rerun syndication, Coogan will always be the bald, fat man in a fur coat who likes to ride a motorcycle through the house, sleeps on a bed of nails, puts his head in a metal vice, plays with dynamite caps, and illuminates light bulbs in his mouth.

We met Coogan without fanfare at the Trancas Restaurant in Malibu Canyon. And no, we didn't eat eye of newt, eels, or fillet of lizard. Coogan ordered a ham, cheese and mushroom omelet with potatoes and an ice tea. After the waitress had taken our order, Coogan leered, "I'd like to rent her ass as a neon sign." No doubt about it, Fester had an acid wit. Pass the Prevacid.

Although we were steps from the ocean, it was hot out. Coogan was dressed in a Hawaiian print shirt, had a few localized strands of long hair falling haphazardly from his bald head and enunciated in a high-pitched squawk through a zeppelin-sized red nose that looked as if it had recently seen service as a Doberman's chew toy.

Coogan was born Oct. 26, 1914, in Los Angeles. Both of his parents traveled throughout the country in vaudeville and during his first few years, Coogan stayed with his grandmother in San Francisco or his other grandmother in Syracuse, New York. "I guess that's where I learned to hate snow," he said. His earliest recollection of performing was in 1918.

"I became part of the act. We only made it look like a surprise. I was a four-year-old kid. I could do imitations, dance and sing. Of course, there weren't many of those types back then and there still aren't."

Besides Coogan's three-year stint on *The Addams Family*, his most noteworthy show business accomplishment was his career as a child actor in silent pictures. His most famous role came in 1920 when he played an orphan who tugged mightily on Charlie Chaplin's paternal heartstrings in *The Kid*.

It was while Coogan was performing with his father, Jack Coogan, at the Los Angeles Orpheum Theater, that Chaplin first got a glimpse of his new co-star.

"About 90 percent of the people in motion pictures came from vaudeville," said Coogan. "Every Thursday night at the Orpheum was like old home week. The film actors would come to the theater to see their friends from vaudeville — to shoot the shit and bring themselves up to date with the latest dirt. Chaplin liked what he saw and signed me to a contract at the magnificent sum of $75 a week."

The Kid proved to be a milestone for Chaplin. It was his first film that was not total slapstick, and he proved that pathos could sell. Jerry Lewis, Red Skelton and Jackie Gleason would all go on to interject pathos into their films, with varying degrees of success.

Coogan recalled how difficult it was for Chaplin to get

the film made.

"He had a deal with First National to produce and direct a picture of his choosing. When these backers found out what he had in mind, they blew up. They thought he was crazy for wanting to make a drama. But Chaplin had an ironclad contract and got his way.

"We never worked from any kind of script," Coogan added. "So consequently he would sit and think. We wouldn't turn a camera on sometimes for two weeks. When he came up with an idea he would put it together. You were never conscious of his direction. He showed me what to do and I did it. I can't remember him ever losing his temper. He was so far and above what we know today. Who have we got now, Chevy Chase, who can't even fall funny?"

A year and three days later the picture was completed at a cost of almost $500,000, which was a fortune in 1920. The film opened to rave reviews and huge box office grosses. And Coogan was an overnight child sensation.

After *The Kid,* Coogan went on to make 29 silent films including the silent classics, *Tom Sawyer, Oliver Twist* and *Peck's Bad Boy.* Careerwise, things went well for Coogan until 1938 when he was involved in a bitter lawsuit with his mother over the money he had amassed as a child performer. The law that resulted was dubbed the "Coogan Law" and has since protected the earnings of minors. The repercussions from the highly publicized trial were severe for Coogan; he was blacklisted by movie producers all over Hollywood.

His career as an actor during the next 25 years was anything but distinguished. It was not until 1964 that his fortunes changed. Coogan auditioned for the television show that would make him, if nothing else, a household oddity — *The Addams Family.*

"I had read Charles Addams cartoons and really enjoyed them," he said. "So when I read they were going to do a show, I told my agent I wanted to try out. He didn't want me to because when you do something weird like that it tends to typecast you for life. But I knew exactly what I wanted to do. I shaved my head and made the test using the high voice. The show lasted three years on ABC. All they had to do was go in color with that impressive set and the show would have stayed on longer."

The only thing Coogan didn't like about the show was that he felt the character of Gomez as played by John Astin was a copy of Groucho Marx. To us, Coogan's comment seemed like a case of the pot calling the kettle black since the character of Fester was a direct ripoff of Curly Howard of Three Stooges fame.

We were utterly relieved, however, when Coogan told us that he still has his Fester fur-lined coat. Next stop Smithsonian ...

Since the cancellation of *The Addams Family,* Coogan has managed to pick up character roles in television and films. He also does voiceovers for commercial products such as Creepy Crawlers.

In assessing his life today, Coogan said, "I have very few friends. I've always kept apart from the establishment. I've always been a loner. The only people I still see are my old nightclub and vaudeville partner, Jimmy Cross, and Gabe Dell, who was one of the Bowery Boys."

The conversation then took a fatal header when Coogan (apparently tired of talking about silent movies and his status as a TV icon) launched into a self-serving panegyric about his World War II experiences in Burma. It was an endless tale of midnight parachute drops and all-out heroics that made Audie Murphy, by comparison, seem like a rear-echelon loafer. It was almost as if Coogan was trying to put some Svengali-like spin on how we handled his story by trying to minimize our embedded perception of him as a pot-bellied guy in a long black coat who had dark circles under his eyes and who never left the Addams house. Fat chance, but we listened to his ramble anyway.

Two hours and six ice teas later, Coogan was almost done pontificating. "You know the good thing now is that I'm in a financial position where I never have to work again if I don't want to," he told us. On that note, he handed us the luncheon tab and traipsed out of the joint. "Coogan's Law" or not, he wasn't taking any chances.

We were left with a creepy, kooky, altogether ooky feeling, but we didn't have the heart to accost Coogan out in the parking lot where he was having trouble backing out from a tight space. That said, for a brief moment, we felt like calling in some paratroopers of our own for retribution, but we let the moment pass. Where's Lurch when you need him!

Taking a Bite Out of Crime
Robert Stack
March 1994

Robert Stack has made a life of crime really pay off.

As host of *Unsolved Mysteries,* the viewer call-in show that fingers fugitives from justice, Stack says it's a nice change to positively affect the outcomes of many real-life instead of reel-life dramas.

"*Unsolved Mysteries* has helped police apprehend more than 40 percent of the fugitives profiled on the series since it premiered in 1987," he told us recently over Cokes and iced teas at Jan's, a nondescript diner in West Hollywood. Fit, trim and surprisingly garrulous considering his taciturn television and movie demeanor, Stack wore a blue and gray warm-up jacket and appeared about a decade younger than his 78 years.

As one of television's first interactive series, *Unsolved Mysteries* has picked up six Emmy nominations as Best Informational Series. By calling the show's toll-free number, viewers aid law enforcement officials in capturing criminals.

To date, Stack has walked the beat in four other major

television series that have dealt, in one way or another, with the criminal element. Starting in 1959 with his Emmy award-winning role as Eliot Ness in the Prohibition-era series *The Untouchables,* Stack went on to portray the editor of *Crime* magazine in *The Name of the Game,* followed by roles on the police action shows *Most Wanted* and *Strike Force.*

"It's truly a heady thing when you realize that millions of people tune in each week to get what amounts to the latest police blotter report," Stack says referring to *Unsolved Mysteries.* "But the show really isn't about acting; it's about making the little moments work on a special level." Making those little moments work has been Stack's stock-in-trade since he began his show business career in the 1942 Jack Benny comedy, *To Be or Not to Be.*

"I approached the acting profession in a totally different way than most actors — almost offhandedly," he says, his voice shifting to a lower register. "You see, I had already succeeded in other areas of my life," he modestly whispers to us across the table.

Stack's self-effacing charm is rare in Hollywood, particularly when his youthful exploits would make prime fodder for a TV movie-of-the-week. At age 16, he was a national skeet-shooting champion, and in college at USC he rode polo ponies, that is, when he wasn't racing speedboats.

Stack is a fifth-generation Californian whose ancestors were among the first U.S. families to settle in the dusty little pueblo that became Los Angeles. Stack's great grandfather was a prominent figure in the early Los Angeles social scene and owned the area's first opera house. His father was an advertising executive who worked on the Schlitz beer account and coined the slogan, "The beer that made Milwaukee famous."

"My father considered the advertising business like show business," he says. "That's why he made my brother and I promise that we would never go into acting. It was only after he passed away and some bills came due that I decided to defy my father's wishes and become an actor.

"I took a different approach to this profession because of my upbringing and exposure to theatrical people," Stack adds. "We had stars at our house all the time, but I just knew these guys as people I could beat at athletics."

Despite growing up with Clark Gable as "practically a surrogate father," Stack says he never planned a career in front of the cameras until financial necessity made it a viable option.

Stack's first professional acting job was in the 1939 film, *First Love,* opposite screen sweetheart Deanna Durbin. After serving in the Navy during World War II as an aerial gunnery instructor, Stack returned to Hollywood to star in a clutch of popular movies, including *Fighter Squadron, The Bullfighter and the Lady, The High and the Mighty* and *House of Bamboo.* His film career reached its apogee in 1957 when he picked up a Best Supporting Actor Academy Award nomination playing a playboy millionaire in the classic melodrama *Written on the Wind.*

"I never got another part like that," he says. "As for not winning the Oscar, Jimmy Stewart once said, 'You never win the one you should. I should have won for *Mr. Smith Goes To Washington.* But I won it for something else.'"

Classically upbeat and forward thinking, Stack, a longtime resident of the exclusive Los Angeles-area celebrity enclave, Bel Air, has been married for 30 years to Rosemarie. They have two grown children, Elizabeth and Charles.

With both feet firmly planted on the ground, Stack recalls the following sage advice:

"I remember what the great acting teacher Stella Adler once said, 'I feel sorry for my gifted ones who were never given the chance to show their gift.' I've never felt that. I've always felt that I was an all-American," Stack says.

Throughout his life Stack has been blessed by profound good fortune, and that lucky aura may help define his insouciant attitude toward his craft. "Acting is like kindergarten recess time," he summed up, "it is fun when it's done right."

That philosophy underscored Stack's work in the hit comedy spoof *Airplane*. "The film's producer's, the Zucker brothers, were gifted but certifiably insane," he said. "During the course of the movie they managed to insult every minority group and no one got mad — God bless them!"

Religious and racial epithets notwithstanding, the movie introduced Stack to an audience that wasn't even born when he was busting the rackets as Eliot Ness. "I came off a golf hole once and ran into a goofy, semi-drunk bunch of college guys who recognized me and then began to spout my lines from the movie — weird!"

However, it is as Eliot Ness, special agent of the FBI, that Stack really hit his stride as a television actor. Although the show ran for four seasons on ABC, it started out as a two-part special.

"I had a lot of friends tell me, don't do a television series, you're a film actor. It will kill you. After a sleepless night, I went to the producer, Desi Arnaz, and asked him, 'What are you going to do with this show because I'm scared?' Desi replied, 'We're going to make the best damn series on television.' I was scared to death about making the transition from film into a weekly series."

Stack's fears proved to be unfounded. His portrayal of the crusty, no-nonsense agent who nailed Al Capone even won the seal of approval from Ness' widow.

"I got a letter from Mrs. Ness when the series aired that I've never published," Stack says. "It went like this: 'Dear Mr. Stack, I was afraid of a television series about my husband. I loved him very much and am very protective of him. But I'm happy to say the show is decent and good. In particular, I was worried about your interpretation of my husband. I don't know how you did it, maybe by osmosis, but you have picked up several of his characteristics that are quite striking. You are very much like him in attitude.'"

Stack says that he based his character on the fact that

Ness was brave and "put his money where his mouth was."
In fact, his inspiration for the character was Audie Murphy
— the most decorated American soldier of World War II.

"When the movie version of *The Untouchables* came out
in 1987 with Kevin Costner, Paramount wanted Kevin and
me to pose for pictures, but I refused," Stack said. "I felt it
was Kevin's movie ... my TV series."

Which brings us back full circle to *Unsolved Mysteries,* a
show that almost did not include Robert Stack.

"I came in as a replacement for Karl Malden," he says.
"You learn to base your decision-making on who's invited to
the party. The audience adopts you and allows you into their
house. If they push that button, you're gone. It's fulfilling for
me to go out, play a tennis tournament and have people yell
that they love the show. That's what it's all about."

"Nerd" is the Word
Henry Winkler
August 1981

Thanks to Henry Winkler, the word "nerd" is now part
of the American vernacular. Although, lately, the term has
gone the way of "groovy" and "far-out," it is still used as a
flip insult by his always cool Fonzie character on ABC's *Happy
Days.* Winkler offered his own definition.

"A nerd is not necessarily a square," he said, "because there
are some very lovely squares. I think the word has two parts.
First, it is someone who doesn't take responsibility for his or
her life. And second, it is someone who doesn't understand
that we're all the same and that we're all in this together.
People who think they are superior are nerds and they should
literally be thrown into a fire."

Winkler's observations came during an interview at his
production company office on the Paramount Studio lot.

If there is any one star in Hollywood who can tell you

what it's like to be at the top, it's Winkler, who's played the leather-jacketed tough for the last nine years. During the mid-'70s, America was literally "Fonzie Crazy." Winkler's Warholian 15 minutes of fame has since been usurped by Bo Derek, Morgan Fairchild and even *Magnum P.I.*'s Tom Selleck. (On second thought, make that about five minutes for Selleck.) Despite Winkler's waning notoriety, he retains his stance as the cool guy with the big heart on *Happy Days.* Winkler commented on the pros and cons of being at the popularity pinnacle, a position he admits he has lost.

"The greatest thing about it is that I really enjoy being a celebrity. I can't even begin to tell you about all the great things. Earning a living. Being able to live out a dream. Meeting people that I'd never met before but had seen all my life. Having dinner with James Stewart. The only thing bad has been the occasional invasion of privacy — like people jumping over my fence and ringing the doorbell at midnight," he said. "Another bad aspect is that you can't make too many mistakes in our business since it's all based on the dollar. So you can't experiment a lot like you can in Europe. You're only as good as the last thing you've done."

For a while it seemed that Winkler would be terminally typecast as a Fonzie-like character. However he has starred in some movies — he played a Vietnam vet in *Heroes* and a wrestler in *The One and Only.* Both proved that Winkler could shed his leather jacket, but he has yet to establish himself as a box office draw or a critics' favorite. Indeed, he went ballistic upon mention of the word "critic."

"Well, critics, they're really interesting, aren't they? There was a guy in Texas who wrote about *The One and Only.* He said, 'After a half hour in the theater, I didn't know whether I wanted to put a bullet through Winkler's head or run out of the theater.' So I called him at three in the morning and said, 'Sir, you asshole, you're reviewing celluloid. You're reviewing entertainment. Why are you writing "put a bullet through my head?"' But you learn to live with such things. You get thick-skinned," he said.

After struggling as a stage actor in New York, Winkler relocated to Hollywood in 1973. He gave himself one month to find a job. Within two weeks he landed a memorable guest spot on *The Mary Tyler Moore Show*. By the end of the month he was offered the role in *Happy Days*.

"I threw caution to the wind and accepted the part," he said. It turned out to be a wise career move, for nine years later the show is still pulling in respectable Nielsen ratings. Winkler takes 90 percent of the credit for developing the Fonzie character.

"It comes out of your own imagination," he said. "What if I was actually in love with a motorcycle? Personally, I like four rubber wheels surrounded by steel. But I like to think that Fonzie has some of the same qualities that I have. He cares for his friends. He stands up for what he believes in. You see, everything that he is based upon is in all of us. He has the heart with the tough guy façade."

Winkler does indeed practice what he preaches and does not hesitate to criticize the medium that has made him a millionaire many times over.

"I think television in general needs to be more real," he explained. "Now I don't mean that it should not entertain or take you away from the stuff that is making you crazy in real life. But children watch television and they want to emulate certain characters. Then they look at real life and try to see where the two gel and, of course, they don't. I also think that television is disrespectful to children. There are 62 million children in America and television talks down to every one of them."

Winkler strongly feels that television viewing should be selected and limited by children's parents. His own 10-year-old son is only allowed to watch one hour a day and absolutely no viewing before school in the morning.

"Watching *Happy Days* is, of course, mandatory," he said.

Does Winkler have his future career plans mapped out?

"No, the only thing I make sure is that I wash every day. I know that there is no planning. I just hope to be a real good, clean father and I would continually like to make good things as an actor, producer, or director."

Stage work is also a possibility. Winkler has been offered the role of Jimmy Durante in a Broadway musical of the comedian's life, and he is seriously considering accepting. New Yorkers soon may be able to see the versatile Winkler once again shedding his leathers to sing "Inka Dinka Doo."

VII.
Shoot to Thrill

Comedy in a Different Vein
Mel Brooks
October 1995

Mel Brooks never met a film genre he didn't like … to
satirize, that is.

From Westerns *(Blazing Saddles)* to suspense films *(High
Anxiety)* to science fiction *(Space Balls)*, his movie spoofs rank
as light-hearted and loving tributes to some of the most defining moments in American pop culture. Although his ef-
forts have met with varying degrees of box-office success, the
real litmus test of a comedy's true worth in Brooks' view has
never varied — immoderate laughter.

"A comedy is successful when people are laughing, even
smiling," he said during a recent interview in his suite of
offices at the Culver Studios in Los Angeles. "The big test, of
course, is how many times they laugh; how often they laugh;
and do they get up and walk out. Even if they walk out, do
they walk out to the concession stand for popcorn or do they
keep going to the parking lot? Those are the barometers."

At 69, with a thick skullcap of gray hair and his impish
grin and raspy voice intact, Brooks is indefatigable. When
not nervously pacing around (for the interview, he was seated
behind an oversize executive desk that wouldn't have looked
out of place on the set of *How to Succeed in Business Without
Really Trying),* his wordplay darts about, seeming to ping off
the walls — so he doesn't have to. To our view, Brooks is a
living testament to the advice that laughter is indeed the best
medicine.

"I've always been a Brooklyn iconoclast," he said. "I saw
the world as too serious a place even when I was three or
four. I knew there should be more fun. Everybody was working too hard, taking life too seriously."

Brooks' antidote to the often-stultifying reality of life in a New York borough, was humor, especially parody. It led him from Borscht Belt club dates in the Catskills to a job writing TV sketches for Sid Caesar on the venerated *Your Show of Shows,* and later to work as co-creator with Buck Henry of *Get Smart* — one of television's funniest half hours and now a staple of *Nick At Nite.*

After winning a Best Screenplay Oscar in 1968 for his first feature film, *The Producers,* Brooks sank down permanent roots in the Hollywood film colony. Almost 30 years later, he's still pitching and producing. His latest directorial effort, *Dracula: Dead and Loving It,* stars Leslie Nielsen as an inept Prince of Darkness with two left fangs. Brooks co-stars as Dr. Van Helsing, Dracula's storied nemesis.

To prep himself for work on the film, Brooks "chain-watched" dozens of horror classics including *M* with Peter Lorre, and the original 1922 German silent version of Bram Stoker's classic Dracula novel, *Nosferatu,* starring the ghoulish Max Shreck.

"I watched them all so I would get good moody backgrounds for the comedy to bounce against," Brooks said.

Although Brooks underscores the fact that his depiction of the novel (Dracula has been filmed 160 times) is true to its Victorian time frame and to the major plotted events, the action admittedly strays into the environs of slap-shtick.

"I told the writers that we better make damn sure we get all the references, but also hedge our bets with physical comedy," he said. "That way, if the references fail, audiences will respond to the fall."

As an example, Brooks laid out for us the first scene of the movie. "At first you see Leslie as Dracula at the top of the staircase," he said. "A bat has just attacked his assistant Renfield. The bat swoops away, EEEE! EEEE! It flies past Leslie who exclaims, 'Children of the night!' — a famous line from the Lugosi version — but Leslie adds, 'What a mess they make!' The camera pans down the staircase and we see bat droppings. Then as a topper, Leslie slips on the stuff and comes tumbling down the stairs."

According to Brooks, Nielsen was the first choice to play Dracula but only if he could affect a Bela Lugosi accent. It was a make-or-break proviso. "I called up Leslie's agent and said it's not about money, it's about the accent. If he can't do it, I can't offer him the part," Brooks said. "About a half-hour later, I got a call, 'Hello, who am I speaking to?' the guy says. It was Leslie doing the best damn Lugosi impersonation you ever heard!"

Brooks has high hopes for the movie, and he bases that enthusiasm on interviews he's conducted with hardcore horror aficionados; readers of magazines like *Fangoria* and *Cinefantastique*. "We wanted to make sure that those guys would start the avalanche, the first push into the theaters," he said. "A faithful, satiric rendition is important to them. I know the words are oxymoronic — faithful spoof — but this movie is just like *Young Frankenstein*. I didn't use any zooms or camera tricks."

The only compromise Brooks admits making in the film is that if a line he didn't like elicited a big laugh, he kept it in anyway. "On the other hand," he said, "I will leave a line or piece of business in that doesn't get a big laugh, but maybe only a chuckle. I know that down the road, when the movie is on video and somebody is watching it for the fifth or sixth time, they're going to get the joke."

Brooks can afford to think about the big picture of his film legacy, after all, he's been working consistently for nearly three decades in a town where many directors don't survive long enough to make three pictures.

"I'm still in good standing as far as audiences and the studios are concerned," Brooks said. "Without bragging, I have no problem commandeering anything under a $50 million budget to make movies."

Such megabucks are a far cry from the relative pennies it took to make his two favorite movies, *The Producers* and *Young Frankenstein*. "They were my most personal films," he said.

"*The Producers* was born strictly out of my brain and out of my heart. And when Gene Wilder and I wrote *Young Frankenstein,* we never thought it would be successful. We were able to sculpt it entirely our way."

Brooks said that David Geffen has approached him with the idea of turning *The Producers* into a Broadway musical. "He could do it. He has more money than God — I've compared both of their bank statements!"

Plans for the future are "vapor that hasn't yet coalesced," according to Brooks. However, one of his New Year's resolutions is to see more of his wife of 31 years, the actress Anne Bancroft. "She's just been in two big films, *How to Make an American Quilt* and *Home for the Holidays,*" he said. "Anne and I wave from passing planes and send a lot of faxes."

If *Dracula: Dead and Loving It* successfully takes wing, it's a certainty Brooks will sink his teeth into another satire coming soon to a theater near you.

The Great Minneapolis Kidnap Caper
Frank Capra
January 1981

We weren't taking any chances.

Uppermost in our minds was the gloomy pall that descended when another great director, William Wyler, died the day before we were scheduled to meet him. The only thing that could keep us from interviewing Frank Capra was if *we* dropped dead. And that wasn't gonna happen. Although, come to think of it, Minnesota was in the throes of a particularly nasty winter with engine blocks freezing in cars all over town and then crashing through their chassis to the icy roadways underneath. Better check the anti-freeze. Did we mention we weren't taking any chances?

Despite the inclement weather, the Minneapolis Film Festival was going full bore with its slate of screenings and seminars. Capra, who had flown in from his home in Palm Springs, California, was the honored guest and celebrity fulcrum around which many of the festivities spun. It was quite a casting coup for the festival organizers and they were milking it for all it was worth, guiding the diminutive director to and fro, albeit willingly, like a beagle on a leash.

Attempting to keep the lid clamped on our maverick tendencies, we tried negotiating through official channels with the frazzled talent coordinator to arrange some time with Capra and were strung along with vague, cheery promises that we'd get "a few minutes sometime ... somewhere."

About midway through the festival, we realized that those minutes were not going to materialize unless we took a preposterous step. We decided to sort of kidnap Capra.

After some checking, we found out that the director was billeted at the Sheraton Ritz Hotel in Minneapolis. We drove downtown, inquired at the front desk and were told outright (without even a trace of suspicion) Capra's room number. In the morning crush of activity with guests checking in and checking out, we guessed that the staff was clueless about Capra's fame as one of Hollywood's great directors and, therefore, didn't have their proprietary antennae up.

We promptly hiked it on up to his floor and knocked on the door. It was around 9 a.m. We didn't hear anything so we knocked again. We repeated this process a couple more times, along with some furtive salutations whispered into the tiny security peephole in the door (as if sound could penetrate the miniscule glass eyepiece), but we got no response — just dead silence.

We started to get worried; Capra after all was in his 80s, and William Wyler's demise was still fresh in our memory banks. So we returned to the front desk and told a hotel manager our concern. He promptly dispatched a worker with a set of keys to accompany us back to Capra's room.

This time there was no knocking as the hotel guy inserted the key and opened the door. We scanned the room and there was no sign of Capra. At about that instant we heard the shower and saw steam coming from underneath the bathroom door. If we had moved as quick as the hotel guy — whose heightened sense no doubt told him to beat a hasty retreat down the hall or risk losing his job — we'd have been home free. But we didn't move fast enough.

Capra (who had heard us enter his room) flung open the door and let loose a stream of invective that would have made Redd Foxx blush. "I was in the fucking shower!" he screamed in a high-pitched voice that sounded like a party balloon, pinched at the nozzle, being deflated. His eyes were fixed and dilated now with more steam pouring out of his ears than from the superheated showerhead. He had a hotel towel hitched around his hips and would have used it as a weapon if his vitriolic rant wasn't already doing a thorough job. "God damn it, get the hell out!" he yelled, white flecks of saliva visible on his lips and chin.

We muttered some half-assed apology and then had the cheek to say we'd wait for him downstairs in the lobby. It was the longest, most abashed half-hour of our lives.

In a film career that spanned four decades and garnered three Academy Awards, Capra provided the American moviegoing public with a style of screen entertainment that was not only grand, but uniquely his. Capra's direct legacy to film was his vision of the triumph of homegrown virtue and morality against all odds.

This ideal found an effective showcase in the cinematic portraits he created for many of his leading men. The Mandrake Falls Vermonter who becomes heir to a large fortune but gives it away free as parceled farm acreage to the unemployed of the Depression; the U.S. Senator who refuses to be corrupted by his fellow politicians in Washington and stands up for his beliefs in front of Congress; the small-town savings and loan banker whose unbending faith in the inherent goodness of humanity enable him to face and defeat crisis after crisis — all are characters he created for such immortal films as *Mr. Deeds Goes To Town, Mr. Smith Goes to Washington* and *It's a Wonderful Life.*

Capra began his career in 1922 as a propman, film cutter, and gagman for the Hal Roach Studios (Laurel and Hardy's alma mater), but later graduated to scriptwriting status while working for Mack Sennett. It was there that he played an instrumental part in forming the comedic style of silent screen star Harry Langdon, a pantomimist many pundits rank as just one notch below Chaplin and Keaton. It is in Langdon's persona of the oppressed underdog that one first discerns the seed that was to germinate fullblown into the character roles of Capra's greatest successes in the 1930s and '40s.

These characters — Mr. Deeds, Mr. Smith, George Bailey of *It's a Wonderful Life* and the rest — were often disparaged by the critics of the time for what was called their "unceasing morality and dedication to virtuous causes." Such characters, critics believed, only existed in folklore and legend. Nevertheless they symbolized the traditional American dream of an idealistic lone eagle that never compromises his beliefs or what he knows to be true. They mirrored closely those rugged individualists of our pioneer past. And in a world being torn apart by the deceit and aggression that was a prelude to World War II, it was a comfort to know that such people existed — even if it was only for a few minutes in a Frank Capra production.

In a few minutes, Capra (dressed more for a shotgun start on Palm Springs' golf links than for a sub-zero Minnesota winter's day) appeared in the lobby. He was minus any kind of wool or downfilled outer layer and was wearing an off-white blazer tailored from a synthetic fabric that probably "breathed" well enough in the desert but would be a miserable breakwater for the cold gusts of wind we'd likely encounter outside (if we ever made it that far.)

We could tell Capra was still upset, but, to his eternal credit, he decided to move past our breaking and entering episode.

"I do about six film festivals a year, and I think I'll have to cut down," he said. "I never get to see any of the cities I visit because I am programmed into doing interviews or seeing films from dawn to dusk. The only time I do get out its usually to some festival coordinator's house."

Jumping at this slight overture to make amends, we offered to squire Capra around on a select tour of the Twin Cities. He told us he wanted very much to see "Mark Twain's river — the Mississippi" and to attend Sunday church services.

We drove to the Cathedral of St. Paul and sidled into a pew (Capra skipped confession rightly figuring that we deserved his early-morning verbal torrent). After services, the recessional hymn was "My Country Tis of Thee." It was a tribute to the American hostages that had just been released from captivity in Iran. Capra sang all the verses from memory without once looking in the hymnal.

After church, we drove Capra around the Summit Hill area just up the incline from the cathedral. We cruised slowly past the governor's mansion, the old Commodore Hotel and F. Scott Fitzgerald's home where the Jazz Age author had completed his first successful novel, *This Side of Paradise*. We discussed the sad fact (in retrospect) that Fitzgerald — along with an army of other talented writers — seemed to have sold out to the sunshine and easy money that Hollywood offered in the late '30s and '40s. Ernest Hemingway was one of the few literary titans of that era who seemed to hold his ground.

"I'll tell you an interesting story about Hemingway that you won't believe," Capra piped up from the backseat. "I wouldn't have believed it myself, but the man who told it to me was Spencer Tracy.

"Spence was filming Hemingway's short story *The Old Man and the Sea* down in the Caribbean when Hemingway invited him in for a drink in a little cantina. They were getting along well when suddenly, for no reason at all,

Hemingway got up, turned around, and slammed his fist into the face of a waiter carrying a tray of food. The waiter went sliding across the floor as Hemingway sat down and continued the conversation as if nothing had happened. Spencer was in a state of shock and asked why he had done that. Hemingway said that he hit one of them every day just to show them who was boss. Spence said, 'Would you like to try that on me?' Hemingway told him that he didn't hit any of his friends, whereupon Spence said, 'I'm no friend,' and got up and left."

We were speechless. It's a good thing Capra wasn't. He continued: "I feel the true aim of any artist is to unify the world through his art, not divide it. I am like a lawyer or doctor. Through the medium of film and my particular work, I try to lobby for all of mankind."

Most of all, Capra wanted to see the Mississippi River. We knew a traverse through the St. Paul neighborhood of Highland Park (where we both grew up) that would take us over the river and afford a nice panoramic view of Fort Snelling. From the bluffs, Capra studied intently the swirls and eddies of the "Big Muddy" as it flowed south of the old, restored 1820s Army outpost and into a confluence with the nearby Minnesota River.

"This is the crux of Twain," Capra said delightedly. "He was a great writer and a great man."

Figuring we couldn't possibly top what Abraham Lincoln once called "The Father of Waters" with any other Twin City hotspot, we drove Capra back to the Sheraton-Ritz and deposited him curbside. "Hey guys, I'm hungry. Do you wanna eat?" he asked before shutting the car door. We reasoned that our unconscionable transgression of kidnapping Capra and obliterating his schedule couldn't possibly be mitigated by any halfhearted show of restraint at this late date, so we accepted his invitation. We all sat down to lunch in the hotel's Cheshire Cheese Restaurant where we discussed Capra's directorial heyday during Hollywood's Golden Era.

Reel to Real: In your autobiography, *The Name Above the Title,* you wrote about many innovations that you devised to improve techniques in filmmaking. Is the teleprompter that we see on modern television cameras your invention?

Capra: Well, it was the first time I ever heard of anybody doing it. I built a primitive model using wire between two spools, in which the cuecards could be rotated. I then placed this on top of the movie camera. I did this for some of General Marshall's speeches during the war.

Incidentally, I put a humorous switch on that idea in *It's A Wonderful Life.* During that scene where Jimmy Stewart and Donna Reed are living in that old dilapidated house without a cooking stove, they use a moving phonograph turntable and a thread spool to slowly roast a chicken over the fireplace.

Reel to Real: An attractive aspect of your film work has always been the attention paid to the minutist details. In *Lost Horizon,* during the scenes in the Himalayan Mountains, the frosty breath of Ronald Colman and the rest of the cast is clearly visible. This is a realistic effect we have seldom seen in movies of the 1930s and '40s that were filmed on backlots.

Capra: The reason you could see the actor's breath was that we shot those winter scenes in an icehouse, with decorated backdrops painted to resemble snowy mountains. Previously I had tried putting little chicken-wire cages of dried ice in the performers' mouths. But as you might imagine the clarity of their dialogue suffered terribly, and I discarded the idea.

Reel to Real: Did Harry Cohn, production boss at Columbia Studios, give you complete autonomy with regard to what film you could direct and which stars would appear in them?

Capra: Yes, he did. Harry Cohn was every kind of a so-and-so, but he was awfully smart. He trusted his talent. If he had confidence in someone, then that person would have complete control. But if anyone under contract ever gave in to him in an argument, then that person was fired. Cohn didn't know how to write or direct a film, so he didn't want his directors saying, "How do you want this Mr. Cohn?" He would say, "What the hell do I know about it!" He trusted people who had confidence in themselves, and who could stand up to his bullying.

Reel to Real: What was the difference when you were under contract to Paramount?

Capra: They dictated absolutely what films I could and couldn't direct. Much of the time this was based on projected production costs. If I presented them with an idea that looked too expensive they would veto it immediately. The only reason I was able to direct the two Bing Crosby pictures, *Riding High* and *Here Comes the Groom,* was that I guaranteed Paramount that I could shoot them for less than one million dollars, which was under their projected budget.

Reel to Real: When you filmed the two Crosby movies, did you record the songs and dialogue live on the set, or did you use playback machines and record them in a soundproof booth somewhere else on the Paramount lot?

Capra: I recorded everything directly on the set. The music department at Paramount raised hell about this; they wanted to take the actors into a beautiful music stage, put them around a microphone, and after hours of rehearsal, record the songs onto a vocal track. A monumental dubbing job I thought unnecessary. I said, "This is ridiculous. Why don't we shoot the songs live on the set?" The music department replied, "The acoustics are bad; we can't." I countered with, "Well, I don't want anyone directing my actors." We were at an impasse.

Reel to Real: Was this situation ever resolved?

Capra: Yes, we arrived at a compromise. In order to placate the music department and yet have full control over my actors, I rigged up a recording system of my own which we used for Jane Wyman's singing of "In The Cool Cool Cool of the Evening" from *Here Comes The Groom.* We shot this scene live on the set. But in order for Jane to hear the orchestra, which was on a separate soundstage at the other end of Paramount Studios, I used two tiny sound wires that we strung along the ground from the orchestra stage, across the lot, to our location. On the ends of the wires were two ear inserts that acted as a kind of miniature headphone set. Jane was then able to hear the orchestra music and sing the song live as we filmed. That song, "In the Cool Cool Cool of the Evening" won the Academy Award for best song that year (1951).

Reel to Real: *Riding High* and *Here Comes the Groom* were essentially movie comedies with music appended. Did you ever want to make a song-and-dance musical?

Capra: My good friend Irving Berlin, one of our greatest songwriters, was always after me to do a musical picture with him. But I kept telling him I wouldn't know what to do with a musical comedy. He said, "What do you mean by that?" I said, "I don't know, all of a sudden some guy starts singing to a tune that materializes out of thin air, Irving, I'd probably break out laughing and never get the film done." Well, Berlin explained that the audience suspends their disbelief in such a case, and that's what makes musicals acceptable. I told him that I loved musicals in the theater and on the screen, but I would still probably break up if I ever directed one. Undismayed, Irving said, "If you ever get an idea for a musical film, call me up."

Well, one day I did come up with an idea for a story in which the songs, I felt, would flow naturally from the plot. The story concerned a group of show people who ran a vacation inn just on the holidays.

Reel to Real: This sounds familiar!

Capra: Yes, my idea became the musical *Holiday Inn* which was released in 1942 starring Fred Astaire and Bing Crosby. I was in the Army at the time making the *Why We Fight* series of films when I told Irving about it. He went wild with delight, exclaiming he could write a different song for each holiday. Since I was in the Army, I wasn't able to direct, but I gave the idea to Irving anyway and the musical was a big hit for Paramount.

Reel to Real: We heard somewhere that when Harry Cohn bought the play *You Can't Take It With You* for you to direct in 1938, you threw out music that had been written for it.

Capra: Cohn couldn't believe it. He said: "Why the hell did you do it, a musical with no music?" I told him that I didn't like the music, and Cohn said the New York critics would eat me alive for tampering with *their* hit play. Well, when my film of *You Can't Take It With You* opened at Radio City Music Hall, I took Irving Berlin to the premiere. He thought it was a hell of a show. We walked home to the Waldorf Astoria, and when the elevator door opened, out came Moss Hart, who along with George S. Kaufman, was the author of the original Broadway version. Moss turned to me and said, "Frank, I liked it," and then walked out of the hotel. I died laughing but Irving was so embarrassed for me that he ran after Hart to get him to apologize.

Reel to Real: You made *State of the Union* with Katharine Hepburn and Spencer Tracy at MGM What were your impressions of working there?

Capra: It would have been impossible for me to be a director contracted at MGM Twice I tried working there and twice they fired me before I started. The production bosses didn't like the idea of any director completely running the show, the old question of limited autonomy again. I made *State of the Union,* one of my best pictures, at MGM, because I wanted to work with Spencer Tracy. I had organized my own independent film company called Liberty Films and had come to an agreement with the studio executives that for the services of Tracy in my picture, MGM would have sole distribution rights when the project was completed. They owned a theater chain that stretched coast to coast, so they stood to gain immensely as their own marketing agents. In addition, my company would rent MGM studio space and facilities, but I would retain complete autonomy on any matters pertaining to the production.

I soon realized that our mutual contract with regard to my undisputed autonomy wasn't — as is said — worth the paper it was written on. There were problems from the very start. I had a scene in the picutre with five people in it and was just about to film when my MGM cameraman approached and said, "I can't shoot that." I asked him why not and he replied: "I can't carry that focus with a 2/4 lens; you'll have to move the actors a little out of line." Well, I wasn't about to re-block a scene I had been working on for the last half hour just to benefit my myopic camerman. I said: "Change the lens to 4/9 and the focus will be perfect. I shouldn't have to tell you that." The cameraman was adamant against changing lenses, so after arguing fruitlessly, I fired him. I then put in a phone call to the production department telling them that I wanted to hire my own cameraman, and not one from MGM. They said the man I had fired was probably the best photographer on the lot. "That makes no difference, I want someone who I can work with," I said.

Later that day, an impeccably dressed white-haired old gentleman, obviously someone of importance, visited me on the set. He asked me what the trouble was, and I told him that my former cameraman had refused to change a 2/4 focal-length lens. He said, "I'm from the photography laboratory and we shoot all pictures here with 2/4 lenses; that way we can use the same developing process on all our movies. I couldn't believe my ears. "You mean you make no exceptions? This is ridiculous!" I said. The lab man told me that if I insisted, I could hire my own cameraman and use whatever lens I desired. I insisted.

As filming progressed on *State of the Union,* I began to see that every technical aspect of the picture was controlled by the department heads. The prop, set, makeup and sound men, to name just a few, all had bosses to account to. It was a machine studio; pictures were churned out with the regularity of a factory assembly line.

Reel to Real: I guess that's why MGM films seem to have a style and sound that is interchangeable.

Capra: Yes, and they were all well done but not very individualistic. MGM pictures seem to exude a shine like mass-made Grand Rapids furniture. Each picture looked like another; that was just their method of production. I believe one man, one film is the only way to make a movie. It is a director's responsibility to exercise complete authority on a film. The director is the only person with an overall conception of the film. It is he who will take the disjointed bits and pieces of film footage and interrelate them into a cohesive whole, the finished product.

Reel to Real: Were there any actors or actresses you wanted to work with but couldn't because they were tenured to other studios at the time?

Capra: Yes, many. One actor I wanted to direct in a film was Jimmy Cagney. I wanted him for everything, but especially for the role of a small-time hood, Dave the Dude, in *Lady for a Day*. Unfortunately, he was contracted to Warner Bros. and our schedules never coincided long enough for us to make a picture together. Another star I would have loved to direct just once was Greta Garbo. But I got my share of fine actors, I have no complaints.

Reel to Real: Do you think Hollywood is still producing fine films with a high level of craftsmanship?

Capra: Oh yes, today's filmmakers are creating some of the best movies. Film mechanics and techniques have advanced enormously since when I first started in this business, but I think the level of screenwriting has slackened recently. An inordinate amount of movies have sex and violence as their only attributes. None seem to have inspiring characters, people fighting for an idea. Instead, I find many films without a single sympathetic character. It's hard to sit through a picture when everyone in it is a jerk. This state of affairs has been brought about because the movie business is now dictated soley by cost and profit. A group of backers with sufficient financial resources decide to invest in a movie with only one motivation in mind: To make a quick buck. This stringent creative attitude allied with low budget outlays afflicts the quality of a film. Occasionally, however, when a director is given free artistic control, independent of business-oriented moviemen, a fine picture will result.

Reel to Real: What advice would you give to anyone aspiring to become a filmmaker nowadays?

Capra: Just submit material and don't get discouraged by rejection; any aspirant will have to face a great deal of it. Films are an art form, so if a person is born without a certain amount of creativity, he or she probably won't be well suited to the more imaginative aspects of moviemaking. Creativity, in most cases, cannot be learned. But skills can be. There are a thousand-and-one jobs that go into making a film, from initial photography to final editing. Qualified and skillful people are always needed to fill these places. Film course such as those offered by the American Film Institute, USC, and UCLA are good starting points for acquiring filmmaking skills.

Our day with Capra was finally winding down. We suggested that it might be a good idea if he checked at the front desk for any messages that came in that morning ... or afternoon ... from festival organizers (which was about as rhetorical as you could get. We half expected to see a sheaf of pink memo slips that would choke a Filofax crammed into the director's mail slot). We had no sooner cleared the lobby than the festival coordinator — the same woman who had strung us along with her vague, verbal promisory notes — accosted us.

"Mr. Capra ... we were ... quite concerned when you didn't show up for your appointments today," she said, addressing Capra but shooting curare-dipped daggers at us with her eyes. Capra, with the classic timing of a silent film gag-man, let us twist in the wind for about two beats short of two seconds and then said, with a cherubic twinkle: "I just spent a wonderful afternoon with a couple of first-rate tour guides."

It was a case of checkmate and exoneration in one fell swoop. Like a topper gag from a Harry Langdon silent comedy, there wasn't a comeback to be had. One man, one film … and a helluva one-liner. Nearly a quarter century after his retirement from directing films, Capra remained true to his credo of standing up for the little guy — this time via a timely, face-saving riposte delivered on our behalf.

We were about two miles, as the crow flies, from the Mississippi River and felt sure that at that moment Twain was smiling.

MGM's Amazing Technicolor Dreamcoat
Vincente Minnelli
August 1981

During his tenure at Metro-Goldwyn Mayer studios in the '40s and '50s, director Vincente Minnelli trailblazed a genre of movie musicals noted for their striking vibrance of color and finely honed visual sophistication. Minnelli wasn't just concerned with the workaday mechanics of filmmaking; he was an artist who painted in a palate of Technicolor and was capable of creating a movie that shimmered like the brushstrokes of Monet's garden at Giverny.

With such films as *An American in Paris, Meet Me in St. Louis, The Bandwagon,* and *Gigi,* Minnelli more than any other director fulfilled the standing MGM commandment: "Do it big, do it right, and give it class."

Dressed in a black shirt and a white blazer, Minnelli ushered us upstairs to the library/office located on the second floor of his home off Sunset Boulevard in Beverly Hills. A slight man with large eyes and sensuous lips but given to small decorous gestures when emphasis was needed to underscore a point, Minnelli seemed to us an aesthete through and through. It was frustrating then (probably more for Minnelli than us), that he was maddeningly inarticulate in conversation. For a director so brilliantly skilled in marshalling the tricky cohesion (on so many complicated fronts) needed to make a film successful, Minnelli just couldn't connect the dots verbally — without a whole lot of patience and prompting. Then again, Minnelli's stunning adroitness with the visual composition of his movies might have been a direct result of his lack of verbal skills — a compensation in one area for the lack in another.

"I guess I set the standard for color in those musicals," Minnelli said, "I knew what I wanted to achieve from my previous experience as an art director doing Broadway shows for the Schuberts. I knew it was possible."

To illustrate his point, Minnelli pulled out from a cabinet in his library a voluminous bound scrapbook of clippings he had gleaned from newspapers and magazines. Yellow and brittle from age and use, the bulging clipbook — which had the girth of a pregnant woman facing her third trimester — chronicled various vogues of interior design and clothing over more than 40 years.

"I got into the habit of making use of the cliproom at the Los Angeles Public Library," Minnelli explained. "By referring to these cutouts, I was able to bring some measure of authenticity to each of my movies — whether they be costume epics or more modern stories."

Minnelli began his directorial career in Chicago, dazzling State Street sidewalk shoppers with his arrangement of the window displays in the Marshall Field's department store. Not long after that, he went to New York City and became the youngest art director in the history of Radio City Music Hall, a certifiable *wunderkind*.

"I was there 3 1/2 years. I did the stage lighting, designed the costumes and conceived the sets. I also did five shows with Beatrice Lillie," Minnelli said. "Arthur Freed (Metro's legendary producer of musicals) saw my work and brought me out to Hollywood in 1941 as a sort of protégé and trouble shooter. I pitched in on any film that needed doctoring. I'm afraid the art department at MGM didn't like me much. They considered me a young upstart from Broadway with fresh ideas. But when I got my own films to direct, they left me alone."

Minnelli's *An American in Paris* and *Gigi* won Oscars for Best Picture of 1951 and 1958. But he feels that to make any real impression on the throngs who cast their Academy Awards votes (or anyone else), a musical must be exceptional.

"Most musicals are lighthearted entertainment with no other pretensions," he said. "I do believe a film should do more than just entertain. *Cabaret* (starring his daughter, Liza) is a marvelous example of a deeply disturbing, ominous, yet entertaining musical-drama."

Lust for Life, the filmization of Irving Stone's biography of Vincent van Gogh, ranks as Minnelli's favorite film. It is truly a homage by one artist to another.

"We shot the movie entirely in Europe. I used locations in Paris and Belgium. I even shot scenes at St. Remy, the mental institution where van Gogh had himself committed toward the end of his life," Minnelli said. "One problem we had to resolve was Vincent's suicide scene in the wheatfield at Arles. I shot it on a cold fall morning. We had to fly in some mature wheat and treat it chemically so it would stay alive while Vincent painted his famous last canvas of black crows flying over the field. All for the sake of accuracy."

The distraction of keeping wheatfields alive in mid-frost would be enough to drive any director to a padded cell at St. Remy. But Minnelli had his own sanity-saving methods.

"I would dissociate myself completely at night," he said. "To take my mind off the job, I'd read detective stories."

Among the many stars with whom Minnelli worked was his wife, Judy Garland, whom he has described as "the consummate performer."

"I tried to direct her as little as possible," Minnelli said. "She would be powdering her nose with a disinterested stare and I wouldn't be sure I was getting through to her. But when the camera rolled, every inflection and nuance was in place — sheer perfection. Gene Kelly was the same way. I'd tell him to make a scene more jaunty. Gene would look quizzically at me. He was, of course, the definition of the word, jaunty."

A pivotal point in the careers of both Minnelli and Garland was the film during which they fell in love, the classic *Meet Me in St. Louis.*

"Judy didn't want to make that film, she wanted to do more sophisticated parts. She thought the teenage role of Esther Smith would set her career back 20 years," Minnelli said. "She asked Louis B. Mayer and Arthur Freed to intercede for her but she couldn't get anywhere, so she came to the set the first day of rehearsal secure in the knowledge that she would at least make life miserable for 'this squirt director Minnelli from New York.' I've been lucky to have great success with things that at first glance didn't seem so good."

In 1945, Minnelli directed the cinema's two greatest dancers, Fred Astaire and Gene Kelly, in their only routine together, "The Babbitt and the Bromide" from *Ziegfeld Follies.* It stands as a unique historical pairing of two legendary hoofers with vastly different styles — a curiosity piece forever captured in the time capsule of film.

"The rehearsals were maddening," Minnelli explained. "Astaire would demonstrate an idea for a step and ask Kelly what he thought of it. Kelly would say, 'fine, great, swell.' They tried to convince each other and be so polite. That dance took three weeks to rehearse, but it turned out well. Fred Astaire is lighter than air you know, and Gene is more earthy. Both are perfectionists to the nth degree. It was a pleasure to direct them."

As to the current crop of film musicals and their talent, Minnelli said that he saw a screening of *The Wiz* starring Diana Ross and decided then and there not to see any more. The movie version of *The Wiz* was adapted from the all-black hit Broadway musical which in turn was based upon the immortal *Wizard of Oz* starring that "consummate performer," Judy Garland.

Alas, like Minnelli himself, some things just can't be improved upon.

A Self-Styled Renaissance Man
George Sidney
September 1980, August 1981, 1994

The lion's mighty roar has been reduced to a barely audible meow. Metro-Goldwyn-Mayer's Culver City, California, dream factory is now owned by another studio. What remains is a film production and distribution company living primarily off its glorious history. It's a past that's being celebrated this year with the selected market release of *That's Entertainment! III*, another in a series of compilation films featuring clips celebrating MGM's faded glory from the Golden Age of movie musicals.

Formed 70 years ago, in May 1924, MGM was a marriage between Metro Pictures, The Goldwyn Company (named for Samuel Goldwyn, although he had no involvement in the merged companies), and pioneering producer Louis B. Mayer. The studio was organized as a subsidiary of the giant New York-based theater chain, Loews, Inc. MGM, which once boasted of having "more stars than there are in the heavens," is today financially troubled, with ownership in the hands of the French bank Crédit Lyonnais.

While some studios could boast of making the finest gangster movies or the best horror films, MGM carved out its special niche from the 1930s through the 1950s with its lavish musical productions.

The director of many of the studio's most successful musicals was George Sidney who worked for MGM for nearly 20 years and is responsible for such pictures as *Anchors Aweigh, The Three Musketeers, The Harvey Girls, Show Boat, Kiss Me Kate, Annie Get Your Gun,* and *Viva Las Vegas* with Elvis Presley. Away from MGM, Sidney directed such films as *The Eddy Duchin Story, Pal Joey* with Frank Sinatra and *Bye Bye Birdie* starring Ann-Margret.

"The first thing you have to understand is that you're talking to an insane man," Sidney warned us as he launched into an epic screed about his dog Rover.

"This dog belongs to every museum in the world," he said. "When I took out my membership in the Museum of Modern Art in New York they asked me if I had any children. I said yes, I have Rover. And they asked me what his age was. I didn't know so I put down 10 years old. Later the president of the museum sent me back a letter that read, 'Unfortunately, your son is too young for a junior membership, but anytime he's in the city, he'll have the run of the museum.'"

Born 78 years ago in Jamaica, Long Island, Sidney grew up in a show business family. His mother started performing when she was four years old as one of the three Mooney Sisters at the Winter Garden Theater in New York. His father held just about every job in show business, ultimately becoming a top executive at MGM's parent company, Loews, Inc.

Before the ripe old age of six, Sidney himself was already a veteran performer. He played the smallest cowboy in the Tom Mix westerns and starred in the silent version of *Little Lord Fauntleroy,* "complete with long blond curls."

Whether meeting in his Beverly Hills office (as we did for the first time in 1980), during subsequent visits over lunch at the posh Hillcrest Country Club, or at his Beverly Hills home, Sidney is the quintessential raconteur.

"By the time I was six-years-old I knew I didn't want to be an actor. I decided to become a director," he said. "During the interim I did odd jobs around Broadway. At the same time I was studying music. I play four instruments. When I was 14, I came out to California and got a job as a messenger boy at MGM."

Through hard work, a good deal of pluck, and the conscious decision not to cash in on his well-placed family connection, Sidney gradually worked his way up through the ranks at MGM. Describing himself as a quiet and polite "what-makes-Sammy-run," he spent 24 hours a day learning everything there was to learn about filmmaking. Soon he was directing *Our Gang* comedies — a chore he recalled with disdain.

"It was impossible working with those kids," he said. "I'd have to listen to the high frequency of their voices all day, then I'd go into a projection room and turn off the sound. I finally went to the studio brass and said, 'Listen, if I make two of these films in one week, do I get two weeks off?' And they said, 'Sure.' So we would write a script with the same sets and costumes and make two shorts at once. I got the supreme luxury of two weeks off before I had to face them again."

After Sidney won Oscars for his direction of two specialty shorts, MGM studio chief Louis B. Mayer promoted him to feature film director. He then went on to direct 27 feature films beginning with *Free and Easy* in 1941 and ending with the British musical, *Half a Sixpence* in 1966.

Perhaps Sidney's most famous musical number of the dozens he directed is Gene Kelly's tap dance with Jerry the cartoon mouse in the 1945 film, *Anchors Aweigh*. Upon completion of the filming, Kelly joined the Navy. It was only then that Sidney realized there was a problem. "We put it all together and ran the number," he recalled. "It looked great, but there was one thing missing. Kelly's reflection appeared on the floor. The mouse was a cell laid onto the film, so there was no reflection. For continuity's sake, we had to go back and make 20,000 mouse drawing reflections.

"While we were doing that sequence, the mouse became so real. We talked to him and panned the camera around to accommodate him. That's why nobody thought about Jerry throwing a shadow."

Sidney described his approach to filmmaking by explaining the shooting of the Academy Award-winning song "On the Atchison, Topeka, and the Santa Fe" from his 1946 film, *The Harvey Girls.*

"In that number Judy Garland does the entire nine-minute song in one shot. But it took us a week to lay the whole scene out. It's easier to make a lot of setups, but then you're going to get chop suey and you're not going to get a seamless flow. When Judy gets off that bloody train and goes into the song, we just swing along with her. The camera should have a fluidity that goes along with her."

Kiss Me Kate, Sidney's 1953 film with Cole Porter songs and featuring a very young Bob Fosse was the only musical shot in 3-D, a short-lived fad that was an attempt by the industry in the early '50s to combat the monolithic menace of television.

"The utmost care was taken making that film," he said. "We really made it twice — in 3-D, and in flat. We'd shoot a scene in 3-D, then we'd pull the cameras back and I would restage it. Now when you look at the film you don't know whether you're watching the 3-D print or the flat one."

Sidney has probably directed more film versions of Broadway musicals than any other person, but he prefers directing original screen musicals over proven Broadway successes.

"It's more of a challenge. In so many Broadway musicals, the first act is really the finish of the musical. The second act will be all musical numbers. Musicals are indigenous to this country. And you have to make a film that the audience thinks is exactly the way they saw it in the theater. When you get a critic who says, 'Oh, he did nothing, he just photographed the stage play,' you've had it. For example, we made *Anchors Aweigh* as we went along. And that's a very exciting way to get up in the morning."

Despite working with virtually every major musical star in Hollywood, people invariably ask what it was like directing Elvis. Presley starred in Sidney's 1964 film, *Viva Las Vegas* (it was also Sidney's last film for MGM). Co-starring Ann-Margret, it was the King's biggest-grossing picture.

"There's not much to say about Elvis," he said. "I never had any trouble with him. He was a nice young man and he approached his job in a professional manner."

Not content with the rock 'n' roll influence that was overtaking the musical tastes of Americans, in 1966, Sidney decided the time was ripe to abandon filmmaking and pursue some other interests, including the study of law, paleontology, medicine and art history. To that end he received an honorary doctorate in the '60s from Hahnemann Medical College in Philadelphia for his film on cardiovascular research.

Away from the camera, Sidney married three show business heavy-hitters. His first wife, Lillian Burns was a famed drama coach at MGM and the person Louis B. Mayer once said was the only woman qualified to run a major studio. His next wife, Jane, was widowed from actor Edward G. Robinson (she died in 1991). The current Mrs. Sidney is the former Corinne Entratter, who was married to the late Las Vegas Sand's Hotel impresario Jack Entratter. It was Jack who headlined friend Frank Sinatra and the Rat Pack at his hotel in the 1960s.

Today, Sidney stays active accepting accolades at film festivals around the world and co-hosting with his wife a Los Angeles cable television program.

George Sidney acts not only as a representative of the bygone days of Hollywood when the studio system reigned supreme, but also as a emissary from an era when the lion's mighty roar was heard throughout the world.

With Sidney at Hillcrest Country Club ...

Hillcrest Country Club in Beverly Hills was founded with vengeance as a motive. In the 1920s, about the only place to play a game of golf in West Lost Angeles was on one of the Los Angeles Country Club's two sprawling 18-hole-courses. Douglas Fairbanks and Joe Schenck, a man who gave definition to the term "movie mogul," were barred from entering the grounds on the grounds that they were "movie people," an unpardonable sin to the highly stratified society of the day that was ruled by a WASP elite.

In response to that ostracism, Fairbanks and Schenck founded the Hillcrest Country Club, which was semitically inclusive and nearby.

"My wife and I are seldom in Beverly Hills for any length of time any more," Sidney said from a lunch table in the men's grill. "I'm an anglophile so we live in London much of the time. I also try to get back to Hong Kong at least twice annually, and then there are always the cruise tours on the Royal Viking Line. Ostensibly I'm retired from the movie business, but we can negotiate free passage anywhere, in the lap of absolute luxury, if I bring along a couple of my films to screen and give a movie lecture to the passengers. You might call it a career dividend."

To the septuagenarians who fill the Viking Line's cabins and staterooms, Sidney's *Eddy Duchin Story* is a perennial favorite. For a couple of hours viewers can nix the deck chairs and shuffleboard and transport themselves back to their era of vitality, when swing music was "Solid Jackson."

"When I was filming that movie we had a bit player under contract at the studio who I felt would be perfect casting for the love interest," Sidney said. "Her name was Kim Novak. We were sitting on a couch discussing the film and I was telling her about my idea of tagging Duchin's arrival in New York City to Lindbergh's transatlantic flight. Kim gave me

the big eye all through my talk and after pondering for a
moment said, 'That's a wonderful story you made up about
that guy who flew across the ocean.' I couldn't believe my
ears. I said, 'But Kim, Lindbergh's flight is a historical fact —
it really happened!' She just replied, 'I suppose it doesn't
matter, I wasn't born then anyway.' Statements like that can
quickly reduce your esteem of humankind."

In a Donkey Kong world where attention spans can be
measured in milli-seconds, Sidney remains a modern day
Renaissance man devoted to the acquisition of knowledge.
Case-in-point: At the age of 50, he enrolled at the University
of Southern California.

"Bored people should use the power of their intellect to
fill up their days," Sidney said. "I get depressed when I think
that I'm about 400 years behind on the information spec-
trum and I'll never catch up on all the things I'd like to know
about. One of my interests is paleontology. I was in Africa
where Dr.Leakey uncovered the remains of earliest man. I
then went down to Pretoria and held the skullcap of "Missy"-
a relic thousands of years old. People say to me in awe, 'Gosh,
you directed Lana Turner.' All I can say to that is, 'Who cares?
I held in my hand the skull of Missy.'"

During our chat, the men's grill filled up to lunchtime
capacity and Sidney began to point out "Jewish movie people"
with the intense glee of a child set loose in a chocolate shop.
In five minutes' time he introduced us to Pandro Berman,
producer of the Astaire-Rogers musicals; Izzy Freedman,
former clarinetist with Paul Whiteman; Irving Brecher, screenwriter for the Marx Brothers movies *Go West* and *At The Circus;* Herman Citron, Hollywood powerbroker; and last (and
least), Monty "Let's Make A Deal" Hall.

We had read our share of unauthorized movie biographies and definitive tell-all tomes, but it was different to see
people "in the industry" in their element — table-hopping
and kibitzing — about points, percentages and million-dol-
lar deals. We felt a kind of nervous excitement, as if we might

suddenly appear in the pages of a Sidney Sheldon novel.

"I've been a club member since 1932, but I don't come here to make deals or bullshit about the pictures I'm going to make," Sidney said, dousing our reverie. "The dues are $35,000 a year, and I don't play tennis, golf, or cards. As far as I'm concerned, they toss a great Cobb Salad."

We noticed that one table was conspicuously crowd-free, George Burns being the only person seated there. Sidney leaned over to us and whispered almost reverently, "What you're witnessing is the end of an era. That used to be the Hollywood version of the famous Algonquin New York roundtable. Burns, Jack Benny, George Jessel, Eddie Cantor, and the Marx Brothers all used to have lunch there regularly. You took your life in your hands if you sat down with them uninvited. Their combined wit could slay you alive. Burns is the last one."

"You just can't live in the past; it's no good," Sidney continued already moving on as we starred transfixed at the hunched-over image of Burns nursing his soup. "Take it from me — a paleontologist who's been around."

A 'NICE' DIRECTOR
Charles Walters
September 1980

In describing the cinematic work of director Charles Walters, *Village Voice* film critic Andrew Sarris, said, "If the word 'nice' could be defined with any precision, it would apply to most of his films." This statement could not be more insightful, for Walters has directed some of the most entertaining musical and light comedy films Hollywood has ever produced.

Walters is a rare breed — a native Californian. He was born in Pasadena in 1911. Fresh out of high school and with no formal dance training, Walters journeyed to New York

City in quest of stardom.

During the '30s and early '40s he enjoyed great success on the musical comedy stage as a performer and choreographer. He appeared in such shows as *Jubilee,* in which he introduced the Cole Porter standard, "Begin the Beguine," and *DuBarry Was a Lady,* where he starred with Betty Grable.

Walters' ambition during his tenure in New York was to someday return home to California and replace George Murphy, whom he considered to be a poor dancer, in film roles. His goal was partially realized in 1943 when he was asked to choreograph a number for the film version of *DuBarry.* Although he never replaced Murphy, Walters did land a long-term contract at MGM. For the next 22 years he would mainly work under the auspices of producer Arthur Freed. The Freed Unit, as it came to be known, consisted of the finest musical talents in the world.

After performing choreographic chores, most notably for *Meet Me in St. Louis,* and occasional on screen dancing roles with Judy Garland, Walters graduated to full directorial status in 1947 when he directed *Good News.* Walters maintained a remarkably high standard for the next 18 years, directing such musicals as *Easter Parade, Summer Stock, The Barkleys of Broadway, Lili, The Tender Trap, High Society, Jumbo* and *The Unsinkable Molly Brown.*

The '60s sounded the death-knell for original Hollywood musicals, and Walters suffered the same fate many of his MGM colleagues did. His workload came to an abrupt halt, except for directorial chores in a few television shows.

Fifteen years later it is a relief to know that his talent and directorial expertise is not going to waste. He is currently teaching students at the University of Southern California in a course called "Film Style Analysis - The Work of Director Charles Walters."

The following is an interview we had with Walters in his Malibu condominium. He seemed to epitomize the laid-back, California beach lifestyle, greeting us at his door wearing a bathrobe and flip-flop sandals. A Marlboro was never far from Walters's reach and between drags he quaffed a limitless amount of decaffeinated coffee from an apparently bottomless pot.

Our discussion with Walters took us through his career, from Broadway up to the present with a special emphasis on his professional and personal relationship with Judy Garland — a friendship that began when Walters worked on the Garland film, *Girl Crazy,* in 1943.

Reel to Real: It has often been said that to crack the entertainment industry you have to be at the right place at the right time. Was that true in your case?

Walters: It couldn't be truer. Being at the right place at the right time and having what is needed at the time. As a for instance, the greatest dancer in New York in my time was Paul Draper, a classical tap dancer. My dance partner and I were appearing in a Theater Guild musical called *Parade.* The scuttlebutt around town at that time was that Sam Harris, Cole Porter and Moss Hart (the biggest names in New York) were on a Caribbean cruise writing a new show to be called *Jubilee.* People were guessing, of course, that Paul Draper would get one of the lead roles. I don't know whether you know this, but the chorus kids get *all* the dirt. All of a sudden, while I was in *Parade,* rumors started that Sam Harris, Monty Wooley, Cole Porter and Moss Hart were out front to see me. Finally, when I leave the stage door there'd be agents and they'd say, "Chuck, sign with me. I think I can get you an audition for *Jubilee.*" Forget it. To me, who could compete with the elegance of Paul Draper? Well to make a long story short, they found out that Draper stuttered. Now that was a real left fielder for them. Now they've got to look around for a juvenile. I had never sung and I had never acted. Now I'm called in to read for Monty Wooley. If you remember Monty Wooley in pictures, he had a beard and was very pompous and ominous. So into a back office we go and I read for him. He came out and said, "All right."

That's how I got *Jubilee*. But I told them I couldn't break
with my partner, we were doing very well. So they said, "We'll
giver her a part in the second act, but we can't pay any more."
So I split my salary with her.

Reel to Real: Your first job at MGM and first association
with the Freed Unit was in *DuBarry Was a Lady?*

Walters: Yes, *DuBarry* was the last show I was in as a
performer and my first Freed film. Again, it's being in the
right place at the right time. My manager-agent-best friend
and I were living together in my house and he also handled
Gene Kelly. Kelly had just done *For Me and my Gal.* He called
our agent and said, "Is Bob Alton (a choreographer) available? I cannot stand Seymour Felix (another choreographer).
I just can't work with this guy again. And he's scheduled to
do my next picture, *DuBarry* with Lucille Ball." Well, my
agent told Kelly that he just signed Felix for *Ziegfeld Follies.*
And Kelly said, "Geez, is Charlie Walters around?" Gene's
the only person in the world who ever called me Charlie. So
Kelly asked me to do this number for him, and I was signed
up for four weeks. I'll show you my contract; it's on an in-
ter-office communication. Well, Kelly liked the number I
did so they took another number away from Felix, gave me
that, took another number away, and I ended up doing the
picture. They liked the picture so they put me under long-
term contract. I was there 22 years, 52 weeks a year.

Reel to Real: The number you were originally signed to
choreograph was to the Cole Porter song, "Do I Love You?"

Walters: Yes, that was the number I was signed to stage.
For some strange reason I asked for a script. "What do you
need a script for, you're just going to do solo staging for Kelly?"
they asked. I might have been curious, having been in the
Broadway show. I might have been curious what they did
with it and if Kelly was playing my part or another part ...
that might have been it! I never thought of that.

Anyway, it so happened that Kelly had a scene in Lucy's
dressing room before the number, and then he left the dress-

ing room and jumped on stage. I thought, gee, wouldn't it be nice if we could start the number in her room with a look of encouragement from her and continue the number out of the dressing room and up on stage. Now he's got a motivation to be up and gay and bright. So I told the producer — Arthur Freed — my idea and he just looked at me. I thought, "Oh Jesus, I really bombed!" Well, he said, "Chuck that's the way directors think. That's very good. I like it."

Arthur was the kind of man who never forgot. The seed was planted in his mind that someday I would be a director.

Reel to Real: How did you land your first directorial assignment, the 1920s college campus musical, *Good News?*

Walters: I was very big in dramatics, if you can imagine, at Anaheim High School. The senior class play was to be of my choice. We've never done a musical, and *Good News* was very popular at the time. So I said, let's do *Good News*. We got the high school orchestra and then we found out that we couldn't afford the rights. So we used the same story line, but different popular music.

Later on at MGM we were running dailies of "Madame Crematon," (a number Walters staged for *Ziegfeld Follies of 1946*) and Arthur Freed, who was always very non-sequiter, said nothing. I looked at him to see what he thought and he said, "I bought a new property today, *Good News.*" It was like somebody had put a firecracker under me. He said, "Chuck that might be a good first picture for you."

Reel to Real: You brought your first three pictures (*Good News, Easter Parade* and *The Barkleys of Broadway)* in under budget. How did you accomplish this, and what kind of impression did this make on the studio brass?

Walters: I had been a dance director for four years, and it was only the last year that I was able to cut and shoot my own numbers. Before that time, I would stage a number, and the director would take it and shoot it his way. When I finally got to shoot my own numbers, I would film them so they couldn't be chopped. I found that I was automatically staging for cutting. Then, when I got into directing, I would shoot only what I wanted, so all the cutter could do was cut off the leader and glue them together. I wanted to protect what I visualized.

Reel to Real: What was it like working with Judy Garland and Vincente Minnelli (who directed) on *Meet Me in St. Louis?*

Walters: Oh, that was a lovely experience. The only funny thing about that was I thought Ralph Blane and Hugh Martin had written an original score. I thought, what the hell is this "Skip to My Lou?" I couldn't get any handle on how to stage it. One evening I had my parents over for dinner, and I told them there was one number in the picture I didn't know what the hell to do with. Well they pounced on it and started singing "Skip to My Lou." That song was around when they were kids. So my square, untheatrical parents helped me choreograph the number.

Reel to Real: Vincente Minnelli is given directorial credit for *Gigi,* but didn't you do much of the filming?

Walters: How did you know I did things on *Gigi?* I never said anything. I never let the cat out of the bag. Wow! I did all the retakes and shot a lot of the numbers like "The Night They Invented Champagne" and Louis Jourdan doing "Gigi." As a matter of fact, I redid the scene where he comes in to propose to her. It was one of the toughest things I've ever done because I had to blend the studio footage into the Paris backgrounds.

Reel to Real: Your choreographic style always seemed to have, for lack of a better term, a kind of upper-class elan or sophistication. How would you appraise your style?

Walters: Pure bastard.

Reel to Real: You directed Astaire and Rogers in their last film together, *The Barkleys of Broadway.* What was your reaction when you were given this assignment. They were childhood idols of yours, we're guessing?

Walters: Once I found out that Astaire was going to be

in it, my knees got weak because he was my hero. So when you say sophistication — I loved the way he danced, the way he walked, his entire style. I never copied a step, but just his whole attitude was wonderful. I think a lot of that rubbed off on me.

Reel to Real: Was Ginger Rogers a good dancer?

Walters: No. She could do the steps, but she was such a good actress you didn't care.

Reel to Real: How about Judy Garland?

Walters: Good faker.

Reel to Real: You always seemed to bring out the best in Judy's dancing.

Walters: The interesting thing about Judy was that she was so insecure, except to get up and sing. For instance, we were doing a number that she was scared to death of. I don't know how I thought of it, but one day I said, "Judy who's your favorite dancer?" And she said, Renee DeMarco, who was part of a famous dance team. I told her, "From now on, whenever we rehearse, you're Renee DeMarco." From then on she was just perfect. Now if you remember "Get Happy" (from *Summer Stock),* I told her to be Lena Horne. This got Judy away from "me dancing" and she felt Lena. It worked beautifully.

Reel to Real: We've read that you and Gene Kelly literally carried Judy through *Summer Stock,* which was her last picture at MGM before the studio cancelled her contract and let her go.

Walters: That's true. The bets around the studio lot were that we wouldn't finish it. So that's an encouraging note on which to go to work every morning. I would look at the dailies and say, "How dare this look like we're having fun!" How dare it when we were just sweating blood. I can't stand watching *Summer Stock.* I was on nothing but coffee and cigarettes during the filming. I ended up getting an ulcer on the film.

Reel to Real: What was your role in Judy's New York

stage triumphs in the early '50s?

Walters: I staged both of Judy's Palace shows. It was my idea to give them more than just a personal appearance, like "Here I am, little Judy Garland." We had a wealth of musical material to draw upon, and Judy loved the idea of having production numbers.

Reel to Real: What do you think of the Garland cultists, which are legion out there?

Walters: Well, she couldn't figure it out, so I don't know how the hell I can. I'll tell you one interesting story about her opening night at the Palace. The impact of opening night hadn't hit us yet. We were at the Plaza before the opening having a steak sandwich and martinis; the martinis came first. We were both a little uptight so we just picked at the steak. And I had to go on that night and do the tramp number with Judy. I thought this was very unfair. I hadn't been on the stage for 10 years, and the Palace meant something to me. So that was an excuse for another martini. Anyway, we got a cab and when we got to the little pie-wedge traffic island at Broadway and Seventh Avenue — all we saw were people jammed on the pie. The cabby said, "I don't know if we can get any farther, they have the fuckin' street blocked off." I asked him what was happening? "Garland's opening at the Palace tonight." It was like somebody punched us in the gut. Anyway, the show was absolutely fantastic. After the show she was getting dressed in a lovely evening gown to go to a big party, which incidentally was for me. Somebody mentioned to us that the people were still standing out in the pie. Judy said, "I don't believe it. What do they want?" "They just want to see you," somebody said. "Well shit," said Judy. "I'm going out the front door instead of the stage exit. If they want to see me, they're going to see me." Well the lobby was filled, as was the pie. As we walked through this sea of humanity — not a word! She's getting into the limousine and says, "What the hell is this, nobody's saying a goddamn word?" A silent tribute … I can't tell that without choking up.

Reel to Real: What in your opinion caused the demise of the Hollywood musical?

Walters: Money; that's my guess. It just got too expensive. In those days at MGM we had a stock company of dancers and other musical talents.

Reel to Real: What do you think of today's films and filmmakers?

Walters: I think that's why I'm not working today. Most of them (the films) I don't understand after I've seen them, let alone read a script and say, I'll do it.

Reel to Real: Do you have a favorite and least favorite among the 21 films you directed?

Walters: I decided the other day that I think *Jumbo* is my favorite because I had done so many intimate and small comedies and musicals. To get a chance at a biggie was a thrill. My least favorite was the *Belle of New York* (a 1953 musical that starred Fred Astaire and Vera-Ellen). I hate it. I just hate it. It was like putting a gun to your head every day. I couldn't stand Vera-Ellen. I would talk to her about a scene and she'd be doing pliés That's the kind of concentration you got.

Reel to Real: Today you are teaching students at USC the lost art of musical film direction. What do you tell them?

Walters: When I started there was no such thing as a school or a book. It had to be on a gut level. For openers I tell the kids, learn all you can, then throw the book over your shoulder and go from your guts. It's the same with you and writing. There is only so much you can learn, then it's up to you — your blood and guts.

A Few of his 'Favorite Things'
Robert Wise
June 1995

Thirty years ago the film version of the long-running Broadway musical by Rodgers and Hammerstein had its unheralded sneak preview at the Mann Theater in Minneapolis. The movie, *The Sound of Music,* generated favorable response from the audience, but director Robert Wise had no idea then that it would be the biggest blockbuster since *Gone With the Wind.*

Three decades later, sitting in his modest office tucked on a commercial street in the flatlands of Beverly Hills, Wise now 81, is still slightly confounded about the root cause for the movie's monolithic success. "*The Sound of Music* had a universality about it that my other films don't have, even *West Side Story,*" he said. "I think it's because it is a family picture from beginning to end. To this day, the film is like an international passport. People in every corner of the world recognize me through the movie."

Mementos collected from the era include a Russian language poster of the film and the disembodied head of one of the marionette puppets featured in the "Lonely Goatherd" song, which acts as a bookend in Wise's office.

"About three years ago Julie Andrews and I were awarded a state medal from Austria because of the movie," Wise said. "I've even had people say to me, in all earnestness, that *The Sound of Music* has done more for Salzburg and Austria than Mozart."

Wise said that he had his heart set on casting Julie Andrews in the lead as Maria Von Trapp from the very beginning. "The only problem was that there was this buzz going around Hollywood at that time that Julie wasn't photogenic," he said. "I called the producer of *Mary Poppins,* which hadn't been released yet, and asked if I could see a reel or two of the film. Ernie Lehman, *Music's* screenwriter, Saul Chaplin, the musical director and I went over to Disney and put those rumors to rest — Julie was our girl."

The casting of the role of Captain Von Trapp, however, was more problematic. "I remember that Yul Brenner desperately wanted to be the captain," Wise said. "But I thought he would be too 'on the nose' somehow. I had seen Christopher Plummer in some plays in New York and thought he could bring a certain edginess to the role that I felt was needed and lacking in the stage version."

Plummer turned the film down, so, at the urging of Plummer's agent, Wise flew to London and over drinks at the Connaught Hotel convinced the actor to take the part. "My only reservation — and it was slight — was over Chris's age," Wise said. "He was only about 35 then, and he refused to do a filmed makeup test. However, he did allow us to come up to his apartment one day with a makeup man and still photographer. We had to convince the studio that Chris could look old enough to be the father of a 17-year-old daughter. We pulled it off."

According to Wise, the search for actors to play the Von Trapp children spanned two continents and included tests of Rex Harrison's granddaughter and a young Mia Farrow. With the exception of Nicholas Hammond, who played Friedrich, all the children ended up coming from Los Angeles.

Wise was initially approached to direct the film when William Wyler dropped out after a dispute with 20th Century Fox over the treatment of several Nazi-related scenes in Lehman's script.

"I think Willie wanted to bear down on those scenes," Wise said. "I, on the other hand loved the script in total. The only problem was that the aerial shots that open the movie were too eerily like the opening aerial shot that began *West Side Story* for which Ernie was also the screenwriter. I told him, 'We can't open the picture that way, we'll be accused of stealing from ourselves!' He couldn't come up with anything better, so we bit the bullet and went with it. To this day, I get more comments on that aerial opening than on the *West Side Story* opening."

The son of a meat packer, Wise had hoped to become a journalist, but was unable to continue his studies during the Depression. Looking for work, he traveled to Hollywood where he found a job as a film porter in the shipping room at

RKO Studios. "One of my main jobs was to carry prints of pictures up to the projection booth for screenings," he said. "After about six months, I was spotted by a man named T.K. Wood, who gave me a start as sound effects editor, then music editor, then assistant editor. It was on-the-job training and I became a full-fledged editor five years after I began."

Among the films Wise "cut" in those early days, were two musicals starring Fred Astaire and Ginger Rogers: *Carefree* and *The Story of Vernon and Irene Castle*. "Years later, when Jerry Robbins and I shared the Oscar for Best Picture for *West Side Story*, Fred was the presenter. I have a picture of that at home, which means a great deal to me." Wise said that early editing experience on the Astaire-Rogers movies effectively demystified musicals — a genre that has perplexed many other directors. In fact, Wise credits those films with giving him the boost of confidence to direct both *West Side Story* and later, *The Sound of Music*."

Wise's high-water mark as a film editor was reached when he worked on *Citizen Kane* with Orson Welles. "Pauline Kael, former film critic of *The New Yorker*, stirred a controversy years ago about who really was responsible for the film's greatness: Orson or Herman Mankiewicz, his co-scriptwriter. To me, Orson's stamp is on every frame of that film — as star, producer, director and writer. I never saw Herman on the set. It's Orson's film, no question about it."

In a directing career that has spanned nearly half a century, totals 39 films and has garnered four Academy Awards, Wise points to only about 12 personal favorites. "*The Day the Earth Stood Still*, is a favorite," he said. "Next to the two musicals, that is perhaps my best-known movie." Another is *The Sand Pebbles* with Steve McQueen.

"He was not the simplest guy to work with. He was moody and you never quite knew where the mood was going to come from one day to the next," Wise said. "He seemed to work from the end of his fingertips. I never knew a star that knew better what worked for him on the screen than Steve. He studied himself and knew exactly what he could do. He would say, 'Bob, I think I can do that bit of business with a look. I don't have to speak the line.'"

Wise said that these days he gets very few offers to direct feature films. "The young studio heads want younger directors," he said with no regrets. He keeps busy by attending film festivals and doing committee work for the Directors Guild of America.

In his clear-eyed view of Hollywood's notorious short-term memory, Wise says he's inspired by Maria's remark as she leaves the convent to embark on her great adventure as governess of the Von Trapp children. "Every time God closes a door," he said, "somewhere he opens a window."

VIII.
Your Hit Parade

Thank God for Little Miracles
Sammy Cahn
1980

Sammy Cahn is one artist who isn't the least bit humble about his accomplishments — and with good reason. One of America's most celebrated lyricists, Cahn has won four Academy Awards for such songs as "High Hopes" and "Call Me Irresponsible." He's also written more hits for Frank Sinatra than any other songwriter, including "The Tender Trap" and "Love and Marriage." Cahn has no reason to downplay his talents. Quite the contrary, he's a self-admitted ham.

"I would have given my soul to have been a performer," he said in a recent interview from his home situated in the Beverly Hills flatlands. "If I would have been born 13 years earlier, in 1900 instead of 1913, I would have been George Burns. So I took out my frustration in demonstrating my songs. And I'm considered a lethal demonstrator."

Admittedly, Cahn's voice does have that common "in the shower" quality of a true amateur, the only difference is he possesses bundles of nerve to sing in public. It was, however, kind of endearing to see him eagerly run back and forth between his desk and his piano to serenade us. To say that Cahn is enthusiastic about his work would be a gross understatement. His kinetic energy is contagious.

A born and bred New Yorker, Cahn (who dispensed with formality and received us naked from the waist up, his slight pot-belly protruding over his belt like a second cousin of Buddha three weeks into the Scarsdale Diet) began his musical education by writing parodies of popular songs. "The greatest exercise for a beginning songwriter is to write parodies," he said. That's how he spent his youth, since he never had a formal education.

"I still hold my high school record for truancy. It's never been approached, passed, or beaten," Cahn boasted. "Education is a tool, especially for a man who deals in words. I started to read voraciously, and, funny enough, I think I know all the important words. As a matter of fact, I'm in the process of putting out a rhyming dictionary."

When his parody days were over he began work at Columbia Pictures with songwriter Saul Chaplin. His most productive years came when he collaborated with Jule Styne and James Van Heusen on such films as *Anchors Aweigh* (starring Gene Kelly and Frank Sinatra), *The Court Jester* (starring Danny Kaye), *The Tender Trap* (again with Sinatra), *Peter Pan* and *Thoroughly Modern Millie* (starring Julie Andrews, Mary Tyler Moore and Carol Channing).

Today Cahn spends most of his time writing special lyrics for benefits, corporate shows or anyone who can afford to hire him. Although he's comfortably ensconced in Los Angeles and has an apartment in Manhattan, Cahn spends most of his time at his desk with his IBM typewriter.

"This is a special IBM typewriter, which was created for me with a special uppercase letter," said Cahn. "Ninety percent of my writing is special lyrics for special occasions. It's also a source of great revenue for me. People send me specific information, and I take the information and reduce it to the songs. And I ask you to believe that they're written as impeccably as I know how to write. I'm not being casual about it."

An example of his cottage industry is a special lyric he wrote for Steven Gray for an IBM banquet in Rochester a few months ago. It's set to the music of "The Tender Trap."

It all began way back in May.
A phone call from a Mr. Gray.
He said my name is Steve and I had to believe the chap.
So you can see it's me and the IBM trap.
And I'm a ham.

Yes I am.
I mean the purest and without shame.
I'll inform you I was flown here tourist.
Some special lyrics I have made.
Please do applaud, don't be afraid.
The applause is how I'm paid in the IBM trap.

Cahn explained his ability to write lyrics as an unexplainable miracle.

"I put the paper in and type. That's it. No margin for error, no paper strewn around the floor. It never fails. It's a miracle, and I'm pleased to be part of the miracle," said Cahn. "I say this most immodestly. I'm not calling myself a miracle. I'm calling *it* a miracle. The point is that I just sit and type, and there's no way in the world that it doesn't come out. And I've learned that after 50 years it will always come out. I don't write the songs as much as the song writes me."

Cahn is also writing songs for Public Television's *Sesame Street,* including an epic called "I Love When it Rains."

Pit pitter pat, pit pitter pat.
I love when it rains.
It's thrilling when it's spilling, just filling the drains.

Though young songwriters often seek advice from Cahn, he advises against them sending him their material.

"If I could ever help amateurs out, I would," he said. "I found out that I can't. You can't help people, because by helping them you don't help and here's the line: If you help salmon upstream you get lousy salmon."

As if Cahn isn't busy enough, he is currently working with Charles Strouse, composer of the score of the hit Broadway musical *Annie,* on another Broadway musical called *Bojangles.* So far they have written 14 songs, but the project seems a long way from completion.

For Cahn, Ma Bell is the source of his inspiration. "People

always ask me, which comes first, the words or the music? It's the phone call. If the phone stops ringing I will stop writing. But the phone is now, for some curious reason, ringing more than ever."

Stardust and Residuals
Hoagy Carmichael
August 1980

"Georgia On My Mind," a song that climbed Hit Parade charts years ago gets mileage even today. As the anthem of the departed Carter Administration and the theme of television's Sheriff Lobo from *BJ and the Bear,* the song holds a special place in composer Hoagy Carmichael's heart: it continues to regularly ring up handsome royalties.

The composer of such standards as "Stardust," "Riverboat Shuffle," "Washboard Blues" and "Rockin' Chair," Carmichael is a popular composer who does double-duty in that many of his tunes have become standards in the jazz canon. Paul Whiteman, Bix Beiderbecke, and Jack Teagarden are just a few of the immortals who have recorded his songs.

"I never had any formal musical schooling," Carmichael said from his summer home in La Costa, California, where he lives in a condominium with an expansive yard that slopes gently to the ocean. "When I was a boy I worked in a 5-and-10 cent store set in the shadow of the Indiana University. A girl played a small piano — an old hurdy-gurdy we used to call it — and all the sheet music that would come in. I also listened to traveling song-pluggers who came through town."

"My mother played ragtime, and when I was about 12 years old, she showed me some basic chord structures. I wish I would have studied fingering the piano. When I hear guys playing jazz now, they are well trained and a helluva lot better than I ever was."

Carmichael developed his piano technique at the Kappa

Sigma fraternity dances while attending the Indiana University. "Hot music" was a pleasant diversion, but certainly not substantial enough to build a career on. So, to please his father, he graduated with a law degree.

"I worked for a firm down in Florida in the early '20s, but kept my hand in at the piano — sort of on the sly," Carmichael said. "I first met Irving Berlin when I was playing a wealthy person's society party in Miami. Berlin was there with Florenz Ziegfeld. Someone asked Irving to sit down at the piano and play a couple of his songs. He did, and his touch was so feathery and lousy that I thought if this guy can write songs, so can I."

"'Georgia On My Mind' slowly grew into a hit," Carmichael said. "I recorded it along with a couple of other people. Jazz bands took to it and suddenly it smashed out when Ray Charles did it."

The proper recording and handling of songs is an aspect of show business over which some composers don't exert much control, and it seems to be especially true for composers contracted to work in the "grist mill" of movie studios.

"Songwriters should be consulted by the A&R man who is directing and recording a song," Carmichael said. "The songwriter knows the song better than anyone and should be present to see that it is being handled correctly. When I was working on tunes for films, I saw many songs that just missed becoming big hits because they were recorded at poor tempos. My song 'Up A Lazy River' was recorded with the lyric, 'Up a lazy river how happy we will be, up a lazy river with me.' It's stinky. It became public domain to sing 'how happy we will be' instead of 'how happy you will be,' which is the way I wrote it."

Quite apart from his wonderful melodies and lyrics, Carmichael has contributed to his own legend by appearing in many movies — not just cameo glimpses but full-fledged supporting roles. He rode a mule, wore a stovepipe hat, and sang his hit "Ole Buttermilk Sky" in *Canyon Passage*. He taught double amputee Harold Russell how to play "Chop-sticks" with his hooks in the American classic of post-World War II readjustment, *The Best Years Of Our Lives.* But per-haps his most memorable role was as the waterfront saloon piano player Cricket in *To Have and Have Not,* starring Humphrey Bogart and Lauren Bacall.

"The wife of director Howard Hawks told him that I would be a good choice for the part of the piano player in *To Have and Have Not,"* Carmichael said. "I didn't know that Bogey was falling in love with Betty Bacall at the time. I had known Betty before he knew her, so when we were making the picture I would go into her dressing room and we'd chat and talk and sometimes I'd get a little intimate with her. Well, Bogey was sitting in the corner of the dressing room one day when I bounded in and patted Betty affectionately on the behind. Did Bogart's expression ever change! His chin just about dropped to the floor."

A footnote to the *To Have and Have Not* saga is that Carmichael suggested to Hawks that a kid singer named Andy Williams be allowed to dub the vocals for Bacall.

"Andy had worked on my radio show with his brothers," Carmichael said. "But Hawks was a stickler for detail and wouldn't allow any dubbing."

Carmichael's recording career has yielded a catalogue of 125 to 130 published songs. He describes this figure as "way low." In the quarter-century that he wrote songs and themes for films, He won only one Best Song Academy Award in 1951 for "In the Cool Cool Cool Of The Evening" from *Here Comes The Groom.*

"The title for that song came from a story a friend told me when I had been in college 30 years earlier," Carmichael said. "The story ended with a donkey saying, ' … in the cool cool cool of the evening, tell him I'll be there.' I never forgot that story — or at least the last line of it. On my way to Palm Springs with lyricist Johnny Mercer, I mentioned that line and an hour later we had written the song."

"I loved winning the Oscar," Carmichael said. "Mercer already had three and I was jealous."

Carmichael quit songwriting and piano playing a few years back. "I got lazy, and the guy who merchandised my songs got lazy. My tunes didn't get any play," he said.

Although he is ostensibly retired, Carmichael keeps himself marginally informed on current trends in the music business.

"I like country music," he said. "As long as Willie Nelson keeps recording my songs. I get some nice residuals from his albums."

THE ART OF PERFECT TIMING
Burton Lane
October 1994

Call it happenstance, harmonic convergence, or maybe just perfect timing, but Burton Lane has certainly been at the right place at the right time throughout his long, rich career as a songwriter of Hollywood and Broadway musicals.

In 1933, he wrote a little ditty called "Heigh-Ho, the Gang's All Here" for *Dancing Lady,* an MGM film starring Joan Crawford and Clark Gable. That song introduced movie audiences to a lithe Broadway hoofer named Fred Astaire, who was on the verge of a harmonic convergence all his own. Thirty-five years later, Lane helped Astaire ring down the curtain on his legendary career when the elder statesman of movie musicals starred in the film adaptation of Lane and lyricist E.Y. Harburg's landmark Broadway show, *Finian's Rainbow.* The show produced several song hits, including the popular standard "Old Devil Moon."

In fact, it was pretty much by chance that Lane, now 83, embarked on a career as a songwriter at all.

"I had a very aggressive father and whenever he saw a piano, he'd say, 'Burt — play!,'" Lane said during a recent interview in his apartment overlooking New York City's Central Park. "One time over the Christmas holidays, we were staying down in Atlantic City at a little inn off the Boardwalk. At the coaxing of my father, I was playing some tunes for the guests at an upright piano in the parlor. Suddenly, a woman came over to dad and announced that she was George Gershwin's mother. She said, 'When I heard your boy play, he sounded like my Georgie, and when I looked up, he looked like my Georgie from the back.'"

The upshot of that chance meeting was Lane being invited to the Gershwin home on the Upper West Side to meet George. A fast friendship developed and Gershwin soon became a mentor to the teenage Lane.

"For my money, George Gershwin is still the greatest songwriter ever," Lane said. "Truthfully, until I met him and his brother Ira, I didn't know there was a career in songwriting for me. I didn't know if I would fit in anyplace."

Lane, like Gershwin before him, landed a job writing songs for Remicks, a large music publisher of the day. He made $17 a week. "I was still going to high school then," he said. "However, I want to point out that I did earn $3 more a week than George did when he worked at Remicks!"

After writing songs for several shows staged by the Schubert Brothers in New York City and environs, a partner of Irving Berlin's in the music publishing business encouraged Lane and his lyric-writing partner, Harold Adamson, to "Go Hollywood."

"After getting the nod to contribute to *Dancing Lady*, I was in the screening room at MGM watching Fred Astaire's famous screen test — the very test that engendered the infamous remark, 'can't act, can't sing, can dance a little' — when a couple of studio executives came in and sat down," Lane said. "I remember one guy said to the other, 'I can walk down the hall and get dancers like this for $75 a week.' I was absolutely incredulous. Those guys didn't have a clue of what they had in Fred."

Lane collaborated with several lyricists throughout his career, including Frank Loesser, Alan Jay Lerner and E.Y. "Yip" Harburg. With Lerner, Lane wrote the score for *Royal Wedding,* a 1951 musical starring Astaire and Jane Powell. One number, "How Could You Believe Me When I Said I Loved You, When You Know I've Been a Liar All My Life!" was, for many years, the longest song title on record.

"Alan was staying at the Bel-Air Hotel when we were writing the score for *Royal Wedding,"* Lane said. "I picked him up in my car to drive to the studio, and before he got in he told me that Astaire wanted to do a low-down vaudeville number in the film. He then hit me with the 'How Could You Believe Me . . .' lyric. I told him I thought it was great and should be sung to a tune something like this. I then repeated the lyric humming a tune made up on the spot. All this occurred in the span of about five seconds; Alan still hadn't stepped foot in the car. Alan replied, 'Not something like that — that!' He got into the car and on the 15-minute drive to the studio, we wrote the rest of the song."

According to Lane, at the film's preview the number literally stopped the show. "The screenplay to that movie was dull, ridden with cliches," Lane said. "But writing for Fred, that was the spark. He was a great deliverer of songs."

Another great singer that Lane personally helped *deliver* to the world was Judy Garland. Lane happened to hear little Frances Gumm (Judy) perform with her sisters on the stage of New York's Paramount Theater in 1934.

"I introduced Judy to the folks at MGM where she sang for the top studio brass for hours. In the crush and confusion of that memorable day, no one thanked me, including Judy," he said. "Flash forward seven years later and I was assigned to write the score for *Babes on Broadway,* co-starring Mickey Rooney and Judy. I was told by producer Arthur Freed to walk over to the sound-stage and help the kids go through some of the songs. As we neared the rehearsal area, a little girl came running up and threw her arms around me. It was

Judy. She apologized for not thanking me that day. 'I was so confused by all the attention,' she said. 'I can't thank you enough for what you did for me.'"

Like Judy, Barbra Streisand has often been touted as having a voice without peer. Lane, who wrote the score for *On a Clear Day You Can See Forever* starring Streisand, readily attests to the "greatness" of Streisand's "vocal instrument." However, he said that she often "sings to herself and forgets what she is singing about." Lane attended Streisand's Madison Square Garden concert last year in which she sang the title tune from *On A Clear Day* and said he enjoyed himself immensely.

One rendition of a song that Lane enthusiastically endorses is a Barbara Cook/Barry Manilow duet recording of "Look to the Rainbow" from *Finian's Rainbow*. "I've kept it on top of my stereo for about two years now," Lane said. "I just love playing it so much I can't put it away."

Still in Tune
Jay Livingston and Ray Evans
March 1994

Sitting on Jay Livingston's grand piano in his Bel Air, California, home are three Best Song Oscars, given to him and his partner Ray Evans for "Buttons and Bows," "Mona Lisa," and "Que Sera Sera." Ironically, their biggest hit of all, "Silver Bells," written in 1951, never took home a statuette.

"No regrets," said Livingston with a wink. "It has sold more than 140 million copies. It's our annuity."

Livingston and Evans, both 84, form the longest running collaboration in the songwriting business. They met 65 years ago, while students at the University of Pennsylvania. In 1945, the two men began a 10-year tenure at Paramount as studio songwriters where they wrote some of their biggest hits, including "Silver Bells."

Chatting with them in Livingston's home, words like collaboration and compromise take on added weight. You can see it in the way career recollections lateral seamlessly between them, in a kind of pianissimo with a rest thrown in only every bar or two.

"Silver Bells," written for the Bob Hope film *The Lemon Drop Kid,* came about almost by accident.

"We were told to write a Christmas song for Hope's film," said Livingston. "We both thought that a Christmas song was doomed to fail, but the studio brass was intractable." Fortunately, sitting on Evans' desk at the time was a small silver bell that provided inspiration for the song.

"Ray and I stared at the bell and wrote a song we titled 'Tinkle Bell,'" Livingston said. "We thought we'd insert it into the film and never hear it played again."

If they had kept that title, their prophecy might have come true. Livingston's wife questioned the choice of the title. "She thought we were crazy titling a song 'Tinkle Bell,'" he said. "She pointed out the fact that tinkle has a bathroom connotation. It was a revelation to us!"

Evans continued, "The next day Jay came into the office and said we have to change the title. Our eyes finally focused on the silver bell on my desk and we changed the title. We never changed a word of the song, except that 'Tinkle Bell' became 'Silver Bells.'"

More than creating a lasting legacy, Livingston said, composing a timeless Christmas song "assures a hit record every year. Not many songwriters can lay claim to that."

The team won their first Oscar for "Buttons and Bows," from another Bob Hope comedy, *The Paleface.* "I was so nervous the night of the Oscar ceremony," Livingston said. "I drank half a pint of whisky on the drive over there. I did it every time we had a nominated song.

According to Evans, a song's real immortality, however, hinges on how it touches the average Joe.

"I once heard a guy singing 'Que Sera Sera' as he washed

the windows of a castle in Salzburg, Austria," said Evans. "That's more thrilling, any day, than hearing it played on the radio."

Two songs perhaps best exemplify the solid underpinnings of Livingston and Evans' lifelong collaboration. From the sublime to the ridiculous they are "Mona Lisa" and the television theme song to the sitcom *Mr. Ed.*

"We chased Nat King Cole around for a year before he recorded 'Mona Lisa,'" Evans said. "He had never done a song quite like it before, and he was a bit squeamish."

"Paramount pulled some strings and we saw him at his house," Livingston added. "I was trying to sing him the song. All the while this little girl is running around the room bugging the hell out of me — that was Natalie. We couldn't have known then that the song would have a wonderful rebirth on her *Unforgettable* album a quarter century later."

As freelancers in the 1960s, Livingston and Evans could write a survival guide on how they rolled with the knockout punch that rock music delivered to the traditional songwriting business.

"We wrote to spec, whatever anyone wanted," said Livingston.

Although the *Mr. Ed* theme was just another assignment designed to put groceries on the table during lean times, the song has lived on in parody as one of the many disposable pop-culture anthems viewed fondly by a generation of babyboomers raised on the boob tube.

The irony isn't lost on Livingston and Evans. "Of the more than 200 songs in our trunk, that goofy novelty song is probably the only one most young people today can sing," said Evans.

"Great songs, drudge assignments, it never mattered," Livingston summed up. "We've had serious arguments, but no real separation. When you have a winning team, you don't break it up," Evans added. "Jay writes the music, but since both of us work on the lyrics, we've learned the art of compromise. After all, two heads are better than one."

Lullabies and Nightmares
Harry Warren
August 1980

If compelled to pick the most underrated living musical
artist, a strong case could be made for 87-year-old Tin Pan
Alley tunesmith Harry Warren. Now retired and living in
luxury in a mansion just off Sunset Boulevard in Beverly Hills,
Warren is enjoying a renewed success thanks to a few ditties
he composed nearly half a century ago.

Unfortunately, the newfound popularity of his songs may
be too little and too late to counterbalance a cantankerous
personality that's the result of professional resentments nurtured over many years. Harry Warren, you see, is a world-
class curmudgeon.

In 1933, along with lyricist Al Dubin, Warren wrote the
score for the film that would revolutionize the Hollywood
musical, *42nd Street*. Last year, producer David Merrick and
the late director-choreographer Gower Champion combined
forces to recreate the simplistic backstage plot for the Broadway stage. The result is the wonderfully entertaining *42nd
Street*, which is enjoying unparalleled success at the Winter
Garden Theater. The show's popularity is due in large part to
such Warren standards as "Lullaby of Broadway," "Shuffle
Off to Buffalo," "We're in the Money," and of course, the
title song.

He also has the distinction of having had more songs on
the top-ten list between 1935 and 1950 on the radio program *Your Hit Parade* than any other composer. Yes, that includes Irving Berlin, Cole Porter and Richard Rodgers! Yet,
why does the name Harry Warren border on anonymity?

"Unfortunately, I guess I wasn't newsworthy," he told us.
"In the first place, the average person that you advertised a
lot wants to have his name known. He's got what they call

chutzpah, which I've never had."

Warren was born on Christmas Eve, 1893, in Brooklyn. He never took a single piano lesson and to this day takes pains to discount his rare, untutored gift. "I think you're just endowed that way, born that way. I think it's a God-given gift. That's the only excuse I can give you."

Warren's contribution to the Hollywood musical goes much further than just *42nd Street*. His music can be heard in over 60 films that were made between 1933 and 1961. Warren has been given the title "Mr. Hollywood Musical," and rightfully so. He was the only composer who conquered all four major Hollywood studios — Warner Bros., 20th Century Fox, Metro-Goldwyn-Mayer and Paramount.

A list of his hits would take up the entire page, but here are a few of them: "I Only Have Eyes For You," "September in the Rain," "Jeepers Creepers," "Chattanooga Choo Choo," "Serenade in Blue," "You'll Never Know," "On the Atchison, Topeka and the Santa Fe" and "That's Amore."

Warren's first musical triumphs came at Warner Bros., where he and Al Dubin wrote most of the music for the Busby Berkeley extravaganzas. Warren recalled one of the more humorous days at Warner.

"I remember one time we were doing a number for Berkeley, and he told the entire set that he was waiting for me. I was holding him up. And there was a Mexican number called 'Muchacha' which had guys on horseback riding on a treadmill. Anyhow, they called me at nine in the morning. In those days I used to get up at noon. So I got dressed and rushed over there.

"I had a piano player who was sort of a musical secretary. I said to him, "I'm going to fake something. Try to remember what I'm going to play." So there's Jack Warner and everybody, about 100 girls and a piano. And they asked me, where's the rest of the number? So I sat down at the piano and faked it. And they thought it was great."

Of the four studios where he worked, Warren said Warner

Bros. provided the worst working atmosphere. "The studio executives knew nothing about musicals. How could they? They didn't have any experience in music. Some people are still around attempting to make musicals, but know nothing about it."

A personal career goal was achieved in 1944 when Warren signed a long-term contract with MGM — the acknowledged king of the movie musical. "My favorite musicals were all at Metro," he said. "I didn't like the other pictures at all. I didn't like the scripts. There was nothing to them. I like a story script where you can write something to it."

Warren deferred telling us which one of his films contains his favorite score. But he did imply that it was the seldom seen and much neglected 1948 MGM film *Summer Holiday* — the musical version of Eugene O'Neill's play, *Ah Wilderness!*

"I was very fond of that film. I think it's the best thing I ever did at Metro. The script to *Ah Wilderness!* lent itself so nicely to music. It just flowed. I think it will be rediscovered," Warren said.

During his years in Hollywood, Warren wrote music for some of the biggest musical film stars. We asked for some short descriptions, and Warren obliged:

Dick Powell: "He was a wonderful guy. I never had any trouble with Dick."

Al Jolson: "He was a little troublesome. He was somewhat of an egotist."

Ruby Keeler: "She was a nice gal."

Fred Astaire: "Nobody danced like Fred. I would say that he really wasn't a vocal singer, but he could put a song over without any effort."

Gene Kelly: "Gene was a little different than Fred. His voice was a bit more brassy."

Judy Garland: "Judy was just fine. We never had any trouble with her."

Bing Crosby: "I like Bing, but he was kind of a distant

guy."

Jerry Lewis: "I wasn't happy working with Jerry Lewis. I watch his telethon just to see if he's still as crass as he used to be. He was a pain in the ass."

Although Warren never won a large measure of personal fame (like Irving Berlin) from his songs, the Motion Picture Academy has recognized his work with three Best Song Oscars. But the coveted awards don't impress Warren. "I only went to receive the first one. Now I use them for doorstops. I'm not proud of them. I quit the Academy."

His most treasured award is the one he received from the National American Theater Owners in recognition of his contribution to popular American films.

By the end of the '50s musicals were on the wane, as were the requests for Warren's services. "I never got a call from a studio anymore. They never even asked me how much I wanted. Well, nobody is making musicals anymore. If they do it's because they know they can make their money back on album sales. I don't know why people buy these albums. I wouldn't be caught with one of them," Warren said.

The bitterness in Warren's voice was palpable when he spoke about contemporary music. When we mentioned that the Beatles, Elvis and the advent of rock 'n' roll were partially responsible for the demise of musical films, Warren launched into a sermonette.

"I can't figure out why the Beatles were such a sensation. Nobody has ever been able to explain that to me. They started all that ragged clothes look, too. My wife just came back from New York and told me that people are walking around in the worst looking clothes. Everybody looks like a tramp comedian. They don't dress for the theater anymore."

Warren has also had the dubious honor of having his hit song, "Chattanooga Choo Choo" go disco. "What can you do?" he asked. "If they buy it you can make some money on it. You see we have funny laws in this country. Copyright laws are supposed to give you a monopoly on your own material. But once a company makes a record you have to let every other company make a record. So naturally it's no monopoly at all. I've heard records of my songs that I thought were horrible."

Harry Warren assiduously avoids the show business limelight, preferring to occasionally tinker at the keyboard if a melody comes to mind. He says his greatest pleasure comes from listening to the symphonic music of Puccini, Verdi, Rachmaninoff and Tchaikovsky. True appreciation of Warren's music may not be fully realized, if ever, for years to come. Fortunately for Warren's psyche if for no other reason, it's a waiting game that holds little interest for him. Call it an occupational hazard of what can happen when, over time, lullabies turn into bad dreams.

The Pen is Mightier Than the Clarinet

Artie Shaw
August 1981, 1994

During the big band era of the late '30s and '40s, Artie Shaw wielded the hottest swing clarinet this side of the weekly Hit Parade poll. When his orchestra struck gold with their legendary recording of "Begin the Beguine," an odyssey of one-night stands quickly led to Tinseltown and a brief fling in B-movies.

Suave and handsome, Shaw attracted a bevy of infatuated starlets including, Judy Garland and Elizabeth Taylor. In the process, he married "Sweater Girl" Lana Turner and then Ava Gardner, sultry star of such pictures as *Mogambo* and *The Barefoot Contessa*.

Nearly half a century later Shaw still lives in Los Angeles but is an expatriate from Beverly Hills and the film colony. He lives in Newbury Park, an upscale suburb in nearby Ventura County, in a house filled with books, art (George

Grosz sculptures) and mementos of his life on the road, including a Japanese battle flag captured on Guadalcanal and autographed by Admiral Halsey. Shaw drives a moped on errands to the grocery store, and is vitally concerned about global overpopulation, the water shortage, and energy conservation.

"When I putter up to a red light and see some blue-haired old lady fiercely idling in her Cadillac en-route to buy makeup, it makes me sick," he says.

The 71-year-old Shaw said he exited moviedom after he awoke one day and realized that the whole Rodeo Drive was "cosmetic bullshit." "Socrates wrote that the unexamined life is not worth living," Shaw said. "I've always been introspective. From the age of 20, I knew I wanted to be a writer. Playing jazz was my method of financing a writing career. I really thought bandleading was a dead-end."

It's been more than 30 years since Shaw last blew a note, but the trade-off of clarinet for Smith-Corona typewriter has reaped dividends. In the interim, Shaw wrote a valedictory of the swing era and its musicians called "The Trouble with Cinderella." For the last 16 years he's been hard at work on an autobiographical account of his life tentatively titled, "The Education of Albie Snow." He showed us three portable fire-proof safes tightly filled with chapters — written in long-hand — and notes for his book.

"I've got 90 chapters so far, and I've done about 20 drafts of each chapter," Shaw said. "I'll be as old as a sequoia when I finish."

In his new novel, Shaw's protagonist Albie Snow (a largely autobiographical character) faces the same kind of anti-Semitic slurs that occasionally dogged Shaw as a bandleader. While on the subject, Tom mentioned that he just finished reading Primo Levi's haunting memoir of the Holocaust, "Survival in Auschwitz."

"I don't know it," Shaw said dismissively. That struck us as hard to believe standing as we were in the middle of Shaw's carefully annotated personal library that canvassed the entire second floor of the house.

We ask him if he's seen Steven Spielberg's new movie of the same, *Schindler's List.* "Little Stevie Spielberg doesn't know a thing about being a Jew," Shaw sputters. "One year on the road 50 years ago would've taught him a thing or two!"

According to Shaw, writing is a thoughtful and measured approach to expression. "Jazz can never be that. It's a spontaneous bag of tricks that you play as fast as you can. You are never where you would ideally like to be. An attraction of writing is that it can make even a stupid person sound halfway intelligent. If only the person will write the same thought repeatedly, improving it a little bit each time. It's like inflating a blimp with a bicycle pump, anybody can do it, it just takes a lot of hot air."

Shaw and his orchestra appeared (often as specialty performers) in several slapdash films during the late '30s and early '40s. One was was a 1940 musical trifle called *Second Chorus* starring Fred Astaire and Paulette Goddard. In a rare position of scrutiny, Shaw saw past the happy-go-lucky elan of Astaire's public persona and into the appalling discipline of a dancer who rehearsed seven days a week 12 hours a day.

"Astaire really sweated — he toiled. He was a humorless Teutonic man, the opposite of his debonair image in top hat and tails. I liked him because he was an entertainer and an artist. There's a distinction between them. An artist is concerned only with what is acceptable to himself, where an entertainer strives to please the public. Astaire did both. Louis Armstrong was another one."

Shaw said that he can remember just four or five times when his own playing skipped the boundary from entertainment into art. "I could play you an eight-bar crescendo at the end of a record released by Decca. The song was 'These Foolish Things' and it achieved perfection purely by accident," Shaw said. "I played it once at a convention of over 300 clarinet players and they absolutely flipped."

The blurring of the boundary between artist and entertainer served as Shaw's wake-up call in the early 1950s. It's
the reason he retired his clarinet.

"I had to get out because I saw the end of my life fore-
told," Shaw says. "When you become a professional you reach
a level of excellence below which you cannot fall. Pretty soon
the audience can't distinguish the difference between super-
lative and mediocre playing, but the artist can discern it if he
remains true to himself and doesn't succumb to his own favorable publicity. You can easily fall into a plush-lined rut
where a form of death occurs. I see creative people who
ended their lives 40 years ago still walking around. When
that happens you'd better get out of the business or resolve
yourself to becoming Lawrence Welk. He's a happy man but
if he could hear with my ears what he is doing, he would
commit hari-kari on his baton."

An indication of how much Shaw regrets his decision to
give up jazz is that he jokes about turning his clarinet into a
reading lamp.

"I'd never dream of performing again; it's too hard," he
said. "It's like asking Muhammad Ali if he does roadwork for
amusement. When I hear something played on the clarinet
I suffer because I can feel the intensity of the effort. I might
remember a bad reed or the trouble I had with the second
trumpet player or God knows what. The quintessential question that people ask me is why I don't play even for fun anymore. I've inured myself to that kind of examination. I just
tune them out like a bad television commercial."

Shaw says that only his last two CDs (*The Last Recordings
- Rare & Unreleased,* Music Masters, 1992 and *More Last Recordings - The Final Sessions,* Music Masters, 1993) measure
up to his supreme critical scrutiny. "If I could erase all the
rest of my work, I'd be happy," he said.

Stepping out of the performing limelight in 1954 didn't
mean passing up television talk show guest spots, the ideal
forum to plug his books. Shaw was a participant on Johnny

Carson's second *Tonight Show* and appeared on every star roster from Dick Cavett to Merv. But even the guest shots went the way of his "licorice stick" after a while.

"You can't really talk on television, no one wants to hear you," Shaw said. "Dick Cavett is a bloody bore. If you want to be a philosopher then get the hell off television. It's the wrong medium. Truthfully, I'm not your ideal TV guest. On the *Merv Griffin Show*, which is all things to all people, I likened the crowds at Woodstock to a bunch of muddy pigs. I was booed off the screen. By and large, TV is a blight. So everyone knows the latest Henny Youngman joke, big deal."

If that sounds like the phlegmatic raving of a misanthrope, Shaw would be the first to confess that he has never lost his maverick streak.

"I guess you could say I don't have much patience with pointless people. Some of my most heated run-ins were with interviewers. One guy desperately wanted me to write a Hollywood expose. I said that I would do it only if he agreed to the title *The Platinum Vagina*. He asked why, and I replied that platinum is expensive, hard, cold, and potentially harmful. I get tired of reporters who only seem interested in the color of Lana Turner's bedspread or what was really under her sweater."

The Great Divide — Media vs. Publicists

The Golden Age of Hollywood is long gone and the modern era in Tinseltown now betrays quite a bit of tarnish on that xanthous glow — at least when it comes to working with celebrity publicists to gain interview access to their gilded clients.

Looking back at all the advance work it took to snag more than 200 interviews, it's hard to fathom that it was easier to arrange a meeting in Lucille Ball's living room 20 years ago than it is to grab 20 minutes on the phone with a "B"-list comedian these days. That's how much the business of celebrity interviewing has changed over the last quarter century.

As reporters for our college newspaper, the *Minnesota Daily*, in the late '70s and early '80s, we carved out a niche as celebrity interviewers. As the popularity of our column grew, we returned to Los Angeles with greater frequency to fill the demand pipeline for our celebrity profiles. Then, as now, personal and sometimes studio publicists acted as gatekeepers who facilitated the logistics in setting up the interviews. Our recollection of working with them during that period is overwhelmingly favorable, and, after presenting our credentials, we seldom found those gates closed off to us.

For stars that were raised on the studio system, people like Charlton Heston and Gregory Peck, doing "publicity" was an accepted part of the job. If they looked at this aspect of their vocation with disdain, they did a good job of hiding it and always cheerfully accepted journalists into their living rooms to talk shop. Stars back then established working relationships with journalists. It was not adversarial. It was seen as an extension of the studio's marketing apparatus.

When we graduated from the University of Minnesota, with some 100 interviews under our belts, we went our own ways and began separate careers in (surprise!) public relations. By no longer wearing the exclusive hat of "journalist," we spent the next 20 years on the "other side" of the divide as corporate public relations practitioners.

We soon found that it doesn't matter if you are representing a corporate entity or an individual celebrity, a publicist's objectives remain the same: To counsel their client on public relations matters and to maximize publicity opportunities that will reflect positively on that client, and if possible, influence buying decisions (i.e., view that personality's TV show or movie).

With bloated film budgets and astronomical salaries, the success of a star's "project," whether a television series or feature film, is hinged more than ever on spin and the positive hype. A film's success today is often predicated solely on the all-important opening weekend. And for a TV series, hitting the 100-episode mark is generally considered the benchmark of success. So why is it that so many of the publicity practitioners working in Hollywood today just don't get it?

After a 10-year hiatus, we rejoined forces about ten years ago and launched our celebrity profile column called "Reel to Real." Dozens of publications from throughout the world have run our profiles.

After being away from the business for a decade, we quickly discovered how the playing field had changed. Yes, publicists still play the vital role of gatekeeper between journalists and their sought-after clients, but the bipartisan mistrust and wariness between the two professions has widened.

Having worked as both journalists and publicists, we found this shift in the balance of power disturbing. Several articles have been written about how "powerful" Hollywood publicists representing "A"-list talent now have brought supposedly credible journalistic publications to their knees by establishing a set of demands that need to be met before that magazine is given permission to conduct an interview. These "demands" often include writer approval, photo approval, a pre-determined list of topics that are taboo to bring up during the interview and even pre-publication approval of the piece. Surprisingly, many of these publications kowtow to these demands, more interested in seeing Tom Cruise on their cover shilling for his latest movie than maintaining any semblance of journalistic credibility.

The playing field has dramatically changed partially because of the explosion of new media vehicles and the increased number of people calling themselves "entertainment journalists." Where there used to be three networks, with cable we now have a zillion stations, many of them looking to fill air time with celebrity content, including some networks (like E!) that are devoted exclusively to entertainment. We also now have the Internet, which devours show business content with the omnivorous appetite of T-Rex at a Jurassic picnic.

And let's not forget about all the print publications that want to feature a celebrity in their pages if not always on their covers. Year's ago, *Reader's Digest, Cosmopolitan* and *Glamour*, to name a few, would never have dreamt of featuring a celebrity on their covers. Now, it's commonplace. It's all about filling the public's seemingly unquenchable appetite for reading about celebrities. Unfortunately, shot-through this mass media clutter has come a pirannha-like zeal on the part of many suspect entertainment venues to hype the lurid, sordid and gossipy story. The proliferation of tabloid journalism drastically impedes the work of legitimate journalists. Characteristically, it makes many publicists gun shy to avail their clients to the media.

Despite all these handicaps, the foundation for a positive working relationship between publicist and journalist hasn't substantially changed. Plain and simple, it's still rooted in trust. That means both parties have to respect each other and honor the commitments they make. Publicists and reporters are meant to work together; they really are two sides of the same coin. Keeping the lines of communication cordial and open at each end makes for a win-win situation.

That said, here are a half dozen suggestions, gleaned from our experience as both entertainment writers and working publicists, which can help build a better bridge between reporters and publicists.

• Return phone calls, faxes and emails in a timely fashion: This may sound self-evident, but this problem is widespread and cuts across both professions. Publicists often don't receive responses when they query editors with story ideas, and journalists often don't receive responses to their particular requests. Whether it's carelessness or laziness, it's irresponsible and unprofessional.

• Put the request in writing: Unless there's a dire time crunch, or if you already have a working relationship with a publicist or journalist, it's best to fax or email that interview request or story idea to the appropriate point of contact. And if the request is coming from a writer, he or she should include publication information (circulation), date of publication, what kind of interview is needed (phone or in-person) and for how long, and if photography is needed.

• Put closure to the request: Whether a request can be granted or not, put closure to it. No one likes to waste valuable time ringing up long-distance phone charges. A simple "yes" or "no" usually works.

• Network Synergy: It's all about relationship building. So it's perfectly acceptable for a journalist or a publicist to get on the phone and arrange a get-acquainted session. When possible, a face-to-face meeting works best. A business bond can be forged quicker that way.

• "Let's Make A Deal": Deal is not a dirty word — this is Hollywood for Pete's sake! For the publicist, it's usually not hard generating publicity for a "name" client. The challenge comes with those up and coming stars that haven't quite hit yet in the public consciousness. Depending on the comfort level between a publicist and a journalist, it may be appropriate for the publicist to make that "name" client available to that writer in exchange for a coverage exchange of that lesser known client.

• There's more than *Vanity Fair* and *Entertainment Tonight* out there: This tip is perhaps better directed to the publicist community. As we mentioned earlier, there is a dizzying array of media outlets available to the publicist. Instead of being unduly wary of the unknown, ask to see a copy of that publication or that Web site address. Any reporter worth his or her salt would be happy to mail or fax you pertinent background articles. And don't forget those collateral publications — like in-flight magazines — that have large readerships and reach a desirable demographic.

Acknowledgments

A quarter-century has passed since our first interview trip to Los Angeles (to meet Fred Astaire and Gene Kelly) and we have many people to thank for making this unforgettable ride possible. To our editors and friends from the *Minnesota Daily*, where our first interviews saw the light of day — Randy Anderson, Eric Lindbom, Sheryl Larson, Ginny Holbert, Jeff Reid, Mike Phillips, Tom Baglien, Jay Walljasper, Jeff Pike, Jerry Creedon, Dave Ayres and Ann Miller — thanks for a big leg up, wonderful editing and a helluva good time. Many thanks to Mary Ann Grossmann and the late Noel BreDahl of the *St. Paul Dispatch*, the first daily paper to publish our work and to the dozens of other publishers and editors who have run (and sometimes run from) our stories through the years. Although it is widely known by people who do what we do that celebrity publicists are often the bane of an interviewer's existence, thanks to the flacks that have been responsive and given us access to their clients. You know who you are! Even bigger kudos should go to the legion of secretaries and personal assistants that helped us cut through the clutter and made their famous bosses available for sit-downs. Lois McClelland (Gene Kelly), Marge Zimmerman (James Cagney), Jack Langdon (George Burns) and Jaye Johnston (Fred Astaire) are several gatekeepers that stand out. Thanks also to Seth Berkowitz for his timely suggestions regarding the book's format and to John Skewes for his awesome cover design. To some eager young future show business journalists who helped retype interviews and transcribe ancient tapes — Kate, Jake and Britt Zarling, Heidi Klotz and Mara Simon-Meyer — we appreciate your unflagging patience. Special thanks to our publisher and editor at Badger Books, Marv Balousek, who saw *Reel to Real's* potential and encouraged us every step of the way, Mary Lou Santovec and to the people at Midpoint Trade Books.

Lastly, although encomiums fall short, we'd like to tip our hats to the stars that have left a legacy of unforgettable work for future generations to enjoy and who met us at the door ... in the den ... by the swimming pool ... or at the restaurant with unfailing good cheer and even better anecdotes.

Index

Symbols